THE

GEORGE SA
Dupin on 1 Ju
was raised at
grandmother'
the greater pa
and frequentl
short stories,
first novel under sole authorship, *Indiana*, in 1832. Sand was a consistent exponent of socialism and agricultural reform, both major concerns in *The Miller of Angibault*. She gave away the equivalent of over £1,000,000, earned from her writings, to exiles from the 1848 revolution, needy peasants, and proletarian writers. She also partially supported her lovers, the poet Alfred de Musset and the composer Frédéric Chopin, providing the latter with the ideal creative climate at Nohant which produced some of his greatest work. When the relationship with Chopin ended after ten years, in 1847, Sand gained a solid support of her own in the engraver Alexandre Manceau, who lived with her for fifteen years and used his own funds to buy her a writing retreat at Gargilesse. After Manceau's death in 1865 and the crushing of the Paris Commune in 1871, Sand, bereaved and distressed at the final failure of her socialist hopes, lived at Nohant until her own death in 1876.

DONNA DICKENSON is the author of *George Sand: A Brave Man, The Most Womanly Woman* (1988). A Lecturer at the Open University, she has also translated the poetry of Louis Aragon and the French Canadian poet Anne Hébert. Her other critical biographies include *Emily Dickinson* (1985) and *Margaret Fuller: Writing a Woman's Life* (1993). She is the editor of Fuller's *Woman in the Nineteenth Century* (World's Classics, 1994).

THE MILLER OF ANGIBAULT

GEORGE SAND was born as Amantine-Aurore-Lucile Dupin on 1 July 1804. From her father's death in 1808, she was raised at Nohant in Berry, France, which was her grandmother's home and where she herself would spend the greater part of her life, although she travelled widely and occasionally stayed in Paris. A prolific writer of plays, short stories, novels, and journal articles, she published her first novel under sole authorship, *Indiana*, in 1832. Sand was a constant ex ... of social life and particular ... chang... ...

THE WORLD'S CLASSICS

GEORGE SAND

The Miller of Angibault

Translated with an Introduction and Notes by
DONNA DICKENSON

Oxford New York
OXFORD UNIVERSITY PRESS
1995

Oxford University Press, Walton Street, Oxford OX2 6DP

Oxford New York
Athens Auckland Bangkok Bombay
Calcutta Cape Town Dar es Salaam Delhi
Florence Hong Kong Istanbul Karachi
Kuala Lumpur Madras Madrid Melbourne
Mexico City Nairobi Paris Singapore
Taipei Tokyo Toronto

and associated companies in
Berlin Ibadan

Oxford is a trade mark of Oxford University Press

First published as a World's Classics paperback 1995

British Library Cataloguing in Publication Data
Data available

Library of Congress Cataloging in Publication Data
Sand, George, 1804–1876.
[Meunier d'Angibault. English]
The miller of Angibault/George Sand; translated with an introduction
and notes by Donna Dickenson.
p. cm.—(World's classics)
Includes bibliographical references.
1. France—Social life and customs—19th century—Fiction.
2. Social reformers—France—Berry—Fiction. 3. Country life—France
—Berry—Fiction. 4. Socialism—France—Berry—Fiction. 5. Berry
(France)—Fiction. I. Dickenson, Donna. II. Title. III. Series.
PQ2411.M4E5 1995 843'.7—dc20 94-27267
ISBN 0-19-283084-8

1 3 5 7 9 10 8 6 4 2

Typeset by Best-set Typesetter Ltd., Hong Kong
Printed in Great Britain
by BPC Paperbacks Ltd., Aylesbury, Bucks

CONTENTS

CONTENTS

INTRODUCTION

The ruin of an aristocratic family, the machinations of ambitious new money, the financial flaying of the few virtuous characters: surely these are incidents which only Balzac could have created? The reckless crushing of an old beggar under the wheels of a wealthy man's carriage, the torture with red-hot irons of a well-to-do peasant by rick-burners, the suffocation and slow death by fire of a demented woman: could these be the main events in one of George Sand's notoriously insipid rural idylls? The answer to the first question is no: greed, neglect, incompetence, and manipulation are the stuff of Sand's *The Miller of Angibault*, as much as of Balzac's *La Cousine Bette* or *Père Goriot*. The second question's answer is yes: these are indeed the climactic events of *The Miller of Angibault*, handled with a restraint and craftsmanship that likewise lifts them above the merely melodramatic and evidences the author's enormous craftsmanship.

How is any of this consistent with the common critical disparagement of George Sand? Despite a recent resurgence of critical interest, the popular image of Sand, particularly in Britain and the United States, still centres on her relationship with Chopin, her trousers, and her cigars: on her sexual reputation. In the English-speaking countries, her literary reputation fell off in the late nineteenth century—or was pushed.

Male novelists in England and America, particularly Henry James, found Sand a tempting subject for target practice in what Sandra M. Gilbert and Susan Gubar have called 'the war of the words'.[1] Men of letters in James's generation were stymied by a Himalayan range of female novelists—George Eliot, the Brontës, Jane Austen, and George Sand—which now stood between them and their forefathers. Whereas Elizabeth Barrett Browning had complained that she sought everywhere

[1] Sandra M. Gilbert and Susan Gubar, *No Man's Land: The Place of the Woman Writer in the Twentieth Century*, i: *The War of the Words* (New Haven, Conn.: Yale University Press, 1988).

for grandmothers and found none, Lawrence, James, and other modernist writers looked for literary fathers and found only 'thinking bosoms'—the phrase which the critic V. S. Pritchett has applied to George Sand ('a thinking bosom and one who overpowered her young lovers, all sybil').[2]

Of these notable women, Sand was the most threatening to male novelists of James's generation and after. She was the only one to enjoy constant and lucrative professional success from her early twenties, and the only one who led much of a sexual life. That this female should have had her cake and eaten it too was almost unbearable. But luckily for the men of James's generation, she was more vulnerable to sexual slurs than the spinsters Jane Austen or Emily Brontë, the late-married Charlotte Brontë, or even George Eliot, despite her association with G. H. Lewes. Besides, Sand was a mother, unlike any of the Englishwomen, and thus open to maternal stereotyping, particularly because her lovers Alfred de Musset and Frédéric Chopin were younger than she.

At the time of Sand's death in 1876, she was accepted as the greatest novelist of her century by such major English-language writers as Walt Whitman, Matthew Arnold, Robert Louis Stevenson, and George Eliot herself. Thomas Hardy, who was told to read Sand by the critic Leslie Stephen if he was serious about the bucolic genre, rated her among the top ten French writers as late as 1899. But none of these authors has been so influential as Henry James in determining the lower opinion of Sand which prevailed for most of the twentieth century. It seems an indicative coincidence that it is James whom Gilbert and Gubar identify as having been most preoccupied with the decline of male literary potency in what *The Bostonians*' Basil Ransom calls 'a feminine, chattering, canting age'.

James was obsessed with Sand, for good or ill. He was her major popularizer in the generation after her death, writing enough essays and reviews on her to make a novel as long as *The Europeans* and affording much publicity to his preoccupations with female domination of the novel. This fixation is

[2] V. S. Pritchett, 'George Sand', *The Myth Makers* (London: Chatto and Windus, 1979), 124.

evident in such James stories as 'Greville Fane', which contrasts a male narrator, a writer whose failure is 'admirably absolute', with a gallingly successful woman novelist 'who could invent stories by the yard but couldn't write a page of English'.

As early as the 1860s—when travellers to Paris were turning back from the capital in the conviction that there was a revolution on, although the mobs were only queuing for Sand's plays—James was trying to write Sand off as over the hill. At this early point in his own development, however, he still admired her style and convictions, ranking her above Dickens and Thackeray, in line with the general evaluation of the time. But later his attitudes hardened into the worst prejudices, which were given play by his extensive publishing and which became the general image of Sand in the English-speaking world: the sexually voracious vampire, the domineering mother-figure, the scribbler of pot-boilers.

In France, Sand continued to be read, but there she was best known as an author of *romans champêtres*, rural novels. Yet, ironically, Sand's reputation as a writer of pretty country tales arose only because she was a political radical. In her lifetime she gained credit and honour at home and abroad from her socialist novels—of which *The Miller of Angibault* (1845) is probably the best known, the one which Sand herself called her 'arch-socialist' work—and from her activity in serving as minister of information during the 1848 revolution and in interceding for clemency towards the revolutionaries with the subsequent government of Louis Napoleon. Particularly in Russia, she was extolled as a prophet of socialism and feminism (even if she was a less than wholehearted feminist). There, although the official censor applied his blue pencil, her novels were admitted when Western socialist non-fiction was barred.

Sand influenced Dostoevsky, Turgenev, Gorky, Belinsky, Herzen, and Bakunin, who called her 'the Joan of Arc of our times, the guiding star, the prophetess of a great future'.[3] Dostoevsky accorded her 'virtually the first place among a

[3] Quoted in Francine Mallet, *George Sand* (Paris: Éditions Bernard Grasset, 1976), 419.

whole pleiad of new writers who at that period suddenly rose
to fame and renown all over Europe'.[4] Although she expresses
some cynicism about utopian socialism in *The Miller of
Angibault*, her high-mindedness appealed to the Russian men
of 1840. As Dostoevsky put it, 'George Sand is one of us, a
Russian idealist of the 1840 generation ... Perhaps some
people may laugh at the great importance I accord her, but the
mockers are wrong.'[5]

The 'great importance' accorded Sand abroad and in France
was precisely the problem. After her death in 1876, the conservative French Senate proposed to issue a ban on all her
work. Following last-minute intercession from her friend the
critic Sainte-Beuve, two novels were exempted from out of the
sixty she wrote: the short bucolic romances *La Petite Fadette*
and *La Mare au diable*. Since only these two novellas were
known to several generations of French readers, she came to
be seen as a 'safe' and dull writer of fictions for schoolgirls.
Had Sand been totally proscribed, she might be remembered
as the communist who was too subversive to be allowed a free
voice.

At least this was certainly the view of the publisher who
originally commissioned *The Miller of Angibault* in 1844.
Véron, editor of the moderate journal *Le Constitutionnel*,
rejected the completed novel as too violent an attack on
property. Although Véron condemned as dangerous the radical sentiments expressed in the admittedly long-winded dia-
logues between the heroine Marcelle and her lover Henri,
Sand was surprised that he had taken these two babes in the
wood, metropolitan innocents abroad in the darkest countryside, so very seriously. '[Véron] claims this is an *attack on
property*,' she wrote in a letter of 10 October 1844 to another
editor, Hetzel. 'When you read it, the simple-mindedness of
my characters' views on the subject, and the artlessness of
manner, will make you laugh at M. Véron's consternation.'

There followed long negotiations and legal threats—which
neatly parallel the bitter and complicated financial wranglings

4   Fyodor Dostoevsky, *Diary of a Writer*, tr. Boris Brasol (New York: Octagon,
1973), i. 340.
5   Quoted in Mallet, *George Sand*, 421.

in the novel itself—before the novel was published in a less 'bourgeois and cowardly' journal (Sand's judgement on *Le Constitutionnel*): *La Réforme*, edited by Sand's fellow social-ist, Louis Blanc. 'I want to sell it for a good price, to compro-mise with Véron without letting him off the hook,' Sand noted acerbically in a letter.[6]

Perhaps this seems hypocritical on Sand's supposedly high-minded part. But the proceeds from the sale of the novel made good the expenses that Sand had incurred from the establish-ment of a printing commune at Boussac, run by the socialist Pierre Leroux (1797–1871), whose ideas percolate through the novel. Co-operatives of this sort were the great hope of many European socialists in the 1840s, after the failure of militancy in the form of the 1830 revolutions and the workers' riots of the following decade. In thirty years Sand spent over £1,000,000 underwriting such projects in practical (and im-practical) socialism, supporting needy peasants on her small estate at Nohant, and offering aid to proletarian poets, exiled supporters of the revolutionary government, and the daughter of the trades-union organizer Flora Tristan, after Tristan's early death.

Thus the external circumstances of the novel's publication mirror its subject and content. Permeated by utopian social-ism, culminating in the establishment of a miniature commune in Sand's native Berry, the symbolic heart of France, *The Miller of Angibault* reflects both the ebullient political move-ments of its period and the despairing conviction that the Revolution had changed nothing. As Grand-Louis the miller himself puts it: 'They say the world is much changed, these past fifty years; I say nothing has changed but the ideas that some of us have' (p. 52).

Her concentration on rural poverty and wage-labour is the most original aspect of Sand's social analysis. Other socialists of her period, such as Flora Tristan, Saint-Simon, Fourier, and, slightly later, Marx and Engels, all concentrated on the plight of the urban proletariat. Although utopian socialist communi-

[6] George Sand, *Correspondance*, ed. Georges Lubin (25 vols.; Paris: Garnier Freres, 1964–91), vi. 661.

ties were established in the countryside, particularly in America (such as Brook Farm in Massachusetts), they were very much imports of townsfolk into a supposedly idyllic rural environment; they did nothing for the situation of local people. This is also the plot of *The Miller of Angibault*: the journey by the naïve Parisians Marcelle and Henri in search of rural utopia, and their awakening to the real state of the country proletarian.

Sand's view is in contradistinction to the dominant position in the political economy of her day, namely that increased production and demand within a capitalist system of private ownership could ultimately benefit both workers and capitalists. Classical economists such as Adam Smith, David Ricardo, and Jean Baptiste Say were most interested in the question of how to increase growth, primarily through industrial production. Those who purchased goods, these economists claimed, were increasing demand and production, thus ultimately employing more workers and increasing the size of the 'cake'. Sand's view, in contrast, depends on a picture of a cake which is fixed in size, as would seem more obviously true of agricultural production than of industry. Although an agricultural revolution, with tremendous growth in output, had preceded the industrial revolution in England, the situation was different in France because landlords of the *ancien régime* did not share their English equivalents' interest in progressive farming practices. The French aristocrats were almost entirely absentee landlords, cultivating court life, lacking the English squires' fascination with domestic-animal husbandry and wild-animal slaughter as hobbies.

In *The Miller of Angibault* the violence inflicted on country people, by country people, during the Revolution has benefited no one but the rural bourgeoisie, the implacably avaricious Bricolins. The class structure is more rigid than ever, if more complex, with previously non-existent but now unbridgeable divisions between rich and poor peasants. Under the revolutionary governments, and even more so under Napoleon, there was an enormous transference of landed property from the old nobility and church to middle-class bureaucrats, lawyers, and speculators; to a lesser degree, some went to wealthy tenant farmers like the Bricolins. However, under the Restoration many estates were returned to their former owners, to the extent that the old nobility made good about half its losses. 'The equation between land and political power remained intact.'[7] This is the subtext of Bricolin's greed for land; it is also a will to power.

Likewise, the gendered structure of power within the family had not changed; if anything, it had become even more inexorable. The modern reader may be surprised that M. Bricolin has such power over his daughter Rose's ability to marry whom she chooses. Why doesn't she simply throw over her wealth and run off with her lover, the miller Grand-Louis? It is important to understand how much authority the French *paterfamilias* enjoyed, supported by the heritage of Roman law, more recent ordinances such as the 1673 statute which gave a father the right to shut his daughter up in a convent until she was 25, and the reactionary Napoleonic Code. '[R]elatively, [French] girls were subjected to a more authoritarian regime than in Britain or the United States.'[8]

I have argued elsewhere that Sand's feminism has been greatly overstated,[9] but it was at its strongest over injustices which had touched her directly, such as legislation on property and divorce. Sand was vividly aware of the powers bestowed by law on husbands and fathers, a theme which recurs throughout her work starting with *Indiana*. Her life, too, was marred by husbands' legal authority: she was unable formally to divorce her husband, Casimir Dudevant. Divorce had been repealed under the Napoleonic Code and was not reinstated until after Sand's death. But on their legal separation in 1836 she was forced to surrender a large portion of her ancestral estate to him and to pay him a yearly income, although he had nearly ruined the estate when he had control of it during their marriage.

[7] David Thomson, *Europe since Napoleon* (Harmondsworth: Pelican, 1966), 106.

[8] Jane Rendall, *The Origins of Modern Feminism: Women in Britain, France and the United States, 1780–1860* (London: Macmillan, 1985), 211.

[9] Donna Dickenson, *George Sand: A Brave Man, The Most Womanly Woman* (Oxford: Berg Publishers, 1988), ch. 3.

Even after the separation, Sand was not free of patriarchal power: although she was awarded custody of her daughter, Solange, at one point Casimir abducted the girl to his home in Gascony. A horrible parallel was to occur in 1855, when Solange's daughter Nini, who had lived with her grandmother at Nohant, was forcibly placed in a boarding-school by Solange's estranged husband, the sculptor Clésinger. The child contracted scarlet fever in the school and died at the age of five.

'When people ask how a conjugal association can survive if the husband isn't the unchallenged head, the judge and party both, with no appeal,' Sand wrote in her *Correspondence*,[10] 'it makes no more sense than when they ask how a free man can get along without a master or a republican without a king. The principle of uncontrolled authority in one individual went out with the divine right of kings.' Thus the attempted liberation of Rose from patriarchal power *by another woman*, Marcelle, is as important a theme in *The Miller of Angibault* as utopian, republican socialism: more important, perhaps, since it is only in the arena of the family rather than that of the polity that Marcelle can actually *do* something.

The insecurity of the landless farmworker in ill health, the transference of land to avaricious speculators, the retrograde movement in women's property rights under the Napoleonic Code: all these recent social factors worsen the natural precariousness of rural existence, where harvest and life itself can be threatened as much by the floods vividly described at the novel's start as by the fire that dominates its end. But this is to ignore the wry humour and gentle lyricism which punctuate the novel, and the sensible realism which prevents Sand from making even its villain Bricolin purely villainous.

Balzac says of Bette, the Lorraine peasant, that 'only her knowledge of the law and of the world enabled her to control that natural quickness of temper with which country people, like savages, pass from feeling to action . . . Cousin Bette, the primitive woman from Lorraine, a little inclined to treachery, belonged to that class of characters which are more common

<hr />

[10] Sand, *Correspondance*, ii. 741.

among the masses than you might think, and may explain their behaviour during revolutions.' Sand is rarely so simplistic about either her characters or her politics. There is a certain revolting grandeur about the rich farmer Bricolin—his name echoing 'bricolage', a ramshackle construction, like his mixed-class background, peasant and bourgeois, and as his own fortune proves to be. Bricolin is introduced to the reader with an even-handed acerbity he himself would approve:

His blunt, strongly accentuated features were marked by unusual energy and sagacity. He had a sharp eye, black and hard, a sensual mouth, a narrow low forehead, curly hair, and a quick, brusque turn of speech. There was no falsity in his glance nor hypocrisy in his manners. This was no double-dealer: his enormous respect for mine and thine, in conventional terms, made him incapable of knavery. Furthermore, the cynicism of his greed prevented him from masking his intentions, and when he had announced to his counterpart, 'My interest is the opposite of yours,' he thought to have demonstrated to him that he acted by the most sacred laws, and that he had shown the highest degree of probity in so speaking. (p. 64)

Sand hates hypocrisy, and although there are elements of self-congratulation in Bricolin's bleak candour, she finds him impossible to dismiss solely as a symbol of the political trends she most dislikes. Much of the sympathy she generates for him, perhaps against her will, lies in his lively use of language. Sand believed in grounding all of her books in research: *A Winter in Majorca* says very little about her time in Valldemosa with Chopin—much to most readers' disappointment—but includes a great deal of scrupulously researched natural history. Similarly, *The Miller of Angibault* records details of country lore and language which derive in part from Sand's own rural upbringing, but also from her study of the history and outlook of the previous century. (This background research plays an even greater part in the last of Sand's bucolic novels, *Les Maîtres Sonneurs* (*The Master Pipers*), since that is set in the eighteenth century, whereas the *Miller* takes place in the present.)

As Béatrice Didier points out in her introduction to the Livre de Poche edition of *Le Meunier d'Angibault*,

The fact that peasant language cannot simply be incorporated willy-nilly, that a novel is something other than a dictionary of terms, obliged her [Sand] to be selective. . . . the use of language not only identifies the character as a peasant, but also makes him an individual, reveals personality characteristics, so that Père Bricolin, Uncle Cadoche, the mother of the miller, all speak *berrichon* but use different expressions, showing how George Sand makes a selection for each of them that reveals character. It is in the matter of language that we can clearly see the subtle mingling of the sociologist's powers of observation and the novelist's particular craft.[11]

Further subtleties occur when the novel's characters are portrayed as self-conscious about their use of language. The miller Grand-Louis

had completed his schooling up to secondary level, and understood a great deal more than he let on. . . . far from showing off his education or priding himself on it, he affected down-to-earth peasant manners rather than the little politenesses with which he was perfectly familiar. Apparently he was afraid the villagers might think him hoity-toity, and he had nothing but scorn for those who turn their backs on their own folk and their simple background, giving themselves ridiculous airs. He spoke with a good accent, as a rule, but did not entirely spurn picturesque local expressions. When he let down his guard, his speech actually became all the more educated, and there was nothing of the miller left. But he quickly resumed his good-humoured jokes and his pleasant familiarity, as if ashamed to have betrayed his station. (pp. 48–9)

If translating this variety of peasant speech in anything but a hackneyed manner raises huge difficulties, setting it down in the original was no easier for Sand. She was well aware that she trod a tightrope: 'If I let the man of the fields speak in his natural manner, the civilized reader will need a translation, and if I make him talk like you and I, he becomes an incredible creature, to whom we must attribute a style of thought which he doesn't actually possess.'[12] That she had not entirely solved the problem was the opinion of Turgenev, though he drew on Sand's use of peasant characters and idiom in *A Sportsman's Sketches*.

---

[11] Béatrice Didier, afterword, in George Sand, *Le Meunier d'Angibault* (Paris: Livre de Poche, 1985), 409–10.
[12] George Sand, *François le Champi* (Paris: Garnier Frères, 1962), pref., 215.

But this is what makes *The Miller of Angibault* such a radical endeavour, not in its politics this time, but in its attempted creation of a new genre. (Balzac was to try a rural setting in *Les Paysans*, serialized in *La Presse* between 3 and 21 December 1844, a few months after Sand had completed *The Miller of Angibault*: but he did not finish the novel.) In the rampantly poetic setting of the Vallée-Noire, described with the full lushness of Sand's rich style, are played out the class dramas of the century: poor peasant against rich peasant, townsman against country dweller, impoverished parents against grown children who have had them declared incompetent, fathers against propertyless daughters. More subtly, the metropolitan visionary Henri begins by hostile verbal jousting with the emblematic working man, the miller of Angibault, and nearly comes to blows with him, but ends up as his mill lad. Grandparents form alliances with grandchildren against the propertied middle generation; the lawyer serves the interests of the beggar; nothing ends up quite the way we would expect.

Abjuring what she sees as the rigid solutions of the Saint-Simonians and the Fourierites, Sand offers no romantic utopias, not even in this idyllic setting where the Parisians hoped to found their own *nouvelle Héloïse*. As always in the work of this writer, who has so unfairly been dismissed as arch-Romantic, the grand gesture has no place. It is only destructive, epitomized in *The Miller of Angibault* by the consuming fire set by the madwoman in what Sand describes earlier as her Romantic mania for the absolute, her fixation. At the novel's close, all the former adversaries who have survived are living more or less peaceably together, within a stone's throw of each other and of the charred ruins of the Blanchemont estate which caused their conflict. As Sand wrote at the end of *A Winter in Majorca*,

I always dreamt of living in the wild, and any frank dreamer like myself will admit to the same fantasy. But believe me, my brethren, we have too much feeling in our hearts to do without each other, and our best course is mutual support; for we are all children of one breast, teasing each other, squabbling, but still unable to separate.

NOTE ON THE TEXT

The text of *The Miller of Angibault* is that of the 1865 edition, published by Michel-Lévy Frères. The novel was first serialized in *La Réforme* between 21 January and 19 March 1845, and published in three volumes by Desesart in the same year. In 1853 Sand's friend the editor Hetzel brought out an illustrated version.

Originally the novel was to be serialized by the publisher Véron in his journal *Le Constitutionnel*, but after putting Sand under considerable time-pressure to complete the novel quickly between July and August 1844, Véron refused to publish it because he thought it was too radical an attack on property. The 1865 edition incorporates corrections and redraftings which Sand had little time to make in the original versions.

The original of the manuscript was given by Sand to Chopin's sister Ludwika and is now in the possession of the Dutch royal family.

SELECT BIBLIOGRAPHY

Primary Sources

George Sand, *A Winter in Majorca*, tr. Robert Graves (1931).

—— *Correspondance*, ed. Georges Lubin (25 vols.; Paris: Garnier Frères, 1964–91).

—— *Indiana*, tr. Sylvia Raphael (Oxford: World's Classics, 1994).

—— *Letters of a Traveller* (Harmondsworth: Penguin, 1992).

—— *Marianne*, tr. Sian Miles (London: Methuen, 1987).

—— *My Life*, tr. and abr. Dan Hofstadter (London: Victor Gollancz, 1979).

—— *Story of My Life: The Autobiography of George Sand*, tr. and ed. Thelma Jurgrau (Albany, NY: State University of New York Press, 1991).

—— *The Master Pipers*, tr. Rosemary Lloyd (Oxford: World's Classics, 1994).

—— and Flaubert, Gustave, *The George Sand–Gustave Flaubert Letters* (Chicago: Academy Chicago, 1979 repr. of 1929 edn.).

With the exception of the definitive Lubin edition of the complete Sand correspondence, all these sources are English translations. An English version of the Sand–Flaubert correspondence, drawing on the Lubin editions of the letters, is forthcoming, replacing the MacKenzie edition.

Most of Sand's novels are available in French paperback editions. The principal publishers include Le Livre de Poche, Garnier Flammarion, and Gallimard Collection Folio. Her political writing is exemplified in *Le Compagnon du tour de France* (Campagnonnage) and *Les Femmes à l'Académie Française* (Les Éditions de l'Opale).

Secondary Sources

James Smith Allen, *Popular French Romanticism: Authors, Readers and Books in the 19th Century* (Syracuse, NY: Syracuse University Press, 1981).

Joseph Barry, *George Sand* (1977).

Elma Marie Caro, *George Sand*, tr. Gustave Masson (Port Washington, NY: Kennikat Press, 1970, repr. of 1888 edn.).

Curtis Cate, *George Sand: A Biography* (London: Hamish Hamilton, 1975).

Claudine Chonez, *George Sand* (Paris: Éditions Pierre Seghers, 1973).

Natalie Datalof (ed.), *George Sand Papers, Conference Proceedings 1976 and 1978* (New York: AMS Press, 1980 and 1982).

Donna Dickenson, *George Sand: A Brave Man, The Most Womanly Woman* (Oxford: Berg Publishers, 1988).

Édouard Dolléans, *Féminisme et mouvement social: George Sand* (Paris: Les Éditions Ouvrières, 1951).

Janis Glasgow (ed.), *George Sand: Collected Essays* (Troy, NY: Whitson Publishing Company, 1985).

Alphonse Jacobs (ed.), *Gustave Flaubert–George Sand Correspondance* (Paris: Flammarion, 1981).

Diane Johnson, 'Experience as Melodrama: George Sand', in *Terrorists and Novelists* (New York: Alfred A. Knopf, 1982), 41–51.

Georges Lubin, *George Sand en Berry* (Brussels: Éditions Complexe, 1992).

Francine Mallet, *George Sand* (Paris: Éditions Bernard Grasset, 1976).

Thérèse Marix-Spire, *Les Romantiques et la musique* (Paris: Nouvelles Éditions Latines, 1954).

André Maurois, *Lélia: The Life of George Sand*, tr. Gerard Hopkins (London: Jonathan Cape, 1953).

Nancy K. Miller, 'Writing (from) the Feminine: George Sand and the Novel of Female Pastoral,' in Carolyn G. Heilbrun and Margaret R. Higgonet (eds.), *The Representation of Woman in Fiction* (Baltimore: Johns Hopkins University Press, 1983), 124–51.

Pierre Moreau, *Le Classicisme des Romantiques* (Paris: Librairie Plon, 1932).

Isabelle Hoog Naginsky, *George Sand: Writing for Her Life* (New Brunswick, NJ: Rutgers University Press, 1991).

Ates Orga, *Chopin* (London: Omnibus Press, 1976, repr. 1983).

Marie-Paule Rambeau, *Chopin dans la vie et l'œuvre de George Sand* (Paris: Société d'Éditions 'Les Belles Lettres', 1985).

Naomi Schor, 'Reading Double: George Sand and Difference', in Nancy K. Miller (ed.), *The Poetics of Gender* (New York: Columbia University Press, 1986), 248–69.

Patricia Thomson, *George Sand and the Victorians: Her Influence and Reputation in 19th-Century England* (London: Macmillan, 1987).

Maurice Toesca, *The Other George Sand*, tr. Irene Beeson (London: Dennis Dobson, 1947).

Pierre Vermeylen, *Les Idées politiques et sociales de George Sand* (Brussels: Éditions de l'Université de Bruxelles, 1984).

Marie-Louise Vincent, *La Langue et le style rustique de George Sand dans les romans champêtres* (Geneva: Slatkine Reprints, 1978).
Adam Zamoyski, *Chopin: A New Biography* (Garden City, NY: Doubleday, 1980).

A CHRONOLOGY OF GEORGE SAND

1804   5 June: Marriage of (father) Maurice Dupin (formerly Dupin de Francueil) and (mother) Antoinette-Sophie-Victoire Delaborde, who has two children by previous relationships. July: Birth at Paris of Amantine-Aurore-Lucile Dupin (George Sand). December: Napoleon proclaims himself 'Emperor of the French'.

1806   Birth and death of baby son in Dupin family.

1808   Heavily pregnant, Sophie travels with Aurore to Spain, where Maurice is with the army. June: birth of son Louis. July: family return to Nohant through great dangers, including near-drowning in Bay of Biscay. September: deaths of baby Louis and Maurice within ten days of each other.

1813   Sophie signs formal contract with Aurore's grandmother renouncing rights to rear her daughter, in exchange for a pension of 1,500 francs.

1815   Fall of Napoleon.

1817   Aurore sent to Couvent des Anglaises in Paris, until 1820, when she returns to Nohant and takes over management of estate.

1821   Death of grandmother, Mme Dupin de Francueil. On eve of burial, Aurore's tutor Deschartres persuades her to view father's remains, since his coffin has been exposed next to hole dug for grandmother, and to kiss his skull. Sand later wrote, 'It filled me with an absolute despair of being able to communicate directly with the beloved dead.'

1822   On visit to James Roëttiers du Plessis and family near Melun, Aurore meets Second Lieutenant Casimir Dudevant, illegitimate son of a minor Gascon noble. Marries Casimir six months later: she contributes 400,000 francs to their common property, he 60,000.

1823   Birth of son Maurice.

1824   Increasing violence by Casimir towards Aurore.

1826   Death of Casimir's father. Casimir inherits only his title, Baron; his stepmother retains life possession of estate. Casimir now completely dependent on Nohant income, and will therefore fight Aurore's later demand for legal separation.

1828   Birth of daughter Solange (probably by Stéphane Ajasson de

Grandsagne).

1829   Aurore writes first novel, *La Marraine* (never published).

1830   Revolution in Paris; fall of Charles X; installation of Louis-Philippe.

1831   With Solange, Aurore leaves for Paris, where she lives with lover Jules Sandeau and begins literary apprenticeship on *Le Figaro*, which pays her 7 francs per article. Publishes *Rose et Blanche*, written in collaboration with Sandeau, published under mutual pseudonym of 'J. Sand' (since mother-in-law objects to her use of name Dudevant).

1832   Publishes *Indiana* by 'Georges Sand', under own sole authorship, drawing on reputation which name 'Sand' has acquired as result of *Rose et Blanche*, and substituting name 'Georges', from Greek for 'farmer'. Begins using 'George' in 1833 because publisher feels that Anglo-Saxon version of name suits English-sounding surname 'Sand'. Publishes *Valentine*.

1833   End of liaison with Sandeau. Publishes *Lélia*, which is pronounced 'the century's assessment of itself'. Begins affair with Alfred de Musset, with whom she travels to Venice in December, sharing coach with Stendhal for part of journey.

1834   Venice sojourn ends disastrously when Musset drinks heavily, uses prostitutes, and attacks Sand with knife. He returns to France in April. Sand returns in August with new lover, Pietro Pagello, but he leaves in October. Publication of *Jacques* and first part of *Lettres d'un voyageur*.

1836   After attempt against her life by Casimir, Sand brings suit for legal separation; wins sole custody of Solange and shared custody of Maurice, but Casimir receives her Paris properties and yearly income from Nohant.

1837   Death of Sand's mother. Solange abducted by Casimir, but Sand recovers her. Publishes *Mauprat* (novel which foretells characters and style of *Wuthering Heights*) and *Lettres à Marcie* (on the Woman Question).

1838   Balzac visits Nohant. Sand begins affair with Chopin. Trip to Majorca, which ends disastrously in February 1839 when Chopin's illness worsens. Publishes *Gabriel* (on Woman Question), and political-religious works *Spiridion* and *Les sept cordes de la lyre*.

1840   *Le Compagnon du tour de France*.

1841   Sets up socialist *Revue indépendante* with Pierre Leroux. *Horace*.

1842   *Un hiver à Majorque*; *Consuelo*.

1844   *La Comtesse de Rudolstadt*; *Jeanne*. Launches republican
        newspaper in Orléans, *L'Éclaireur de l'Indre et du Cher*.
        Writes *Le Meunier d'Angibault* (published in January 1845)
        during summer at Nohant with Chopin. 'Young Europe'
        movement founded by exiles in Paris, headed by Sand's
        friend Giuseppe Mazzini.

1846   *La Mare au diable*, *Lucrézia Floriani* (often said to contain
        portrait of Chopin as 'Prince Karol', although Chopin him-
        self denied it).

1847   May: Solange marries sculptor Auguste Clésinger at Nohant.
        Summer: scenes between Clésinger, Maurice, and Sand, dur-
        ing which Clésinger punches Sand in chest. Solange inter-
        venes on her mother's behalf but complains in letter to
        Chopin that Sand is being unreasonable in refusing addi-
        tional dowry. Chopin fails to arrive at Nohant this summer,
        for whatever reason, and relationship fades away.

1848   Abdication of Louis-Philippe. Sand leaves Nohant for Paris,
        to press new government for reforms in Berry. Becomes
        caught up in Revolution as unofficial minister of informa-
        tion. *La Petite Fadette*.

1849   October: death of Chopin.

1850   Beginning of Sand's most enduring relationship, with en-
        graver Alexandre Manceau, seventeen years her junior.
        Death of Balzac.

1851   Coup by Louis Napoléon, with whom Sand intercedes on
        behalf of exiled and imprisoned republicans.

1853   *Les Maîtres Sonneurs*.

1854–5 *Histoire de ma vie*.

1856   Sand warned by official censor for publication of anti-papist,
        pro-Republican novel *La Daniella*.

1857   Death of Musset. Manceau buys Sand a writing retreat at
        Gargilesse, near Nohant.

1860   Near-fatal attack of typhoid. Publishes *Le Marquis de
        Villemer*; *Valvèdre*.

1861   Maurice marries Lina Calamatta at Nohant.

1862   *Laura*; *Voyage dans le cristal*.

1863   *Mademoiselle la Quintinie*, anti-clerical novel. Manceau fa-
        tally ill with consumption.

1864   *Villemer* produced in Paris: provokes pro-Sand, anti-regime
        riots by 5,000 demonstrators. Maurice forces Manceau from
        Nohant, asserting that his marriage has made him master
        there. Sand goes with Manceau.

1865   Death of Manceau at Palaiseau, near Paris.

1866   Growing friendship between Sand and Gustave Flaubert produces famous correspondence.

1868   Visits of Flaubert and Turgenev to Nohant.

1870   War declared against Prussia; siege of Paris.

1871   Death of Casimir Dudevant. Paris Commune ends with murder of 15,000 and exile of 125,000 supporters. Sand, greatly distressed by this bloody end to her socialist visions, publishes *Journal d'un voyageur pendant la guerre*.

1876   June: death of Sand at Nohant from an inoperable intestinal occlusion. She continues to write until morning of day on which she takes to her bed and never rises again. Burial at Nohant: address by Victor Hugo; attendance by Prince Jérôme Buonaparte, Alexandre Dumas *fils*, and Flaubert. Sand's American friend Henry Harrisse describes the scene: 'this ill-tended graveyard, this throng of peasant women wrapped in their dark cloth mantles and kneeling on the wet grass, the gray sky, the cold drizzle which kept pelting our faces, the wind whining through the cypresses and mingling with the aged sexton's litanies'.

THE MILLER OF
ANGIBAULT

CONTENTS

NOTICE

This novel, like so many others, is the outcome of a stroll, a chance meeting, a day of leisure, an hour of *far niente*.* All those who have written imaginative works, good or bad, are aware that intellectual perception often proceeds from sensory awareness. Newton's apple, falling from its tree, led him to discover one of the great laws of the universe. All the more likely is it that the plan of a novel should arise from the encounter with some fact or material object. In works of scientific genius, it is reflection which draws the inner essence out of the simple fact. In humbler imaginative works of art, it is reverie which attires and embellishes the solitary fact. The complexity or simplicity of the work is irrelevant. The working of the spirit is the same for both.

Now in our valley there is a fine mill called Angibault,* whose present miller I do not know, though I did use to know the owner. He was an elderly gentleman, who, since his acquaintanceship in Paris with *M. de Robespierre** (for so he always called him) had allowed his mill-dam to be overgrown with whatever vegetation sprouted naturally there: the alder and the bramble, the oak and the reed. The river, left to its own devices, had carved out of the sand and grass a network of tiny torrents, whose lower reaches were covered in summertime by sturdy tufts of aquatic plants. But the old gentleman is dead; the hatchet has done its work; there was many a faggot to chop, many a plank to saw in this miniature virgin forest. There still remain a few fine trees, some running water, a fresh-smelling little lake, and thickets of those enormous brambles that are the lianas of our climate. Still, this corner of a wild paradise that my children and I came upon one day in 1844, with exclamations of surprise and joy, is now but one pretty place like so many others.

The castle of Blanchemont,* with its countryside, its hunting-park and its home farm, is real, and I have painted it faithfully; only it is called by another name, and the Bricolin family are fictional types. The madwoman who plays a part in this story, I encountered elsewhere; she, too, had been driven mad by love. She made such a painful impression on myself and my travel companions that, despite having crossed twenty leagues* of country in order to explore the ruins of a magnificent Renaissance abbey, we could not endure the place more than an hour. This unhappy woman had adopted the melancholy spot for her mechanical, unceasing and eternal round. Fever had singed the grass under her stubborn feet, the fever of despair!

GEORGE SAND

*Nohant, 5 September 1852**

TO SOLANGE*

My child, let us search together.

The First Day*

=====

I. INTRODUCTION

The bell of St Thomas Aquinas church was just sounding one
o'clock in the morning, as a slight, swift black shape slipped
along the looming wall of one of those fine gardens that are
still found in Paris on the left bank of the Seine, and which are
worth so much in the middle of a capital city. The night was
warm and calm. Exhaling their sensuous odours, daturas in
full bloom stood like great white ghosts under the brilliant
gaze of the full moon. The columns of the wide flight of steps
leading up to the Hôtel de Blanchemont still retained their old
elegant air, and the large well-maintained garden heightened
the opulent appearance of this silent dwelling, where not a
light shone from the windows.

This circumstance of superb moonlight roused some disquiet in the young woman wearing mourning who was
making her way along the most sombre avenue towards a
little gate in the far corner of the wall. But her resolve was
undiminished, as this was not the first time she had risked her
reputation for the sake of a pure and henceforth legitimate
love; she had been a widow for the past month.

She made good use of the rampart thrown up for her by
a clump of acacias, arriving soundlessly at the little private
gate opening on to a narrow and little-travelled lane. At
almost the same moment, this gate opened, and the assignation guest entered furtively. Saying nothing, he followed his
mistress to a little orangery, where they shut themselves
away. But out of an irrational propriety, the young Baroness
Blanchemont, drawing a pretty little Russian copper box
from her bag, struck a match and lit a candle which had been
placed in a corner, hidden in advance, and the nervous, respectful young man foolishly helped her to light up the in-

terior of the pavilion. He was so pleased to be able to look at her!

The summerhouse had large shutters of plain wood. A bench, a few empty crates, some garden tools, and the little candle with no other holder than a cracked flower pot, such were the furnishings and lighting of this abandoned boudoir which had served some long-gone marquise as a voluptuous retreat.

Their descendant, the blond Marcelle, was chastely and simply dressed, as befits a modest widow. Her only ornament was her beautiful golden hair, tumbling over her black crêpe shawl. Only the delicacy of her alabaster hands and her satin-shod foot gave away her aristocratic origins. Otherwise she could have been taken for a little Parisian milliner, the natural companion of the young man on his knees before her: for it is grisettes whose brows are marked by regal dignity and saintly guilelessness.

Henri Lémor had a pleasant face, intelligent and distinguished rather than handsome. His abundant black hair made his sallow complexion seem even paler. Anyone could see that here was a child of Paris, strong of will, delicate of constitution. His attire, proper and modest, told of a humble middle station; his carelessly folded cravat betrayed either an entire want of style or a habit of absent-mindedness; his brown gloves alone went to show that this was not a man fit to be Madame's husband or lover, if the servants of the Hôtel de Blanchemont had their say.

In this pavilion the two young people, the one scarcely older than the other, had often spent sweet moments together during the mysterious nocturnal hours; but during the month that they had been separated, great troubles had cast a shadow over the tale of their love. Henri Lémor trembled, like one full of consternation. Marcelle de Blanchemont seemed frozen with fear. He knelt before her as if to offer his thanks for her willingness to grant him one last interview, but rose again quickly without having spoken a word, his manner constrained, well-nigh cold.

'At long last! . . .' she said with effort, holding out her hand, which he brought to his lips with an almost convulsive movement, without showing the least trace of pleasure in his expression.

He no longer loves me, she thought, covering her eyes with both hands. And she remained mute, frozen with terror.

'*At long last*?' Lémor repeated. 'Perhaps you mean *already*? I should have had sufficient fortitude to wait longer; pardon me, for I lacked the strength.'

'I fail to understand you!' said the young woman, overwhelmed, letting her hands drop again.

Lémor saw her moist eyes and mistook the cause of her emotion.

'Oh! yes,' he replied, 'I am indeed guilty; your tears show plainly what remorse I have caused you. To me these four weeks seemed so endless that I lacked the courage to tell myself that they were in fact too few! Thus, hardly had I written to you this morning, requesting permission to see you, when I repented. I blushed for my cowardice, I blamed myself for the pangs which I was forcing your conscience to endure; and when I received your reply, so grave and good, I understood that pity alone summoned me to you.'

'Oh! Henri, how you pain me when you talk so! Is this some game, some pretext? Why did you ask to see me, if you return to me with so little joy and trust?'

The young man trembled and fell again at the feet of his mistress.

'I could endure haughtiness and reproaches better,' he said. 'Your kindness strikes me to the quick!'

'Henri! Henri!' cried Marcelle. 'Have you done something for which I should reproach you? Oh! you have a guilty air! I see it clearly, you have forgotten me, or scorned me!'

'Neither one; to my eternal misery, I respect you, I adore you, I believe in you as I believe in God, on all the earth I can love only you!'

'Well then!' said the young woman, throwing her arms around her poor Henri's dark head. 'This is no great catastrophe, your loving me so, since I love you in the same manner. Listen to me, Henri, I am free now; I have no cause to reproach myself. So little did I desire the death of my husband, that not once did I allow myself to think of what I

would do with my liberty if I happened to find myself free. As
you well know, we never once talked of that, you were not
unaware that I loved you passionately, and yet this is the first
time that I have boldly told you so. But my friend, how pale
you are! your hands are icy, you seem to be suffering so! You
terrify me!'

'No, no, pray continue,' replied Lémor, collapsing under
the weight of emotions at once delicious and painful.

'Well then,' continued Mme de Blanchemont, 'I cannot
entertain such scruples and torments of conscience as you
attribute to me. When they brought me the bleeding body of
my husband, killed in a duel for another woman, I was as-
sailed by consternation and horror, I admit; in telling you this
dreadful news and ordering you to stay away from me for
some time, I thought to do my duty; oh! if it is indeed a crime
to have found this time terribly long, your scrupulous obedience has punished me enough for it! But during the month
when I have withdrawn from the world, thinking only of
bringing up my son and comforting the parents of Monsieur
de Blanchemont as best I could, I have sounded my heart
thoroughly, and I no longer find it so guilty. Never could I
love that man who did not love me, and all that I could do was
to respect his honour. At present, Henri, I owe to his memory
no more than a superficial respect for propriety. I shall see you
secretly, not often, that cannot be! . . . till the end of my period
of mourning; and after a year, two years, if necessary . . .'

'What! Marcelle, after two years?'

'Are you asking me what we shall be to each other then,
Henri? I have already told you, you no longer love me.'

This reproach had no effect on Henri. It was so little deserved! Attentive to the point of anxiety towards all his
mistress's words, he begged her to continue:

'Well then!' she went on, blushing with the modesty of a
maiden. 'Don't you want to marry me, Henri?'

Henri let his head fall on to Marcelle's lap, and remained
thus for a few moments, as if overwhelmed with joy and
gratitude; but he lifted himself up brusquely, his face expressing the deepest despair.

'Haven't you already had enough unhappy experience of marriage?' he said with some harshness. 'Do you mean to submit to the yoke again?'*

'You frighten me,' said Mme de Blanchemont after a moment of apprehensive silence. 'Are you then aware of tyrannical instincts within yourself, or is this your own hesitation before the yoke of eternal fidelity?'

'No, no, nothing of the kind,' replied Lémor despondently. 'You are well aware of the thing I fear, the thing to which I cannot subject you or myself; but you will not, or cannot, understand that. And yet we have talked of it so often, at a time when we did not dream that such discussion could have any personal meaning for us, or become a matter of life or death for me!'

'Is it possible, Henri, that you should still be so attached to your utopias? What! is love itself powerless against them? Ah! how little you love, you men!' she added with a deep sigh. 'If it is not vice which shrivels your souls, then it is virtue, and in either case, whether you are cowardly or sublime, you love only yourselves.'

'Listen to me, Marcelle, had I but asked you, one month ago, to abandon your own principles, if my love had demanded that which your religion and your beliefs judge an immense crime, never to be made good . . .'

'You never asked it,' said Marcelle, blushing.

'I loved you so that I could never ask you to suffer and weep for me. But if I had done so . . . Answer me then, Marcelle!'

'Your question is indiscreet and out of place,' she replied, attempting gentle coquetry in order to avoid having to reply.

Her grace and beauty made Lémor tremble. He pressed her to his heart with passion. But tearing himself instantly away from this drunken moment, he stood apart, and continued in an altered voice as he strode up and down behind the bench on which she sat:

'And if I were to ask now for this sacrifice which the death of your husband has certainly made less terrible . . . less fearsome . . .'

Once more Mme de Blanchemont became pale and grave.

'Henri,' she replied, 'I should be offended and wounded to the core of my being by such a thought, at a time when I have just offered you my hand, which you appear to decline.'

'I am indeed unfortunate, to be so unable to make myself understood, and to be taken for a wretch, when I feel heroism and love pervading me! . . .' he answered bitterly. 'The word will seem ambitious to you; it must make you smile in pity. Nevertheless it is true, and God will take account of my suffering . . . which is atrocious, perhaps beyond my strength.'

And Henri burst into tears.

The young man's grief was so deep and genuine that Mme de Blanchemont was aghast. In these scalding tears there was something like an invincible refusal ever to be happy, a farewell for ever to all the illusions of love and youth.

'Oh my dear Henri!' cried Marcelle. 'What evil have you resolved to do to both of us? Why such despair, when you are the lord of my life, when there is longer any bar to our being united before God and man? Is my son the obstacle between us? Cannot you muster sufficient greatness of soul to give him some part of the affection which you have for me? Do you fear that you will someday have to reproach yourself with having abandoned the unhappy child of my blood?'

'Your son!' sobbed Henri, 'I should have a graver fear than not loving him. I should be afraid of loving him too much, and of being unable to resign myself to seeing him take the opposite path to mine at the crossroads of the century. Custom and public opinion would have me leave him to the world, whereas I want to snatch him away from it, even if it meant making him as unfortunate, poor, and ruined as I . . . No, I could never regard him with sufficient indifference or egotism to allow him to become a man like the rest of his class; no! no! . . . that, and other things, everything, your position and mine, all these are insurmountable obstacles. From whatever aspect I survey such a future, I can see nothing but hopeless struggle, misery for you, anathema to me! . . . It is impossible, Marcelle, for once and for all, impossible! I love you too much to accept sacrifices whose outcome you cannot predict and whose number you cannot measure. You do not know me, I realize. You take me for an indecisive, weak dreamer. Perhaps you have occasionally thought me guilty of affectation; you have believed that one word from you would bring me back to reason and truth, as you see them. Oh! I am more miserable than you can think, and I love you more than you can presently understand. Later ... yes, later, you will thank me from the bottom of your soul for having known how to be unhappy alone.'

'Later? but why? and when? what do you mean?'

'Later, I tell you, when you awake from this grim, ill-omened dream which I have brought upon you, when you return to the world, when you resume your easy, sweet intoxications, in short, when you cease being an angel and descend again to earth.'

'Oh yes, yes, when I shall be drained by egotism and corrupted by flattery! That is your meaning, that is your prophecy for me! In your wild arrogance, you think me incapable of embracing your ideas and empathizing with your heartfelt desires. Let us be frank, you think me unworthy of you, Henri!'

'What you say is frightful, Madame, and this struggle can continue no longer. Allow me to take leave of you, for we are beyond understanding each other.'

'Will you leave me thus?'

'No, I shall not leave you; far from your presence, I shall contemplate you in my spirit and adore you in my heart's core. I shall suffer eternally, but with the hope that you will forget me, with guilt at having desired and sought your affection, with the consolation that at least I did not take advantage of you like a poltroon.'

'Why then did you wish to see me?' she asked him in a cold, hurt voice as she watched him preparing to take his leave.

'Yes, yes, you have cause to reproach me for that. It was a final cowardice on my part; I was aware of it, though I gave in to the need to see you one last time ... I hoped that I should find you altered for me; your silence had given me to hope that; I was eaten up with sorrow, and I thought that your coldness would have power to cure me. Why did I come? Why do you love me? Am I not the grossest, the most ungrateful, the most savage, the most detestable of men? But it is better that you should see me so, and that you should know that there is no cause to regret losing me . . . Things are better so, and I have done well to come, have I not?'

Henri spoke as if in a delirium; his grave, unspoiled features were all disordered; his voice, normally full of gentleness and sympathy, now had a flat, metallic timbre that grated on the ear. Marcelle perceived his suffering, but her own was so poignant that she could do or say little that would relieve either of them. She remained pale and silent, her hands clenched together and her body rigid as a statue. Just as he was leaving, Henri turned round, and when he saw her in this state, he fell at her feet, covering them with tears and kisses. 'Adieu,' he said, 'the most beautiful and pure of all women, the best of friends, the most noble of lovers! May you find a heart worthy of your own, a man who loves you as I do, and who does not bring discouragement and trepidation as his contribution to your mutual fortunes! May you be happy and benevolent, without enduring the struggles of an existence like mine! Finally, if there be any traces of fidelity and human feeling in the world that you inhabit, may you rekindle them with your divine breath, and find grace before God for your caste and your century, which you are worthy to redeem through your own endeavours alone!'*

Having spoken thus, Henri plunged out, overlooking the despair to which he was abandoning Marcelle. He seemed as one pursued by the Furies.

Mme de Blanchemont remained stricken to stone for some time. When she returned to her apartments, she walked up and down her own chamber until the first rays of dawn, shedding no tears, troubling the night's stillness with no sighs.

It would be too grandiose to claim that this beautiful twenty-two-year-old widow, well-to-do, distinguished in her milieu by her grace, accomplishments, and wit, was in no wise humiliated and outraged at having her proposal of marriage spurned by a man of no birth, no fortune, and no fame. In the first moments the outraged pride of the young woman probably served her in place of courage. But soon the genuine nobility of his sentiments suggested more serious reflections to her and, for the first time, she was plunged into a thorough examination of her own life and that of the other personages around her. She reminded herself of what Henri had said to her at earlier meetings, when there was no question of anything between them but unrequited love. She was amazed at her flippancy towards what she had thought mere fantasies, in a young man actually of serious mind. She began to judge him with that calm which a generous and strong will brings to bear on the most violent emotions of the heart. As the night hours slipped away and the distant clocktowers tolled them in succession, in tones of silvery clarity, Marcelle attained that spiritual lucidity which contemplation and a long vigil bring to grief. Educated by other principles than Lémor's, she was none the less destined in some measure to share this plebeian's love, and to find refuge in it from all the tedium and melancholy of aristocratic life. She was one of those simultaneously tender and strong souls who need to devote themselves to something, and who can conceive of no greater happiness than that which they themselves confer. Unhappy in her household, bored by the world, she had abandoned herself with the romantic trust of a young girl to this sentiment, which soon became her religion. Sincerely devout in her adolescence, she had perforce become passionately attached to a lover who respected her scruples and worshipped her chastity. Piety itself had urged her to devote herself to this love and to want to see it sanctified by indissoluble bonds, as soon as she found herself free. With joy she had thought to make a brave sacrifice of those material interests that the world prizes so, and of those narrow prejudices of her birth, which had never misled her judgement. She thought to do much, poor child, and in fact it *was* much; for the world would have blamed or scolded her greatly for it. She had not foreseen that it was nothing none the less, and that the poor man's pride would reject her sacrifice as if it were an insult.

Suddenly enlightened by fright, misery, and Lémor's resistance, Marcelle reviewed in her anxious mind all that she had glimpsed of the social crisis that shakes this century. The women of our time are no longer strangers to these higher realms of thought. According to the bent of their minds, and without affectation or mockery, all of them can now read* daily in the great, sad, amorphous, contradictory, but profound and significant book of real life: in all forms—journal or novel; philosophy, political discourse, or poetry; official statement or private conversation. So she was well aware, as are we all, that this bloated, diseased present time is at odds with the past which holds it back, and the future which calls it forward. She had seen lightning-flashes hurtling over her head, she could foresee a monstrous battle, more or less distant. She was not of a timid nature: she had no fear and kept her eyes wide open. Her grand-parents' discontents, complaints, dreads, and grudges had worn her out and left her disgusted with cowardice! Youth has no wish to blight its bloom, and its charmed years are dear to it, no matter how storm-tossed. The brave and gentle Marcelle told herself that even in thunder and hail, one could smile in the shelter of the first bush with the person one loves. Thus the threatening battle between material interests seemed to her but a game. What did ruin, exile, or prison matter? she asked herself, as terror hovered over all the supposed happy souls of the time. Love can never be exiled; and then, thank heaven, I love a man without means, who will be spared.

Yet she had never thought that she could be wounded deep within her affections, by that veiled and mysterious battle that continues despite all formal constraints and all apparent obstacles. The struggle of feelings and ideas is well and truly joined from this time onward, and Marcelle found herself thrown into it with sudden force, all her illusions clinging to her, as one wakes from a dream. Intellectual and moral war had been declared between the classes, steeped in their opposing beliefs and passions, and Marcelle had encountered a sort of irreconcilable enemy in the man she loved. Astounded at first by this discovery, gradually she came to terms with the idea, which suggested to her new plans, more generous and romantic still than those which had nourished her for over a month, and at the end of her long walk through the silent and empty apartments, she found a calm resolution, which she alone, perhaps, might look on without a smile of admiration or pity.

All this happened quite recently, perhaps only last year.

II. THE JOURNEY

Having married her first cousin, Marcelle was known as de Blanchemont both before and after her marriage. The lands and castle of Blanchemont formed part of her patrimony. The land still retained its importance, but for farming alone, and even the tenant farmers no longer lived in the tumbledown castle, which, abandoned over a century ago, would have required too much expense to make good. Orphaned early, educated in a Paris convent, married very young, and ignorant of her husband's financial affairs, Mlle de Blanchemont had never seen this ancestral estate. Resolved to leave Paris and to seek a bucolic life consistent with her newly formed aspirations, she wished to begin her pilgrimage by visiting Blanchemont, thinking to take up residence there in good time if that suited her designs. She was well aware of the castle's state of disrepair: indeed, that constituted a reason for preferring it. The disarray in which her husband had left both his and her own affairs afforded her a pretext for undertaking a journey to which she publicly appointed a term of some few weeks, but to which she privately assigned neither goal nor limit; her real aim was to leave Paris and the life to which she was fettered.

Happily for her plans, no one in her family was in any position to take on the duty of accompanying her. As an only daughter, she was not obliged to defend herself against the protection of a sister or elder brother. Her husband's parents were well on in years; taken aback by the debts incurred by the deceased man, which only clever management might put right, they were both astonished and delighted that a young woman of twenty-two, who had previously demonstrated neither a talent nor a taste for business, should be resolved to administer her own affairs and to examine the state of her properties for herself. None the less there were several objections to the idea of her setting out on her own with her child. They thought that she ought to be accompanied by her financial adviser; they feared that the child might take ill on the journey, in such warm weather. Marcelle replied to the elderly Blachemonts, her father- and mother-in-law, that a prolonged conversation with an ancient lawyer would do little to offset the tedium which she was imposing on herself; that the local notaries and attorneys could provide her with more trustworthy information and advice better suited to the locality; finally, that it was no terribly difficult matter to settle accounts with the farmers and renew the leases. As for the child, the Paris air was making him progressively more delicate. The country, an active life, and sunshine could only do him much good. Unexpectedly adroit at vanquishing objections, which she had foreseen and considered during the vigil related in the previous chapter, Marcelle then adduced the duties imposed by her role as her son's teacher. Moreover, she could not be certain of the state of the inheritance: whether M. de Blanchemont had made the farmers advance him considerable sums, whether he might not have raised heavy mortgages on his lands, etc. Her duty was to set forth and verify all these matters, relying entirely upon herself, in order to know on what footing she must live henceforth, so as not to compromise her son's future. She spoke so wisely of these interests, which, deep down, conerned her but little, that after twelve hours she had gained her victory and persuaded all the family to approve and praise her resolution. Her love for Henri had been so well disguised that no suspicion troubled the grand-parents' trust.

In this unremitting, unaccustomed activity and wholehearted hope, Marcelle slept little better the night following her final interview with Lémor. She had the strangest dreams, sometimes pleasant, sometimes painful. At last, with the dawn, she awoke, and as she cast a sleepy look around the interior of her apartment, she was struck for the first time by the vain and superfluous luxury displayed everywhere. Satin draperies, excessively soft and overstuffed furnishings, a thousand expensive niceties, a thousand gleaming trinkets, in short, all the gilt, porcelain, panelled, fantastic pomp that encumbers the dwelling of today's elegant woman. 'I should really like to know,' she thought to herself, 'why we profess so much scorn for courtesans.* They merely earn those things that we can afford by other means. They sacrifice their modesty to possess objects which should have no value for a wise and virtuous woman, but which we none the less regard as indispensable. They share our tastes, and degrade themselves for the sake of appearing as rich and fortunate as we are. We should set them the example of a simple and austere life, rather than condemning them! And if we were to compare our own indissoluble marriages with their passing liaisons, would we actually see any more principled behaviour in the young ladies of our own class? There, no less than among prostitutes, one observes a child tied to an old man, beauty sullied by repulsive vice, wit in the thrall of foolishness, all for the love of a diamond tiara, a carriage, and a box at the Italiens!* Poor girls! They say that for your part you scorn us; you have good reason!'

But the pure and pale blue daylight passing through the curtains lent an enchanted air to the sanctuary which Mme de Blanchemont had decorated with her own hand and with an exquisite taste. She had almost always lived apart from her husband, and this pretty bedchamber, so chaste and fresh, where Henri himself had never dared to enter, brought back to her only sweet and melancholy memories. It was here in this refuge, scented by those blooms of unparalleled beauty, found only in Paris, which are essential to the life of today's well-to-do woman, that she had read and dreamed. She had made this retreat as artistic as she could; she had ornamented and decorated it to suit her own taste; she was devoted to it as her secret haven, where her life's sadnesses and her soul's storms had always responded to the calming influence of isolation and prayer. Casting a long, affectionate look around her, she silently pronounced an expression of eternal farewell to these mute witnesses of her inner life . . . a life as private as that of the flower that has no blemish for the sun to expose, but that hangs its head under the leaves for love of the cool shade.

'My chosen retreat, ornaments according to my taste, I once loved you,' she thought, 'but I no longer can, for you accompany and sanctify wealth and idleness. Henceforth you stand in my eyes for all that separates me from Henri. No longer can I survey you without disgust and bitterness. Let us part before we begin to detest one another. Austere statue of the Virgin, no longer could you protect me; profound and pristine mirrors, you would make me loathe my own image; beautiful vases of flowers, you would lose all charm and perfume!'

Then, before writing to Henri, as she had resolved to do, she went on tiptoe to look at her son and to bless his slumber. The sight of this pale child, whose precocious intelligence had flourished at the expense of his physical well-being, tugged violently at her heart. She spoke to him silently, as if, in his sleep, he might hear and understand his mother's thoughts.

'Have no fear,' she said to him, 'I do not love *him* more than you. Do not be jealous of him. If he were not the best and worthiest of men, I should never allow him to be your father. There, my little angel, you are loved with loyalty and strength. Sleep well, we shall never separate!'

Bathed in delicious tears, Marcelle returned to her chamber and wrote these few lines to Lémor:

'You are right, and I understand you completely. I am not worthy of you, but I shall become so, for so I wish to be. I am embarking on a long voyage. Have no fears for me, and love me still. In a year, on the same day, you will receive a letter from me. Arrange your life so as to be free to come search for me in the place to which I shall summon you. If you still judge me insufficiently redeemed, you will give me another year . . . one year, two years, sustained by hope, such is almost happiness for two beings who loved for so long and so hopelessly.'

She had this letter delivered early that same morning. But Lémor was nowhere to be found. He had left the evening before for an unspecified place and period. He had given notice at his modest lodgings. But she was assured that the letter would reach him, as one of his friends had been asked to call every day for his correspondence and to send it on to him.

Two days later, Mme de Blanchemont, accompanied by her son, a lady's maid, and a groom, were crossing the wastes of Sologne* in a mail coach.

At eighty leagues from Paris,* the traveller reached the virtual centre-point of France, and stopped for the night in the first village this side of the Blanchemont domain. Blanchemont itself was another five or six leagues hence,* and in the centre of France, despite all the new roads created in the past few years, the rural areas still have so little commerce with each other that it is difficult to obtain clear information from the inhabitants about other interior districts. Everyone is familiar with the road to the market town or the county seat to which business sometimes calls them. But if you ask the inhabitants of a hamlet which is the track to a farm a mile distant, you put them to the utmost test. There are so many tracks! . . . and they all look alike. Awaking early to attend to their mistress's departure, the servants of Mme de Blanchmont could obtain no enlightenment on the Blanchemont estate from either the innkeeper or his servants or the drowsy rural travellers there. No one knew exactly where the estate was. One came from Montluçon,* another was familiar with Château-Meillant;* all of them had been through Ardentes* and La Châtre a hundred times; but none of them knew anything more of Blanchemont than its name.

'The name is familiar,' mused one, 'I know the farmer, but I have never been there. It is very far away, at least four full leagues.'*

'Good Lord!' boomed another, 'I saw the Blanchemont cattle at La Berthenoux* fair, no more than a year ago, and I was talking with the farmer, Monsieur Bricolin, as plain as I speak to you now. *Indeed! Indeed!* I do indeed know Blanchemont; but I have no idea where to find it.'

The serving-maid, like the serving-maid at every hostelry, knew nothing of her surroundings. Like all inn-maids, she had only been in the area a short time.

The lady's-maid and the groom, accustomed to following their mistress to stately homes famed for over twenty leagues round, and located in civilized regions, began to think themselves in the middle of the Sahara. Their faces lengthened and their self-respect suffered cruelly at these rebuffs to their quest for information about the road to the chateau which they were to honour with their presence.

'I suppose it must be a hut or a foxhole?' said Suzanne scornfully to Lapierre.

'It is the palace of the Corybantes,'* replied Lapierre, who had been much taken in his youth with an enormously popu-

lar melodrama entitled *The Château of Corisante,** and who
applied this name, mangling it, to every ruin he saw.

Finally the stable-lad had a flash of brilliance. 'There's a
man in the hayloft who can tell you,' he said, 'as his job is
running round the country, day and night. Grand-Louis, we
call him, the big miller.'

'Go and fetch the big miller,' commanded Lapierre majestically. 'It would appear that his bedchamber is at the other end
of the ladder?'

The big miller descended, stretching, from his corn-loft,
cracking the joints of his long arms and legs. When he
glimpsed this athletic structure and resolute face, Lapierre left
off his lordly mien and approached him with all politeness.
The miller was in fact among the best-informed; but his
clarifications induced Suzette to bring him to Mme de
Blanchemont, who was taking her chocolate in the dining-
room with little Édouard, and who, far from sharing the
consternation of her household, was delighted to learn that
Blanchemont was an abandoned and well-nigh lost world.

The specimen of the countryside who was presently standing before Marcelle was five feet eight inches in height, remarkable for a region whose inhabitants are generally on the
short side. He was well-proportioned, robust, easy in his
movements, and strikingly featured. The local girls called him
the handsome miller, and this epithet was as well earned as the
other. When he wiped his cheeks free of their usual flour with
the back of his sleeve, he laid bare a tanned complexion
glowing with lively health. His features were regular,
big-boned like his limbs, his eyes were black and wide-set, his
teeth sparkling, and his long chestnut hair, wavy and crinkled
as strong men's hair often is, surrounded squarely a broad full
forehead that betokened shrewdness and common sense
rather than poetic ideals. He wore a coarse blue smock,
unbleached linen trousers, hob-nailed boots, and no stock-
ings. In his hand was a heavy, knobbed sorb-wood walking-
stick which doubled as a club.

He entered with an assurance which might have been taken
for effrontery, were it not that the softness of his clear blue

eyes* and the smile on his wide ruddy lips testified that openness, kindness, and stoical insouciance were the bedrock of his character.

'Greetings, Madame,' he began, tipping his broad-brimmed grey felt hat without going quite so far as to lift it altogether; for while the older peasant is obsequious and inclined to salute anyone better dressed than he, the post-Revolutionary peasant is notable for the adherence of his head-covering to his head.* 'They tell me you want to know the road to Blanchemont?'

The tall miller's loud sonorous tones made Marcelle jump, for she had not seen him enter. She turned round smartly, taken aback at first by his aplomb. But the privilege of beauty is such that in mutual examination the young miller and the young gentlewoman quickly forgot that wariness which a difference in rank always inspires at the first meeting. Still, seeing him thus disposed towards familiarity, Marcelle thought it necessary to remind him with great gentility of the niceties due to her sex.

'I thank you greatly for being so obliging,' she said, greeting him, 'and I should be grateful, Monsieur, if you would be so kind as to tell me if there is a route from here to Blanchemont which our carriages might manage.'

Without a by-your-leave, the tall miller was already making ready to sit down; but when he heard himself called 'Monsieur', he grasped with his unusual perspicacity that he was dealing with a decent personage deserving of respect in her own right. Softly and smoothly he removed his hat and rested his hands on the back of the chair, as if to give himself a more dignified bearing.

'There's a local track, not a very good one,' he said, 'but at least you won't tip over if you're careful; the thing is to follow it and not turn off. I'll tell your postilion that. But the best would be to hire a rattletrap here, because the last rains of the storm have done more damage than you might think to the Vallée-Noire, and I'm not sure that your carriage's dainty wheels could get out of the ruts. Perhaps they might, but I wouldn't vouch for it.'

'I can see that your ruts are no laughing matter, and that it would be prudent to follow your advice. Are you quite certain that with your "rattletrap" I shall not tip over?'

'Oh! have no fear, Madame.'

'I am not afraid for myself, but for this little child. That is what makes me careful.'

'It's true that it would be a great shame to crush this little fellow,' said the tall miller, coming up to young Édouard with an air of genuine benevolence. 'How genteel and delicate he is, this little man!'

'Delicate indeed, wouldn't you agree?' said Marcelle, smiling.

'Ah, my Lord! he isn't strong, but pretty as a girl. Are you coming to our country then, Monsieur?'

'Come here, big man!' shrilled Édouard, climbing on to the miller as he bent down. 'Help me touch the ceiling!'

'Take care!' warned Mme de Blanchemont, a bit taken aback by the carelessness with which the rustic Hercules was handling her child.

'Oh, have no fear!' replied Grand-Louis. 'I'd rather break every *alochon** on my mill than a single finger on this little Monsieur.'

This word *alochon* delighted the child, who repeated it, giggling, without understanding.

'So you don't know that word?' asked the miller. 'Those are the little wings, the pieces of wood that ride along the mill wheel, and that the water pushes to make it turn. I'll show you them if ever you come to see us.'

'Yes, yes, *alochon*!' said the child, bursting into laughter and wriggling in the miller's arms.

'What a joker this little rascal is!' laughed Grand-Louis, setting him back down on his chair. 'Well, Madame, I must return to my business. Is that all I can do for you?'

'Yes, my friend,' answered Marcelle, her reserve overcome by good will.

'Oh! I ask nothing better than to be your friend!' replied the miller chipperly, his look implying clearly that such familiarity would not have been to his taste had it come from someone less young and lovely.

'Fair enough,' thought Marcelle as she blushed and smiled, 'I have been warned.' And she added, 'Farewell, Monsieur, though doubtless not for ever, for surely you live at Blanchemont?'

'Nearby. I am the miller of Angibault, a league from your castle, for I believe you are the lady of Blanchemont?'

Marcelle had forbidden her servants to betray her incognito. She wanted to enter the country unperceived; but she now realized, from the miller's manner, that her position as landowner would not create the sensation she had feared. A non-resident landowner is a stranger who gives no cause for concern. The tenant farmer who represents him and with whom one deals all the time is another character altogether.

Although she had planned to leave early and arrive at Blanchemont before the heat of midday, Marcelle was obliged to spend most of the day at the inn.

Every 'rattletrap' in town had gone to a great fair on the outskirts, and she had to wait for the first one to return. Not until three in the afternoon did Suzanne announce, in mournful tones, that the only available vehicle was a sort of wicker dog-cart, shameful and disgusting.

Much to the astonishment of her amazed maid, Mme de Blanchemont promptly accepted this offer. She took along the most essential parcels, left the keys of her *calèche** and her trunks with the inn-keeper, and left in a simple *patache*,* that respectable relic of our forefathers' plain tastes, becoming rarer with each passing day, even on the tracks of the Vallée-Noire. The one which it was Marcelle's unhappy fate to encounter was of the purest native construction, and an antiquarian would have contemplated it with respect. It was as long and low as a coffin; no springs of any sort diminished its charms; the wheels, as tall as the cowl, were a fit match for the muddy ditches carved out alongside our roads, those trenches that the miller, doubtless from regional pride, had dignified with the name of ruts; finally, the cowl itself was made of a sort of wattle and daub, so that every little bump rained clods of clay down on the travellers' heads. A thin but ardent little stallion drew this rural carriage quite nimbly, and the *patachon*, that is, the driver, seated on the cart-shaft with his legs dangling down (since our forefathers found it easier to draw up a chair for climbing into a carriage, rather than getting all tangled up in a footboard) was the least crowded and most secure member of the party. Two or three *pataches* of this sort are still to be found in our region, in the possession of rich old peasants who see no reason to change their habits, and who maintain that carriages with springs give you 'ants', that it, pins and needles in your calves.

Nevertheless the voyage was more or less bearable, as long as they stuck to the high road. The *patachon* was a lad of fifteen, carrot-headed, snub-nosed, brazen-faced, fearing nothing, never hesitating to goad his horse with every oath in his rich vocabulary regardless of the ladies present, and taking pleasure in draining the energy of the brave pony who had never had a taste of oats in his life, and who was cheery enough so long as he could see the meadows greening up. But as soon as they penetrated more barren countryside, he began to lower his head, more in discontent than in disheartenment, and to pull his burden with a sort of fury, taking no heed of the road's roughness, lurching the cart harshly from side to side.

III. THE BEGGAR

Things got much worse when they left the sandy countryside and descended into the damp, fertile lands of the Vallée-Noire. On the outskirts of the barren plateau, Mme de Blanchemont had admired the immense and marvellous landscape that rolled away beneath them, only to rise again in zoned horizons of pale violet, bounded in golden bands by the setting sun. There are few lovelier vistas in France. In close detail the vegetation is not particularly lush. No great rivers water these fields, whose slate roofs reflect little sunlight. There are no picturesque mountains, nothing striking, nothing extraordinary in this quiet landscape; only a broad sweep of arable farmlands, an infinite parcelling-out of fields, paddocks, coppices, and wide parish roads with all manner of line and turning, in a palette of dark green verging on blue; a hotch-potch of overgrown walls, chimneys hidden away in the orchards, lines of poplars, thickly wooded pastures in the distance; on the wolds paler fields and more distinct hedge-rows setting off the neighbouring masses; all in all, a unity and harmony visible for a range of fifty square leagues, the whole of which the eye can see from the thatched cottages of Labreuil* or Corlay.

But our traveller would quickly have lost this magnificent panorama from her sights. Once one is down in the twisting lanes of the Vallée-Noire, the scenery changes. Alternately descending and ascending the high-hedged lanes, one skirts no precipices, but the lanes are themselves precipitous. The sun, setting behind the trees, gives them a strangely fey and wild air all their own. Receding mysteriously away under their thick shade, *traînes** of an emerald green lead only to blocked paths or stagnant swamps, bends which a carriage cannot mount again once it has gone down them, all in all, an unending enchantment for the imagination, but with very real risks for those who adventure down its seductive, capricious, and perfidious byways by any other means than foot, or at best on horseback.

So long as the sun was above the horizon, the ginger-topped Automedon* acquitted himself honourably. He took the most heavily travelled road: therefore the roughest, but also the surest. He crossed two or three little streams by following the tracks left on the banks by cart-wheels. But once the sun had set, night fell quickly in these sunken lanes, and the last peasant they met had said nonchalantly, 'Go on! go on! it's only another short league or so, and the track is good all the way.'

Unfortunately this was the sixth peasant in two hours who had told them that it was only another short league or so, and the track, always pronounced a good one, was such that the horse was exhausted and the travellers at the end of their tether. Marcelle herself began to fear that they would be thrown over; for although in broad daylight the driver and his nag picked out their route skilfully, in the dead of night it would be impossible to avoid the wrong turnings which the lay of the land renders more dangerous than picturesque, and which, ending suddenly in nothing, drop the traveller over a ten- or twelve-foot bluff. The lad had never been so far into the Vallée-Noire; he was losing his temper, swearing like a lunatic each time that he had to turn back to find the way again; he was complaining about his thirst, his hunger, his horse's fatigue, all the while raining blows on the beast, and giving himself citified airs in cursing this wild country and its doltish inhabitants to the furthest corners of hell.

Several times Marcelle and her party had got down when the track looked quick and dry; but they could not walk for more than five minutes without coming on to one of those hollows where the path first narrowed and then was entirely taken up by a spring with no outflow, creating a swamp that a delicate woman could not cross on foot. Suzette, a Parisian, said that she would rather tip over than leave her shoe in that mire, and Lapierre, who had spent his life in dancing-shoes on gleaming parquet floors, was so awkward and dispirited that Mme de Blanchemont no longer trusted him to carry her son.

The peasant's usual response on being asked for directions is: *Walk straight on, straight on.* This is no more than a facetious witticism meaning *walk straight on your own two legs*, for there is no such thing as a straight road in the whole of the Vallée-Noire. The numerous cuttings of the Indre,* the Vauvre, the Couarde,* the Gourdon, and a hundred other minor streams that change their names as they flow and that have never submitted to the yoke of any bridge or causeway, force you into a thousand detours in order to find a fordable crossing, so that you are often obliged to turn your back on your destination.

When the beleaguered travellers arrived at a crossroads with a wayside crucifix, an evil spot which the peasant imagination always peoples with devils, warlocks, and monsters, they encountered a beggar sitting on the 'dead man's stone',* who called out to them in monotonous tones, 'Good folk, take pity on a poor unfortunate!'

The tall stooped frame of this ancient but still robust man, together with his huge stick, presented a disarming prospect in the event of solitary attack. His stern features were barely visible, but in his harsh voice there was something more imperious than grovelling. His melancholy attitude and filthy rags were at odds with the evidently jocular intent behind his withered boutonnière and the faded ribbon in his hat.

'My friend,' Marcelle said to him as she gave him a silver coin, 'show us the way to Blanchemont, if you know it.'

Instead of replying, the beggar continued gravely reciting an Ave Maria, which he had begun as a sly dig at her.

'Come on, answer,' ordered Lapierre, 'you can mutter your prayers later.'

The beggar turned towards the lackey with a scornful air and carried on with his orison.

'Don't bother talking to that man,' said the driver. 'He's an old tramp who wanders around, you see him all over, never in his right mind.'

'The way to Blanchemont?' the beggar finally replied, when he had done with his prayer. 'You've missed it, my children; you must turn back and take the first track that goes down the hill on the right.'

'Are you certain?' enquired Marcelle.

'I've been that way six hundred times or more. If you don't believe me, suit yourselves; it's all the same to me.'

'He seems certain of his facts,' said Marcelle to the driver. 'We had best listen to him; why should he want to trick us?'

'Humph! For the pleasure of his own wickedness,' exclaimed the worried driver. 'I don't trust that man.'

Marcelle insisted on following the beggar's advice, and soon they had plunged into a narrow, sunken lane, twisting rapidly downhill.

'I still say, I do,' the driver repeated, swearing as his horse recoiled before each step, 'that sly old bastard is leading us astray.'

'Go on,' commanded Marcelle, 'we can't turn back.'

The further they went, the more impossible the track became; but it was too narrow to turn the cart around; two impressive hedges fenced it in. After performing miracles of strength and loyalty, the little horse got to the bottom, under a stand of ancient oaks which appeared to be the outskirts of a forest. Suddenly the track broadened out, and there before them was a great pool of stagnant water, nothing like a river ford. None the less the driver plunged in; but right in the middle, he sank deeply and tried to pull to one side; this was the last exploit of his bony Bucephalus.* The driver sank in up to the hub of the cart-wheel, and the horse fell heavily, severing the harness. They had to unhitch him. Lapierre plunged into the water up to his knees, groaning like a man in his final agony; and though he helped the driver out of the worst of it, they were not able, neither being strong, to lift the cart up again. So the *patachon* leapt nimbly on to his horse, and, wishing eternal damnation on that sorcerer of a beggar, took off at a fast trot, promising to go and look for help, but in a tone of voice which indicated that he would have little compunction in leaving his travellers mired until daybreak.

The *patache* had remained upright. Calmly standing in the marsh, it was still perfectly habitable, and Marcelle stretched out on the back seat with her son on top of her to let him sleep more comfortably, for Édouard had been demanding his supper and his bed, and after his hunger had been calmed by a few sweetmeats from Suzette's pocket, stored in reserve, he was not long in dropping off. Reckoning that the young driver would be in no haste to return, if he found good lodgings, Mme de Blanchemont sent Lapierre off to see if he could obtain hospitality at this hour from any of the cottages secreted under the greenery, so closed and silent after dusk that one must touch them to believe them real. Old Lapierre had only one concern: finding a fire to dry his feet and ward off rheumatism. So he did not have to be asked twice, fleeing the swamp as soon as he had ascertained that the cart, settled on the fallen trunk of an old willow, would sink no further.

The most inconsolable was Suzette, who was terrified of highwaymen, wolves, and snakes, three scourges never encountered in the Vallée-Noire but ever-present in the mind of a lady's-maid on a journey. However, the sprightly sang-froid of her mistress forbade her to give way completely before her fears and, wedging herself as comfortably as she could on to the front seat, she resigned herself to weeping quietly.

'Come now, what is it, Suzette?' urged Marcelle when she saw her crying.

'Alas! Madame!' she sobbed, 'can't you hear the bullfrogs croaking? They might jump in, all over the cart . . .'

'And eat us alive, I suppose?' exclaimed Mme de Blanchemont with a burst of laughter.

In fact the green swamp-dwellers, briefly disturbed by the horse's fall and the driver's shouts, had resumed their monotonous droning. Dogs could also be heard barking and howling, but so far away that there seemed little reason to expect swift assistance. The moon was not up yet, but the stars glittered in the stagnant water of the swamp, limpid once more. A warm breeze stirred the huge reeds growing in thick clumps on the bank.

'So, Suzette,' said Marcelle, abandoning herself to poetic reverie, 'things are not so bad in the mire as you might think, and if you were so disposed, you might sleep as soundly as in your own bed.'

'Madame must have lost her wits,' thought Suzette, 'to subject herself to such a situation.'

'Oh, heavens, Madame!' she screamed after a moment's silence, 'I'm sure I heard a wolf howling! Aren't we deep in the middle of a wood?'

'The wood is nothing more than a clump of willows,' Marcelle replied, 'and as for your howling wolf, it is a man singing. Were he to pass this way, he might help us back to dry land.'

'But what if it is a robber?'

'If so, it is a kindly robber who sings to warn us he is coming. Listen now, Suzette, quite seriously, he *is* coming this way, his voice is getting nearer.'

In fact a full and melodiously masculine voice, though an uninstructed one, was floating over the silent fields, to the percussive beat of a horse's slow and steady clopping; but this voice was still distant, and there was no certainty that the singer was making his way towards the swamp, which was probably nothing more than a cul-de-sac. When the song ended, they heard nothing more, whether because the horse moved on to the grass or because the villager turned aside.

At that moment Suzette, prey again to her fears, saw a silent shadow sliding along the pool, magnified to giant stature in the water. She let out a cry, and the shadow, plunging into the marsh, made straight for the cart, slowly and deliberately.

'Have no fear, Suzette,' said Mme de Blanchemont, although she herself was far from reassured at this moment. 'It is the old beggar we met a short while ago; perhaps he will tell us of a house which might send out help.'

'My friend,' she called to him with much presence of mind, 'my serving-man, *who is over there*, will accompany you so that you may show him the path to some dwelling-place.'

'Your serving-man, my girl?' the beggar replied familiarly. 'He's not over there, he's already far away... And in any case he's too old, silly, and weak to be any possible use to you.'

This time Marcelle was afraid.

IV. THE SWAMP

This answer sounded like the fierce threat of a man with evil intent. Marcelle seized Édouard, resolved to defend him with her life, if necessary: and she was about to jump into the water on the other side of the cart from which the beggar was approaching, when the rustic song started again, a second chorus, this time much closer.

The beggar stopped short.

'We are lost,' murmured Suzette, 'here comes the rest of the gang.'

'On the contrary, we are saved,' replied Marcelle, 'for that is the voice of an honest peasant.'

In fact the voice was reassuring, and the quiet simple song proclaimed a conscience at peace with itself. The horse's hoof-beats likewise drew nearer. Evidently the villager was coming down the path that led to the swamp.

Marcelle leaned out over the cart to call the peasant; but he was singing too loudly to hear her, and if his horse had not stopped with a fierce whinny, taking fright at the black shape of the *patache* ahead, the master would have ridden on without noticing.

'What the devil is that?' cried an intrepid stentorian voice, which Mme de Blanchemont recognized immediately as that of the tall miller. 'Ho there! Friends! Your carriage has stopped short. Are you all dead in there, that you say nothing?'

When Suzette recognized the miller, whose handsome presence had favourably impressed her that morning, despite his rough-and-ready dress, she became all graciousness. She retailed to him the pitiable state to which she and her mistress were reduced, and Grand-Louis, laughing unconcernedly about their little adventure, assured her that nothing would be simpler than pulling them out. But first he went to unload a big sack of wheat which he was carrying behind him on his horse. Catching sight of the beggar, who seemed indifferent about hiding, he said in a friendly tone: 'Oh, is that you there, Père Cadoche? Stand aside so that I can throw down my sack!'

'I came to try to assist these poor children!' replied the beggar; 'but there is so much water that I can go no further.'

'Don't worry, old fellow, and don't get wet for nothing. At your age that's dangerous. I can get the women out without your assistance.' Turning back to fetch Mme de Blanchemont, and sinking in the mud up to his horse's breast, he said gaily: 'Come now, Madame, step down the shaft a bit and slip up here behind me; nothing could be simpler. Though you'll wet more than the tips of your shoes, for your legs are not as long as your servant's. Your driver must be an idiot to have mired you there, when two paces to the left, there's no more than six inches of mud!'

'I am terribly sorry to make you undergo such a nasty soaking,' said Marcelle, 'but my child . . .'

'Oh, the little monsieur? Of course! him first. Hand him over to me . . . like that . . . there he is, up in front of me. Have no fear, the saddle will not bruise him, my horse doesn't believe in saddles and neither do I. There you are, sit here behind me, my little lady, and have no fear. Sophie has a strong back and a sure gait.'

The miller lifted the mother and child softly down on to the grass.

'What about me?' cried Suzette. 'Do you intend to leave me here?'

'Not a bit, Mademoiselle,' boomed Grand-Louis, turning back for her. 'Give me your parcels as well, we'll get everything out, have no fear.'

'Now,' he continued when he had finished unloading everything, 'that wretched driver can come for his carcass of a cart whenever he likes. I have no way of harnessing Sophie to it; but I shall take you wherever you like, my little ladies.'

'Are we very far from Blanchemont?' enquired Marcelle.

'Aye, s'truth! your driver took an odd road, he did! It's a good two leagues of country from here, and by the time we got there all the folk would be in their beds; it would be no easy matter to rouse them. But if you like, here we are, no more than a short league from my mill at Angibault; it's not grand, but it's clean, and my mother is a good woman who'll make no fuss about getting up and putting clean white sheets on your beds and twisting a couple of pullets' necks. Will that suit you? Let's be off then, ladies! You must take the rough with the smooth, the mill with the miller. By tomorrow morning they'll have pulled the cart out and wiped it clean, it won't take cold in the swamp, and you shall be driven to Blanchemont whenever you like.'

In the miller's brusque invitation lay cordiality and even a kind of tact. Marcelle, won over by his good heart and the mention he made of his mother, accepted gratefully.

'That's all right then,' exclaimed the miller; 'I don't know you, you may be the lady of Blanchemont, but I don't mind; even if you're the devil himself (and they say the devil can make himself fine and lovely when he likes), I only want to save you from spending a miserable night. Oh yes! I can't leave my sack of wheat; I shall put it on Sophie, the little fellow can sit on top and mama behind him; that will do you no harm, you can lean on the sack. The girl will come with me, on foot, and have a little chat with Père Cadoche, he may not be so well turned out, but he has a good wit about him. But where has he got to, the old lizard? Ho there! Père Cadoche! Are you coming to stay with us? No answer; well then, he has other plans for tonight. Let's go now, ladies.'

'That man gave us quite a fright,' said Marcelle. 'Do you know him?'

'I've known him since I was born. He's not an evil man, you had no reason to be afraid of him.'

'But I do think he was threatening us, and the way he called me "my girl" . . .'

'He called you "my girl"? The old rascal! He has no shame! But that's just his way; take no notice. He's not got an evil bone in his body, oh he's one of a kind, Père Cadoche! *Everybody's uncle*, they call him, and he promises to make everybody his heir, though he's poor as a church mouse.'

Marcelle rode along quite comfortably on the sturdy, even-tempered Sophie. Little Édouard, whom she held firmly before her, 'was much pleased by this style of travel,' as the good La Fontaine* puts it. He kicked the mare's withers with his two little feet, but she felt nothing and went no faster. She walked on like a true miller's horse, with no need of the reins, knowing the road by heart, and finding her way through the shadows, over water and rocks, without a single false step. At the behest of Marcelle, who was afraid that her old serving-man might have to spend a night under the stars, the miller called out several times in his thunderous tones, and the little party of travellers was soon rejoined by Lapierre, who had got lost in a neighbouring thicket and had been going round and round the same acre of land for the past half-hour.

After an hour's march, they heard the rush of the mill-race, and the first pale beams of the moon lit up the vine-covered roof of the mill and silvered the river banks, covered with wild mint and soapwort.

Marcelle jumped lightly down on to this scented carpet, having handed the miller back her child, who was full of the joy and pride of his equestrian adventure. Throwing his little arms around the miller's neck, Édouard exclaimed, 'Hello, Alochon!'

Just as Grand-Louis had predicted, his elderly mother got up without a murmur and made the beds with the help of a servant-girl, perhaps fourteen or fifteen years old. Mme de Blanchemont was more eager for rest than supper: she would not let the old woman give her anything more than a glass of milk, and, overcome with fatigue, she was soon sleeping, with her child by her side, in a featherbed of the sort called a *couette*, of boundless height and infinite softness. Together with a well-filled straw pallet, these beds, whose only fault is that they are too warm and soft, form the sleeping-arrangements of all the inhabitants, rich or poor, of a province in which geese abound and the winters are very cold.

Exhausted by her long voyage of some eighty leagues, covered very rapidly, and particularly by the culmination, the ride in the *patache*, the lovely Parisienne would happily have slept late; but dawn had scarcely broken when the crowing of the cocks, the tic-tac of the mill, the deep voice of the miller, and all the sounds of rustic labour prevented her from sleeping any longer. Besides, Édouard was already jumping about on the bed, not in the least tired and already invigorated by the country air. Despite all the din outside, Suzette, who was sleeping in the same room, was slumbering so soundly that Marcelle thought it a pity to rouse her. So, making a start on the new life which she had vowed to begin, she rose and made her toilette without her maid's assistance, dressed her son with great pride and pleasure, and went down to wish her host and hostess good morning. But there she found only the mill-lad and the serving-girl, who told her that the master and mistress had just left for the bottom of the meadow, where they were busy getting the meal ready. Curious to know what sorts of preparations these might be, Marcelle crossed the mill-pond over the rough bridge and entered the field, passing a fine plantation of young poplars on her right and keeping to the course of the river, or rather the brook, which was no more than ten feet across at this point, though up to the top of its banks and lapping against the blooming meadow. At the outskirts of the mill, this stream, slender but powerful, forms a lake of considerable breadth, still, deep, and harmonious as a mirror, in which the ancient willows and mossy roofs of the dwelling are reflected. Marcelle sat in contemplation of this peaceful, pleasant spot, which spoke more to her than she knew. She had seen more beautiful scenes; but there are places which leave us open to some inexplicable and powerful affin-

ity, where it seems that fate draws us so as to prepare us to
accept certain joys, griefs or duties.

V. THE MILL

Making her way into the massive thickets where she expected
to find her hosts, Marcelle thought herself in a virgin forest.
One piece of land followed another, all overgrown with thick
vegetation and riddled with flood damage. Clearly the little
river had ravaged the earth greatly during the rains. Tumbled
together in vainglorious disorder, huge half-fallen alder,
beech, and trembling poplar trees exposed their roots, twined
together like serpents, on the wet sand. The river, splitting
into many rivulets, had carved out a capricious array of little
clearings, where hardy brambles lay tangled on the dewy grass
with a hundred kinds of wild flowers, tall as hedges and
allowed to grow with their own unique, savage grace. No
English garden* could ever imitate the prodigality of nature,
the shapes arranged by happy chance, the many little basins
that the river had carved out in the sand and the flowers,
the bowers of branches joining over the current, all those
fortuitous natural accidents, the ruined dams, the few piles
still upright, devoured by moss, seemingly dropped there to
complete the beauty of the scene. Marcelle was rapt and
would have remained so a long while, were it not for young
Édouard careering about like an escaped fawn, eager to leave
his little footprints as the first marks in the sand freshly
deposited on the riverbank. But fear of his falling into the
water reawakened her solicitude; and following him at a run,
deeper and deeper into this enchanted wilderness, she thought
herself in the middle of one of those dreams in which the
beauty of nature appears an earthly paradise.

At length she glimpsed the miller and his mother on the
other bank, one casting his net to fish for trout, the other
milking her cow.

'Ah! already awake, my little lady!' exclaimed the miller.
'As you can see, we are taking care of your wants. My mother

is ashamed to have nothing dainty to give you; but I told her that you would be happy with our good will. We are not cooks, or innkeepers, but when one side has a hearty appetite and the other a good will . . .'

'You are a hundred times too kind to me, my good people,' said Marcelle as she carried Édouard over to them, risking the plank that served as a bridge. 'I have never had such a sound night's sleep, nor ever seen such a beautiful morning. What fine trout you get here, *Monsieur le meunier*! And such creamy white milk, *la mère*! You are spoiling me, and I know not how to repay you.'

'We shall be repaid if you are content,' smiled the old woman. 'We never see such grand folk as you, and we know few fine words; but we can see that you are an honest woman who makes no unreasonable demands. Come, let us go back to the house, the *galette** will soon be ready, and I am sure the little boy likes strawberries. We have a corner of the garden where he can pick them himself.'

'You are so kind, and your countryside so beautiful, that I should like to spend my life here,' blurted Marcelle recklessly.

'Really?' said the miller with a good-natured smile. 'Oh well! if your heart says so . . . You see, Mother, our land is not so unattractive as you think. If I tell you that a rich lady feels at home here!'

'Oh yes!' exclaimed the mill-wife, 'so long as she can build a castle, and a poor place to choose for a castle, I should say.'

'Can you possibly mean that you are not happy here?' asked the astonished Marcelle.

'Oh, I'm happy enough,' the old woman answered. 'I have lived here all my life and here I shall die, God willing. I have got used to it, over the seventy-five years of my reign, so to speak; and besides, you must get used to whatever country you find yourself in. But as for you, Madame, if you were to spend a winter here, you would not think our land so beautiful. When the floods cover our fields and we can't even get out into our own farmyard, no, that's not so very fine!'

'Rubbish! women are always frightened about something,' barked Grand-Louis. 'You know very well that the floods can't carry the house away, and the mill is solid enough. It's time enough to worry about the bad weather when the bad weather comes. All winter you long for summer, Mother, and while summer lasts you have nothing better to do than worry about the coming winter. I say that we can live here happy and carefree.'

'Why not practise what you preach, then?' replied his mother. 'Are you so carefree? Are you always content with being a miller and having the house flooded so often? Ah! let me tell you everything you have ever said about how miserable it is to have a poor house and no prospects!'

'It's no good you repeating every stupid thing I ever said, Mother, save your breath.' Although he spoke plainly, the tall miller was looking at his mother with a gentle affection, almost beseechingly. To Mme de Blanchemont their conversation seemed less banal than the reader may think it thus far. With her inclinations towards the rural life, the least harsh existence for the poor, she wanted to know how it felt for those who had to endure it. She did not approach country living with too many romantic illusions. Henri, who doubted her ability to live simply, had drilled into her its privations and genuine sufferings. But she did not think such sufferings beyond her spirit, and what intrigued her in the opinions of her hosts at the mill was the extent to which they were armed with natural stoicism or insensitivity, as against the support she might expect from poetic sensibility and love, that still more religious and powerful sentiment. So she allowed some curiosity to show as soon as Grand-Louis had taken his trout in to 'fry on the cookstove', as he put it.

'You are not happy, then?' she asked the old mill-wife. 'Nor your son, who is sometimes tormented despite his cheerful mien?'

'Well, Madame, as for myself,' began the good woman, 'I should be quite rich, and perfectly content with my fate, if my son was happy. My poor dead husband was content; his trade was going well; but he died before the children were grown, and I had to raise them all myself as best I could and set them up in life. And so none of them got very much; the mill went to my Louis, him they call Grand-Louis, as they called his father Grand-Jean, and me Grand'Marie. For, God be thanked, we grow tall in our family, and all my children are a good height. But that's the best of our fortune; the rest is nought to hope on.'

'But why do you want to be any richer? Are you in poverty? You seem to be well lodged, you eat good bread, you enjoy excellent health.'

'Aye, aye, thank the Good Lord, we have what we need, and many a better one, it may be, is in want; but you see, Madame, you're only as happy or unhappy as you think you are.'

'That is the real question,' sighed Marcelle, who had observed good sense and native perspicacity in the face and speech of the mill-wife. 'Since you understand so well what really matters, why do you complain?'

'I don't complain, it's my Grand-Louis! or to put it better, I do complain because I see him discontented, and he holds his tongue, because he is a brave lad and doesn't want to hurt me. But sometimes it all gets too much for him, and he blurts it out, poor child! He says but one word, and that one breaks my heart: "*Never, never*, Mother!" and that means he's lost all hope. But then, being naturally of a happy disposition (like his poor dear dead father) he seems to make the best of a bad job, and he tells me all sorts of tales, as if to comfort me, or as if he imagines his dreams might come true.'

'And what dreams are those? Is it ambition?'

'Oh, aye! a great ambition, a piece of madness! but not greed for money, for he's not greedy, far from it! When the inheritance was divided, he let his brothers and sisters have anything they wanted, and whenever he's earned a little something he'll give it away to the first one who asks. Nor is it vanity, for he still wears the smock, though he's an educated man and could afford to dress as well as a bourgeois. No, nor is he a wrong 'un, nor a spendthrift, for he's content with what he has and never sticks his nose in where it's not wanted.'

'Well, then, what is it?' asked Marcelle, unconsciously inducing the old woman's confidence by her gentle face and friendly tone.

'Well, what else should it be but love?' said the mill-wife with an enigmatic smile and an indescribable delicacy, which immediately negated the differences of age and rank between the two women and established a mutual freedom of manner and common interest between them, in the matter of feelings.

'How right you are,' replied Marcelle, coming closer to Grand'Marie, 'it is indeed love which is the great spoil-sport of youth! And this woman he loves, is she better off than he?'

'Oh, it's no woman! My poor Louis is too honourable to pay his addresses to a married woman! No, it is a girl, a young girl, a pretty girl, my word, and a good one, I have to say. But she is well off, rich, and it's no good thinking about it, her parents would never marry her to a miller.'

Struck by the parallel between the miller's story and her own, Marcelle was filled with curiosity and emotion. 'If she really loves your son,' she suggested, 'this good, beautiful girl, she will marry him in the end.'

'So I sometimes think; for she does love him, I know that much, Madame, though my Grand-Louis is not so sure. She's a good girl, and would never tell a man she wants to marry him against her parents' wishes. And then, she's also a bit of a flirt, a bit of a tease: well, it's her age, she's only eighteen! Her impish ways drive my poor boy mad; so to cheer him up, when I see he isn't eating or when he's scolding Sophie (our mare, to speak of her more respectfully), I can't stop myself telling him what I think. And he believes me a little, for he sees that I know more than him about a woman's heart. I can see that the pretty thing blushes when she meets him, and that she looks his way when she walks past here; but I have no business saying that to the lad, it but inflames his madness, and I should do better to tell him he must put it out of his mind.'

'Why?' asked Marcelle. 'Love conquers all. You can be certain, good mother, that a woman in love is stronger than any obstacle.'

'Oh yes, I thought that when I was young. I said to myself, a woman's love is like the river that knocks all down before it, that makes light of dams and barriers. I was better off than my poor Grand-Jean, and yet I wed him. But there wasn't the difference between us as between Mademoiselle . . .'

Just then little Édouard interrupted the mill-wife, calling out to his mother, 'Look! Is Henri here?'

VI. A NAME CARVED ON A TREE-TRUNK

Flinching at the child's exclamation, Mme de Blanchemont was hard pressed not to cry aloud. What could have prompted it?

Looking the way Édouard was pointing, Marcelle saw a name carved with a penknife on the bark of a tree. The child was just learning to read, particularly familiar words and names that he might have been taught to spell. He was right: the name Henri was inscribed on the smooth trunk of a white poplar, and he thought it was his friend who had carved it. Carried away by her child's imaginings, Marcelle too thought for a moment that she might see Henri Lémor emerge from the thickets of alder and trembling poplar. But she was not long in realizing, with a sad smile, how vulnerable she was to self-delusion. Still, hope being slow to die, no matter how illusory, she could not help but ask the mill-wife who in her family or her acquaintanceship bore the name of Henri.

'No one that I know of,' answered mother Marie. 'I know nobody at all by that name. In the village of Nohant* there is a family called Henri, but they are folk like me, and cannot write, on paper or trees . . . Unless it was their son who's back from the army . . .* but never! he's not been by here for more than two years.'

'So you have no idea who might have written that name?'

'I didn't even know something was written there. I never noticed. And if I had noticed, I couldn't have read it. I did have the means to get an education, but it wasn't the thing in my day.* You made a cross on your deeds or your will, instead of signing, and that was good enough in law.'

The miller had returned to announce that breakfast was ready. Although he had not noticed the name before, he knew perfectly well how to read and write, and he tried to devise an explanation that might satisfy Marcelle's curiosity.

'It must be some prank by that fellow who was here the other day,' he opined, 'for no other cityfolk ever come.'

'And who was this fellow the other day?' asked Marcelle, forcing herself to feign indifference.

'It was a gentleman who didn't give his name,' the old woman replied. 'We don't know much, but we know that curiosity killed the cat. Louis agrees with me there. There are folk in our part of the world who quiz any traveller they see, but we never ask to know more than a being wants us to know. This gentleman seemed to want to keep his name and his business to himself.'

'Although he did ask a lot of questions, that lad,' observed Grand-Louis, 'and we'd have been within our rights asking him a few in turn. I don't know why I didn't venture it. He looked harmless enough, and hanging back's not my nature; but he had an odd look, as made me feel right sad.'

'What kind of look?' queried Marcelle, her interest and curiosity growing with every word the miller uttered.

'I couldn't say,' he replied. 'I didn't take a lot of notice at the time, but afterwards I got to thinking. Do you remember, Mother?'

'Aye, you said to me, "There's one like me, he's not got what he wants."'

'Poppycock! I never said that,' Grand-Louis exclaimed, fearful that his mother might reveal his secret, and unaware that she already had. 'I just said, "There goes a queer stick, not much content with his lot."'

'Did he look terribly sad?' asked Marcelle sympathetically.

'He looked like he was thinking a good deal. He sat on the ground, just where you are now, oh, three hours or more, all by himself, and he watched the river flowing along, like he was trying to count up all the drops of water. I thought he might be sickening for something, so I went out twice to ask him into the house for a cool drink. When I got close he jumped up like I'd woke him from his sleep, and he didn't seem any too pleased. But then he looked all calm and peace-

able again, and he thanked me. I got him to take a bit of bread
and a glass of water, no more.'

'It *was* Henri!' shrilled little Édouard, clinging to his mother's dress and listening attentively. 'You know very well,
Mother, Henri doesn't drink wine.'

Mme de Blanchemont blushed, went pale, blushed again,
and, in a voice which she could not entirely control, asked
what the stranger was doing in this part of the world.

'I haven't an inkling,' said the miller, attentively observing
the lovely, emotion-stricken face of the young woman, and
saying to himself, 'Here's another soul like me, with a certain
idea in her head!'

So, willingly satisfying Marcelle's inquisitiveness about the
stranger and his own curiosity about her feelings, he happily
told her all the details that she awaited so anxiously.

The stranger had arrived on foot about fifteen days ago.
He had roamed about for two days in the Vallée-Noire, and
no one had seen him since. Where he had spent the night
no one knew; out in the open, the miller supposed. He
didn't look very well off for money. But he had offered to
pay for his meagre repast at the mill; when the miller refused, he had thanked him in the simple way of a man
who has no compunction about accepting hospitality from
one of his own social station. He was dressed in the fashion
of a respectable working man or a rural shopkeeper, in a
smock-frock and straw hat. He carried a small rucksack,
and from time to time he knelt down and drew paper out
of it, as if he were making notes. He had been to Blanchemont, from what he said, although no one had seen him
there. But he talked about the farm and the old castle like
a knowledgeable man. While he was eating his bread and
drinking his water, he asked the miller a great many questions about the extent of the acreage, how much the farm
brought in, what sort of mortgages there were, what kind
of a man the farmer was, how much the late M. de
Blanchemont had spent, what other lands he owned, etc.; in
the end they made him out to be an agent sent by some
purchaser to get information and evaluate the quality of the
land.

'For it appears that the Blanchemont estate will be put up for sale, if it hasn't been already,' added the miller, who was not quite as exempt from the local peasants' intimate curiosity as his mother made him out to be.

Marcelle, racked by other worries, barely listened to this final surmise. 'What age might this stranger have been?'

'If his face told true,' replied the mill-wife, 'he was about the same age as Louis, twenty-four or twenty-five.'

'And what kind of face does he have? Does he have brown hair, is he about average height?'

'He's not tall and he's not blond,' said the miller. 'His face is not unpleasant, but he's pale, like a man whose health's not good.'

'It could well be Henri,' thought Marcelle, even though this rather rough sketch did not match the ideal she carried in her heart.

'He might be a bit of a sharp customer,' Grand-Louis continued: 'for to please Monsieur Bricolin, the farmer at Blanchemont, who wants to buy the place, and to put the stranger off a bit, I teased him by talking down the property, but there were no flies on this lad. The land is worth such and such amount, he said, and he counted out income, outgoings, expenses on his fingers like someone who knows his stuff, and who needs no long chat, glass in hand, as we do round here, to know what's what.'

'Come now, I must be losing my wits,' thought Mme de Blanchemont; 'this stranger is some newcomer, some agent sent to make land purchases in the area, and his sad mien and his reverie on the water's edge were caused by no more than heat and fatigue. As for the name, Henri, that is mere coincidence, if indeed it was he who carved it. Henri never had any head for business; he had no idea of any property's value, or the acquisition and cultivation of riches of any sort. No, no, that wasn't him. Besides, wasn't he in Paris fifteen days ago? I saw him three days since, and he said nothing about having been away lately. And what would he have been doing in the Vallée-Noire? Did he have any idea that the estate of Blanchemont was in this province? I don't remember telling him anything about it.'

Tearing her eyes forcibly away from the mysterious inscription that had so taxed her thoughts, she followed her hosts back to the house, and found an excellent meal laid out on a massive table covered with a snow-white cloth. *Fromentée*, that typical dish of the region, a cracked-wheat milky porridge; a pear cake with cream and nutmeg; the trout from the Vauvre; thin but tender chickens, laid still warm on the grill; salad with hot walnut oil; goat's cheese and slightly underripe fruit; little Édouard thought all this exquisite. They had laid places for the two servants and the two hosts at the same table with Mme de Blanchemont, and the mill-wife was greatly amazed at Lapierre and Suzette's refusal to sit next to their mistress. But Marcelle insisted that they conform to country ways, and she embarked gaily on this egalitarian life, still fresh in her thoughts.

The miller's manners were brusque, frank, but never rude. His mother's were somewhat more deferential, and despite scolding from Grand-Louis, for whom common sense counted more than politeness, she pressed her guests somewhat to make them eat more than their appetites dictated; but her concern was so sincere that Marcelle did not think her at all importunate. This old woman had a good heart and mind, and her son took after her in those respects. He also had a sounder basic education.* He had completed his schooling up to secondary level, and understood a great deal more than he let on. In his conversation Marcelle found more sensible ideas, healthy notions, and natural taste than she would have expected from her meeting with him in the inn the day before. All this was the more noticeable because, far from showing off his education or priding himself on it, he affected down-to-earth peasant manners rather than the little politenesses with which he was perfectly familiar. Apparently he was afraid the villagers might think him hoity-toity, and he had nothing but scorn for those who turn their backs on their own folk and their simple background, giving themselves ridiculous airs. He spoke with a good accent, as a rule, but did not entirely spurn picturesque local expressions. When he let down his guard, his speech actually became all the more educated, and there was nothing of the miller left. But he quickly resumed his good-humoured jokes and his pleasant familiarity, as if ashamed to have betrayed his station.

Marcelle was none the less rather embarrassed when she attempted to pay her hosts for their expense, on taking her leave of them when the *patachon* returned about seven o'clock to put himself at her disposal. They refused to accept anything.

'No, no, my dear lady, no,' said the miller mildly but firmly; 'we are no innkeepers. We might well be, as that's not above our station. But we aren't, and there's an end to it, and so we'll not take your money.'

'Come now!' exclaimed Marcelle. 'I have caused you all this fuss and expense, and you will not allow me to make it good? For I know perfectly well that your mother gave me her own room, and she took over your bed, and you slept in the mill-loft hay. You had to put your other business aside this morning to go fishing. Your mother had to heat up the cooking-stove, think of the trouble she took, and we ate a good deal of your food.'

'Oh! my mother slept perfectly soundly and I slept even better,' answered Grand-Louis. 'Trout from the Vauvre cost nothing; today is Sunday, when I always fish all morning long.* A little milk, bread, and flour for your breakfast, and a scrawny fowl, that won't ruin us. So your debt to us is not great, and you may accept it with no regrets. We shall not hold it against you, still less as we may see you again.'

'I hope we shall,' replied Marcelle, 'for I expect to remain at Blanchemont for at least a few days; I intend to come back and thank you and your mother for your cordial hospitality, although I feel quite ashamed of accepting it.'

'And why should you feel ashamed of accepting a little help from honest folk? If you are satisfied with our good will, then you owe us nothing more. I know that in the big city they pay for everything, even a glass of water. It's a shameful custom, and in our part of the world we'd be very miserable if we didn't help each other out. Come, come, say no more about it.'

'So you would prefer that I should not ask you to dine in return? You force me either to abstain from that pleasure or to become indiscreet.'

'That's another matter altogether. We did no more than our duty in giving you what you call hospitality; for indeed we're raised to think that our duty; and although the good old ways are slipping a bit, although poor folk accept whatever a guest gives them, though they may not ask to be paid, my mother and I aren't minded to give up a custom if it's a good one. If there'd been a decent inn hereabouts, I'd have taken you there last night, as you'd be more comfortable than with us, and I could see you'd got money to pay for your lodgings. But none there is, good nor ill, and I'd be a heartless wretch to let you stay out all night. Do you reckon I'd have asked you back to our place if I'd had a mind to make you pay? No, for as I say, I am no innkeeper. As you see, we have neither holly nor broom* over the door.'

'I should have observed that, and been more discreet in my conduct here. But what is your reply to my question? Would you prefer that I should not return?'

'That's another matter. You're welcome to come back whenever you please. You find this a pretty place; your little boy likes our cakes. So I make bold to say that whenever you return, we shall be glad to see you.'

'And shall you force me to accept all this gratis?'

'Didn't I just invite you? Perhaps I didn't make myself clear.'

'But can you not see that by my code, that would be to abuse your good will?'

'No, I see nothing of the kind. If you're invited, you've a right to come.'

'Well then,' replied Mme de Blanchemont, 'yours is the true courtesy, I see it well, and that of our world is false. You have shown me that our much-vaunted discretion, such a necessary quality among us, is only so because benevolence has become mere flattery, and good manners are no longer the expression of a sincere desire to oblige.'

'You do speak well,' blurted the miller, his face lit up by a shaft of pure intelligence, 'and I'm ever so glad I had the chance to oblige you, 'pon my word!'

'In that case, you will allow me to receive you in turn when you come to Blanchemont?'

'Oh, as for that! beg pardon, but I'll not visit you. I shall stop with your tenant farmers, as I go there all the time to fetch the wheat; and I shall greet you gladly, no more.'

'Oh! Monsieur Louis, do you not wish to dine with me?'

'Yes and no. I often dine with your farmers, but if you're there, that changes everything. You're a noblewoman, that's all.'

'Explain yourself, I fail to understand you.'

'Well then, don't you keep to the old lordly ways? Wouldn't you send your miller down to the kitchen to eat with your servants, and never with you? As for me, I've no objection to eating with them, for I've done the same today in my own house; but I'd think it a poor thing to have sat you down at my table but not to sit at yours, in a corner by the fire, your chair by mine. As you see, I'm just a touch proud. No fault on your part, each has his own ways and ideas; which is why I've no mind to obey others' customs unless I must.'

Marcelle was much struck by the miller's common sense and candid pluck. She was aware that he was giving her a useful lesson, and she was glad that she had adopted plans that would allow her to accept his teaching without embarrassment.

'Monsieur Louis,' she said to him, 'you are wrong about me. It is hardly my fault if I am a member of the nobility; but it so happens, by good fortune or chance, that I no longer wish to follow aristocratic ways. If you will visit me, I shall not forget that you received me as an equal, that you waited on me like a neighbour, and to show you that I am not lacking in gratitude, I shall, if necessary, lay the table for you and your mother myself, as you did for me here.'

'Would you really do that?' asked the miller, looking at Marcelle with a blend of surprise, respectful doubt, and friendly sympathy. 'In that case I'll go . . . no I won't, for I see that you are an honest woman.'

'I have no idea what you mean by that statement.'

'Oh! heavens! if you don't understand . . . I don't really know how to explain it to you.'

'Come now Louis, I believe you've lost your wits,' said old Marie, who sat knitting and listening to the whole of the conversation, with a serious air. 'I've no idea what makes you say such things to our good lady. Excuse him, Madame, the lad is a careless fellow who speaks his mind to all, high or low. Please take no offence, he means well, believe me, and I see by his face that he would throw himself into the fire for you at this very moment.'

'Into the fire, I'm not so sure,' laughed the miller, 'but into the water, that's my element. You see, Mother, Madame is a woman of spirit, and I can say to her whatever I will. I do that to Monsieur Bricolin, her farmer, who's more to be reckoned with than she is here!'

'Tell me then, Master Louis, speak up! I am eager for your instruction. Why is it that you will not visit me, if I am indeed an honest woman?'

'Because we'd be wrong to hobnob with you, and you'd be wrong to treat us as equals. It would bring trouble down upon you. Your peers would blame you; they would say you'd forgot your station, and I know that's a great sin in their eyes. And then if you were kind to us, you'd have to be kind to everybody else, or there'd be jealousy and we'd make enemies. Let everyone take his own way. They say the world is much changed, these past fifty years; I say nothing has changed but the ideas that some of us have. We won't submit any more, and my mother here, much as I love her, the good woman, thinks other than me about most things. But the well-off folk and the aristocrats haven't changed their ideas, not a jot. If you have changed yours, if you don't feel just a whit superior to poor folk, if you really respect them as much as your own kind, it may well be the worse for you. I used to see your husband, the late Monsieur de Blanchemont, as some called the lord of Blanchemont. He came to this region every year and stayed for a day or two. He called me "my lad". If that was meant in friendly fashion, all well and good; but it was done out of scorn; you had to speak to him standing up and holding your hat. I didn't take to that at all. One day he met me in the road and ordered me to hold his horse. I pretended not to hear, he called me a lout, I looked at him slantways; if he hadn't been so poorly and thin, I'd have told him a thing or two. But that would have been cowardly of me, so I went on my way, singing. If that man was alive and could hear you talking to me as you do now, he'd not be at all happy. You know, even your servants, I could see from their faces, they reckoned you weren't grand enough with us today, nor with them neither. So, Madame, it's up to you to come back to the mill for a little stroll, and up to us who regard you highly not to go dine at the castle.'

'That one phrase, which you just said, excuses all the rest, and I shall endeavour to convince you,' said Marcelle, stretching out her hand with an expression whose noble purity demanded respect, whilst her tone induced affection. The miller blushed as he took that delicate hand in his massive one, and for the first time he became rather timid in front of Marcelle, like a bold but well-intentioned child whose audacity is suddenly overwhelmed by emotion.

'I'll put the bridle on Sophie and guide you as far as Blanchemont,' he blurted after a moment's embarrassed silence. 'That wretched driver will only lead you astray again, even though it's no distance.'

'Very well, I accept,' said Marcelle. 'Do you still think me proud?'

'I think, I think,' cried Grand-Louis, leaving the room hastily, 'that if all rich women were like you . . .'

The last of his sentence died away inaudibly, and his mother took it on herself to finish it.

'He is thinking,' she said, 'that if the girl he loves were as lacking in pride as you are, he'd have much less torment.'

'And could I not be of some use to him?' enquired Marcelle, considering, with some satisfaction, that she was rich and generous.

'Perhaps by saying good things about him to the girl, for you'll meet her soon . . . But nonsense! she's too rich!'

'We shall talk of that again,' promised Marcelle, seeing her servants come in for the baggage. 'I shall return very soon, for that purpose, perhaps tomorrow.'

The ginger-haired, hot-tempered driver had spent the night under a tree, not having been able, in the dark, to find a single house anywhere in the Vallée-Noire. At break of day he had glimpsed the mill, and there he and his horse had been lodged and refreshed. Still in a bad mood, he was minded to return insolence to the reproaches that he expected to receive. But for her part Marcelle offered him none, and for his, the miller showered him with so much mockery that he had nothing more to say, and climbed, crestfallen, on to the shaft. Little Édouard begged his mother to let him ride horseback in front of the miller, who took him tenderly in his arms, saying under his breath to old Marie:

'What if we had such a one to delight us here at the house, eh, Mother? But that will never happen!'

And his mother realized that he would never marry anyone but the girl who was beyond his rightful expectations.

VII. BLANCHEMONT

Having embraced the mill-wife and tipped the mill-servants generously but secretly, Marcelle climbed into the hellish *patache* again, but with a cheerful heart. Her first efforts for equality had gladdened her soul, and in her mind she began painting in the most poetic colours the next chapter of the novel she wanted to live.* But the mere sight of Blanchemont darkened her thoughts considerably, and her heart tightened as soon as she crossed through the gate of her domain.

Following the Vauvre upstream, and ascending a steep little hill, one comes to the *tré* or *terrier*, that is, the castle mound of Blanchemont. It is a fine lawn shaded by ancient trees, looking out over a charming site, not one of the most extensive in the Vallée-Noire, but fresh, melancholy, and rather wild of aspect, surrounded only by one or two dwellings whose thatch or tiles can barely be glimpsed through the trees.

A poor church and the cottages of the hamlet enclose this mound as it slopes towards the river, which traces graceful bends at this spot. From there a wide rough track leads to the castle, situated somewhat behind and down from the mound, in the middle of wheat-fields. One descends again to the plains and loses the view of the fine blue horizons of Berry and the Marches,* which can only be seen again from the castle's second floor.

This castle never had strong defences: the walls are no more than five or six feet thick at the base, the slender towers corbelled. It dates back to the end of the feudal wars. Nevertheless the narrowness of the doors, the scarcity of windows, and the plentiful debris of turrets and walls that had formerly circled it all attest to a suspicious epoch, when force was still the surest shelter. It is quite an elegant castle, of squarish shape, with a single large hall on each floor, four angled towers containing smaller chambers, and another tower at the rear enclosing the only staircase. The chapel is now set apart, the old outbuildings having been demolished; the defensive ditches are partly crumbled, the surrounding towers half destroyed, and the pond that once lapped at the castle's northern flank is now a pretty, oblong meadow with a little spring in the middle.

But the picturesque aspect of the old castle* only struck the heiress of Blanchemont at second glance. The miller, helping her to get down from the wagon, directed her towards what he termed the new castle and the numerous outbuildings of the farm, situated at the foot of the old manor, and bordering a very wide courtyard bounded at one end by a crenellated wall, and at the other by a hedge and a ditch full of muddy water. Nothing could be more gloomy and ugly than this rich farmers' dwelling. The new castle was no more than a large peasant's house, built perhaps fifty years ago with the debris from the fortifications. But the solid, newly plastered walls and the roof covered in fresh tiles of a loud red indicated recent repairs. This rejuvenated exterior clashed with the tumbledown outbuildings and the filthy farmyard. These grim buildings, with their remnants of solid, older architecture, made up a range of granges and stables which were the pride of the single tenant-family that possessed them all, and the envy of every other farmer in the country. But this enclosure, well-suited to agricultural industry and convenient for bringing in livestock and harvest, also enclosed one's sight and mind in a gloomy, prosaic space of a repulsive dirtiness. Foul trickles of manure ran freely down towards the lower ground, feeding the kitchen-garden vegetables, from huge middens, stacked ten or twelve feet high in square pits walled in with rough stone. These stores of muck, the farmer's dearest wealth, gladden his sight and make his contented heart palpitate gloriously, particularly when another tiller of the soil admires them with envy. On a rural smallholding such details offend neither the eyes nor the spirit of the artist. Their disorder, the piled-up agricultural tools, the grass that covers all, either camouflage them or set them off to advantage; but on a larger scale and on an open plain, there is nothing more unpleasant than this vista of refuse. Clouds of turkeys, geese, and ducks take it upon themselves to prevent you from putting your foot safely down on a patch of land which the copious streams of muck have spared. The uneven earth is crossed by a metalled road, which in this case was no better than the bare ground. The rubble of the old roof of the new castle remained scattered on the soil, so that one walked over a field of broken tiles. The roofers' work had been complete for nearly six months, but those repairs were paid for by the proprietor, whilst the work of carrying off the debris and cleaning up the courtyard was left for the tenant farmer. He had told himself that it could be done when the summer's work was over, and that his servants would take care of it. On the one hand there was the saving to be made by not hiring workmen for a few days; on the other the profound apathy of the Berry man, who always leaves something undone, as if after such effort his drained energies require a period of rest and the delights of negligence before he completes his task.

Marcelle compared this gross and repulsive agricultural opulence with the poetic well-being of the miller; and she would have offered him these reflections, had she been able to make herself heard above the distressed cries of the terrified but immobile turkeys, the hissing of the mother geese with their broods, and the barking of four or five scrawny yellow dogs. As it was Sunday, the cattle were in the barn and the labourers on the doorstep in their best clothes, thick Prussian-blue linen from head to foot. They observed the entry of the *patache* with much astonishment but without any inclination to disturb themselves sufficiently to make the travellers welcome or tell the farmer that he had visitors. It was left for Grand-Louis to introduce Mme de Blanchemont; he did so unceremoniously, entering without knocking and saying, 'Madame Bricolin, come here! Madame de Blanchemont has arrived to see you.'

This unexpected news seized the three Bricolin ladies abruptly. They had just returned from mass and were about to tuck into a light collation, still on their feet. So they stood there dumbfounded, looking at one another as if to ask what should be done in such circumstances; and they had not yet budged from the spot when Marcelle entered. The group which presented itself to her eyes was made up of three generations. Mother Bricolin, who could neither read nor write, and who wore peasant dress; Mme Bricolin, the farmer's wife, a little more elegant than her mother-in-law, with something of the manner of a priest's housekeeper; she knew how to sign her name legibly, and find the timetable for the sunrise and the moon's phases in the Liège* almanac; finally, Mlle Rose Bricolin, as lovely and fresh as a May rose itself, who could read a novel perfectly well, do the household accounts, and dance the quadrille. Her hair was fashionably dressed, and she wore a pretty frock of rose-coloured muslin which set off her charming figure to good advantage, although rather artificially, with its exaggerated bust and tight-fitting sleeves in the fashionable mode. This lovely face, with an expression both noble and naïve, dispelled Marcelle's discomfort at the hard, embittered visage of the mother. The grandmother, weatherbeaten and wrinkled like a hardened countrywoman, had an open and frank expression. These three women stood there with their mouths open; mother Bricolin asked herself in all sincerity if this beautiful young woman was the one who had visited the castle occasionally some thirty years before, that is, Marcelle's mother, though she knew her to have died some time ago; Mme Bricolin, the farm-wife, became aware that on her return from mass she had been too quick to don her kitchen apron over her maroon merino gown; and Mlle Rose took rapid stock of her impeccable dress and shoes, thanking her stars that because it was

Sunday she could be taken unawares by an elegant Parisienne without having to blush at some vulgar domestic occupation.

To the Bricolin family Mme de Blanchemont had always been a mystery, possibly an imaginary being, whom they had never seen and certainly never would see. They had known her husband well enough, disliking him because he was high and mighty, disdaining him because he was a spendthrift, and scoffing at him because he was forever in need of money and would do anything to obtain it. After his death they had expected to deal only with his agents, since the deceased had often produced his wife's willing signature and said, 'Madame de Blanchemont is a mere child and never troubles herself about business; so long as I bring her enough money, she cares not where it comes from.' Of course the husband made a habit of charging to his wife's expensive tastes the prodigal sums which he spent on his mistresses. Thus no one had any idea about the true character of the young widow, whose appearance here at the hub of the Blanchemont farm convinced Mme Bricolin that she must be dreaming. Ought she to be glad or troubled? Was this strange apparition a sign for good or ill in the Bricolin fortunes? Had she come to reclaim her wealth, or to beg?

While the farm-wife, troubled by these unexpected dilemmas, stared at Marcelle like a goat taking up its defensive stance against a strange dog harassing the herd, Rose Bricolin, quickly won over by the pleasant manner and the simple dress of the stranger, had mustered up the courage to take a few steps towards her. The grandmother was the least embarrassed of the three. Once her first surprise was over, and her weakened mind had made an effort to understand who this was, she went up to Marcelle with a brusque candour and welcomed her in roughly the same terms as had the mill-wife of Angibault, although with less elegance and grace. The two others, reassured by the gentle, kindly manner in which Marcelle requested a few days' hospitality in order to discuss business with M. Bricolin, hastened to offer her some breakfast.

Marcelle's refusal was moved by the excellent meal which she had enjoyed an hour earlier at the mill of Angibault, and it was only then that the three Bricolin ladies noticed Grand-Louis standing by the door, talking about flour with the maidservant in order to have some excuse for staying a while. Each looked at him in a very different way: the grandmother companionably, the mother scornfully, Rose uncertainly and in an indefinable manner, as if with a mixture of inner feelings.

'What!' exclaimed Mme Bricolin in a whining, sarcastic voice, when Marcelle had briefly recounted last night's adventures. 'So you were obliged to stay the night at the mill? And we had no idea! Ah, why didn't that fool of a miller bring you here right away? Oh! my Lord! what a terrible night you must have had, Madame!'

'Delightful, on the contrary. I was treated like a queen, and I am obliged a thousand times over to Monsieur Louis and his mother.'

'Well, that comes as no surprise to me,' exclaimed old mother Bricolin. 'Grand'Marie is such a fine woman, and keeps her house so spotless! She was my friend when I was a girl; we tended our sheep together, begging your pardon; two pretty girls we were then, they all said, though you'd never credit it now, would you, Madame? Green as grass, we were: spinning, knitting, making cheese, we knew no more than that. Our husbands had different expectations: hers was poorer than she was, mine was better off. In those days we married for love, that was the thing; now they marry for money, crowns count more than feelings. And they're none the better for it, are they, Madame de Blanchemont?'

'I am entirely of your opinion,' agreed Marcelle.

'Oh, my Lord! Mother, what kind of tales are you spinning for Madame?' Mme Bricolin screeched in her vinegary voice. 'Surely you don't think she's amused by your old wives' stories? Hey there! miller!' she added imperiously, 'Go and see if Monsieur Bricolin is in the hunting-park or the field of oats behind the house. Tell him to come and pay his respects to Madame.'

'Oh, I know,' said old mother Bricolin, 'he must be at the priest's. *Monsieur le curé* is always very thirsty and hungry after high mass, and he likes a bit of company. Louis, my child, would you go and look for him, like the good lad you are?'

'I'm off right away,' exclaimed the miller, who had not moved a muscle at the farm-wife's orders. And he set out at a trot.

'If you think he's a good lad,' muttered the farm-wife, giving her mother-in-law a vexed glance, 'you can't be very hard to please.'

'Oh, Mother, don't say that,' blurted lovely Rose Bricolin in her low voice. 'Grand-Louis has a very good heart.'

'And what good will that do you?' countered Mme Bricolin with growing annoyance. 'What is this affection you both have for him lately?'

'But Mother, you're the one who's been unfair to him lately,' replied Rose, who seemed to have little fear of her mother, habitually backed up as she was by her grandmother. 'You're always rude to him, and yet you know that Papa thinks a great deal of him.'

'As for you,' shrilled the farm-wife, 'you'd do better to stop your arguing and get your room ready for Madame, as it's the most comfortable in the house and Madame might like to lie down before dinner. I'm sure Madame will excuse us if she's not well lodged here. It was just last year that the late Monsieur de Blanchemont gave his permission for the new castle to be done up a bit, it was almost as dilapidated as the old one, and so it was only when we'd renewed our lease that we could begin getting the house furnished a bit more comfortably. Nothing's finished yet, some of the rooms still aren't papered, and we're waiting for some chests of drawers and beds to come from Bourges.* But we do have a few bits of furniture that are just about presentable. Things are all topsy-turvy here since the workmen left us in such a state.'

The domestic discomforts at which Mme Bricolin hinted in this tale of woe were real enough, like those that Marcelle had observed outside the house. Parsimoniousness combined with apathy to postpone any spending and put off indefinitely the moment for enjoying that comfort which was wanted, which could be managed, and which was yet too precarious to be permitted. The gloomy, smoky room in which the chatelaine had surprised the family was the ugliest and filthiest in the new castle. It served at the same time as kitchen, dining-room, and parlour. The hens were free to come and go there, since the ground-floor door was always open; the job of chasing them away was an everlasting task for the farm-wife, as if the angry state and the perpetual harsh measures to which the fowls' repeated trespasses obliged her were vital to her need for fluster and chastisement. It was there that the family received the peasants with whom they had their daily dealings; and as muddy feet and rough manners would inevitably have ruined parquet floors and good furniture, there were only a few rough straw cushions and wooden benches on the bare tiles, swept, to no avail, ten times a day. The flies, to whom the place was Liberty Hall, and the fire, always lit, whatever the hour or season, in the huge chimney studded with pot-hooks of all dimensions, made the room highly disagreeable in summer. And yet it was the family's usual abode, and when they showed Marcelle into the next-door room, it was obvious to her that this sort of front parlour had never been used, although it had been furnished a year since. It was decorated with the ostentatious luxury of an inn's bedchambers. The brand-new wood flooring had not seen a trace of beeswax or polish. The gaudy chintz curtains were hung from poles ending in moulded copper finials of detestable taste. The fire-place tiles reflected the sparkle of ugly imitation Renaissance ornaments. The gilt-and-brass legs of an ornate pedestal table, on which coffee was meant to be served, were still encased in paper and twine. The furnishings were covered with checked red-and-white dust-sheets, under which fine damask wool was destined to become moth-eaten before it saw the light of day; and since these farmers are still unaware of the distinction between a salon and a bedroom, two mahogany beds, not yet curtained, were stretched out with the foot to the window, right and left of the entry door. In the family, it was whispered that this would be Rose's bridal chamber.

Marcelle found this house so unpleasant that she resolved not to stay there. She announced that she did not wish to cause her hosts the slightest discomfort, and that she would find some peasant dwelling where she might lodge in the hamlet, unless there was perhaps one habitable room in the old castle. This last notion appeared to worry Mme Bricolin considerably, and she spared no pains in trying to dissuade her guest.

'It is certainly true,' she suggested, 'that there is still a room in the old castle that we call the master's chamber. Whenever your late husband, *Monsieur le baron*, did us the honour of passing this way, he always wrote in advance to warn us, and we took pains to clean everything so that he shouldn't be too uncomfortable. But that miserable castle is so gloomy and dilapidated! . . . The rats and owls make such an unholy row in it, and the roof-tiles are in such a dreadful state, and the walls are so shaky, that you'd not be safe sleeping there. I can't imagine what *Monsieur le baron* saw in that room. He wouldn't accept our hospitality, and you might have thought he reckoned himself too good to spend the night here and not under the roof of his old castle.'

'I shall have a look at this chamber,' answered Marcelle, 'and so long as one can sleep under cover there, I shall be content. While you wait, please do not take any trouble. I have no wish at all to be a burden on you.'

Rose expressed her countervailing desire to surrender her bedroom to Mme to Blanchemont in such gracious terms and with a prepossessing countenance that Marcelle took her hand gently to thank her, but without changing her mind. The appearance of the new castle, together with her instinctive dislike of Mme Bricolin, had convinced her to refuse the hospitality which she had accepted so gladly at the mill.

She was still defending herself against the ceremonious requests of the farm-wife when M. Bricolin arrived.

VIII. THE PARVENU PEASANT*

M. Bricolin was a man of fifty, robust and with regular features. But his once-sturdy limbs were now stout, as occurs with all well-off farmers: passing their days in the open air, generally on horseback, leading an active life but not undergoing hard labour, they are just tired enough to enjoy their good health and hearty appetites. Thanks to the stimulus of out-door life and frequent exercise, these men can endure daily culinary excess for some time without mishap, and although in their rural occupations they may be dressed much like the peasantry, there is no confusing the two classes, even at first glance. Whereas the peasant is always thin, well-pro-portioned, and agreeably swarthy, the country bourgeois, from forty upwards, is cursed with a large gut, a heavy gait, and a ruddy colouring which make the handsomest individu-als gross and ugly.

Among those who have made their own fortunes and who began their lives in the enforced sobriety of the peasant, there are no exceptions to this thickening of the form and alteration of the complexion. For it is a proverbial truth that when the peasant begins to eat meat and drink wine to his taste, he becomes incapable of work, and that if he were to return to his early habits, it would be promptly and certainly fatal. Thus, one might say, money passes into their bloodstreams, leeching on to them body and soul, and that either their lives or their reason would inevitably succumb to the loss of their fortunes. Any thought of devotion to humankind, any religious sense, is well-nigh incompatible with this trans-formation effected in their physical and spiritual being by prosperity. It is useless to rail against them. They cannot be otherwise. They fatten themselves up for apoplexy or senility. Their faculties for the acquisition and cultivation of riches, initially so well developed, are extinguished in mid-career, and having made their fortunes with remarkable speed and skill, they quickly fall into apathy, chaos, and incapacity. They are sustained by no societal awareness, no sense of progress. Digestion becomes their life's work, and their wealth, bought with such vigour, is tangled in a thousand misfortunes and squandered by a thousand misjudgements, before they can consolidate it . . . not to mention the vanity which hurls them into speculations exceeding their credit; to the extent that all these rich men are nearly always ruined by the time they excite the greatest envy.

M. Bricolin was not yet at that stage. He was of that age where full powers of energy and will can still do battle against the double inebriation of arrogance and intemperance. But his narrowed eyes, his wide belly, his shiny nose, and the nervous trembling of his strong hands (produced by his habitual morning refresher, that is, two bottles of white wine on an empty stomach, rather than coffee)—all signalled the coming time when this man, now so alert, wide-awake, canny and implacable in business, would lose his health, his memory, his judgement, and his strength of character, to become a worn-out drunkard, a thick-witted prattler, and an easily outwitted master.

His face had once been handsome, although entirely without distinction. His blunt, strongly accentuated features were marked by unusual energy and sagacity. He had a sharp eye, black and hard, a sensual mouth, a narrow low forehead, curly hair, and a quick, brusque turn of speech. There was no falsity in his glance nor hypocrisy in his manners. This was no double-dealer: his enormous respect for mine and thine, in conventional terms, made him incapable of knavery. Furthermore, the cynicism of his greed prevented him from masking his intentions, and when he had announced to his counterpart, 'My interest is the opposite of yours,' he thought to have demonstrated to him that he acted by the most sacred laws, and that he had shown the highest degree of probity in so speaking.

Something between the countryman and the town dweller as he was, his Sunday best was half that of the peasant, half of the merchant. His hat was lower than the one's, and its rim narrower than the other's. On his stocky form his grey shirt, with belt and ruffles, gave him the look of a hooped barrel. His gaiters gave off an indelible smell of the stables, and his black silk cravat shone greasily. This personnage, short and bluff, made a disagreeable impression on Marcelle, and his wordy conversation, always touching on money, was even less to her taste than the dire predictions of his better half.

This was roughly the substance of the two hours' worth of tattle which she had to endure from Master Bricolin. The Blanchemont estate was weighed down with mortgages on over a third of its total worth. In addition the late baron had demanded considerable advances on the rents, at enormous rates of interest which M. Bricolin 'had no choice but to accept', given the difficulty of borrowing money and the usurious levels prevailing. Mme de Blanchemont would have to accept still harsher conditions if she intended to continue the system which she had authorized her husband to establish; or rather, before demanding her revenues, she would have to pay off arrears, capital, interest, and interest on interest, a total of more than 100,000 francs. As for the other creditors, they wanted either to get all their money back or to hold on to the debt as an investment. It would therefore be necessary either to sell the estate or to come up with the capital straightway; in brief, the land was worth 800,000 francs, it was encumbered with 400,000 francs in debts, not counting those owed to M. Bricolin. There were 300,000 francs remaining, henceforth all of Mme de Blanchemont's fortune,* apart from that which her husband might or might not have left to his son, of which she knew nothing as yet.

Although Marcelle was unprepared for such disasters, the worst was yet to come. The creditors had not yet put in their claims; well-armed with their documents, they had been waiting—with M. Bricolin at the head of the queue—for the young widow to learn her position, at which point they would demand either payment in full or continued revenue from their loans. When she asked Bricolin why he had given her no indication of the state of her affairs during the month she had been a widow, he answered with brutal frankness that there was no reason for haste, that her credit was good, and that each day of indifference on the proprietor's part was a day of profit for the farmer, during which his interest was accumulating at no risk to himself. This peremptory logic gave Marcelle instant insight into the ethics of M. Bricolin.

'Well and good,' she replied with an ironic smile whose import the farmer did not deign to comprehend. 'I see that it is my own fault if each day that I allow to pass eats further into the income which I had thought to possess. But in the interests of my son, I must put an end to this sort of disaster, and I await from you, Monsieur Bricolin, some wise counsel on the subject.'

Dumbfounded by the calm with which the lady of Blanchemont had received the news that she was well-nigh ruined, and still more by the boldness with which she had requested his opinion, M. Bricolin stared her straight in the eye. He saw in her face a sort of malicious challenge to his avarice, born from the most perfect candour.

'I see perfectly well that you want to lure me on,' he said, 'but I won't let myself be humiliated by reproaches from your family. It's wrong to accuse a man of deliberate complicity in usurious loans. I must speak seriously to you, Madame de Blanchemont, but the walls are too thin here, and I don't want this to get out. If you'll pretend to come and look over the old castle with me, I'll tell you, first, what I would advise you to do if I were your father; second, what I want you to do, as your creditor; you'll see there's no third opinion to consider. I think not.'

If the old castle had not been surrounded by nettles, stagnant smelly ponds, and a thousand broken bits of rubbish that looked like nothing other than a scene of barbaric pillage, it would have been quite a picturesque remnant of the past. There was part of a defensive ditch, overgrown with tall reeds; magnificent ivy covering a whole wall of the building; and a rockfall where wild cherries flourished. Its aspect was not wanting in poetry. M. Bricolin showed Marcelle the chamber in which her husband had been accustomed to stay on his visits. There were a few bits of Louis XVI furniture, very faded and dirty. But the room was habitable, and Mme de Blanchemont resolved to spend the night there.

'This won't please my wife much, as she was looking forward to the honour of receiving you in her own home,' said M. Bricolin, 'but I don't know anything less helpful than pestering people. If you like the old castle, there's no accounting for tastes, as the saying goes, and I'll have your things brought over. We'll put a camp-bed in for your chambermaid.* In the meantime, I must speak seriously to you about business matters, Madame de Blanchemont; that's the great hurry.'

And, pulling up an armchair, Bricolin sat himself down and began thus: 'First, can I make bold to ask if you've some other fortune in your possession than the lands at Blanchemont? I don't believe so, if I'm rightly informed.'

'I have nothing else of my own,' answered Marcelle tranquilly.

'And do you expect your son to inherit a large fortune on his father's account?'

'I have no idea. If the estates belonging to Monsieur de Blanchemont are as heavily encumbered as mine . . .'

'Oh! so you've no idea? You don't bother much with business? How amusing! But then all the nobility are like that. As for me, it's my business to know your position. That's my occupation and my interest. Well then, when I saw that *Monsieur le baron* was living on the grand scale, never dreaming he'd die so young, I was obliged to find out what dents he'd already made in his fortune, so as to protect myself against loans that might exceed the residual value of these lands, and leave me with no guarantee. So I got my advisers to scurry and ferret around a bit, and I know within a sou what's left for your little man, in the light of day today.*

'Then give me the pleasure of hearing it, Monsieur Bricolin.'

'Easily done, and you can inspect it yourself if you like. If I'm off by 10,000 francs, that's the end of it. Your husband had a fortune of about a million, and that's still there, except the 980,000 or 990,000 francs of debts to pay.'

'So my son has nothing?' exclaimed Marcelle, upset by this additional revelation.

'Just as you say. Added to what you have, he'll get 300,000 francs one day. That's still a pretty sum if you want to consolidate it and free up the equity. As land, it represents 6,000 or 7,000 livres* in rent. If you want to eat it all up, better still.'

'I have no intention of destroying my son's only future. It is my duty to extricate myself as promptly as possible from the embarrassments in which I find myself.'

'In that case, listen here: your lands and his bring in two per cent. You're paying interest at fifteen and twenty per cent on the debts; with the accumulated interest, you're eating into the capital very rapidly. What are you going to do?'

'I shall have to sell, shan't I?'

'Just as you like. I would think that's certainly in your best interests, unless you prefer to live on your son's money, profit from the disorder, and add to it.'

'No, Monsieur Bricolin, such is not my intention.'

'But you can still draw money out of his fortune, and since the little boy has grandparents from whom he'll inherit, maybe he won't be bankrupt when he reaches majority.'

'That is exceedingly logical,' said Marcelle coldly, 'but I wish to proceed otherwise. I intend to sell everything, so that the debts of his inheritance do not exceed the capital; and as for my own fortune, I want to make it all liquid, so that I may raise my son in comfort.'

'In that case, you want to sell Blanchemont?'

'Yes, Monsieur Bricolin, immediately.'

'Immediately? Oh, no doubt; people in your position, who need to get out of it quickly, never want to lose a single day, because each day eats a hole in their purse. But do you really think it's so easy to sell an estate of this size right away, in one lot or several? You might as well say you could build a castle like this one between today and tomorrow, and build it solid enough to last five or six hundred years. You might as well know that in the light of day today nobody shifts their capital anywhere except into industry, railways, and other big business where they can realize a hundred per cent, or lose it. Big estates are the devil to unload. In our part of the world everybody wants to sell up and nobody wants to buy; they're all fed up with sinking big money into the fields and harvesting practically nothing. Land is all right for those who live on it and from it, if they're frugal: that's for country folk like me. But for you city lot, it brings in nothing at all. So, a property worth 50,000 or 100,000 francs at the most will find some eager buyers among my sort. A property worth 800,000 is generally beyond our means, and you'll have to ransack your Paris lawyer's chambers for a capitalist who doesn't know what to do with his money. Do you really think you'll find many people, in the light of day today, when they can play the market, or roulette, or dabble in jewellery, or invest in the railways, or get high office, or a thousand other big games! You'll have to come up with some worried old lord who'd rather earn two per cent on his money, for fear of a revolution, than have a go at all those tempting speculations that attract everybody, in the light of day today. And furthermore there'd have to be a fine stately home where an old squire could end his days. Have you seen your castle? I wouldn't even touch it for the building materials. The trouble of knocking it down wouldn't be repaid by what you'd get for the rotten woodwork and the smashed stones. All in all, if you put your estate up, you might sell it in one lot some fine day; or you could just as well wait another ten years; because your lawyer can proclaim on the placards that it'll bring in three or three and a half per cent, till he's blue in the face; people will see my lease, and they'll realize that after tax it won't bring in more than two.'

'Did you perchance agree the lease with a view to the advances you had made to Monsieur de Blanchemont?' asked Marcelle with a smile.

'And why not?' replied Bricolin coolly. 'My lease is good for twenty years; one's up, there's nineteen to go. You should know, you signed it. Although perhaps you didn't read it . . . Good Lord! It's your own fault.'

'And therefore I blame no one else. So, I cannot sell in one lot, can I sell in several?'

'In several lots you could sell at a good price, but no one will pay you.'

'Why not?'

'Because you'll be forced to sell to several people, of whom the majority won't be solvent, to peasants. The better-off will pay you lengthily sou by sou, and the poorer ones will have been tempted beyond their means by their desire to own a little bit of land, as they do in the light of day today, and you'll have to foreclose after ten years without having seen a bit of your money. You'll wear yourself out badgering them!'

'And that I am resolved never to do. So, Monsieur Bricolin, your view is that I can neither sell nor hold on to the land?'

'If you want to act rationally, sell cheap and get ready money, you can sell to someone I know.'

'Who?'

'Me.'

'You, Monsieur Bricolin?'

'Me, Nicolas-Étienne Bricolin.'

'As a matter of fact,' said Marcelle, recalling a few words the miller of Angibault had let slip, 'I had heard as much. And what is your offer?'

'I settle up with the creditors on the mortgages, I split up the land, I sell to some people and buy from others, I keep whatever suits me and I pay you whatever's left over.'

'And you can settle the creditors' accounts in cash? You must be terribly rich, Monsieur Bricolin!'

'No, I'll make them wait, one way or another, don't you worry about it.'

'I thought they all wanted to be repaid straightaway; didn't you tell me as much?'

'With you they'll demand that; they'll advance me credit.'

'Fair enough. I suppose they think me insolvent?'

'Possibly! in the light of day today, nobody trusts anybody else. So then, Madame de Blanchemont! you owe me 100,000 francs, I'll give you 250,000, and we're quits.'

'You mean you would pay 250,000 for a property worth 300,000?'

'A little bonus, it's only fair you should give me that: I'm paying cash. You'll say that it's to my advantage not to deal with interest payments. It's also to your advantage, getting cash in hand for your fortune, because if you wait much longer you won't see hide nor hair of it.'

'So you would profit from the discomfort of my position to reduce by a sixth the little that remains to me?'

'I've a perfect right, and anybody else would demand more. You can rest assured that I've taken your interests into account as much as possible. I've no more to say. Think about it.'

'Yes, Monsieur Bricolin, I do need to think about it.'

'The devil take it! I should think so! First of all you need to be sure that I'm not tricking you, and that I'm not fooling myself about your situation and the value of your property. You're here now: you can get information, see everything for yourself, even go visit your husband's lands at Le Blanc,* and when you understand matters thoroughly, in a month or so, come back to me with your answer. Let's just reckon up my offer, and I've no fear about your verifying this calculation:

you can either, first, sell what you've got left over at twice what I'm offering, but not see the half of it, or wait ten years, during which you'll have to service such high interest-charges that you'll have nothing left; or, second, sell to me, taking a loss of one sixth, and get 250,000 francs in solid gold or silver or pretty little banknotes, whatever you please, all within three months from now. So, I've said my piece, now let's go back to the house for an hour, you will dine with us. Our house is your house, you know, *Madame la baronne*. We're doing business together, and if you don't ask me for any more favours, we can rub along nicely.'

Marcelle found herself henceforth on such a footing with the Bricolins that she had no further scruples, and was obliged to accept this offer. Thus she promised to make good use of it; but she requested that she might stay at the old castle and write a letter whilst awaiting the dinner hour, and M. Bricolin took his leave of her to attend to her servants and baggage.

IX. AN UNEXPECTED FRIEND

During the few moments that she was left to herself, many thoughts went rapidly through Marcelle's mind, making her aware that love had given her an energy of which she might never have thought herself capable, without its all-powerful inspiration. At first glance she had been rather frightened by this gloomy manor, the only home that she could rightfully call her own. But once she had learned that even this ruin would not be hers for long, she began to smile, looking at it with an entirely disinterested curiosity. The seigneurial escutcheon of her family remained intact over the mantel of the huge chimneys.

'So,' said she to herself, 'all links between myself and the past shall be sundered. Wealth and nobility part company, *in the light of day today*, as Bricolin says. Oh just God! thank you for having made love as eternal and immortal as yourself!'

Suzette came in, bringing in the travel writing-desk that her mistress had requested for her letter. But as she was opening it, Marcelle glanced by chance at the maid and could not help but laugh, so bizarre was the expression the girl wore as she stared at the bare walls of the old castle. Suzette's face reddened further, and her voice took on a pronounced accent of insubordination. 'So,' she muttered, 'Madame has made up her mind to sleep here?'

'As you see,' answered Marcelle, 'and you have your own little closet, with a magnificent view and plenty of air.'

'I am greatly obliged to Madame, but Madame can be certain that I shall not sleep there. It frightens me enough in broad daylight; what would it be like at night? They say he comes back, and that's not hard to believe.'

'You must have lost your wits, Suzette. I shall protect you from ghosts.'

'Madame will have the goodness to install some farm servant here, for I should rather depart instantly, on foot, from this dreadful country...'.

'There is no need to put on a tragic manner, Suzette. I have no wish to force you, you may sleep where you will; however, I should like to point out to you that if you continually refuse me your services, I shall be obliged to dismiss you.'

'If Madame expects to remain in this province very long, and live in this hovel . . .'

'I am forced to remain here a month, perhaps more; what will you make of it?'

'That I shall ask Madame to be so good as to send me back to Paris or to one of her other estates, for I swear that I shall die here after three days.'

'My dear Suzette,' replied Marcelle quite gently, 'I have no other estates, and it is unlikely that I shall ever return to Paris to live. I have lost my fortune, child, and most probably I shall not be able to retain you in my service for long. Since staying here is odious to you, it is pointless for me to impose it on you any longer. I shall pay your wages and travel costs. The wagon that brought us has not yet left. I shall give you excellent references, and my relations will help you find a situation.'

'But how can Madame intend me to go off like this, all alone? Truly, there was no point bringing me so far into this forsaken country!'

'I had no idea then that I was ruined, and I have only just been made aware of it,' answered Marcelle calmly. 'Do not reproach me, it is not by my own choice that I have caused you this vexation. Further, you shall not go alone; Lapierre will return to Paris with you.'

'Madame is also dismissing Lapierre?' wailed Suzette.

'I shall not dismiss Lapierre. He will go back to my mother-in-law, who gave him to me, and who will receive her loyal old servant with open arms. Go and have dinner, Suzette, and prepare to depart.'

Astounded by her mistress's calm and her quiet serenity, Suzette burst into tears, and, with a recurrence of affection, perhaps spontaneous, she begged to be pardoned and retained in service.

'No, my dear girl,' answered Marcelle, 'your wages are beyond my means from now on. I shall miss you, despite your little ways, and perhaps you will miss me as well, despite my faults. But this is a necessary sacrifice, and the times call for strength.'

'And what will become of Madame? without her fortune, without her servants, and with a little child in her arms, in such a wilderness! Poor little Édouard!'

'Do not torment yourself, Suzette; you will certainly find a situation with one of my acquaintances. We shall see each other again. You will see Édouard. Do not weep in front of him, I beg of you!'

Suzette left; but no sooner had Marcelle dipped her pen in the ink to begin writing than the tall miller appeared before her, carrying Édouard on one arm and a travelling-bag on the other.

'Ah!' exclaimed Marcelle, taking the child, whom he placed on her lap, 'are you still taking pains on my behalf, Monsieur Louis? I am so glad that you have not yet left. I have hardly had a chance to thank you, and I should have been sorry not to have said goodbye.'

'No, I've not left yet,' said the miller, 'and to tell truth, I've no great mind to go. But look here, Madame, if it's no matter to you, you're not to call me Monsieur. I'm no Monsieur, and I'm getting a bit put out with all this folderol. You can call me plain Louis, or Grand-Louis, like everybody else.'

'But I must point out to you that this contradicts the idea of equality, and after your thoughts this morning . . .'

'This morning I was a fool, an ass, and a miller's ass to boot. I had my prejudices . . . because you were an aristocrat, and your husband . . . what do I know about it? Now if you'd called me Louis, I suppose I'd have called you . . . What's your name?'

'Marcelle.'

'I like that name, Madame Marcelle! Well then! that's what I'll call you; it won't bring to mind *Monsieur le baron*.'

'But if I may not call you Monsieur, will you then call me Marcelle, no more?' said Mme de Blanchemont with a laugh.

'No, no, you are a woman . . . and a woman like few others, devil take me! . . . Well, I'll make no bones about it, you're close to my heart, especially since a moment ago.'

'Why since a moment ago, Grand-Louis?' enquired Marcelle, who had begun writing and was only listening to the miller with half an ear.

'Because when you were talking with your chambermaid just now, I was out on the staircase with this imp of yours, who was playing all sorts of tricks to stop me walking on, and against my will I heard everything you were saying. I must beg pardon.'

'There is no harm in that,' Marcelle assured him. 'My position is no secret, since I have told it to Suzette, and besides, I am certain that a secret would be safe in your hands.'

'Any secret of yours would be graven on my heart,' answered the miller in a flush of tenderness. 'So you had no idea before coming here that you were ruined?'

'No, I had no idea. Monsieur Bricolin has just told me. I was expecting losses, but thought I could make them good; nothing more.'

'And you're no more bothered than that?'

Marcelle, who was still writing, did not reply, but after a moment she raised her eyes to Grand-Louis and saw him standing before her with his arms folded, looking at her with a kind of ingenuous enthusiasm and profound astonishment.

'Is it so very surprising,' she said to him, 'to see someone lose her fortune without losing her spirit? Besides, don't I have enough left to live on?'

'What you have left, I'm pretty much aware. It may well be I know your affairs better than you do; for Père Bricolin does like to talk when he's drunk a few, and he's filled my head with all that often enough, before it was of any interest to me. But all the same, a person who can watch a million vanish in one way and half a million in another, all without raising an eyebrow . . . snap! in the twinkling of an eye! . . . I've never seen the like, and I still can't make it out!'

'You would find it still more incomprehensible if I were to say to you that so far as my deepest concerns go, it gives me extreme joy.'

'Oh! but so far as your son's concerned!' exclaimed the miller, lowering his voice, so that the child, who was playing in the next room, might not hear his words.

'At first I was rather taken aback,' replied Marcelle, 'and then I quickly found consolation. For a long while I have felt that it was a misfortune to be born rich and to be destined for idleness, the hatred of the poor, selfishness, and the rich man's impunity. I have often regretted not being the daughter and mother of a working man. But now, Louis, I shall be of the people, and men like you will distrust me no longer.'

'You'll never be of the people,' laughed the miller. 'You've still got a fortune a man of the people would think tremendous, though it may not strike you as much. Besides, this little boy has rich relations who'll never let him grow up a pauper. All this, Madame Marcelle, is just fairy stories you're making up! but where the devil did you ever get such ideas? You must be a saint, the deuce take me! It has the strangest effect on me to hear you say such things, when every other rich person thinks only of getting richer. You're the first of your kind I've seen. Are there other rich people and nobles in Paris who think like you?'

'None at all, I must admit. But do not give me such credit for it, Grand-Louis. Perhaps the day will come when I can make you understand why I feel as I do.'

'Begging your pardon, but I doubt it.'

'Oh, but yes.'

'No indeed, and the proof is, I can't even say it outright. Those matters are too delicate, and you'll tell me I'm too bold, asking you about them. But if you only knew how humble I am on that subject, how well I can understand others' troubles! I'll tell you all my concerns, I will! Yes, strike me dead! so I will. It'll only be you and my mother who know. Perhaps you can restore my spirits with a few kind words.'

'And if I told you in my turn that I doubt it?'

'You'd have a right to! which proves that all these things are for love and money.'

'I should like you to tell me your secrets, Grand-Louis; but here comes old Lapierre, climbing the stairs. We shall meet again soon, shan't we?'

'So we must,' said the miller, lowering his voice, 'for I want to ask you a thing or two about your business with Bricolin. I fear that old shyster may be treating you hard, and who knows! my being a peasant through and through may be of use to you. Will you treat me like a friend?'

'Certainly.'

'And will you do nothing unless you tell me first?'

'I promise, friend. Here is Lapierre.'

'Ought I to go?'

'Go stand aside here, with Édouard. Perhaps I shall need to consult you, if you can spare a few minutes more.'

'It's Sunday . . . Besides, I'd do it any day!'

X. CORRESPONDENCE

Lapierre came in. Suzette had already told him everything. He was pale and shaking. Elderly, incapable of heavy work, he was merely an ostensible male protector on the trip, so far as Marcelle was concerned. But although he had never said so openly, he was deeply attached to her, and though he, like Suzette, had taken a dislike to the Vallée-Noire and the old castle, he refused to leave his mistress, declaring that he would remain in her service, at whatever small wage she judged feasible.

Marcelle, touched by his noble devotion, clasped his hands affectionately in her own and overcame his resistance by showing him that he could be of more use to her by returning to Paris than by staying on at Blanchemont. She wished to sell off her luxurious furniture, and Lapierre was competent to preside over the sale, take the money, and use it to pay off the few small ongoing debts which Mme de Blanchemont might have left behind in Paris. Upright and businesslike, Lapierre was flattered to play the part of a man of the world, someone to be relied on, without fail, and to do a service for the mistress whom he left so unwillingly. The arrangements were made for their departure. Marcelle, considering all the details of her situation with remarkable coolness, called Grand-Louis back and asked him if he thought the *calèche* left behind at —— could be sold.

'So, you're burning your bridges behind you?' answered the miller. 'All the better for us! Seems you might stop here, and I ask no more than to look after you. I'm always in —— on business, or on a visit to one of my sisters, who's settled there. I know most everything that goes on, and I've observed that all our townsfolk are mad for luxury goods and fine carriages, have been for years. I know one chap who wanted to have one sent from Paris; yours is here on the spot, that'll save him transport costs, and in our country they'll spend a fortune on expensive foolishness but worry about piddling sums. It looked fine and handsome to me, your carriage did. What's it worth, this business?'

'Two thousand francs.'

'Would you like me to go as far as —— with Monsieur Lapierre? I can put him in touch with the sellers, and he can get cash, for in our country no one pays cash except to strangers.'

'If it is not taking advantage of your time and trouble, you are the only one capable of the business.'

'I'll go with pleasure; but don't say a word to Monsieur Bricolin; he might just want to buy it himself, that *calèche*!'

'Well, why not?'

'Oh, never! that would be the last straw, it'd turn her head all right . . . I mean, turn their heads . . . And anyway, Bricolin would find some means of paying you no more than half what it's worth. I promise you, I'll look after it.'

'In that case, will you bring the money to me if possible? for I thought I should be able to obtain some here, whereas it is now certain I shall have to pay some back.'

'Well then, we'll be off this evening; as it's Sunday, that's no bother; and if I'm not back tomorrow evening or the morning of the next day with 2,000 francs, you can call me an idle boaster.'

'You are such a good person,' said Marcelle, thinking of the rich farmer's rapacity.

'Shall I bring back the trunks you left there, as well?' enquired Grand-Louis.

'If you like to hire a wagon and send them on to me . . .'

'Not a bit of it! Why hire a man and a horse? I'll hitch Sophie to the cart, and I wager Mademoiselle Suzette would rather travel out in the open air on a bale of straw with a good driver like me than with that mad *patachon* in his salad basket. Now, that's not the end to it. You must have a servant, Monsieur Bricolin's are too busy to amuse your little devil from morn till night. Oh, I wish I'd not got my work! We'd have a fine time together, as I love children and he's even more full of it than me! But I'll lend you little Fanchon, my mother's serving-girl. We can manage without her for a bit. That girl will look after him like the apple of her eye, and she'll do anything you ask. She's only got one fault, and that's saying "Pardon?" three times whenever you speak a word to her. But there you are, she reckons it's good manners and thinks she'd be in for a scolding if she didn't pretend she was deaf.'

'You must be sent from heaven,' exclaimed Marcelle, 'and I find myself amazed that such a good soul should happen my way when I am in such a potentially delicate situation.'

'Tosh! they're just little bits of help from a friend, and you'll pay me back some other way. You've already been a great help to me since you arrived, though you may not know it!'

'What do you mean?'

'Oh, Lord! we'll talk about it later,' shrugged the miller with a mysterious air and a smile in which the gravity of his love contrasted oddly with the buoyancy of his character.

Once the departure of the miller and the servants had been arranged by common consent for this evening, 'in the cool', as Grand-Louis put it, Marcelle had a few minutes to write the two letters that follow, before dinner at the farm:

FIRST LETTER

Marcelle, Baronne de Blanchemont, to the Comtesse de Blanchemont, her mother-in-law.

'Dear Mama,

I direct this to you, as the bravest of women and head of the family, requesting you to inform the estimable Count and our other beloved relations of facts which will doubtless affect you more than they do me. You have so frequently told me of your apprehensions, and we have discussed the subject of my current preoccupation too often for you to require more than a hint from me. *There is nothing left* (absolutely nothing) *of Édouard's inheritance.* Of mine, there remains 250,000 or 300,000 francs.* As yet I only know my situation through the medium of a man whose own interests would lead him to exaggerate the catastrophe, if such were possible, but who is too sensible to attempt trickery, since tomorrow or the day after I can find out for myself. I am returning the good Lapierre to you, and have no need to ask that you should take him on again. You sent him to me in hopes that he might introduce a modicum of order and economy in my household's expenses. He did his best; but what good were his domestic savings when prodigality raged uncontrolled outside the household? Minor reasons which he will explain himself have forced me to send him precipitately; thus I write to you in haste, and without recounting the details, which I barely know myself and which will reach you later. I insist that Lapierre should see you alone and give this into your hands, so that you will have a few hours or days, if need be, to prepare the Count for this revelation. Soften it by telling him a thousand times over what you know of me, how indifferent I am to the delights of wealth, and incapable I am of bitterness against any person or thing in the past. How shall I not pardon him who was unfortunate enough to die before he could make all good! Dear Mother, let his memory be entirely and easily forgiven in your heart and mine!

'Now, a word or two about Édouard and me, who are as one in this trial sent by fate. I shall have enough, I hope, to provide for his needs and his education. He is not old enough to trouble himself about his losses, of which he knows nothing and should continue to know as little as possible, for kindness's sake, when he is of an age to understand. Is it not fortunate for him that this reversal of his situation has occurred before he could develop habits of ostentatious living? If it is a misfortune to be reduced to the bare necessities (which it is not, in my estimation), he will not be aware of it, and, accustomed henceforth to living modestly, he will think himself rich. Since he is destined to drop to the middle ranks, it is a blessing from Providence that he has been thus reduced at an age when the lesson, far from being a hard one, can only do him good. You will tell me that other inheritances will be his. I know nothing of this future and have no desire whatsoever to profit from it in advance. I should refuse, almost as an insult, the sacrifices which his family may wish to impose on themselves in order to give me what is called a respectable way of living. In apprehension of the news I have just heard, I had already formed my plans. I shall follow them, and nothing in this world can make me change. I am determined to settle in the provinces, deep in the country, where I shall mould my son's early years in hard work and simple living, and where neither sight nor experience of wealth in others can ruin the good effect of my example and my lessons. I have not lost hope that I may take him to visit you from time to time, and it will give you pleasure to see a lively, strong child, rather than that frail, dreamy creature, who, we always feared, held but an insecure purchase on life. I realize that you have rights over him and that I owe respect to your wishes and counsel; but I hope that you will not think amiss of my project, and that you will allow me to determine his childhood, in which the assiduous care of a mother and the happy influences of the country will be of more value than the superficial lessons of an overpaid tutor, riding-school, and carriage drives in the Bois de Boulogne.* As for me, have no fear; I do not regret my old lazy life and idle companions. I love the countryside with a passion, and I shall spend the long hours which the world will no longer steal from me in educating myself, the better to educate my son. Before this you have had some little confidence in me; now you should have an entire trust. I make bold to count on it, believing that you have only to sound your own energetic spirits and deeply maternal heart in order to understand my designs and resolves.

'All this will certainly meet with considerable opposition from the family; but when you announce that you think me right, all the others will be convinced. Thus I entrust our present and future into your hands, and I am yours forever in devotion, tenderness and respect.

MARCELLE'

There followed a postscript about Suzette and a request to send the family lawyer to Le Blanc, to certify the ruin of the provincial estate and to wind it up formally. As for her own affairs, Marcelle wanted to settle them personally, aided by competent local people.

The second letter was addressed to Henri Lémor:

'Henri, what happiness! what joy! I am ruined. No longer can you reproach me for my wealth; no longer will you detest my golden chains. Once again I am a woman whom you may love without compunction, and who needs to make no further sacrifices for you. My son no longer has expectations, at least not in the near future. Henceforth I have the right to bring him up in the manner you approve, to make a man of him, to entrust you with his education, and to surrender his whole soul to you. Make no mistake, we may well have a minor battle with his father's family, whose blind tenderness and aristocratic pride will call for returning him to the world, making him rich against my will. But we shall win out through soft words, a little tact, and much strength of will. I shall remain at a sufficient remove from their influence to paralyse it, and we will envelop the growth of this young soul in sweet mystery. It will be like the infancy of Jupiter in the sacred grottoes.* And when he leaves this holy retreat in order to test his powers, when he is tempted by wealth, we shall have made him proof against the temptations of the world and the corruption of gold. Henri, I am lulled by the sweetest hopes, do not destroy them with cruel doubts and what I might call pusillanimous scruples. You owe me your support and protection, now that I am to hide myself away from my family, who are full of care and kindness, but whom I must abandon and indeed combat, only because they do not share your views. The letter which I wrote you two days ago, when I left Paris, is thus entirely and clearly confirmed by this one. I shall not call you to me at present, I must not, and prudence also requires me to remain some time without seeing you, so that no one can attribute my self-chosen exile to my feelings for you. I shall not tell you the retreat I have chosen, indeed I do not know it myself. But in a year, Henri, dear Henri, after 15 August, you will come join me wherever I shall have settled, whenever I call you. Till then, if you do not share my confidence in myself, it would be better if you did not write... But have I the strength to live through a year, knowing nothing of you? No, nor will you! Write me a few words to say: '*I am alive and I love you!*' And address it to me through my faithful old servant Lapierre at the Hôtel de Blanchemont. Adieu, Henri. Oh! if only you could look into my heart, and see that I am worthier than you think!—Édouard is well, he does not forget you. Henceforth he will be the only one who speaks about you to me.

M.B.'

Having sealed these two letters, Marcelle, whose only worldly vanity was her son's angelic beauty, straightened Édouard's clothes a bit and crossed the farmyard. They were expecting her for dinner, and to pay her homage they had laid the table in the parlour rather than in their usual eating-place, the kitchen, although they were habitually afraid of dirtying the furniture. Besides, Mme Bricolin generally preferred to be within reach of the food which she had cooked herself, with the help of her mother-in-law and maidservant; Marcelle noticed this departure from the family's customs. Mme Bricolin, whose attentiveness was naturally tainted with ill grace, the worst breach of etiquette, showed her true colours by continually begging pardon for the poor quality of the service, putting her servants off completely. Marcelle requested that from now on, starting tomorrow, they should resume the normal ways of the household, and her request was granted, after she remarked with a playful smile that she would dine at the mill of Angibault if they insisted on standing on such ceremony with her.

'Oh, and speaking of the mill,' blurted Mme Bricolin, after several mangled polite phrases, 'I must have a word with Monsieur Bricolin.—Ah! here he comes now! Tell me, Monsieur Bricolin, have you lost your wits? You asked the miller to dine with us, the day when *Madame la baronne* has done us the honour of accepting our humble meal.'

'Devil take it! That never crossed my mind,' mumbled the farmer naïvely, 'or rather . . . I thought, when I invited Grand-Louis, that Madame wouldn't grant us that honour. *Monsieur le baron* always turned us down, you know... we served him in his chamber, which wasn't very comfortable, by the way... Anyhow, Thibaude, if Madame doesn't care to eat with the lad, you tell him so, you've got a tongue in your head; I can't be bothered; it was my mistake, I'd look a fool admitting it.'

'Oh it's up to me, as usual!' said Mme Bricolin bitterly. (Thibaut was her maiden name, and, being the eldest girl in her family, she was called by its feminine form, according to local custom.) 'Well then, I'm sending your fine Louis back to his flour.'

'That would offend me deeply, and I should probably leave myself,' said Mme de Blanchemont in a firm, and even rather harsh, tone, but one that impressed itself on the farm-wife. 'This morning I had breakfast with the lad, at his own house, and I found him so helpful, polite, and kind that it would hurt me considerably to dine without him this evening.'

'Really?' said the lovely Rose, who had listened very attentively to Marcelle and whose sparkling eyes expressed a surprise blended with pleasure; but she lowered them and blushed deeply when she noticed her mother's penetrating glare.

'As Madame wishes,' said Mme Bricolin; and she added under her breath to her servant, who was privileged to hear her confidential remarks when she was in a temper, 'It's a fine thing to be a handsome man!'

La Chounette (a nickname for Fanchon) smiled maliciously, making herself look even uglier than usual. She too thought the miller a fine handsome man, and was annoyed that he didn't return her admiration.

'Well then!' barked M. Bricolin, 'so the miller will dine with us. Madame's right not to be proud. That's the best way to make folk go along with you. Rose, go call Grand-Louis, he's in the farmyard. Tell him the soup's on the table. Do you know, *Madame la baronne*, I've been proved right, sticking with that miller. He's the only one who doesn't hold back double measure and switch grains on you. Aye, the only one hereabouts, devil take me! They're all rogues, every last one of them. As the old saying goes, "Catch a thief, catch the miller." I've tried them all, and he's the only one that doesn't fiddle the accounts and add cheap grain. And he's very eager to please, besides. He never grinds my wheat on the millstone when he's just done barley or rye. He knows that ruins the flour and takes away the whiteness. He's set his reputation on pleasing me, for he knows I like fine bread on my table. That's my only fancy, you know! I feel ashamed when someone comes here and doesn't say, "Ah, what beautiful bread! Nobody grows such fine wheat as you, Master Bricolin!"—"It's all Spanish wheat, my lad, and I'm proud of it!"'

'Your bread certainly is magnificent,' said Marcelle, as much to praise the miller as to flatter the vanity of M. Bricolin.

'Oh, heavens! what a lot of bother for the sake of a few holes more or less in the bread, and a bushel more or less each week!' screeched Mme Bricolin. 'When we have millers much closer by, one at the bottom of the castle mound, to use a man who lives a league away!'

'What business is it of yours?' exclaimed M. Bricolin. 'He comes for the sacks and brings them back without so much as a grain missing on top of his milling-fee.* Besides, he has a fine handsome mill, two great new wheels, a top-notch mill-pond, and there's never any shortage of water. It's nice not to have to wait.'

'And also, since he comes from so far away,' said the farm-wife, 'you always feel obliged to invite him in for dinner or supper; there's a fine saving!'

The miller's arrival put paid to this conjugal discussion. When his wife scolded him, M. Bricolin contented himself with shrugging his shoulders and speaking a little faster than usual. He pardoned her shrewish humours because her frugality and industry were highly useful to the household.

'Come now, Rose,' shrilled Mme Bricolin to her daughter, who was walking back with Grand-Louis, 'we're waiting for you before we can sit down at table. You could easily have asked Chounette to tell him, rather than run out yourself.'

'My father told me to do it,' said Rose.

'And you'd never have come otherwise, I'm sure,' whispered the miller to the girl.

'Is this the thanks I get from you, when I've been scolded for your sake?' said Rose in the same tone.

Marcelle could not hear what they were saying, but these furtive words that they exchanged, Rose's high colour, and Grand-Louis's visible emotion confirmed the suspicions already awakened in her by Mme Bricolin's aversion for the poor boy: the lovely Rose was the subject of the miller's thoughts.

XI. DINNER AT THE FARM

Eager to advance the romantic interests of her new friend, and seeing no risk therein to Mlle Bricolin, whose father and grandmother appeared to favour Grand-Louis, Mme de Blanchemont made a point of addressing him at length during the meal and of bringing the conversation round to subjects in which his education and intelligence did in fact outshine those of all the Bricolins, perhaps including the charming Rose herself. On agriculture, considered as one of the natural

sciences rather than as a matter of commercial exploitation;
on politics, taken as the pursuit of happiness and of social
justice; on religion and ethics, Grand-Louis's ideas were of the
right stamp, high and just, sensitive and noble, if unsophisti-
cated, and they came as a complete surprise to the farm folk.
The Bricolins' conversation was crude, and the only wit that
marked it was put to the service of mocking their neighbours.
Grand-Louis, who had no inclination towards shady haunts
or nasty rumours, had little to say on such subjects and had
never made any great impression. M. Bricolin had announced
that he was a fool, like all handsome men, and Rose, who had
always found him a backward or niggling suitor, either teasing or timid, could only make excuses for his lack of spirit by
pointing out his good-heartedness. So they were all astounded
that Mme de Blanchemont preferred to direct her conversation towards him, and even more surprised to hear him
speak so well, once she had helped him overcome the nervous-
ness brought on by Rose's presence and her mother's ill will.
Five or six times M. Bricolin, who had no doubts about the
miller's feelings for his daughter, heard him out with benevolent astonishment, thumped the table and shouted, 'You mean
you know *that*? Where the devil did you fish that one up
from?'

'Oh well! The river, of course!' laughed Grand-Louis
flippantly.

Mme Bricolin retreated bit by bit into a sombre silence,
seeing her enemy's success; she resolved to warn M. Bricolin
that very evening of her genuine or imagined discovery about
this peasant's feeling for her *young lady*.

As for old mother Bricolin, she did not understand a bit of
the conversation; but she thought the miller spoke with a
silver tongue, for he could muster several sentences at once,
without stumbling or stopping for breath. Rose appeared not
to listen, but she missed nothing; and her eyes were involuntarily fixed on Grand-Louis. There was a fifth Bricolin there,
although Marcelle took little notice of him. This was old
father Bricolin, who wore peasant dress, like his wife, ate a
great deal, said very little, and appeared to think not at all. He
was well-nigh deaf and blind, and seemed quite senile. His
better half had led him to the table, talking to him like a child.

She took great pains with him, filling his plate and his glass, and removing the crumb from his bread, since he had lost all his teeth and his tough hardened gums could only grind down the hardest crusts; all the while saying not a word to him, as if it were a waste of time. When he sat down she had managed to make him understand that he must remove his hat, as a sign of respect for Mme de Blanchemont. He obeyed but seemed to have no idea why, and he put it on again immediately afterwards, a liberty which his son M. Bricolin also allowed himself, after the custom of the country. The miller, who had not departed from this usage that morning at home, stuffed his cap in his pocket when he thought no one was looking, out of a new-found deference for women, inspired by Marcelle, and a fear of looking the bumpkin, for the first time in his life.

But although he admired the tall miller's gift of the gab, as he put it, M. Bricolin found himself entirely at odds with his opinions. On the subject of farming he maintained that there was no point trying anything new, that inventors had never discovered anything worthwhile, that innovation led to ruin; that since *there's nothing new under the sun, in the light of day today*, things had always been thus and would never be any better.

'All right then!' exclaimed the miller. 'But the first men to do what we do today, the ones who yoked oxen to plough the land and sow the seed, they did something new, all the same, and they might have been put off it if someone had said to them that uncultivated land wouldn't ever be fertile, wouldn't they? The same as in politics: tell me then, Monsieur Bricolin, suppose a hundred years since, someone had told you you'd not be paying tithes or rents, and all the monasteries would be rubble . . .'

'Claptrap! twaddle! I shouldn't have believed it, I give you that; but it happened because it had to happen. All's for the best *in the light of day today*; everyone's free to seek his own fortune, and there'll never be anything better than that.'

'And the poor, the idle, the weak, the simpletons, what are you going to do about them?'

'I don't intend to do anything about them, the good-for-nothings. So much the worse for them!'

'And if you were one of them, Monsieur Bricolin, Heaven forbid! (you're a long ways off it) would you say to yourself, "So much the worse for me!" Not a bit, you didn't speak your true mind when you said so much the worse for them! You've too good a heart for that, you're a religious man.'

'A religious man? Me? I've no time for religion, nor do you neither. I can see perfectly well it's trying to make a comeback, but I don't fret over it. Our *curé* likes the good life, and I don't stand in his way. If he was one of the preaching sort I'd soon send him packing. Who believes any of that foolishness *in the light of day today?*

'And your wife and mother and daughter, do they reckon it's foolishness?'

'Oh, they like it, it keeps them happy. Seems women need that sort of thing.'

'And the rest of us peasants, we must be like women, we also need religion.'

'Fine and good, you've got one ready to hand; go to mass, I'm not stopping you, so long as you don't make me go.'

'But they may force you, if our religion becomes strict and fanatical again, as it's often been in the past.'*

'If it's worthless, let it go. I can manage without.'

'But since the rest of us must have one, shall we have a different one?'

'A different one! a different one! devil take it! you do go on! All right then, make yourself one!'

'I'd like one that stopped men hating and fearing and hurting each other.'

'Oh, that'd be something new! Well, I'd like one that stopped my tenants pinching my corn at night and my labourers spending three hours over their soup at dinner.'

'All that would stop if your religion ordered you to make them as well-off as you are.'

'Grand-Louis, you have true religion in your heart,' said Marcelle.

'That's true!' exclaimed Rose warmly.

M. Bricolin did not dare say anything more. He was much concerned to gain Mme de Blanchemont's confidence and good opinion. Grand-Louis, seeing how moved Rose was, looked at Marcelle with a spirited glance, as if to say: I thank you.

The sun was going down, and the copious meal drawing to a close. M. Bricolin, lowering himself heavily into his chair after many hearty helpings of food and full bumpers of wine, would have liked to indulge in his favourite pleasure of several cups of coffee, spiked with *eau-de-vie* and interspersed with liqueurs, spread out over two or three hours of the evening. But Grand-Louis, on whose company he had been counting, rose from the table and went out to prepare for the departure. Mme de Blanchemont took leave of her servants and settled their wages. She handed them the letter for her mother-in-law, and, taking the miller aside, entrusted him with the one addressed to Henri, asking him to put it in the post himself.

'Have no fear,' he assured her, aware that this was something secret. 'It won't leave my hand till it goes in the letterbox, and no one'll see hide nor hair of it, not even your servants, eh?'

'Thank you, my good Louis.'

'Thank you! You say that to me, when I'm the one as ought to be thanking you on my knees. Have you any idea how much I owe you? I'll stop off at our house, and little Fanchon'll be with you in two hours. She's neater and gentler than that clumsy Chounette here.'

When Louis and Lapierre had left, Marcelle had a pang of moral distress, alone and at the mercy of the Bricolin family. She felt overwhelmed with sadness, and, taking Édouard by the hand, went off to a little wood which she could see on the other side of the meadow. It was still daylight, and the old castle's high towers cast long shadows in the declining sun. But she had not gone far when she was joined by Rose, who felt a great attraction to her, and whose pleasant face was the only object which she found it agreeable to contemplate at the moment.

'May I have the honour of showing you the hunting-park?' asked the girl. 'It's my favourite spot, and you'll like it too, I know for a fact.'

'Whatever it may be like, your company will make it pleasant for me,' answered Marcelle, passing her arm familiarly under Rose's.

The ancient seigneurial park of Blanchemont, which had been cut down during the revolution, was now fenced off by a deep ditch full of running water and by huge thriving hedges, where Rose left a bit of the trim on her muslin dress, with the haste and carelessness of a girl whose wardrobe is ample. The ancient trunks of the old oaks had sprouted suckers everywhere, and the plantation was now a dense thicket dominated by a few *specimens* which the axe had spared, like venerable ancestors stretching out their robust knotty arms over their numerous new progeny. Pretty paths wound up and down over natural steps in the rock and trailed off into the thick low shade. This was a mysterious wood. Here one might wander freely, supported by a lover's arm. Marcelle chased away this thought, which made her heart beat, and fell into a reverie as she listened to the songs of the nightingales, linnets, and blackbirds that inhabited this placid secluded copse.

The only avenue which the undergrowth had not invaded was at the far boundary of the wood; it served as a lumbering road. Marcelle approached it with Rose, and her child ran on ahead. Suddenly he stopped and turned round slowly, indecisive, serious, and pale.

'What is the matter?' asked his mother, accustomed as she was to guess all his thoughts, when she saw him torn between fear and curiosity.

'There's a horrid woman there,' answered Édouard.

'One may look horrid but be nice,' replied Marcelle. 'Lapierre is nice, although not handsome.'

'Oh, Lapierre isn't ugly!' shrilled Édouard, who, like all children, thought the objects of his affection handsome.

'Give me your hand,' continued Marcelle, 'and we shall go and see this horrid woman.'

'No, no, don't go, it's no good,' urged Rose, dejected and embarrassed, but apparently not fearful. 'I'd no idea *she* was there.'

'I want Édouard to get used to conquering his fears,' answered Marcelle in a half-whisper.

And since Rose did not dare stop her, she hastened her steps. But when she reached the middle of the avenue she halted, overcome with a sort of terror at the sight of the strange being advancing slowly towards her.

XII. CASTLES IN SPAIN

Under the majestic bower formed by the huge oaks that lined the avenue, which the setting sun carved into stark shadows and trenchant gleams, a woman was walking with measured paces; or rather, a nameless thing, swept up in some fierce meditation. It was one of those figures that have been brutalized and driven wild by misfortune, of indeterminate age and sex. Yet the regular features had once possessed a certain nobility which was not entirely lost, despite the terrible ravages of misery and disease, and the long black hair, spilling out chaotically under a white bonnet topped with a man's straw hat, ripped and torn in a thousand places, gave a sinister appearance to the swarthy narrow features which it partially shrouded. Of this face, yellow as saffron and devastated by fever, there was nothing to be seen but two huge dark eyes, frighteningly intense but focused on nothing; a straight nose of a good shape, though very pronounced; and a livid red mouth, half open. The costume, of a repulsive filthiness, was of the bourgeois class; a badly fitting yellow gown, dragging in the dirt on one side, outlined a malformed body, whose constantly hunched high shoulders had developed out of all proportion to the emaciated remainder. The scrawny black legs were bare, the hardened feet ill-protected against pebbles and thorns by muddy shoes with splitting soles. She walked gravely, head down, eyes fixed on the ground, hands busy rolling and pressing a handkerchief spotted with blood.

She made straight for Mme de Blanchemont, who disguised her fear so as not to spread it to Édouard, but waited in anguish to see if the woman would swerve right or left so that she might pass her. But the spectre—for this creature resembled some evil apparition—kept on walking, apparently unaware of them, and her visage, which bore no trace of idiocy but rather a grim despair that had progressed to a state of blank contemplation, showed no impression of external objects. However, just as she came up to the foot of Marcelle's shadow, she stopped abruptly, as if she had encountered a barrier that she could not cross, and, turning her back brusquely on them, resumed her incessant dull march.

'That's our poor Bricoline,'* said Rose without lowering her voice, although the woman was within earshot. 'She's my older sister, whose mind is unsettled (as we say hereabouts, meaning mad). She's no more than thirty, though she looks an old woman, and it's twelve years since she's spoken a word to us, or seemed to hear our voices. We don't know but what she's gone deaf. She's not mute, for when she thinks herself alone, she talks a bit, but it makes no sense. She wants to be left alone, and she does no harm unless you cross her. Don't be frightened; so long as you pretend as you don't see her, she'll not look at you. It's only when we try to clean her up a bit that she gets angry and fights us off, screaming, as if we were hurting her.'

'Mama,' shivered Édouard, trying to hide his fear, 'take me back to the house, I'm hungry.'

'How can you be hungry? You just got down from the table,' said Marcelle, no more eager than her son to contemplate this sad spectacle any longer. 'You must be mistaken; let us enter some other avenue: perhaps there is too much sun here, and the heat is tiring you out.'

'Yes, yes, let's go back in the glade,' sighed Rose, 'this isn't a pretty sight. There's no chance of her following us, once she's on a track she doesn't often leave it; you can see for yourself, the grass in this one is brown in the middle, she's been back over it so many times, always the same spot. My poor sister, what a pity! She used to be so pretty and kind! I can remember when she carried me in her arms and looked after me like you do with your fine boy. But since her troubles she doesn't know me any more, she doesn't even remember I'm alive.'

'Ah, my poor Mademoiselle Rose, what a terrible misfortune! And what has caused it? Is it some sorrow or sickness? Does anyone know?'

'Oh, we know all too well. But no one talks about it.'

'I ask your forgiveness if the interest I take in you has led me to pose an indiscreet question.'

'Oh, with you, Madame, it's completely different. I think you're so gentle that nobody could feel ill at ease with you. So I shall tell you, just between ourselves, my poor sister went mad from being crossed in love. She was in love with a young man who was honest and kind, but who had nothing, and our parents wouldn't consent to the marriage. The young man enlisted and went off to get himself killed in Algiers. Poor Bricoline had been sad and quiet ever since he left, but they reckoned it was just flightiness, time would heal it. But she heard about his death in the cruellest way. My mother thought that if all hope was taken away from her she'd come round at last, and so she just threw the news at her, didn't soften it at all, though she was in such a state that it could have killed her. My sister didn't seem to understand and didn't answer. We were having our evening meal, I remember like it was yesterday, though I was only little. She dropped her fork and stared at my mother a good quarter of an hour, never looking down for a minute, and so oddly that my mother took fright and screamed, "Doesn't she look as if she wanted to eat me up?" "It's your doing," said my grandmother, who's a good woman and wanted Bricoline to marry her young man. "You've given her such a fright, you'll have driven her mad."

'My grandmother had judged only too well. My sister had gone mad, and since that day she's never eaten with us. She won't touch anything we give her, and she lives on her own, she runs away from us, and she feeds herself on old scraps that she keeps in the bottom of the pantry cupboard, when there's nobody in the kitchen. Sometimes she pounces on a hen, kills it, tears it apart with her fingers, and wolfs it down, all bloody. That's what she's just done, I know it, she's got blood on her hands and handkerchief. Other times she pulls vegetables out of the garden and eats them raw. She lives like a savage and everybody's afraid of her. That's what happens when you're crossed in love, and my poor parents have been punished for judging their daughter's feelings wrongly. Though they never say a word about what they'd do if it all started over again.'

Marcelle thought that Rose was referring to herself, and, eager to learn to what extent the sentiments of Grand-Louis were mutual, she encouraged her confidences with a tone of affectionate kindness. They had arrived at the opposite boundary of the plantation from where the madwoman was walking. Marcelle felt more at ease, and little Édouard had already forgotten his fright. Once again he was frolicking madly about, under his mother's eye.

'Your mother does seem rather strict to me,' suggested Mme de Blanchemont to her companion; 'but Monsieur Bricolin appears more ready to indulge you.'

'Papa makes less of a fuss than Mama,' replied Rose, nodding her head. 'He's more cheerful, more affectionate; he gives me more presents, more signs of love, and all in all he is fond of his children, he's a good father!. . . But when it comes to his fortune, and what he calls propriety, his will might be even more unshakeable than my mother's. I've heard him say a hundred times over that it's better to be dead than miserable, and that he'd kill me rather than consent . . .'

'To marry you according to your wishes?' enquired Marcelle, seeing that Rose could not find words to express her thoughts.

'Oh, he never puts it like that!' answered Rose, a bit prudishly. 'I've never given a thought to marriage, so I've no idea if my wishes would be the same as his. But it's true he's very ambitious for me and he's already tormented by fear that he'll never find a son-in-law worthy of him. Which means that I shan't be married soon, and that suits me, as I've no wish to leave my family, even if Mama does have her little ways.'

Marcelle thought that Rose was concealing her feelings somewhat, and, not wishing to disrupt their intimacy, she observed that Rose was doubtless quite ambitious for herself as well.

'Oh, not in the least!' exclaimed Rose with abandon. 'I find myself far richer than I have any need or desire to be. It's no good my father saying that there are five of us (for I have two other sisters and a brother, all settled), and so none of us will get a very big share, I don't care. I have simple tastes, and besides, I can see plainly from what things are like at home, the richer you are, the poorer you are.'

'What do you mean?'

'With farmers like us, at any rate, that's the simple truth. You aristocrats, you make a great thing of your wealth as a rule; we even accuse you of splashing it about, and when we see so many ancient families ruined, we tell ourselves we're wiser than that, and we aim ever so carefully, how can I put it?... ever so passionately to set our children up comfortably. We always want to double or triple what we own; well, at least, that's what my father and mother, and my sisters and their husbands, and my aunts and my cousins have harped on about since I was born. So, not wanting any interruptions to the business of getting rich, they subject themselves to all kinds of hardships. Sometimes they make a great show of wealth in front of other people, and then at home, in secret, they dine on an egg, as the saying goes. They're afraid they might ruin the furniture or their clothes, and get too self-indulgent. At least that's my mother's way, and it's hard, saving all your life, but then not allowing yourself any pleasures when you're in a position to afford them. And when it's a matter of being mean with your workers' well-being, their wages, and their appetites, it's even sadder. As for me, if I were the mistress and could do as I think best, I'd not refuse anything to anyone, nor myself. I'd eat up my income, and perhaps the capital wouldn't be any the worse for it. For then everyone would be fond of me, and they'd work for me gladly and loyally. Isn't that what Grand-Louis was saying at dinner? He was right.'

'My dear Rose, he was right in theory.'

'In theory?'

'I mean in applying his altruistic ideas to a society which does not yet exist but will certainly do so some day. As for actual practice, that is relative to what might be accomplished today. You would be deluding yourself if you thought it enough for some to be good, in the midst of so many others who are not, if they would be understood, loved, and rewarded in this existence.'

'What you say astonishes me. I thought that you would share my beliefs. Do you believe that it is right to crush those who labour to line our pockets?'*

'I do not share your beliefs, Rose, and yet I am far from holding the opinions you may suppose. I should like no one to work for anyone else, but each for everyone, and thus for God and himself as well.'

'And how is that to be done?'

'It would be too long a business to explain to you, my child, and I should fear to do it badly. Until the future that I envisage takes shape, I feel it a great misfortune to be wealthy, and for my part I am entirely relieved to be so no more.'

'This is peculiar,' wondered Rose. 'A rich person might none the less do good to the poor. That is the highest happiness!'

'One single person of good will can do so little good, even if she were to give away all she possessed, and then she would quickly be reduced to powerlessness!'

'But suppose everyone did the same?'

'Oh yes, if everyone did! That is what would be required; but there is no way at present to induce all the wealthy to make such a sacrifice. Even you, Rose, would not be inclined to do so whole-heartedly. Within your income you would be happy to relieve as much suffering as you could, to rescue a few families from destitution; but only on condition of preserving your capital, and I, sermonizing to you now, cling to the last shreds of my fortune in order to save what is called *honour*, so that my son will have something with which to meet his father's debts without falling into absolute penury himself, ending in paltry education, excessive struggle, and, quite probably, premature death for a delicate creature from a line of idlers, heir to a sickly constitution greatly inferior to that of the peasant. So you may see that even with our good intentions, those of us who cannot tell how society might resolve such quandaries can do very little except choose a middle state for ourselves rather than riches, and work rather than idleness. It is one step nearer virtue, but how few praises we deserve for it, and how little it does for the countless miseries that strike our eyes and sadden our hearts!'

'But the remedy?' said Rose, stunned. 'Isn't there any remedy? There must be some king who can find one, a king can do anything.'*

'A king can do nothing, or very nearly nothing,' answered Marcelle, smiling at Rose's innocence. 'A people must find that in their hearts.'

'All this feels like a dream to me,' sighed Rose. 'This is the first time I've heard such things discussed. Sometimes I wonder about them, on my own, but in our house no one ever suggests that all's not well with the world. They say that you have to look after yourself, because your happiness is the last thing anybody else cares about, and that everyone is your natural enemy; that's frightening, don't you think?'

'And a peculiar contradiction. All is indeed not well with the world, precisely because it is full of beings who fear and detest one another!'

'But what's your plan of improvement? for anyone who's aware of something evil must have an idea of something better.'

'One may have a definite idea of that kind when all the world shares it and strives to further it. But we are one or two against many, all of whom mock our dreams and call it a crime to speak of them, and so we can only have a vague and foggy view. Such is the case, I shan't say with the great minds of our times, I know nothing of them, I am only an ignorant woman,* but with the most benevolent hearts, and that is where we stand today.'

'Yes, *in the light of day today*! as my papa says,' replied Rose with a smile. Then she added sadly, 'But what shall I do? What shall I do to be virtuous, being wealthy?'

'You will hold locked in the treasure chest of your heart, my dear Rose, your sorrow in others' suffering, the love of your neighbour which the Gospels teach you, and the ardent desire to sacrifice yourself for the common good, on that day when one person's sacrifice can aid all of us.'

'Will that day come?'

'Never doubt it.'

'Are you certain?'

'As of justice and God's mercy.'

'That's true, God cannot let evil last for ever. All the same, *Madame la baronne*, you've filled my head with dizziness till it hurts, but now it seems to me that I understand how you can bear the loss of your fortune with such tranquillity, and I begin to see, in fits and starts, that I could happily live a little more frugally myself.'

'And if you had to live on a pittance, suffer, work?'

'Oh Lord! if it was for no purpose, it would be horrible.'

'And if you nevertheless began to see that it might be for some purpose? If it were necessary to pass through a crisis of great distress, a sort of martyrdom, in order to save humanity?'

'Oh well!' said Rose, looking at Marcelle with astonishment, 'then you'd bear it patiently.'

'You would throw yourself into it enthusiastically,' exclaimed Marcelle with a tone of voice and an expression that made Rose tremble but swept through her like an electric shock, much to her surprise.

Édouard began to tire of his games, and the moon was rising on the horizon. Marcelle thought it time to put her child to bed, and Rose followed her silently, still overwhelmed by the conversation which they had just had; but as she descended again into reality, approaching the farm and hearing her mother's shrill voice in the distance, she thought to herself as she looked at the young woman walking before her, 'Mightn't she be mad as well?'

XIII. ROSE

Despite her fears, Rose began to feel an irresistible attraction towards Marcelle. She helped her put her son to bed, showered her with a thousand little attentions, and took her hand to kiss when she left. Marcelle, who was already fond of her, as of a child full of grace, prevented this by kissing her on both cheeks. Delighted and encouraged, Rose hesitated on the doorstep.

'I should like to ask you something,' she said at last. 'Does Grand-Louis have enough wit to understand you?'

'Of course, Rose. But what does that matter to you?' teased Marcelle.

'Because it seemed strange to me, to see that of all of us today, it was our miller who was so full of ideas. It's not as if he's had a great deal of education, poor Louis!'

'But he is so good-hearted and intelligent!' exclaimed Marcelle.

'Oh, good-hearted, yes. I know him inside out, that boy. I was raised with him. His older sister was my nurse and I spent my early years at the mill of Angibault... Didn't he tell you?'

'He said nothing of you to me, but I surmised that he was entirely devoted to you.'

'He was always very good to me,' blushed Rose. 'The proof of his good character is that he's always loved children. He was only seven or eight when I was put out to nurse with his sister,* and my grandmother says that he looked after me and played with me as if he was old enough to be my father. Apparently I took such a liking to him that I didn't want to leave, and my mother, who didn't hate him then like she does now, had him come to our house when I was weaned, to keep me company. He stayed with us two or three years, though we'd only agreed two or three months originally. He was so enterprising and helpful that they found him a good deal of use at our place. His mother was in financial difficulties, and my grandmother, who was her old friend, thought it a good idea to relieve her of one child. So I remember very clearly the time when Louis, my poor sister, and I were always running and playing together, in the meadow, in the hunting-park, in the castle attics. But when he was old enough to be useful with the flour to his mother, she fetched him back to the mill. We were so sad to part company, and I was so miserable without him, and his mother and his sister (my nurse) were so fond of me, that they took me over to Angibault every Saturday evening and brought me back here every Monday morning. That lasted till I was old enough to go to school in town, and when I left, it was no longer fitting, a friendship between a boy like the miller and a girl who'd been brought up as a young lady. But we went on seeing a good deal of each other, especially when my father made him his miller, despite the distance, and he began coming here three or four times a week. For my part I've always enjoyed seeing Angibault again, and the kind mill-wife I love so much! . . . Well, Madame, would you credit it, for some time now my mother has taken it into her head that all this is dreadful, and she won't let me walk over there any more. She thinks poor Grand-Louis really shocking, she does her best to humiliate him, and she won't let me dance with him at the *assemblées*,* on the grounds that he's too much below me. But young ladies from the country, as they call us, we always dance with any peasant who asks us; and besides, you can't call the miller of Angibault a peasant. He's worth 20,000 francs, and he's better educated than most. To be frank, my cousin Honoré Bricolin doesn't write as fine a hand, despite the money they spent teaching him, and I can't see why I should be so proud about my family.'

'I am equally at a loss to understand it,' mused Marcelle, aware that a certain delicacy would be necessary with Mademoiselle Rose, and that she would not unburden herself with the same ardent candour as Grand-Louis. 'Have you remarked nothing in the good miller's manner that would have occasioned your mother's dislike?'

'Oh, nothing at all! He's a hundred times more decent and honest than all our rich farmers, who mostly drink heavily and are often very uncivilized. I've never heard him say a single word to make me blush.'

'But perhaps your mother might have formed the strange idea that he is in love with you?'

Rose was nonplussed; after a pause, she finally admitted that her mother might have persuaded herself of that.

'And if your mother had supposed correctly, would she not have been right to warn you against him?'

'But that's as may be! If it was so, and he'd told me about it! . . . But he's never said a word to me except as a friend, pure and simple.'

'And if he were greatly taken with you but had never dared to tell you so?'

'Well, where would be the harm in that?' said Rose, rather coquettishly.

'You would be very wrong to entertain his overtures if you did not wish to encourage him,' answered Marcelle, quite severely. 'That would be playing with a friend's misery, and your family above all others, Rose, should take care never to cross someone in love!'

'Oh!' exclaimed Rose with a rebellious air, 'men don't go mad for love! Although,' she added innocently, with a nod of her head, 'you do have to admit, he often looks sad, poor Louis, and he speaks like a desperate man . . . though I haven't an inkling why! It does give me pain.'

'Although not enough that you deign to understand him?'

'But if he did love me, what could I do to console him?'

'Quite. You must either love him or avoid him.'

'I can't do either. Love him, that's almost impossible, and avoid him, he's too good a friend for me to hurt him like that. If you only knew the expression he takes on when I seem not to be paying him any attention! He goes quite pale, and it hurts me to see him.'

'Then why do you say that it would be impossible to love him?'

'My Lord! How can you love someone you can't marry?'

'But you can always marry someone you love.'

'Oh, no, not always! Look at my poor sister! Her example terrifies me too much, I can't risk following in her footsteps.'

'You risk nothing, my dear Rose,' said Marcelle with some slight bitterness. 'Anyone who can so easily dispose of their love and free will is not in love and runs no risk.'

'Don't say that,' replied Rose spiritedly. 'I'm as capable as the next girl of loving and risking unhappiness. But would you really advise me to be so brave?'

'Heaven forbid! I only want to help you discover the true state of your feelings, so that your imprudence should not result in misery for Louis.'

'Poor Grand-Louis! . . . But tell me, Madame, what am I to do? Let's suppose that my father consents to give me to him, after a great deal of bluster and temper; that my mother is frightened by my sister's case and would rather sacrifice her scruples than see me fall into a decline, not that all that's very likely; but to get to that stage, just think of all the quarrels, the scenes, the trouble!'

'You are frightened, and you do not love him, I tell you; perhaps you are correct, and thus you must send Grand-Louis away.'

This piece of advice, to which Marcelle kept returning, was not at all to Rose's taste. The miller's love was highly flattering to her self-esteem, particularly since Mme de Blanchemont had called it so much to her attention, and perhaps also because of the rarity of the occurrence. Peasants rarely fall victim to passion, and in the bourgeois world which Rose inhabited, passion was becoming more and more unknown and unheard-of, compared to the abiding concerns of self-interest. Rose had read novels; she was proud to have inspired an unbalanced, impossible love that might one day astonish all the locality. Finally, Grand-Louis was the darling of all the peasant girls, and the distance between that race and the newly rich Bricolins was not so great as to dispel the intoxication of besting the prettiest girls around.

'Don't think me a coward,' said Rose after a moment's reflection. 'I know perfectly well what to say to Mama when she maligns the poor boy unfairly, and if one day I took it into my head, with the help of all your spirit and my father's great desire to please you . . . I could triumph over everything. For a start, I can assure you that I shouldn't lose my mind like my poor sister! I'm stubborn, and they've always spoiled me too much not to be a bit nervous of me. But I shall tell you what would cost me the dearest.'

'Go on, Rose, I am listening.'

'What would people think of me if I created such trouble in the family? My friends would be jealous that I'd inspired his love, such as they'll never find when they marry for money, and they'd be the first to cast stones. My cousins and suitors would be furious that I'd preferred a peasant to them, when they think so much of themselves; all the mothers would be fearful of the example I was setting their daughters; even the peasants themselves would be jealous of one of their number making what they call a grand marriage, and they'd persecute me with their ill words and mockery.

'"She's mad," one would say, "it's in the blood, and she'll soon be eating raw meat like her sister." "She's a fool," another would say, "to take a peasant when she could marry one of her own!" "She's a wicked girl," they'd all say, "to hurt her parents so, when they've never refused her anything! Oh! the brazen thing, the slut, making such a scandal for the sake of a bumpkin, just because he's five feet eight inches tall! Why not her father's ploughman? Why not Uncle Cadoche, who goes around begging from door to door?" There'd never be an end to it, and I don't think it's seemly for a young girl to expose herself to all that for a man's love.'*

'My dear Rose,' said Marcelle, 'these last objections do not seem so serious to me as the first, and yet I can see that you would find it much more repugnant to brave the ill opinion of the world than the resistance of your parents. We must consider this together carefully, for and against, and since you have told me your story, I owe you mine. I wish to tell it to you, although it is a secret, the entire secret of my life! but it is so pure that a young girl may hear it. In a little while it will be secret to none, and until that time, I am certain that you will guard it faithfully.'

'Oh, Madame!' cried Rose, throwing her arms round Marcelle's neck, 'you are so good to me! No one has ever told me any secrets, and I've always wanted to know one so that I could keep it well. So you see how sacred yours will be to me! It will teach me much of which I am ignorant; for it seems to me that there must be a moral in love as in everything, and no one has ever wanted to tell me about it, on the pretext that there's no place where love is not. Though it seems to me... but tell me, tell me, dear Madame Marcelle! I imagine that if I have your confidence, I'll have your friendship too.'

'And why not, if I may expect payment in return?' said Marcelle, returning her embrace.

'Oh, my Lord!' exclaimed Rose, her eyes filling with tears. 'Can't you see that I love you? Since I first saw you my heart has been drawn to you, and it's all yours, even though I've only known you a day. How did that happen? I've no idea. But I've never seen anyone who could please me as much as you do. I've only seen such people in books, and you seem to me to be all the beautiful heroines of the novels I've ever read, all in one.'

'And so, my dear child, your noble heart does need to love someone! I shall try not to be unworthy of this fortunate occasion for me.'

Little Fanchon was already installed in the next-door box-room, and was snoring loudly enough to drown out the barn-owls and nightjars who were beginning to stir in the rafters of the old towers. Marcelle sat down by the open window, with its view of the serene stars shining in a magnificently pure sky, and, taking Rose's hand in her own, spoke as follows:

XIV. MARCELLE

'My story, dear Rose, is somewhat like a novel; but a novel of such simplicity and familiarity that it is like all the novels in the world. You shall have it in as few words as possible.

'When my son was two, his health was so delicate that I despaired of saving him. My concern, my sorrow, the continual tasks of caring for him, with which I trusted no one else, provided a natural occasion for me to retire from the world, for which I had in any case little taste and in which I had only made a brief appearance. The doctors advised me to live in the country with my child. My husband had a fine estate twenty leagues from here,* as you know; but the boisterous and licentious life he led with his friends, horses, dogs, and mistresses* did not induce me to settle there, not even during the times whilst he was in Paris. The disorder of the house, the insolence of the valets, who were allowed to develop thieving ways because they could not be paid a regular wage, the ill manners of the neighbouring nobility, all were described to me so vividly by my old Lapierre that I had long since abandoned any thought of establishing myself there. Monsieur de Blanchemont, not caring for me to come and live here, where

I might learn of his abandoned ways, led me to believe that this place was appalling, that the old castle was uninhabitable, and on that last count he merely exaggerated slightly, as you will agree. He talked of buying me a country house on the outskirts of Paris, but where would he have found the money for such an acquisition, when, although I was yet ignorant of the fact, he was already nearly ruined?

'Seeing that his promises amounted to nothing and that my son was wasting away, I made haste to rent the first thing I could find, indeed the only one at that time: half of a house at Montmorency (a village near Paris, in an admirable situation, near healthy forests and well-elevated hills). These dwellings are in great demand among more than modestly rich Parisians, who come for some time during the good weather. My friends and relations came to see me quite often at first, then less and less, as happens when the person being visited loves her retreat and makes no effort of luxury or coquetry to attract others. Towards the end of the first season, a fortnight might go by without my seeing anyone from Paris. I had not established relations with any of the notables in the area. Édouard was better, I was calm and content; I read a good deal, I went for walks in the woods with him on his donkey, led by a peasant woman, accompanied by a book and a large dog, a very assiduous guardian of our safety. This life was greatly to my taste. Monsieur de Blanchemont was delighted not to have to concern himself with me. He never came to see me. From time to time he would send a servant to get news of his son and to enquire after my needs for money, which were extremely modest, happily for him: he could not have satisfied them.'

'Well, I never!' exclaimed Rose. 'He said to us here that it was for your sake that he was running through both your incomes; that you required horses, carriages; and all the time you were probably going on foot through the woods to save the hire of a donkey!'

'You have guessed rightly, dear Rose. Whenever I did ask my husband for money, he told me such complicated and far-fetched tales about his poverty-stricken farmers, who had been utterly ruined by the winter frosts and summer hailstorms, that to spare myself all these details and, for the most part, duped by his generous concern for you, I concurred and forbore from claiming my proper revenues.

'The old house where I lived was respectable but very modest, and no one noticed me there. It had two floors. I occupied the first. On the ground floor two young men lived, one of them ill. A very shady little garden, surrounded by high walls, was common to both tenants, myself and Monsieur Henri Lémor; Édouard played there with his nursemaid, and I sat watching from my window.

'Henri was twenty-two. His brother was only fifteen. The poor boy was consumptive, and his elder brother cared for him with admirable diligence. They were orphans. Henri was a true mother to the poor sufferer. He never left him for so much as an hour, he read to him, he took him for walks, supporting him in his arms, and since poor Ernest hardly slept at all any longer, Henri looked almost as ill as he: pale, exhausted, racked by his vigils.

'The landlady of the house, an excellent old woman who occupied part of the ground floor, was very obliging and devoted to these unhappy young people; but she could not do everything, and I felt obliged to be her helpmate. I did it with zeal, without sparing myself, as you would have done in my place, Rose; and even in the last days of Ernest's life I hardly left his bedside. He showed me a touching affection and gratitude. Not realizing and no longer feeling the gravity of his illness, he died almost without noticing, still speaking. He had just told me that I had cured him, when his breathing stopped and his hand went cold in mine.

'Henri's grief went deep; it sent him into a decline, and I was obliged to tend and watch over him, in his turn. The old landlady, Madame Joly, was at the end of her strength. Happily Édouard was well, and I was able to divide my caring between him and Henri. The duty of aiding and consoling poor Henri fell on me alone, and towards the end of autumn I had the joy of restoring him to life.

'You may well imagine, Rose, that a deep and inalterable friendship bonded the two of us in the midst of all these griefs and dangers. When winter, and my relatives' insistence, forced me to return to Paris, we had fallen into such sweet habits of reading, conversing, and walking together in the little garden, that the separation wrenched our hearts. Yet we did not yet dare to promise each other that we would find ourselves at Montmorency the following year. We were still timid with each other, and we would have trembled to give this affection the title of love.

'Henri had never thought to enquire after my rank, nor I after his. Our household expenses were much the same. He had asked permission to visit me in Paris; but when I gave him the address of my mother-in-law, the Hôtel de Blanchemont, he seemed surprised and afraid. When I left Montmorency in the carriage with a heraldic crest, sent by my relations, he appeared much perturbed, and when he realized that I was wealthy (as I believed myself to be, and so appeared), he considered himself estranged from me for ever. Winter went by without my seeing him, or hearing anything about him.

'In fact Lémor was actually richer than I at the time. His father, who had died a year before, was a man of the people, a craftsman whose little business and great skill had made him quite comfortable. His children had received an excellent education, and the death of Ernest left Henri an income of 8,000 or 10,000 francs. But his businessman father's mercenary ideas, his indelicacy, his terrible harshness and profound egotism had revolted Henri's enthusiastic and generous spirit from his early youth. The winter after Ernest's death, he made haste to sell the business for a pittance to a man whom father Lémor had ruined through the most rapacious and disloyal schemes of an unpitying competition. Henri shared out the proceeds of the sale with the workers whom his father had long harried; spurning their gratitude with a kind of aversion (for he often said to me that these unfortunates had themselves been corrupted and debased by the example and manoeuvres of their master), he uprooted himself and took up an apprenticeship, to become a worker himself. The previous year, before his brother's illness had forced him to live in the country, he had already begun his studies to become a mechanic.*

'I learned all these details from the old woman at Montmorency, whom I visited once or twice at the end of winter, as much, I admit, to hear news of Henri as to pay her the respects of friendship which were entirely her due. This woman worshipped Lémor. She had looked after poor Ernest as if he were her own son; when she spoke of Henri, it was with hands joined and eyes full of tears. When I asked her why he never came to visit me, she replied that my wealth and worldly rank did not allow the establishment of natural relations with a man who had voluntarily thrown himself into poverty. That was when she told me all she knew of him, which I have just told you.

'You must see, dear Rose, how struck I was by the conduct of this young man, who had shown himself so simple, modest, and blind to his own moral stature. I could think of nothing else; in society or my lonely bedchamber, at the theatre or in church, the thought and image of him were always in my heart and mind. I compared him with all the other men I saw, and he seemed so superior!

'At the end of March I returned to Montmorency, never thinking to find my interesting neighbour there. I experienced a moment of deep sadness when, on descending to the garden with a female relation who had accompanied me, against my will, to help install me in the country again, I learned that the ground floor had been let to an elderly lady. But when my companion was a few paces off, good Madame Joly whispered that she had made up this white lie because my relation seemed a gossip and a snoop, but that Lémor was hidden there, and that he would emerge when I was quite alone.

'I thought I would faint with joy, but I endured my poor cousin's kind attentions with a patience that nearly finished me. At length she left, and I saw Lémor again, not only that day but every day and at almost every hour of the day, from the end of winter until the very end of the following autumn. In all, rare brief callers and necessary business in Paris cost us at most two weeks of our delicious intimacy.

'I shall leave you to judge whether our life was happy and whether love seized absolute mastery of our friendship. But this last sentiment was as chaste, before the eyes of God and my son, as our friendship, forged at the bedside of Henri's dying brother. Perhaps tongues wagged somewhat among the inhabitants of Montmorency; but the sound reputation of our landlady, her discretion about our feelings, which she knew well, the retired life we led, and the care we took never to appear together in public; in all, the absence of any scandal prevented the gossip from becoming malicious; not a word reached the ears of my husband or relations.

'Never was a love more spiritual and salutary for two souls. Henri's ideas, though singular in the eyes of the world, were the only true and Christian beliefs to me, and they transported my spirit into a new sphere. I experienced the enthusiasm of faith and virtue along with that of love. These two sentiments were linked inseparably in my heart. Henri adored my son, forgotten, neglected, and barely known to his father! Thus Édouard felt for Lémor the tenderness, confidence, and respect which his father should have evoked in him.

'Winter again tore us away from our earthly paradise, but this time it did not separate us. Lémor came to see me secretly from time to time, and we wrote to each other almost every day. He had a key to the garden of the Hôtel, and when we were unable to meet there at night, a crack in the pedestal of an old statue was the receptacle for our correspondence.

'It was quite recently, as you know, that Monsieur de Blanchemont lost his life, in a tragic and unexpected manner, in a duel to the death with one of his friends for an extravagant mistress who had betrayed him. A month afterwards I saw Henri, and it was then that my sorrows began. I had thought it so natural to pledge myself to him for life! I wished to see him for a moment and agree with him the date when the duties of my position would allow me to give him my hand and person, as he already had my heart and spirit. But would you think it, Rose? his first action was a refusal full of terror and despair. The fear of being wealthy, yes, a horror of wealth, won out over love, and he fled from me in panic!*

'I was offended, distraught, I could not convince him, I did not wish to hold him back. And then on reflection I realized that he was right, that he was being consistent, faithful to his principles. I honoured and loved him the more for it, and I resolved to arrange my life in a fashion that could not offend him, to quit society altogether, to hide myself away in the country, far from Paris, and to break off all relations with the powerful and wealthy people whom Lémor considers enemies of humanity, sometimes implacable, sometimes unwitting and foolish.

'But to this project, which was only secondary in my thoughts, I tied another, which would dig out the root of the evil and destroy all the scruples of my lover, my future husband. I wished to imitate his example, to use up my own fortune* on what were called good works at the convent school, what Lémor calls the work of remuneration, what is just towards men and pleasing in God's eyes, in all religions and at all epochs. I was free to make this sacrifice without harm to what the wealthy would call my son's future happiness, as I then thought him destined for a considerable inheritance; and besides, in my own thoughts, I would also be working towards his happiness by leaving his income intact during the long years of his minority, allowing it to accumulate and investing it. That is, by educating him in habits of sobriety and simplicity, and exposing him to the inspiration of my charity, I should one day have given him a considerable fortune for these same good works, augmented by my frugality and by my self-imposed refusal to enjoy any of his income for myself, whatever rights the law might allow me. I believed that my child, that innocent and tender soul, would respond to my enthusiasm, and that I would be amassing this worldly wealth for his future salvation. You may laugh a little, dear Rose, if you wish; but I still believe that I shall succeed in convincing my Édouard of this, under more sober conditions. He will inherit nothing now from his father, and the little that remains to me will henceforth be consecrated towards the same end. I cannot think I have the right to despoil myself of the little comfort that remains for both of us.* It seems to me that none of it is mine any longer, since my son has no certain expectations except through me. This poverty, a vow which I could have made for myself alone, is a new baptism which God may not permit me to impose on my son before he is of age to accept or reject it of his own free will. May those of us who were born in this century, and who have given birth to creatures destined for pleasures and power in society, violently deprive them without their consent of what society considers great advantages and sacred rights? In the universal *sauve-qui-peut* to which the corrupting effect of money has reduced all humanity, if I should die and leave my son in penury before I have had time to teach him the love of work, should I not risk abandoning his good but feeble instincts to all sorts of abject vices? Some speak of a religion of fraternity and community,* in which all men will be happy through mutual love and rich through self-deprivation. They say that the greatest saints of Christianity and the wisest sages of antiquity* were on the brink of resolving the problem. They say further that this religion is set to descend into men's hearts, although all seems to conspire against it in reality; because from the immense and terrifying clash of all these selfish interests there must come a realization that all must change, a weariness of evil, a need for truth and a love of goodness. I believe in all that fervently, Rose! But as I was saying to you a short while ago, I do not know how long God has appointed to the accomplishment of his design. I know nothing of politics,* I cannot see bright enough glimpses of my ideals there; and sheltered in the Ark like the dove from the deluge, I wait, pray, suffer, and hope, caring nothing for the jibes which the world dispenses to those who will not approve its injustice and rejoice in the misfortunes of their time.

'But in my ignorance of tomorrow, in this unleashed tempest of all human forces set against each other, I must press my son to my breast and help him to swim the wave that may carry us to the banks of a better world here on earth. Alas! dear Rose, at a time when money is all, all can be bought and sold. Art, science, all light and hence all virtue, religion itself, all are barred to him who cannot pay for the advantage of drinking from these divine fountains. Just as one pays for the sacraments in church, one must pay a monetary price for the right to be a man, to know how to read, to learn to think, to know good and evil. The poor man is condemned to vegetate without knowledge or teaching, unless he is of an exceptional genius. And the beggar, the poor child whose entire apprenticeship is in the art of holding out his hand and raising his voice plaintively, with what false and obscure notions his weak and powerless intelligence is forced to struggle! There is something frightful in the idea that superstition is the only religion accessible to the peasant, that his entire cult can be reduced to practices which he does not understand, of which he will never know the meaning or origin, and that for him God is merely an idol who favours the harvests and flocks of the man who devotes a candle or a picture to him. On my way here this morning I met a procession which had stopped around a fountain to pray for an end to the rains. I asked why they were praying there rather than somewhere else. A woman showed me a little plaster saint hidden in a niche and decked with garlands like a pagan god,* which this *good woman* called "the best of them all for rain".

'If my son becomes indigent, must he then be an idolater, reversing the way of the first Christians, who embraced true religion and holy poverty? I realize that the poor man would be entitled to ask me, "Why should your son know God and truth when mine cannot?" Alas! I have no answer, except that I could only save his son at the cost of my own. What a harsh reply to him! Oh! these stormy times are terrible! Each runs to save what is dearest to him and abandons the others. But again, Rose, what can we do, we poor women, who can only weep for all this?*

'Thus the duties imposed by family ties contradict those we owe to humanity. But we can yet do something for our families, while for humanity we can do nothing more without being hugely rich. For in our time, when the great fortunes eat up the little ones so rapidly, the middle station is all encumbrance and powerlessness.

'This is the reason,' continued Marcelle, rubbing away a tear, 'why I shall be forced to modify the fine dreams I had when I left Paris two days ago. But I shall still do my best, dear Rose, not to surround myself with useless little pleasures at others' expense. I shall reduce my needs to the most basic, buy a peasant's cottage, live as soberly as possible without threat to my health (since I owe it to Édouard to live), restore some order to this small capital so that I may give it to him one day, after having shown him the pious and beneficial uses to which it may be put at such a time as God shall reveal to us; and while waiting, I shall devote the least possible part of my little income to my needs and my son's proper education, so that I may always have something to give the poor when they knock at my door. That, I think, is the most I can do, unless some truly holy society is formed in the near future, a new church, in which a few inspired believers call their brethren to live communally under the laws of a religion and a morality which touch the noblest needs of the soul and the laws of true equality. Do not ask me exactly what those laws might be. It is not my mission to enunciate them, since God has not bestowed on me the talent for discovering them. My entire intelligence is limited to comprehending them once they are revealed, and my good instincts require me to reject those systems bandied about today, rather too arrogantly, under various titles.* I have yet to see one in which moral freedom is tolerated, in which atheism and ambition to dominate do not creep in somewhere. Perhaps you have heard of the Saint-Simonians and the Fourierites.* Those are systems without religion or love, abortive philosophies, roughly sketched, in which the spirit of evil seems to lurk beneath the appearance of philanthropy. I shall not judge them absolutely, but they repel me, as a new trap laid for the simplicity of humanity.

'But it is growing late, my good Rose, and although your lovely eyes still gleam, they are battling the fatigue of listening to me. I have no conclusion for you from all this; except that both of us are loved by poor men, and that one of us hopes to free herself from her alliance with the well-off, whilst the other hesitates and fears their bad opinion.'

'Ah, Madame!' sighed Rose, who had listened to Marcelle with a religious attentiveness, 'How worthy and good you are! You know how to love, and now I understand why I love you! I feel as if your story and the explanation of your actions have made my head swell up half as large again! What a petty, miserable life we lead, compared to the one you dream of! My Lord, my Lord! I think I shall die the day you leave here!'

'Without you, dear Rose, it would be very hard for me to go and build my little cottage next to that of the poor, I confess;

but you shall teach me to love your farm, and even this old castle ... Ah! I hear your mother calling you. Embrace me again and pardon the harsh words I said to you. I reproach myself for them, when I see how sensitive and loving you are.'

Rose embraced the young baroness effusively and left. Giving in to a wayward child's habit, she allowed herself the pleasure of letting her mother shout whilst she made her way slowly towards her cries. Then she felt badly about it and began to run; but she could not bring herself to speak to her before she arrived; that shrill voice grated on her like a false note after the sweet harmony of Marcelle's words.

Still weary from her journey, Mme de Blanchemont slipped into the bed where her child lay, and pulling the floral cretonne curtains about her, she dropped off to sleep without thinking of the inevitable ghosts at large in the old castle, when an unexplained noise forced her to lend an ear, and to wake up in some fright.

The Second Day

XV. THE MEETING

The sound which had troubled our heroine's sleep was that of some body or other going past her chamber door, turning and returning with remarkable obstinacy and awkwardness. The touch lacked the warmth and intelligence of a human hand trying to locate the keyhole in the dark, and yet as the sound was nothing like a rat, Marcelle could arrive at no other hypothesis. She thought that perhaps somone from the farm slept in the old castle, perhaps a drunken servant who had mistaken the floor and was fumbling blindly for his bed. Remembering that she had not removed the key from the lock, she rose to make good her omission, as soon as the person might absent himself. But the sound went on, and Marcelle did not dare open the door halfway for fear of being insulted by some sot. This little vexation became quite unpleasant when the unknown hand grew impatient and scratched at the door in such a manner that Marcelle thought it must be a cat's claws. Smiling at her fear, she decided to open the door to welcome or eject this *habitué* of her apartment. But she had barely opened the door a chink, still somewhat cautious, when the door was pushed back violently in her face, and the madwoman stood before her on the threshold.

This visitation was the most unpleasant of the possibilities Marcelle might have considered, and she wondered momentarily if she ought to repel this disquieting person by force, despite what she had been told of the usual tranquillity of her mania. But she was stopped by disgust at the unfortunate woman's filthy state, and by an even more powerful sense of compassion. The madwoman seemed oblivious to her presence, and it was quite likely that, given her taste for solitude, she would withdraw as soon Marcelle made herself visible.

Mme de Blanchemont thought it best to wait and watch, observing the fancy of her inconvenient guest, and so she retreated and sat on the edge of her bed, having closed the bedcurtains behind her so that if Édouard awoke, he might not see the *horrid woman* who had frightened him in the hunting-park.

Bricoline (we have already mentioned that in our part of the world, the eldest daughters of peasants and wealthy farmers are known by the feminine form of the family name) hastily crossed the bedchamber to the window, which she tried to open with a great deal of superfluous effort, hampered as she was by the weakness of her emaciated hands and the length of her nails, which she would never allow to be trimmed. When she finally managed it, she leaned out, and called *Paul* in a deliberately muffled voice. This was apparently the name of her lover, whose return she still awaited, and whose death she could not bring herself to accept.

When her lamentable cry awoke no echo in the nocturnal silence, she sat down to wait resignedly, still rolling her blood-stained handkerchief, on the stone bench typically found in the window recess of these antique buildings. After about ten minutes she arose and called again, still in a low voice, as if she thought her lover might be hiding in the undergrowth of the ditch and she feared to alert the farmfolk to his presence.

For over an hour the unhappy woman continued in the same manner, at times calling Paul and on other occasions waiting for him with remarkable patience and resignation. The moonlight shone full on her ravaged features and mis-shapen body. Perhaps she found some slight happiness in this pointless hope. Perhaps she slipped into some waking dream that he was beside her, that she could hear him and answer him. And when the dream grew dim, she brought it back by calling again to her dead lover.

Marcelle observed her with a deep wrenching of the heart; she would have liked to unravel all the secrets of her madness, in hopes of finding some means of moderating such suffering; but lunatics of this sort offer no clues, and no one can guess whether they are absorbed in one thought that torments them unendingly, or whether the very action of thought is suspended by intervals.

When the miserable girl finally left the window, she began walking up and down the room with the same slow gravity that had impressed itself on Marcelle in the avenue of the hunting-park. She no longer seemed to be thinking of her lover, and her strongly set expression resembled that of an ancient alchemist lost in the pursuit of the absolute.* This ceaseless march went on so long that Mme de Blanchemont became exhausted, but she dared neither go to bed nor leave her son long enough to wake little Fanchon. Finally the madwoman took her leave and climbed the stairs to a window on the next floor, where she again began calling Paul and awaiting his return, as she paced back and forth.

Marcelle thought she must warn the Bricolin family. No doubt they were unaware that their daughter had escaped from the house and that she ran the risk of killing herself or of falling involuntarily from a window. But when she aroused little Fanchon, not without difficulty, to ask the girl to keep watch at Édouard's bedside while she went to the new castle herself, the maid dissuaded her.

'Oh, no, Madame!' she said. 'The Bricolins won't fret over that. They're quite used to the poor girl running about all the night long, and the day as well. She does no harm, and she's long since given up the idea of killing herself. They say as she never sleeps. It's no surprise she's more wide awake when there's a full moon. Close your door tight, then she won't bother you. You did right to say nothing; that might make her angry, if you surprised her. She'll carry on up above till daylight, like the owls; but now that you know what it is you won't lose any sleep over it.'

Little Fanchon took it all in her stride; being fifteen years old and of an easy-going disposition, she could have slept through cannonfire if she had known what it was. Marcelle had some difficulty in following her example, but at length fatigue overcame her, and she dropped off to the regular and continual tread of the madwoman's steps above her, rattling the shaky joists of the old castle.

The next day Rose learned of the night's incident with regret but little surprise. 'Oh Lord!' she exclaimed. 'We did shut her in, as we knew she'd a mind to wander, and liked the old castle in moonlight best. (That's why my mother would have rather you'd not lodged there.) But she's found some way to open her window and climb out. She may not be strong or nimble with her hands, but she's got no end of patience! She's only the one idea, and never leaves off. *Monsieur le baron*, who wasn't as tender-hearted as you and used to find things funny that weren't, he'd pretend that she was looking for ... wait, I'm not sure I remember the word he used ... the square ... Oh yes, that's it, squaring the circle; and when he saw her go by, "Well then!" he'd say to us, "so your philosopher still hasn't solved the problem?"'

'I am in no mood to joke about a matter that could break one's heart,' sighed Marcelle, 'and I have had dismal dreams. Dear Rose, we are good friends and shall become better ones, I hope. Since you have offered me your bedchamber, I accept, on condition that you do not leave it and that we share. A couch for Édouard, a trestle-bed for me, we need nothing more.'

'Oh! you've given me such joy!' exclaimed Rose, clasping her round the neck. 'That'll cause no trouble at all. There are two beds in all our bedchambers, it's the country custom, that way we're always ready to welcome a friend or relation, and I shall be so glad to chat with you every night!'

The friendship between the two young women did progress substantially that day. Marcelle was all the more unrestrained because it was the only pleasure she might permit herself with the Bricolins. The farmer took her to view some of her lands, talking continually of money and arrangements. He tried to hide his eagerness to buy, but in vain, and in order to have done with concerns so antipathetic to her spirit, Marcelle was disposed to concede some of the sacrifices he urged, as soon as she could verify the correctness of his calculations. But she maintained a certain shrewdness with him, so as to keep him on edge. Rose had given her to understand that she might use her circumstances for beneficial influence, and in any case Grand-Louis had made her promise that she would decide nothing without consulting him. Mme de Blanchemont trusted her unexpected friend implicitly, and she resolved to await his return, when he would help her choose a good lawyer. He knew everyone and had too excellent a judgement to fail of putting her in excellent hands.

We left the good miller on his way to the town of ——, with Lapierre, Suzette, and the *patachon*. They arrived about ten in the evening, and the next day, at dawn, Grand-Louis put the two servants on board the diligence for Paris and made his way to the home of the merchant to whom he intended to sell the *calèche*. But as he had to pass the post office, he decided to go in and deliver Marcelle's letter by hand to the clerk. The first person he saw was the young stranger who had come to the Vallée-Noire on his wanderings a fortnight before, visiting Blanchemont, and whom fortune had brought to the mill at Angibault. This young man was paying no attention to the miller; standing at the door of the post office, he was reading a letter he had just received, with eagerness and deep emotion. Grand-Louis held in his hands the letter Mme de Blanchemont had given him, and, remembering that the young woman had been much discomfited at seeing the name Henri carved on a tree by the banks of the Vauvre, he cast a furtive glance at the address on the letter which the young man was reading. The stranger was holding this piece of paper in such a way as to hide the contents completely but to leave the exterior perfectly visible. With one quick glance, motivated by a kindly curiosity, the miller saw the name of M. Henri Lémor written in the same hand as on the letter which he was charged to carry: there was no doubt that both letters were from Marcelle, and that the stranger was... the miller made no more ado about it, the young widow's lover.

Grand-Louis was not mistaken; the first letter was the one which Marcelle had written in Paris, and which one of Lémor's friends, whom he had entrusted with this duty, had addressed to the poste restante at ——. The young man had only just collected it, and he had no expectations of any such joy as receiving a second one, when Grand-Louis flippantly slid this treasure between his eyes and the first letter, which he was perusing for the third time.

Henri started, and threw himself impatiently on the second letter. But just as he was about to clutch it, the miller snatched it away, saying, 'No, no, not so fast, my lad! The postmaster might be watching us out of the corner of his eye, and I've no wish to pay a fine, it's no light one. We'll go have a little talk somewhere else, for I don't reckon you've got the patience to wait till this pretty little letter comes back from Paris, where they'll certainly send it, even if you do claim it and produce your papers, as it's not addressed to the poste restante. Follow me to the end of the avenue.'

Lémor followed him, but the miller was already troubled by second thoughts. 'Hang about,' he said, when they had reached a suitably isolated spot, 'are you sure you're the one the letter's addressed to?'

'I am sure you cannot doubt it, and you apparently know me, since you presented the letter to me.'

'All very well, but have you got papers?'

'Obviously, I have just shown them at the post office to obtain my letters.'

'Still all very well; take me for a police officer in disguise if you like, I want to see them,' said the miller as he held out the letter. 'Come on, tit for tat.'

'You are of a very suspicious nature,' said Lémor, hastily giving him his papers.

'Just one moment more,' continued the prudent miller. 'I want to be able to swear, just in case the clerk saw me hand you this letter, that I gave it you unsealed.' And he broke the seal quite unceremoniously, but without allowing himself to open the letter, which he gave to Henri as he took his papers.

Whilst the young man read eagerly, the miller, not displeased at this chance to satisfy his curiosity, made himself acquainted with the full particulars of the stranger.

Henri Lémor, aged twenty-four, native of Paris, profession mechanic, travelling to Toulouse, Montpellier, Nîmes, Avignon, and perhaps Toulon and Algiers, to look for work and exercise his craft.*

'Devil take it!' the miller said to himself. 'A baroness in love with a mechanic! Looking for work, and yet perhaps about to wed a woman who still has 300,000 francs! So it's only in our part of the world that money is preferred to love, and women are so high and mighty! There's not so great a distance between the granddaughter of Père Bricolin the farmworker and the grandson of a miller, as between the baroness and this poor devil! Ah! Mademoiselle Rose! if only Madame Marcelle could teach you how to love!' Then, describing the young man's identifying characteristics to himself before he looked at those in the passport, Grand-Louis studied Henri, absorbed in his reading, and thought to himself, 'Height middling, complexion pale... handsome enough, I suppose, but that black beard is a poor thing. These Paris workmen look like they carry all their strength on their chins.' And with a secret self-satisfaction the miller compared his own athletic limbs to Lémor's more delicate frame. 'It seems to me,' he said to himself, 'that if you've not got to be any more remarkable than that to turn the head of a spirited woman... and a beautiful lady... Mademoiselle Rose might take notice of her very humble servant, who's no worse featured than many. Though these Paris lads do have a certain something, their turnout, their black eyes, I don't know what, but we look like bumpkins next to them. And no doubt this fellow has the more wit for being so small. Well, if he could only spare me a bit of it, and teach me the secret of making yourself loved!'

XVI. DIPLOMACY

At the deepest point of his ruminations, Master Louis realized that the young man, moved by much livelier preoccupations, was disappearing without giving him a second thought.

'Hey there! My friend!' shouted Grand-Louis, running after him. 'Did you mean to leave me your papers?'

'Ah, my good friend, I had forgotten you, and I do beg your pardon,' stuttered Lémor. 'You have done me the service of giving me this letter, and I owe you a thousand thanks... But now I remember you. I have seen you before, not so very long ago. It was at your mill that I was treated so hospitably . . . A superb location . . . and your excellent mother! You are a happy man! and honest and obliging as well, that is clear!'

'Ah yes, treated so hospitably, let's discuss that!' exclaimed the miller. 'After all, you only had yourself to blame if you'd take no more than bread and water . . . That didn't give me much of an opinion of you, no more your Capuchin goatee! But still you've no more of a Jesuit's face than I have, and if you remember my features, I know yours as well . . . As for being a happy man, you're a fine one to envy others, me especially! Or perhaps that's your little joke?'

'I have no idea what you mean. Have you experienced some misfortune since I saw you last?'

'Devil take it! My misfortune's long-standing, and Lord knows how it'll end up! But I've no more wish to talk about it than you have to listen to me, I can see you've got a lot of vexation going on in your head. Well, aren't you going to give me a word or two in answer for the person who wrote to you? if only to say I've carried out my errand?'

'Do you know that person?' asked Lémor, trembling.

'Oh, there! you'd not thought to ask me, had you? Where have your wits got to?'

Lémor was beginning to be troubled by the benevolent banter of Grand-Louis. He was afraid he might compromise Marcelle, although the peasant's features were not such as to inspire distrust. But Henri thought best to feign a kind of indifference.

'I am not very well acquainted,' he began, 'with the lady who has done me the honour of writing to me. Since chance has recently brought me to the locality wherein lie her lands, she thought that perhaps I might be in a position to offer her some information . . .'

'Balderdash,' interrupted the miller. 'She's no idea you're here, still less why you've come, and that's what I'd like you to tell me, unless you want me to guess at it.'

'Perhaps another time,' said Lémor with a certain impatient and sarcastic arrogance. 'You are curious, my friend, and I have no idea why you wish to impute any mystery to my conduct.'

'Because it's there, my friend! I assure you it's there, because you didn't tell *her* that you were in the Vallée-Noire!'

The miller's persistence was becoming more and more of an embarrassment, and Henri, fearful of falling into a trap or of committing some imprudence, cast about for a way to rescue himself from this bizarre interrogation. 'I know neither whom nor what you mean,' he shrugged. 'I repeat my thanks and take my leave. If the letter which you have given me demands either an answer or a receipt, I shall send it by post. I must leave for Toulouse within the hour, and I have no leisure to spend with you any longer.'

'Oh, so you're leaving for Toulouse,' called the miller, lengthening his stride in pursuit. 'I thought you might like to come to Blanchemont with me.'

'Why Blanchemont?'

'Because if you've got some business advice for the lady of Blanchemont, as you claim, it'd be more polite to explain it to her in person, not scribble a couple of lines in a rush. She's worth going a couple of leagues out of your way for, if you can do her a service, and though I'm only a miller, I'd go to the ends of the earth for her if I had to.'

Lémor, informed almost against his will of the spot which Marcelle had temporarily chosen for her retreat, could not bring himself to take an abrupt leave of a man who was acquainted with her and who seemed so inclined to tell him more of her. This invitation or advice, of a sort, to go to Blanchemont, brought dazzling thoughts to a mind which had voluntarily chosen stoicism but was deeply shaken by passion. Shaken by contradictory desires and resolutions, he allowed his face to reflect the confusion which he thought to keep secret in his soul, and the perceptive miller observed it all. 'If I thought,' said Lémor at last, 'that verbal explanations were required . . . but in truth I think not . . . *this lady* has said nothing of the kind . . .'

'Oh yes,' joked the miller, '*this lady* thought you were still in Paris, and no one makes a man come that far for a few words. But perhaps if she'd known you were so near, she'd have ordered me to bring you back with me.'

'No, my good miller, you are mistaken,' blurted Henri, terrified by the acuity of Grand-Louis. 'The questions which she honours me with are not of sufficient importance to warrant that. I shall certainly reply by post.'

And in coming to this last resolve, Henri felt his heart break. For despite his obedience to Marcelle's commands, the notion of seeing her one more time before they separated for an entire year had made his energetic young blood boil. But this accursed miller, with his gossip, might make such a step compromising for the young widow, whether by malice or flippancy, and Lémor felt obliged to abstain.

'You may do as you please,' said Grand-Louis, a bit annoyed at this coldness, 'but since *she* will no doubt ask me some questions about you, I'll have to say that the idea of coming to see her didn't suit you at all.'

'That will doubtless upset her greatly?' asked Lémor with a forced laugh.

'Oh yes, play games with me, my friend!' replied the miller. 'But that's a two-faced kind of laugh.'

'My good miller,' answered Lémor, losing patience, 'your insinuations, in so far as I understand them, are quite uncalled for. I have no idea whether you are as devoted to the personage in question as you claim to be; but it did not appear to me that you spoke of her with as much respect as I do, although I am barely acquainted with her.'

'Getting het up, are you? Fine, let's have it out, that bothers me less than your joking. Now I know what to expect from you.'

'This is the final straw,' exclaimed Lémor with irritation, 'and that sounds like a personal insult. I shall ignore the mad notions you attribute to me, but I tell you that I am beginning to find this game tiresome and that I shall not endure your impertinence any longer.'

'Oh, now you're getting well and truly het up,' said Grand-Louis calmly. 'I'm the man to take you on. I'm a good deal stronger than you; but no doubt you belong to some *Devoir* and you know how to handle a single-stick. They say you

Parisians wield a quarterstaff like masters of the art. Down here we don't know the theory but we do know the practice. You're more agile than me, I expect; I hit a bit harder than you; we'll be well matched. Let's go behind the old ramparts, if you like, or to Père Robichon's café. There's a little court-yard where you can settle your account without witnesses, there's no risk of him calling the guard, he's too wise for that.'

'Well then,' said Lémor to himself, 'I wished to become a worker, and the code of honour is as strict with cudgels as with rapiers. I am as ignorant of the fierce art of killing my fellow man with one kind of arms as another. But if this gallic Hercules wants the pleasure of knocking me senseless, I shall not escape by speaking reasonably to him. In any case, this is the only means of putting an end to his questions, and I cannot see why I should be any more patient than a gentleman.'

The generous and peaceable miller had no wish to provoke a quarrel with Henri, as the latter supposed, in his ignorance of Louis's genuine concern for Mme de Blanchemont, and himself in consequence; but this benevolence was mingled with distrust, and only a frank explanation from Lémor would clear the miller's mind. Being balked in his turn, he thought himself insulted, and as they made their way towards the Café Robichon, each of the two adversaries was convinced that he was obliged to reply to the other's belligerent fantasy.

It was striking six, by the belltower of a neighbouring church, when they arrived at the Café Robichon. This was a cottage decorated with the ostentatious title to be seen these days on the most humble taverns in the most remote back-waters: *Café de la Renaissance*. One entered through a narrow path planted with young acacias and superb dahlias.* The little courtyard for settling accounts backed on to the wall of the Gothic church, covered at that point in ivy and rambling roses. Cradles of honeysuckle and clematis blocked the neigh-bours' view and perfumed the morning air. This flowery hiding-place, still empty and freshly strewn with clean sand, seemed more fitting for lovers' meetings than tragic scenes. Showing Lémor in, Grand-Louis closed the gate behind him, then sat down at a little green wooden table.

'Well now!' he barked. 'Are we here to beat each other's brains out or have coffee together?'

'As you please,' answered Lémor. 'I shall fight you if you so desire; but I shall not take coffee.'

'You're too proud for that, it's plain!' shrugged Grand-Louis. 'Getting letters from a baroness!'

'Are you starting again? Come then, either let me depart, or let us fight immediately.'

'I can't fight you,' sighed the miller. 'You have only to look at me to see that I'm no coward, but all the same I refuse your offer. Madame de Blanchemont would never forgive me, and that'd be the ruin of all my plans.'

'Never mind that! If you think that Madame de Blanchemont will blame you for being quarrelsome, you needn't tell her you picked a fight with me.'

'Oh, so now I'm the one who picked a quarrel with you? Who was the first to talk about fighting?'

'I thought you were the only one who mentioned it, but no matter. I accept your proposition.'

'But who insulted the other one? I never gave you any but honest talk, and you treated me as if I was insolent.'

'Your manner of interpreting my words and thoughts was uncivil. I asked you to leave me in peace.'

'Yes, right, you ordered me to shut up! And what if I don't choose to?'

'I shall turn my back on you, and if you find that an insult, we shall fight.'

'This lad is stubborn as the devil!' shouted Grand-Louis, striking his large fist on the little table, which cracked halfway along. 'Come on now, *Monsieur le Parisien*! You can see what a heavy hand I've got! Your pride makes me curious to see if your head is as thick as this oak plank; for there's nothing in the world so rude as saying to a man, "I don't want to listen to you." And yet I mustn't, I can't hurt a hair on your iron head. Come on, let's have done with this. I wish you well all the same, I wish it in particular to a certain person for whom I'd break my arm or leg and who has a fancy of being interested in you, I'm sure of it. Let me explain: I'll ask you no more questions, as it's a lost cause, but I'll tell you everything in my heart, for and against you, and when I've spoken, if you don't like what I've said, then we'll fight; and if what I suspect you of is true, I'll have no regrets in breaking your jaw. You see, we've got to agree before we square off, so we know why we're doing it. We'll take some coffee, for I've fasted since yesterday and my stomach is pleading poverty. If you're too great a gentleman to let me pay the bill, let's say the one who's taken the lesser drubbing will settle it afterwards.'

'Agreed,' said Henri, who still considered himself at logger-heads with the miller and was of no mind to be unselfishly benevolent.

Père Robichon brought the coffee himself, with many little signs of friendship towards Grand-Louis. 'So this is a friend of yours?' he said, looking Lémor over with the curiosity of the country landlord who has little else to occupy him. 'I don't know him, but no matter; he must be a good fellow, if you've brought him here. See here, my lad,' he added, addressing Lémor, 'you've made a good acquaintance there, you've started off right in our part of the world. Everybody thinks the world of Grand-Louis. As for me, I love him like a son. He's straight, sensible and kind ... gentle as a lamb, even though he's the strongest man around; he never makes any trouble, wouldn't hurt a flea, I've never heard him so much as raise his voice in my place. Lord knows, we get plenty of troublemakers here, but he spreads peace wherever he goes.'

This eulogy made the two young men smile, coming as it did at the moment when Grand-Louis had brought the stranger to the Café Robichon to settle their differences.

XVII. THE FORD AT THE VAUVRE

Nevertheless this panegyric seemed so heartfelt that Lémor, who had initially been disposed to like the miller greatly, was obliged to reflect on the singularity of his conduct in these circumstances, and he began to think that the man must have very powerful reasons for interrogating him. They drank their coffee together with great mutual politeness, and when Père

Robichon had relieved them of his presence, the miller opened thus:

'Monsieur (so I must call you, for I've no inkling whether we're friends or enemies), I want you to know, first of all, that I'm in love, begging your pardon, with a girl who's too well off for me, and who likes me just enough not to hate me. So I can tell you about her without compromising her reputation; and besides, you don't know her. I've no great liking for talking about love, it bores other folk, especially when the same thing is biting them and they think only of their own troubles and don't give a fig for others', as is usually the way with this sickness. But as you get nowhere trying to move a mountain on your own, I reckoned that something might be done by working together in friendly fashion. That's why I wanted your confidence, as I've got that of the lady you know, and why I put mine in you, even though I've no idea if it's safe there.

'The fact is, I'm in love with a girl who'll have 30,000 francs more dowry than I've got, and as things stand these days, that's as bad as if I wanted to marry the empress of China. I don't care a straw about her 30,000 francs; in fact I'll tell you I'd happily send them down to the bottom of the sea, since that's what keeps us apart. But there's no hindrance can make a lover see sense, and it's no good my being poor, I'm in love; that's all I can think of, and if the lady you know doesn't come to my assistance as she's given me grounds to hope she will . . . I'm a lost man . . . I could! . . . I don't know what I could do!'

And with these words the miller's usual lively expression changed so profoundly that Lémor was impressed with the strength and sincerity of his passion.

'Well then,' he said to him warmly, 'since you are under the protection of such a gracious and enlightened lady . . . so they say she is, in any case . . .'

'I've no idea what *they say she is*,' broke in Grand-Louis, irritated at the young man's continued stubborn reserve; 'I know what I think of her, and I tell you that woman is a heavenly angel. Too bad for you if you don't know that.'

'In that case,' continued Lémor, inwardly recognizing that he had been defeated by this sincere homage to Marcelle, 'what do you wish to happen, my dear Monsieur Grand-Louis?'

'For a start, to tell you that when I saw that this woman, with her goodness, her respectability, and her pure heart, was well disposed towards me, and already beginning to give me hope when I thought I'd lost everything, I just took to her, all of a sudden, once and for all. Friendship overwhelmed me, like they say about love in novels, at first sight; and now I'd like to pay this woman back, in advance, for all the good she means to do me. I want her to be happy, as she deserves to be, happy in her affections, for that's all she cares for in the world, she's no longing for money; happy in the love of a man who'll love her for herself and not calculate what's left of her wealth, since she's delighted to have lost that; not trying to wheedle out of her what she's got or hasn't got . . . before he decides whether he'll go back to her or leave her . . . and forget her, no doubt, and see whether his handsome face can win him some richer prize . . . for in the end . . .'

Lémor interrupted the miller: 'What reason have you to fear that this respectable lady has entrusted her love so ill-advisedly?' he asked, growing pale. 'Who is the coward you suspect of such shameful secret calculations?'

'I know nothing of that,' said the miller, carefully observing Henri's agitation but still uncertain whether to attribute it to the indignation of a sound conscience or the shame of being found out. 'All I know is, about a fortnight ago a young man came to my mill, honest enough in his face and manner, but worried about something, and then all of a sudden he began to talk about money, ask questions, take notes, all in all, to reckon out in francs and centimes, on a bit of paper, that the lady of Blanchemont still had a nice little bit of her fortune left.'

'Really, so you think that this lad was only prepared to declare his love if the marriage looked advantageous to him? In that case, he is a miserable wretch; but to suspect him of such a thing one would have to be equally . . .'

'Go on, city boy! don't stand on ceremony!' barked the miller, his eyes flashing like lightning. 'After all, we're here to settle our accounts!'

'I mean,' replied Lémor, equally annoyed, 'that to interpret a man's conduct in such a fashion, a man whom one has never met before, one would have to be equally smitten with the dowry of one's own beloved.'

The miller's eyes darkened, and a cloud passed over his face. 'Oh,' he sighed, 'I know they *could* say that, and I wager many a one *would* say it, if I did succeed in making myself loved! But just let her father disinherit her, as he certainly would if she loved me, and then we'll see whether I reckon out how much she's lost!'

'Miller!' exclaimed Lémor brusquely but frankly, 'I do not accuse you myself. I have no wish to suspect you. But with your honest mind, why did you fail to come to more truthful and worthy conclusions?'

'The real test of the young man's feelings is how he acts afterwards. If he runs joyfully to his darling lady's arms! . . . well and good, but if he goes to the devil, that's another matter!'

'One might suppose,' answered Lémor, 'that he regards his love as an act of lunacy, and that he does not wish to risk a rebuff.'

'Ah! Caught you!' cried the miller. 'You're starting your lies again! I happen to know a very pertinent fact, that the lady's overjoyed to have lost her fortune, that she's even taken her son's total ruin with a good heart, and all because she's in love with somebody who it would have been a crime for her to marry, if it weren't for all these disasters.'

'Her son is ruined?' said Henri, shivering. 'Completely ruined? Is that possible? Are you sure?'

'Absolutely sure, my lad!' blurted the miller mockingly. 'The guardian who might have used her son's minority to share the interest from his enormous capital with a lover or a husband, now only has debts to pay, to the extent that she means, as she told me yesterday evening, to teach her son some trade so he can earn his living.'

Henri had risen. He was pacing agitatedly around the little courtyard, with an indefinable expression on his face. Grand-Louis, who never let him out of his sight, wondered whether he was at the height of joy or in the depths of disappointment.

'Let's find out,' he said to himself, 'is he a man like *her* and me, hating money when it gets in the way of love, or is he a schemer, who's used some trickery to win her love and who has higher ambitions than the little bit of income she has left?'

Eager for the honour of either giving Marcelle great joy or ridding her of a treacherous lover by unmasking him, Grand-Louis hit upon a stratagem after a few moments' thought. 'All right, my lad,' he said, softening his voice, 'so you've been balked! nothing wrong with that. Everybody can't be romantic, and if you've had an eye to solid reality, you're no different from anybody else these days. As you see, I've not done you such bad service in quarrelling with you; I've told you the widow's dowry has dried up. I expect you were counting on the profits from the young heir's guardian, for you must know that those famous 300,000 francs were the widow's complete and last delusion?'

'What are you saying?' cried Lémor, stopping his troubled pacing. 'Her last resource has been taken from her?'

'Of course; don't pretend you don't know; you've been too busy getting information not to realize that the debt to farmer Bricolin is four times what they thought, and that the lady of Blanchemont will be obliged to set up as a postmistress or a tobacconist to pay for her son's schooling.'

'Can this be?' repeated Lémor, stupefied by the news. 'Such a quick about-face in her fate! A thunderbolt!'

'Yes, a thunderbolt!' laughed the miller bitterly.

'Well then, tell me, is she not at all worried?'

'Oh, not a whit. *Not by a long way, on the contrary*, she imagines you'll only love her the more for it. But will you? You're not so daft, are you?'

'My dear friend,' answered Lémor, without listening to what Grand-Louis was saying, 'what have you told me? And to think I was ready to fight you! You have done me a great service! when I was going to . . . You have been sent to me by Providence.'

Grand-Louis, attributing this effusion to Lémor's satisfaction at being warned in time that his grasping schemes were spoiled, turned away in disgust and remained plunged for some moments in a deep sadness.

'Such a trusting, selfless woman,' he said to himself, 'to be abused by such a whippersnapper! She must have as little sense as he has heart. I should have realized she must be very imprudent, since in a single day, when I met her for the first time in my life, she let me find out all her secrets. She's capable of handing her kind heart over to the first comer. Oh! I must scold her, warn her, I must put her on her guard against herself in everything! and to begin with, I must rid her of this amusing fellow. I could tear this scoundrel's ear a little, I could put a scratch on his pretty mug to stop him sidling up to another beauty in a hurry . . .' 'Well, then, *Monsieur le Parisien*,' he said without turning round, trying to keep his voice calm and clear, 'now that you've heard what I had to say, you should know what store I set on you. I've found out what I wanted, you're nothing but a cad. That's my opinion, and now I'll prove I'm right, if you permit me.'

As he was speaking the miller had calmly rolled up his sleeves, intending to use nothing but his fists; he rose and turned round, surprised that his antagonist was so slow in replying. But to his huge surprise he found himself alone in the courtyard. He went down the dahlia path, searched every corner of the Café Robichon, strode along every nearby street; Lémor had vanished. No one had seen him leave. Grand-Louis, indignant nearly to the point of fury, hunted for him in vain throughout the town.

After an hour's empty chase the miller was beginning to be out of breath, tired, and discouraged.

'All right then,' he said, sitting down on a milestone, 'not a single diligence or farm wagon will leave town today without my counting every passenger personally! This gentleman won't get away without . . . oh, what's the point! I must be mad! He's travelling on foot, of course, and a man who makes a point of avoiding debts of honour will skulk through the forests . . . And anyhow,' he added, calming down somewhat, 'my dear Madame Marcelle won't be grateful to me for roughing up her gallant. You don't get over such an *attachment* that quickly, and the poor woman might not believe me when I tell her that her Parisian is a true *Marchois*.* How shall I break it to her? It's my duty, but when I think how much it will hurt her . . . The Good Lord and his lady!* How can anybody be so mistaken?'

While he was arguing thus with himself, the miller remembered that he had a *calèche* to sell, and went in search of a wealthy ex-farmer, who, after looking it over thoroughly and bargaining a long time, was eventually swayed by fear that M. Bricolin might get hold of this luxury item cheaply. 'Buy it, Monsieur Ravalard!' said Grand-Louis with the admirable patience given to the *Berrichons*,* when, understanding perfectly well that the buyer wants to take advantage of their product, they pretend to have been taken in by his sham uncertainty, all for the sake of politeness. 'I've told you two hundred times now, but I'll say it again, as often as you want. This is the genuine article, the real thing. It comes from the best makers in Paris, but there's no carriage to pay. You know me too well to reckon I'd be involved in a fiddle. And I'm not asking any commission, which you'd have to pay anybody else. So you see, it's pure profit.'

The buyer's hesitations dragged on until the evening. Shelling out his *écus** rent his very soul. When Grand-Louis saw the sun setting, he said: 'Come on, I don't want to spend the night here, I'm leaving. I see perfectly well, you've no interest in this pretty little wheelbarrow, all gleaming and reasonable though it is. I'll hitch Sophie up to it and go back to Blanchemont as proud as Lucifer. That'll be the first time in my life I've travelled in a carriage; I'll enjoy that, and I'll enjoy it even more when I see Père and Mère Bricolin rolling along to La Châtre in it on Sundays! Though I do reckon you and your lady would have cut a finer figure in it.'

At length, with night falling, M. Ravalard counted out the money and put his fine carriage in the barn. Grand-Louis stowed Mme de Blanchemont's belongings in his wagon, tucked the 2,000 francs into a leather belt, and set off, sitting on a trunk and singing at the top of his voice over the noise of Sophie at full trot and the enormous wheels rattling along the road.

He made good time, not running the risk of getting lost like the *patachon*, and he had passed the pretty hamlet of Mers*
before the moon rose. The cool mist that rises above the many

close-thicketed little streams of the Vallée-Noire, even on hot summer nights, criss-crossed the vast sombre plains in the distance with white sheets that might have been taken for lakes. The cries of the reapers and the songs of the shepherds had ceased. Glow-worms sprinkled at intervals through the bushes bordering the track were soon the only living things the miller might expect to encounter.

And yet as he was crossing one of the swampy patches formed by the river's meanderings through this countryside that is otherwise so carefully cultivated and so fertile, he seemed to see a wispy shape run through the rushes before him and stop by the banks of the ford at the Vauvre, as if in wait for him.

Grand-Louis was not normally prey to vague fears. But tonight he had a little pot of money to defend, and he was more devoted to it than if it had been his own. He made haste to catch up with his wagon, having fallen a bit behind, since he had come part of the way on foot, as much to relieve the pins and needles in his legs as his faithful Sophie. The leather belt, which chafed him, had been stashed in a sack of wheat. When he had regained the wagon, which he called flippantly in the country style his equipage of *wheelbarrow leather*, that is, pure and simple wood, he planted himself firmly on his feet and armed himself with his whip, whose heavy grip made a two-ended weapon. Standing like a sentry at his post, he walked straight towards the night-time voyager, singing a gay comic operatic couplet which Rose had taught him in their childhood.

> Our miller, weighed down with wealth,
> Was returning through woods to his village
> When what should he hear but the stealth
> Of some villain intending pillage.
> Our miller was brave, of course,
> But they say he hid under his horse . . .
> So listen to me, my friends,
> If my advice you'll hear,
> From the Vallée-Noire keep clear!

I believe the song goes, 'from the Forêt-Noire'; but Grand-Louis, who was as little bothered by scansion as by thieves and ghosts, was pleased to adapt the words to his own situation; and this naïve couplet, which had once been much in vogue but was now only sung in the mill at Angibault, often lightened the boredom of his lonely rides.

When he came abreast of the man who was waiting steadily prepared for him, he realized that the situation was well chosen for an ambush. Although the ford was not deep, it was littered with huge stones that would force a horse to step cautiously, and furthermore, in order to enter the water, the driver would have to lead the animal by the bridle down the steep bank.

'Well, we shall see,' said Grand-Louis to himself with great prudence and calm.

XVIII. HENRI

The traveller approached the horse's head, and Grand-Louis, who had dexterously attached a lead weight to the whip's lash while he was singing, was just raising his arm to release the blow, when a familiar voice called out in a friendly manner:

'Master Louis, allow me to climb into your wagon to get over the ford.'

'Oh ho, my dear Parisian!' exclaimed the miller. 'What a pleasure to meet you again. I spent enough time looking for you this morning! Climb up, climb up, I have a thing or two to tell you.'

'And as for me, I have more than a thing or two to ask you,' answered Henri Lémor as he jumped up in the cart and sat himself down on the trunk next to the miller, with all the confidence of a man who expects no ill.

'This is a bold fellow,' said the miller to himself, barely able to contain the first flush of his returning anger till they reached the other bank. 'Are you aware, comrade,' he said, putting his robust hand on Lémor's shoulder, 'that I've no idea what's stopping me turning half-way round to the right and giving you a nice little bath under the mill-dam?'

'What a pleasant thought,' mused Lémor tranquilly, 'and practical to a certain degree. But I do believe, my dear friend, that I should defend myself rather well, because for the first time in a very long while I am fond of my life this evening, passionately so.'

'Hang about!' exclaimed the miller, pulling up on the sand after crossing the stream. 'Now we've more leisure for a chat. First and foremost, do me the goodness, my dear sir, of telling me where you're bound.'

'I'm not entirely sure,' laughed Lémor. 'I think I'm wandering aimlessly. Isn't it a fine evening for a stroll?'

'Not so fine as you think, my man, and you may yet go back under a cloud, if it pleases me. You wanted to ride in my cart; it's my own movable fortress, and not so easy to leave as to enter.'

'No more of your witticisms, Grand-Louis,' answered Lémor, 'and do give your horse a prod! I cannot laugh, I am too shaken by emotion . . .'

'Frit, are you?'

'Oh, yes, frightened enough to hide under your horse, like the miller in your song, and you'll understand why when I tell you... if I can talk . . . I can barely keep my thoughts straight.'

'Where exactly are you bound?' asked the miller, beginning to recover his reason, after his rage, and to fear he had misjudged Lémor. Would a guilty man have put himself voluntarily in his hands?

'Where are you bound yourself?' countered Lémor. 'To Angibault? quite close to Blanchemont? . . . and I am headed that way as well, although I have no idea whether I shall dare to go there. But you may have heard it said that the magnet attracts iron.'

'I haven't an inkling whether you're made of iron,' answered the miller, 'but I do know that there's a powerful magnet for me as well, in that same place. Come then, my lad, you want to . . .'

'I want nothing, I dare want nothing! and yet she is ruined, utterly ruined! Why should I leave?'

'Why did you want to go so far away, to Africa, to the devil?'

'I thought she was still rich; 300,000 francs, as I have told you, is opulence compared to my own position.'

'But since she was in love with you in spite of that?'

'What about me, do you think I could accept her wealth with her love? For I shall disguise it from you no longer, my friend. I see that you have been entrusted with secrets which I should never have confessed to you, even if we had come to blows. But I thought again, after I had left you rather unceremoniously, not entirely aware of what I was about, and overwhelmed with such joy that I could no longer keep silent . . . Yes, I thought over all you told me, I saw that you knew all and that I was mad to fear any indiscretion from such a devoted friend of . . .'

'Marcelle!' cried the miller, rather proud to be sufficiently familiar with her to use her Christian name, as he did in his thoughts, as opposed to the hereditary title of the lady of Blanchemont.

The mention of her name made Lémor tremble. This was the first time it had echoed in his ears. Never having had any dealings with the entourage of Mme de Blanchemont, and never having dared to confide the secret of his love to anyone, he had not heard the sound of this beloved name on anyone else's lips, although he had read it with veneration at the end of many a love-letter and repeated it to himself in his moments of deep despair and delirious joy. He clasped the miller by the arm, torn between the desire to ask him to repeat that name, and the fear of sullying it in the echoes of this lonely spot.

'Well then!' blurted Grand-Louis, touched by his emotion, 'so you've realized you couldn't and shouldn't distrust me? But do you want to know the truth? I still distrust you a bit. Maybe in spite of myself, but the feeling's on my tail, it leaves me and then it comes back again. Tell me, where did you spend today? I thought you'd hidden in some cellar.'

'I think I should have done, if there were one within reach,' said Lémor with a smile, 'for I was in such great need of hiding my agitation and my delirium. Do you know, my friend, I was going to Africa with the intention of never seeing . . . the lady whom you have just named. Yes, despite the letter you gave me, which ordered me to return after a year, I felt that my own conscience commanded a dreadful sacrifice. And even today I still experienced a good deal of terror and doubt! for although I am no longer obliged to combat the dishonour of marrying a wealthy woman, when I am a proletarian, there still remains the racial enmity of the plebeians and the patricians, who will persecute this noble lady because they consider her choice unworthy of her. But perhaps it would be cowardly to flee this battle. It is not her fault that she is of the oppressors' stock, and in any case the power of the nobility has passed into other hands. Their ideas have lost their force, and perhaps . . . she who deigns to love me . . . will not be traduced by everyone. But it is appalling, is it not, to bring the woman one loves into strife with her family, and to expose her to the censure of all those with whom she has lived before! With what other affections can I replace those: secondary ones, it may be, but numerous, pleasant, so that a generous heart abandons them with regret? For I am alone on earth: as the poor man always is, for the people still do not understand how to welcome those who come to them from so far away and through so many barriers. Alas! I spent part of the day in a thicket, I have no idea where, in a secluded spot where I had wandered, and it was only after several hours of anguish and painstaking thought that I resolved to search you out, in order to request you to obtain an hour's interview with her for me . . . I searched for you in vain, perhaps you were looking for me as well, for it was you who had put into my mind this burning urge to visit Blanchemont. But I believe that you are imprudent and I am mad, for *she* forbids me to know where she has hidden herself away, and she has established a year's delay for the proprieties of mourning.'

'As much as that?' exclaimed Grand-Louis, now a little alarmed at the clever idea he thought he had that morning, when he tempted Marcelle's lover to visit her. Are these proprieties you're telling me of really as serious as all that, do you think? Does an honest woman who's lost an evil husband really have to wait a full year before she can look on the face of an honest man who wants to marry her? Is that the way of things in Paris?'

'No more so in Paris than anywhere else. The religious sentiment which the mystery of death inspires is no doubt the private judge of how much time one should devote to the memory of the funeral ceremonies.'

'I know that there's a decent feeling behind the custom of wearing mourning, and saying the right words, and doing everything properly; but isn't the bad side of it the way it becomes hypocrisy, when there wasn't much to mourn in the dead man, and love speaks honestly in another man's favour? Is it a consequence of a widow's propriety that her suitor has to go abroad, or at least never pass by her door, and not even look at her out of the corner of his eye when he thinks she's not noticing?'

'You are unacquainted, my good man, with the nastiness of those who call themselves *men of the world*, an interesting title, is it not? and correct in their eyes, for the people counts for nothing, they claim to rule the world, since they always have done so and will do so for a while longer!'

'It's no hardship for me to believe they're a good deal nastier than us!' sighed the miller. 'And yet,' he added mournfully, 'we're none of us as good as we ought to be! Sometimes we gossip, or we make fun, or we've no charity for the weak. Yes, you're right, my friend, we should be careful of exposing this dear lady to slander. She'll need some time to get herself known, cherished, and respected as she deserves; it takes only a day for her to be accused of behaving badly. So my advice is, don't show yourself at Blanchemont.'

'You are a man of good counsel, Grand-Louis, and I knew I could count on you to keep me from ill conduct. I shall have the courage to obey the dictates of your reason, as I had the folly to lose my temper at the first impulses of your good will. I shall chat with you until we come to your mill, and then I shall return to ——, leave on the morrow, and continue my voyage.'

'Come now, you go from one extreme to another!' said the miller, who had been guiding the patient Sophie along the track while talking to Lémor. 'Angibault is a league from Blanchemont, and you can spend the night there without compromising anybody's reputation. There's no other woman about tonight but my old mother, and that won't make people talk. You've had a nice stroll from —— to here, and I'd be a heartless soul if I didn't force you to take forty winks with us, and a frugal supper, as the *curé* would put it, though he doesn't like his suppers frugal. Besides, haven't you got something to write? You'll find everything you need at our place . . . though perhaps not perfumed letter-paper! I'm the deputy mayor of the parish council, and I don't do my records on vellum; but even if you do have to set down your amorous prose on paper with the town-hall seal, that won't stop her reading it, and twice over. Come on, I can see the smoke from my supper rising up through the trees; we'll trot a bit, for I wager that my old mother is hungry and doesn't want to eat without me. I promised her I'd be home in good time.'

Henri was dying to accept the miller's kind offer. He made a few polite protestations; lovers are dissemblers, like children. He had abandoned the folly of going to Blanchemont, but he was drawn that way as if by enchantment, and each step of Sophie's that brought him nearer to this centre of attraction gladdened his heart, which had been broken by a struggle beyond his strength.

Lémor gave in at last, inwardly blessing the miller's hospitable insistence.

'Well, Mother!' exclaimed the latter, jumping down from the cart, 'didn't I keep my word? If the Good Lord's timepiece is still aright, the stars of the Cross make it ten o'clock on Saint James's Path.'*

'Not much more,' agreed the good woman. 'It's only an hour later than you promised. But I'll not scold you; I can see you're doing our good lady's work. Do you reckon on carrying that load to Blanchemont tonight?'

'Good Lord, no! it's too late. Madame Marcelle told me that one day more or less wouldn't matter to her. Anyway, how can you get into the new castle after ten o'clock? Haven't they repaired the battlements on the courtyard wall and put iron bars on the main gate? Next thing they'll put a portcullis over the old moat. Devil take me! Monsieur Bricolin already thinks he's the lord of Blanchemont, and he'll soon be sticking his coat of arms on the hearth. I expect he'll call himself *de* Bricolin . . . But look, Mother, I've brought you some company. Do you remember this lad?'

'Oh, the gentleman from last month!' exclaimed Grand' Marie, 'the one we thought was the factor for the lady of Blanchemont? But it seems she's not acquainted with him.'

'No, no, she's not acquainted with him at all,' sputtered Grand-Louis, 'and he's not her factor; he's a surveyor for the new tax-registration. Come, geometer, sit down and have something hot to eat.'

'Tell me, sir,' asked the mill-wife after they had finished the first course, celeriac soup, 'was it you who wrote your name on one of our trees by the river bank?'

'Yes, it was I,' said Henri. 'I must beg your pardon; perhaps my foolish schoolboy fancy killed the young willow?'

'With respect, it was a white poplar,' the miller broke in. 'You're a true Parisian, and no doubt can't tell hemp from potatoes. But no matter. Our trees laugh at your penknife, and my mother only asked you that to make conversation.'

'Oh, I'd not take you to task over a little tree. We've got plenty of other ones here,' said the mill-wife. 'It's only that our young noblewoman was in such a tizzy to know who'd put that name there. And her little boy read it himself! yes, Monsieur, a child of four, who can make out what I've never been able to, in letters!'

'So she came here?' asked Lémor dazedly, having temporarily lost his faculties.

'What do you care? You don't know her,' barked Grand-Louis, giving him a heavy jab with his kneecap to remind him to dissimulate, especially in front of the mill lad.

Lémor thanked him with a glance, although the warning was a shade impolite, and, fearing another misstep, did not open his mouth again except to take in food.

When they had 'bidden each other good night', as Grand'Marie put it, Lémor, who was to share the miller's little ground-floor bedchamber facing the mill door, asked Grand-Louis not to lock up yet, but to let him stroll for a bit by the banks of the Vauvre.

'By my faith, I'll take you myself,' offered Grand-Louis, greatly taken by his new friend's story, so like his own. 'I know where you'll choose for your wool-gathering, and I'm not so minded to sleep that I can't spare time for a stroll with you by the moon: for here it is, just risen, showing its face in the water. Come see, my Parisian, how white and proud it is in the Vauvre pond, and tell me whether you have such a beautiful moon and such a fine river anywhere in Paris! Hold on!' he added when they reached the foot of the tree, 'here's where *she* leaned while she read your name; like that, against the gate, with her eyes wide like . . . well, I can't do it, even if I spent two hours opening mine. Come to think of it, did you know she'd be coming here, when you left your signature?'

'That is the strangest thing of all, I had no such idea, and it was mere chance . . . a child's caprice, that suggested to me the thought of marking my passage through this lovely spot which I had no expectation of ever seeing again. I had heard in Paris that *she* was ruined. I hoped so! I had come here to find out what to expect, and when I learned that she was still too rich for me, I had no other thought than to bid her adieu.'

'Well then! there's a God for lovers; otherwise you'd never have returned. It was the way Madame Marcelle pumped me about the young traveller who'd written this name, that made me see, all of a sudden, she was in love, and her lover was called Henri. That was the first clue that let me guess the rest, no one told me any of it, I guessed it all; I blame myself, but I'm proud of it.'

'What! she said nothing of it to you, and I told you all? May God's will be done! I recognize his hand in all this, and I shall no longer resist the absolute trust you inspire in me.'

'I'd like to say the same to you,' exclaimed Grand-Louis, taking his hand, 'for may I burn in hell if I'm not fond of you! But there's still something worrying me.'

'How can you still suspect me, when I have returned to your Vallée-Noire expressly in order to breathe the air she has breathed, knowing as I do at long last that she is poor?'

'But mightn't you have made the rounds of the lawyers and notaries while I was looking for you this morning all over town? And suppose you learned that she's still pretty well off?'

'What are you saying, is that true?' cried Lémor in tragic tones. 'Do not play with me in this manner, my friend! You accuse me of such ridiculous charges that I shall not bother to defend myself. But there is one matter I shall sum up in two or three words. If Madame de Blanchemont is still wealthy, even if she were to accept the love of a proletarian such as I am, I should be obliged to leave her forever! Oh! if such is the case, if I must learn . . . but not yet, in God's name? Allow me to dream of my happiness, at least until tomorrow, when I shall leave this land for a year, or perhaps for good!'

'You know, you're a mite touched, my friend,' said the miller. 'In fact, you're so outlandish that I reckon you might be putting it all on to trick me.'

'So you are not like me! You have no hatred for wealth?'

'No, I swear! I don't hate it and I don't love it, not as such, but only because of the harm or good it might do me. For example, I detest the *écus* of Père Bricolin, because they stop me marrying his daughter . . . Oh, damnation! I've let slip names I should have kept from you . . . But I know your business, to be fair, and you might as well know mine . . . So I say, I detest those *écus*; but I'd be quite happy if 30,000 or 40,000 francs fell out of the sky and allowed me to court Rose.'

'I am not of your mind. Even I possessed a million, I should not keep it.'

'Oh, so you'd throw it in the river rather than use it to claim equality between yourself and *her*? You're an odd fellow, all right.'

'I think I should distribute it to the poor, like the Christian communists of the early era,* in order to be rid of it, although I realize quite well that I should not be accomplishing truly good works; for in abandoning their wealth these first disciples of equality founded a society. The legislation they brought to the poor was at the same time a religion. Their wealth was the bread of both the soul and the body. This redistribution was their doctrine, and it won them converts. Today there is nothing similar. We dream of a holy community, guided by Providence, but its laws are unknown to us. We cannot re-create the little world of the first Christians, we are aware that it would require doctrine; we have none, and besides, men are not now disposed to receive it. Distributing wealth to a little handful of the poor would only give birth to selfishness and idleness in them, unless we could make them understand their communal duties. On the one hand, I tell you again, my friend, there is insufficient enlightenment amongst the initiators; on the other, insufficient faith, sympathy, and impetus among the new recruits. This is why, when Marcelle . . . (and I, too, dare to name her, since you have named Rose) suggested that she should do as the apostles did and give to the poor this wealth which I found repugnant, I recoiled before a sacrifice which I felt myself incapable, in knowledge and genius, of turning into a productive contribution for human progress. To possess wealth and make it useful in the manner I mean, one must be more than a man of good heart, one must be a man of genius. I am not such a man, and when I think of the heavy vices and the stunning egotism which wealth creates in those who possess it, I feel permeated by fear. I thank God that he made me a poor man, that I did not inherit much money, and I swear never to possess more than my weekly wage!'

'So you give thanks to God for having made you virtuous purely through his own benevolence, and it's only this lucky chance that keeps you from doing evil? That's an easy kind of goodness, and it doesn't astound me as much as you might think. Now I understand why Madame Marcelle was so pleased when she heard yesterday that she'd been ruined. You've put all these fairy-tales into her head! They're pretty, but they don't mean a thing. What is it about these people who say, "If I was rich, I'd be an evil man, and I'm so pleased not to be"? It's the same story as my grandmother, who used to say, "I don't like eels, and I'm glad of it, because if I did like them, I'd eat them." Just tell me this, why couldn't you be well off and open-handed? Even if you didn't do any greater good than putting bread in the mouths of those around you who lack it, that'd be somewhat, and the riches'd be better placed in your hands than some miser's. Oh, I know your game! I understand: I'm not so stupid as you think, sometimes I read journals and pamphlets that tell me a little of what's going on outside our part of the world, where it's fair to say nothing new ever happens. I can see you're a maker of new systems, an economist, a brainbox!'

'No. Perhaps it is my misfortune; but I know less of the science of numbers than of anything else, and I do not understand political economy as it is practised today. It is a vicious circle, and I cannot imagine why anyone is content to turn round and round in it.'

'So you've not studied the science you'd need to attempt something new? In that case you're an idler.'

'No, though I am a dreamer.'

'I see, you're what they call a poet.'

'I have never written verse, and now I am a working man. Do not take me so seriously. I am a child, and a child in love. My only virtue is that I did learn a trade, and I intend to practise it.'

'Fine! Earn your living, like I do, and stop tormenting yourself about the way of the world, since you can do nought about it.'

'What reasoning, my friend! If you saw a boat capsize on this little river, and there was a family in it, but you could do nothing because you were roped to this tree, would you watch them perish, with indifference?'

'No, Monsieur, I'd break the tree, even if it was ten times broader. My good will would be so strong that God would do this little miracle for me.'

'And yet the family of man is perishing,' sighed Lémor tragically, 'but God performs no further miracles!'

'I should think not! nobody believes in him any more. But I believe in him, and I shall tell you, since we've got to the point of hiding nothing from each other, that I've never given up hope of marrying Rose Bricolin. Getting her father to accept a poor son-in-law would be more of a miracle than splitting this thick tree-trunk with my bare hand, without an axe. But there we are! this miracle *will* happen, I don't know how: I'll get 50,000 francs. I'll find them in the earth when I'm planting my cabbages, or in the river when I'm casting my nets; or some idea will come to me . . . never mind what. I'll work something out, because it only takes one idea, so they say, to shake the world.'

'You will discover the means of applying egalitarianism to a society which survives only through inequality, perhaps?' said Henri with a mournful smile.

'Why not, Monsieur?' replied the miller with playful vivacity. 'When I've made my fortune, as I've no wish to become stingy and greedy, and as I'm sure I never will, no more than my grandmother ever came to like eels, which she never could abide, well, I'll have to become more learned than you, overnight, and find that in my own head which you've not found in your books, the secret of creating justice with my power, and happiness with my wealth. Does that surprise you? And yet, my Parisian, I tell you I know even less than you about political economy, not the first thing about it. But what does it matter, when I've got faith and good will? Read the gospel, Monsieur. I reckon you talk well, but you've forgot, the first disciples were people with nothing, who knew nothing, like me. Our good Lord breathed on them, and they knew better than all the schoolmasters and all the priests of the time.'

'O people! You are prophesying!' cried Lémor, pressing the miller to his heart. 'It is for you that God will perform miracles, it is on you that the holy spirit will descend! You know nothing of discouragement, you doubt nothing. You feel that the heart is more powerful than the head, you sense your own strength, your own love, and you count on inspiration! And this is why I have burned my books, why I wished to return to the ordinary people, from whom my parents had separated me. This is why I shall search among the poor and humble of heart for the faith and zeal which I lost when I was educated among the rich.'

'I see!' said the miller. 'You're a sick man looking for a cure.'

'Oh, I should find it if I lived near you!'

'Gladly, I'd give it to you, only promise not to give me your sickness. And for a start, try to talk reasonably; tell me that whatever the position of Madame Marcelle, you'll marry her if she accepts you.'

'You have revived my anguish. First you told me that she had nothing; then you seemed to change your mind and imply that she was still wealthy.'

'All right, you may as well know the truth, it's a test. The 300,000 francs are still there, and despite the wiles of Père Bricolin, I'll advise her so well that she'll hang on to them. With 300,000 francs, my comrade, you could do some good, I hope, since I reckon I could save the world with the 50,000 I've not got!'

'I admire and envy your gaiety,' sighed Lémor, over-whelmed; 'but your words have dealt death again to my soul. I adore this woman, this angel, but I could never be the husband of a wealthy woman! On the subject of honour the world has prejudices which I have imbibed in spite of myself and which I cannot shake. Thus I could not consider making myself useful through my wealth, without failing in what is regarded as probity. And then I would have certain scruples in condemning to poverty a woman for whom I feel an infinite tenderness, and a child whose future independence I respect. I should suffer from their privations, I should be continually chilled by the thought that they might succumb to a life too spartan for them. Alas! this child, this woman, they do not belong to our race, Grand-Louis. They are the dethroned masters of the earth, and they would demand of their former slaves the treatment and the affectations to which they are accustomed. We would see them languish and perish under our thatch. Their feeble hands would be broken by hard work, and our love might perhaps not sustain them until the end of this battle in which we ourselves may be broken . . .'

'There you go again, your sickness is back, and your faith has left you,' interrupted Grand-Louis. 'You've even lost your faith in love; don't you think *she* would go through anything for you and be happy that way? You're not worthy to be loved so much, not a whit!'

'Ah, my friend, if she were to become poor, completely impoverished, without my involvement, then you would see if I lacked the courage to sustain her!'

'Oh, I see! so you'd work to earn a little money, no more than we all do. Why such scorn for the money she's got, which is already earned?'

'It has not been earned by the poor man's labour; it is stolen money.'

'How do you reckon that?'

'It is the inheritance of her ancestors' plunder in feudal times. The blood and sweat of the people were the mortar of their castles and the fertilizer for their fields.'

'That's all true, but that sort of rust doesn't stick to money. It's cleansed or dirtied by whatever kind of hand touches it.'

'No!' exclaimed Lémor fervently. 'There is dirty money, which dirties the hand that receives it!'

'That's just a metaphor,' said the miller calmly. 'All money comes from the poor man, because it was extorted by pillage, violence, and tyranny. But why shouldn't the poor man take it back, just because it's been handled by robbers for so long? Let's go to bed, my friend, your mind is wandering; better not go to Blanchemont. That's more than ever my opinion, because you've nought but foolishness to say to my dear lady; but God's wounds! you won't leave here till you renounce your... hang about, what's the word . . . your utopias! Is that right?'

'Possibly,' said Lémor pensively, led by love to submit to his new friend's influence.

The Third Day

XIX. A PORTRAIT

We do not know whether it accords with the rules of our craft to describe in minute detail the characteristics and costume of the characters introduced in a novel. It may well be that the narrators of our time (and we in particular) have somewhat abused the style of drawing portraits in their accounts. None the less it is an ancient usage, and whilst we hope that future craftsmen, scorning our minutiae, will sketch their characters in broader and plainer terms, we do not feel sufficiently skilful to follow any but the accustomed path, and we shall now make good our previous forgetfulness in omitting the portrait of one of our heroines.

Does it not seem that the capital is wanting, though the interest present, when a love-story, no matter how truthful, fails to make it clear whether the female character is blessed with a particular or a mediocre degree of beauty? It is not sufficient to be told: *she is beautiful*; if her adventures or the eccentricity of her situation interest us greatly, we want to know whether she is fair or dark, tall or short, dreamy or vivacious, elegant or simple in her apparel; if we are told that she is passing down the street, we run to the windows to see her, and according to the impression which her physiognomy produces on us, we are minded to love her or to absolve her for having attracted public attention.

Such, no doubt, was the opinion of Rose Bricolin; for after the first night that she had shared her chamber with Mme de Blanchemont, she was still stretched out languidly on her pillow whilst the young widow, more inclined towards activity in the morning, was already completing her toilette. Rose examined her attentively, asking herself whether this Parisian beauty was likely to eclipse her at the village fête, which was to take place the following day.

Marcelle de Blanchemont was smaller than she appeared at first, thanks to the elegance of her figure's proportions and the distinction of her posture. Her hair was of a very fresh blond, not sandy or even ash blond, a colour which is too often admired but which almost always drains colour from the face, indicating as it does a constitution of little strength. She was of a warm, golden blond, and her hair was one of the crowning beauties of her person. As a child she always made a great impression, and at the convent school they called her the cherub; at eighteen she was no more than a rather pretty girl, but at twenty-two she had inspired many a passion, although she remained unaware of it. And yet her features were by no means perfect, and her freshness was sometimes exhausted by a slightly febrile animation. Around her startlingly blue eyes could be seen shadows which marked the labours of an ardent soul, and which the unintelligent observer would have put down to the agitation of a sensual nature; but one cannot oneself be chaste* without realizing that this woman lived more by the heart than by the mind, and by the mind more than the senses. Her variable complexion, her open and honest gaze, a little blond down at the corners of her mouth, all were the certain signs of an energetic will, a devoted, courageous, and disinterested character. She pleased at first glance, though she did not dazzle; she became progressively more dazzling, without ceasing to please; and he who had not thought her pretty at first, soon found that he could not take his eyes or thoughts off her.

The second transformation which had been effected in her was the work of love. Diligent and sprightly at school, she had never been melancholy or dreamy before meeting Lémor; and even since she had been in love with him, she had remained active and decisive in the smallest matters. But this deep affection, in directing all the force of her will towards a single objective, had accentuated her character and given a strange mysterious charm to all her ways. No one knew that she was in love; everyone believed that she was capable of loving passionately, and each man who had become acquainted with her hoped to inspire in her either love or friendship. Because of her strong powers of attraction, there was a time when the women of her society had accused her of coquetry, since they were jealous of her but unable to find any fault in her behaviour. No reproach was ever less deserved. Marcelle had no time to waste on the puerile and immodest amusement of inspiring desire. She was not even aware that she could inspire any, and when she cut herself off so suddenly from the world, she had no reason to reproach herself for having wilfully blotted her passage through it.

Rose Bricolin, who was undeniably more beautiful, but whose childish emotions were less difficult to divine, had heard of the young Baronne de Blanchemont as a beauty of the Paris salons, and she could not understand how, with such simple dress and such natural manners, this careworn blonde had created so high a reputation. Rose was unaware that in highly civilized and therefore blasé societies, an inner vivacity gives a certain aura to a woman's exterior being, which always outshines the classic majesty of cold beauty. Yet Rose was aware that she loved Marcelle to the point of madness; she had not fully taken into account the attraction of her firm lively gaze, of the affecting sound of her voice, of her gentle and benevolent smile, of all the decisive and generous charms of her whole nature. 'She's not as beautiful as I thought!' Rose thought. 'Why is it then that I want to look like her?' In fact Rose found herself putting up her hair in the same fashion, and involuntarily imitating Marcelle's walk, her quick and gracious way of turning her head, even the inflexion of her voice. She succeeded sufficiently well to lose, in a few days, some remnants of rural gaucherie, though they had a certain charm; but it is true to say that this liveliness was inspired rather than merely imitated, and that she knew how to adapt it so as to bring out her own natural gifts. Rose, too, did not lack for courage and honesty; Marcelle's role was to develop her natural bent, which external circumstances had stifled, rather than to provide an artificial model.

XX. LOVE AND LUCRE

As she was walking up and down the room, Marcelle heard a strange voice in the adjoining bedchamber, strong as a bull's and hoarse as an old woman's. Choked, laboured, and hollow, it repeated over and over:

'Because they've taken everything away from me!... everything, down to my clothes!'

And a firmer voice, clearly that of grandmother Bricolin, answered:

'Be quiet, our master!* I won't talk to you about that!'

Seeing her companion's astonishment, Rose took it upon herself to explain this dialogue. 'There has always been misfortune in our house,' she said, 'even before my poor sister and I were born. You saw my grandfather, who looks so old, so very old. It's him you just heard. He doesn't say much; but as he's deaf, he shouts so loud the whole house echoes. It's the same thing, just about all the time: *They've taken everything away from me, stolen everything, robbed me of everything!* He never leaves off, and if my grandmother, who can control him, hadn't made him quiet down, he'd have said the same to you yesterday, rather than wishing you good day.'

'And what does it mean?' asked Marcelle.

'Haven't you ever heard the story?' replied Rose. 'There was enough said about it; but it's true, you've never come down this way before, and never took an interest in what was going on. I don't imagine you know that the Bricolins have been the tenants at Blanchemont for over fifty years?'

'I did know that, and I even know that your grandfather, before settling here, had a considerable holding over towards Le Blanc,* which belonged to my grandfather.'

'Well then, in that case you've heard the story of the rick-burners?'

'Yes, but it was a long time ago, for it was already an old tale when I was a mere child.'

'It happened over forty years ago, as far as I know myself, for they don't talk much about it in my family. It's too upsetting and frightening. At the time of the *assignats*,* my lord your grandfather entrusted to my grandfather Bricolin a sum of 50,000 francs in gold, asking him to stow it away in some ancient wall of the castle, while he went into hiding in Paris. He managed to avoid getting denounced, as you know better than I. Well then, my grand-dad had hidden this gold with his own in the old castle at Beaufort, where he was the tenant, about twenty leagues from here. I've never been there. Your grandfather was in no great hurry to pick up his deposit, and in trying to get a letter to him about it, my grandfather was unlucky enough to put a rascally lawyer on its trail. The next night the rick-burners came and put my poor grandfather through a thousand tortures to get the money's whereabouts out of him. They took it all, yours and his, right down to the household linen and my grandmother's wedding jewellery. My father, who was only a child, was half-strangled, and thrown on his bed. He saw everything and nearly died of terror. My grandmother was locked up in the cellar. The farm lads were beaten and tied up. They held pistols to their throats, so they wouldn't cry out. Finally, when the robbers had made a clean sweep of everything they could carry away, they left. They made no bones about what they'd done, but they were never punished, we still don't know why not. And after that, my grandfather, who was only a young man, became old overnight. He never regained his reason, his mind is feeble; he hardly remembers anything at all, except this dreadful adventure, and he can't open his mouth without mentioning it. That shaking you see, he's had it since that night, and his legs were so scorched by the fire that they've stayed thin and weak, and he's never been able to work since. Your grandfather, who was a good squire, so they say, never asked for his money back, and my grandmother, who suddenly became head of the family through her courage and good business-sense, was even allowed to keep the rents that were due for the five years before, he didn't ask to be paid. That put us back on a good footing, and when my father was old enough to take over the farm at Blanchemont, he was already a bit in credit. That's our story: added to my sister's, you can see it's not a very happy one.'

This narrative made a great impression on Marcelle, and the Bricolin household seemed even more sinister to her than the day before. In the midst of their prosperity these people seemed destined for darkness and tragedy. Between the madwoman and the idiot, Mme de Blanchemont was overwhelmed by instinctive terror and deep sadness. She was amazed that Rose's careless, luxurious beauty could have developed in this atmosphere of catastrophe and violent struggle, in which money had played such a fatal part.

Seven o'clock was just sounding on the cuckoo clock which mother Bricolin kept lovingly in her next-door bedchamber, which was encumbered with all the old rustic furniture that had been removed from the public rooms in their redecoration, when little Fanchon came in with great joy to announce that *her master* had just arrived.

'She means Grand-Louis,' said Rose. 'Why is she telling us this as if it was some great piece of news?'

But despite her disdainful tone, Rose went as scarlet as the fullest-blown of the flowers whose name she bore.

'Because he's got important business, and needs to talk to you,' said Fanchon, a bit flustered.

'To me?' asked Rose, blushing even deeper red and shrugging her shoulders.

'No, to Madame Marcelle,' said the girl.

Marcelle was about to go out through the door which little Fanchon had left wide open, when she was forced to step back in order to admit a farm lad carrying a trunk, then Grand-Louis carrying an even heavier one, which he deposited on the floor with great ease.

'And all your errands are done!' he said, putting a sack of *écus* down on the chest of drawers.

Then, without waiting for Marcelle's thanks, he looked over at the bed she had just vacated, where Édouard was sleeping, lovely as an angel. Carried away by his love of children, particularly for this one, with his irresistible graces, Grand-Louis went over to the bed to look at him more closely, and Édouard, opening his eyes, held out his arms, calling him by the name Alochon, which had taken his fancy.

'Just see how well he looks since he's been here with us!' said the miller, taking one of the little hands to kiss. But there was a brusque movement of the bedcurtains behind him, and, turning round, Grand-Louis saw the pretty arm of Rose, who, embarrassed and irritated at this invasion of her bedroom, had shut herself in behind the embroidered curtains with a great swish of sound. Grand-Louis, unaware that Rose had offered to share her room with Marcelle, and having no idea that he would find her there, stood rooted to the spot with shame and repentance, unable to detach his eyes from the white hand gripping the edges of the curtains in a rather awkward position.

Marcelle understood what a nuisance she had let the miller commit and reproached herself for the aristocratic habits which had ruled her unawares. Because she was unaccustomed to treating someone carrying a trunk as a man, she had not thought to forbid Rose's chamber to the farm lad and the miller as they carried her possessions in. Ashamed and embarrassed in her turn, she was about to warn Grand-Louis, who stood as if made of stone, to withdraw as quickly as possible, when Mme Bricolin appeared bristling on the threshold and stopped stock-still in horror when she saw the miller, her mortal enemy, standing indecisively between the young women's twin beds.

She said not a word, but turned abruptly, like someone who finds a thief in the house and runs for the police. In fact she ran to find M. Bricolin, who was in the kitchen, drinking his *morning refresher*, as he called it—his third jug of white wine.

'Monsieur Bricolin!' she said in a stifled whisper. 'Come quickly, quickly, do you hear!'

'What's the matter?' said the farmer, who disliked being disturbed from his refreshment. 'Is there a fire in the house?'

'Come, I tell you, come see what is going on in your house!' answered the farm-wife, almost speechless with fury.

'Oh! My Lord! If there's something to get angry about,' said Bricolin, accustomed to his better half's histrionics, 'you'll manage very nicely on your own. Doesn't bother me.'

Seeing that he would not be moved, Mme Bricolin came up to him and, making a massive effort to swallow in order to relieve the fury that threatened to choke her, she said, 'Will you move or not?' Retaining enough control to lower her voice so that the servants could not hear as they came and went, she added, 'I tell you, your boor of a miller is in Rose's bedchamber, and Rose is still in bed.'

'Ah, that is *unproper*, very *unproper*,' said M. Bricolin, getting up, 'and I'll tell him a thing or two... But not a sound, wife, do you hear? because of the girl!'

'Get along with you, and don't make a sound yourself! Well, I hope you believe me now, and that you'll treat him like the ill-mannered lout he is!'

Just as M. Bricolin was about to leave the kitchen, he found himself face to face with Grand-Louis. 'My Lord, Monsieur Bricolin,' said the latter, with an irresistible air of candour, 'you see before you a man who is completely astounded by his own stupidity.' And he told him frankly what had happened.

'You can see, he didn't do it on purpose!' said Bricolin, turning to his wife.

'Is that how you're going to take it?' screamed the farm-wife, giving free rein to her fury. Then she hastily closed both doors and planted herself between the miller and M. Bricolin, who was already offering the guilty party a bit of his *refreshment*. 'No, Monsieur Bricolin,' she screeched, 'I can't understand how you can be such an imbecile! Don't you see, this scoundrel takes liberties with our daughter that aren't suitable for folk of his station; we can't put up with them any longer! So I'll have to be the one to tell him what's what!'

'Don't tell him anything, Madame Bricolin,' roared the farmer, taking his turn to raise his voice, 'just let me get on with my business, being the head of the family. If you had it your way, you'd wear the trousers, and you'd like to stick pins in his heels, wouldn't you? Go away, don't give me a headache this time of morning. I know what needs to be said to this lad, and I don't want anybody else taking charge. Go on, wife, tell Chounette to bring us a fresh jug of wine, and see to your chickens.'

Mme Bricolin was on the brink of answering, but her husband took up a thick holly stick, which he always kept propped up by his chair when he was drinking, and began thumping the table rhythmically. This racket drowned out Mme Bricolin's voice so thoroughly that she was obliged to take her leave, slamming the doors noisily behind her.

'What is it you want, our master?' asked Chounette as she came running.

M. Bricolin took up the empty jug and handed it to her, rolling his eyes in terrible fashion. The stout Chounette grew light as a bird as she ran to execute the will of the potentate of Blanchemont.

'My poor Grand-Louis,' the portly gentleman began when they were alone together, 'you must know my wife is furious with you; she hates you to death, and if it weren't for me, she'd show you the door. But you and I are old friends, we need each other, so we won't fall out. Now tell me the truth: I'm certain my wife is mistaken. All women are mad or stupid, what do you expect? Come now, tell me, hand on heart!'

'Go on, what?' said Grand-Louis as if he were looking forward to this, making a great effort to put on a calm untroubled expression, contrary to his actual feelings.

'Well then! I'm a plain man!' barked the farmer. 'Are you or aren't you in love with my daughter?'

'Odd sort of question!' shrugged the miller, brazening it out. 'What kind of answer do you expect? If I say yes, I look disrespectful to you; if I say no, I'm insulting Mademoiselle Rose, because she's well worth being in love with, as you're worth respecting.'

'Oh, you're joking! A good sign; I can see you're not in love with her.'

'Hold on, hold on!' said Grand-Louis. 'I never said that; on the contrary, I say that everybody's got to love her, because she's beautiful as the sunlight, because she's the image of you, because everybody who sees her, old or young, rich or poor, feels something for her, without being sure whether it's the pleasure of being in love with her or the pain of not allowing himself to.'

'He's got as much wit as thirty thousand men!' roared the farmer, turning round in his chair with a guffaw that nearly split his bulging waistcoat. 'Devil take me if I didn't wish you was 100,000 *écus* richer! Then I'd give you my daughter in preference to any other man.'

'I should think so! but since I'm not, you won't, eh?'

'Not on your life! but I'm sorry about it, and that just shows you how much I value your friendship.'

'Many thanks, you're far too good to me!'

'Well, it's just that my nag of a wife has got it into her head that you're making love to Rose!'

'Me?' said the miller, this time speaking with the accents of truth. 'I've never said a word to her that wasn't fit for your ears.'

'I'm sure of it. You're too sensible not to see that you can't aim at my daughter, and that I can't give her to a man like you. It's not that I don't think much of you, not a bit of it! I'm not a proud man, and I know we're all equal before the law. I've not forgot that I come from peasant stock, and that when my father began getting his wealth, which he lost in that luckless way you've heard, he wasn't so great a gentleman, he was a miller too! But *in the light of day today*, old boy, money is everything, as they say, and I've got it and you haven't, so we can't do business together.'

'Well, that sums it all up nicely,' said the miller with bitter gaiety. 'It is fair and right we should glorify thy name, as the priest says.'

'My Lord! Listen, Grand-Louis, everybody's the same. You wouldn't marry Fanchon if she took a shine to you, would you?—seeing as you're quite well off, for a peasant, and she's a servant.'

'No, but if I took a shine to her, that would be different.'

'Are you telling me, you rogue, that my daughter might be fond of you?'

'Did I say that? When?'

'I'm not accusing you of saying it, though my wife maintains you're capable of insubordination if we let you get too familiar with us.'

'Come now, Monsieur Bricolin!' exclaimed Grand-Louis, beginning to lose patience and finding it brutal enough to be detained in this fashion, without being insulted as well. 'Is this or isn't it a *laughing matter*, as the saying goes? Why have you been telling me all this for the past five minutes? Are you serious? I've not asked for your daughter's hand, so I don't see why you're taking so much trouble to turn me down. I'm not the sort of man who'd speak disrespectfully of her; so I can't see why you're telling me all about the poor opinion Madame Bricolin has of me. If you mean to tell me to go about my business, I'll go. If you want to deprive me of your custom, I don't mind; I've got plenty of other customers. But tell me straight, and let's take leave of each other like honest folk, because frankly this strikes me as a sham quarrel you're trying to pick with me, like somebody here wants to put me in the wrong to make themselves look in the right.'

While he was talking, Grand-Louis had risen and begun to leave. But falling out with him was not to M. Bricolin's taste, nor in his interests.

'What are you on about, you great oaf?' he bantered, pushing him down again. 'Have you gone off your head? What's bothering you? Do I pay any heed to my wife's foolishness? As a rule, a wasp that buzzes about your ear, a wife who plagues and contradicts you, there's not much to choose between them. Let's finish up our jug and stay friends, fair and square, Grand-Louis. My business is good, and I'm pleased with myself for giving it to you. We can do a good number of little favours for each other, it would be stupid to fall out over nothing. I know you're a young man of wit and sense, and you'd never court my daughter. Besides, I've too good an opinion of her not to think she'd tell you off if you didn't show her the proper respect.'

'That's enough!' shouted Grand-Louis, striking the table with his glass in a quick angry movement. 'All this useless palaver is beginning to bore me, Monsieur Bricolin! The devil take your business, your little favours, and my interests, if you so much as hint that I'm capable of showing disrespect to your daughter. I may only be a peasant, but I'm as proud as you, with respect; and if you can't find some politer way of talking, allow me to wish you good day and go about my business.'

It was only with difficulty that M. Bricolin placated Grand-Louis, who was incensed not so much by the farm-wife's suspicions, which he was conscious of deserving in one sense, nor by Bricolin's gross manner, to which he was accustomed, but by the cruelty with which the latter had unintentionally twisted the knife in his heart. At length he calmed down after extracting an honourable apology from the farmer, who had his own reasons for turning the other cheek and disregarding his wife's fears, at least for the time being.

'Well now!' said Bricolin, inviting Grand-Louis to start on some cheese and a fresh jug of rosé wine, 'so you're great friends with our young baroness?'

'Great friends!' sputtered the miller with a shred of wit, but without drinking, despite his host's insistence, 'That's about as reasonable as the love which you forbid me to mention to your daughter!'

'Oh, Lord! if the word is *unproper*, I'm not the one who made it up; for she told us herself, several times, yesterday (which made Thibaude furious!) that she was a great friend of yours. Well, why not! you're a handsome lad, Grand-Louis, that's well known, and they say these high-flown ladies... Oh, Lord, are you getting het up again?'

'I reckon you've had a drop too much to drink this morning, Monsieur Bricolin!' said the miller, pale with indignation. He had never been so disgusted by Bricolin's cynicism, though he had borne his share of it before.

'And as for you,' answered the farmer, 'I think you must have swallowed one of your mill-sails, you're jumpy as a teetotaller. So you can't take a joke any more? That's new! All right, let's talk seriously, if you want. It's certain that one way or other, you've got the young lady's confidence and esteem, and she trusts you with her commissions without telling anybody else about them.'

'I don't know what you mean.'

'Oh come now! you go to —— for her, you bring back her goods and her money! . . . Chounette saw you give her a big sack of *écus*! You do her business for her.'

'As you like; all I know is, I did my own, and if at the same time I brought back her purse and her trunks from the inn where she left them, and you want to call it doing her business for her, well and good.'

'What's she got in the sack? Is it gold or silver?'

'How should I know? I didn't look.'

'It wouldn't have cost you any trouble, and it wouldn't have done her any wrong.'

'Then you should have told me you were interested. I can't read your mind!'

'Listen, Grand-Louis, my boy, be open with me! Did the lady tell you her affairs?'

'Where'd you get that idea?'

'From here!' said the farmer, putting his index finger to his narrow, sunburnt forehead. 'There's a smell of secrets and mysteries in the air. The lady seems not to trust me but to consult you!'

'If you like!' answered Grand-Louis, staring fixedly at Bricolin with the intent of confronting him.

'If I like, Grand-Louis. You wouldn't do me down, would you?'

'What do you mean?'

'You know perfectly well. I've always had faith in you, you wouldn't want to abuse it. You know I want the land, and I don't want to pay too much for it?'

'I know you don't want to pay the full price.'

'The full price! the full price! that depends on the position of the people involved. What would be a bad bargain for another woman would be good for her, she needs to get out of the stew her husband left her in!'

'I know all that, Monsieur Bricolin, I know what you've got in mind. You want to defraud her of 50,000 francs, as the lawyers say.'

'No! not defraud her at all! I've put my cards on the table. I've told her what her property is worth. I've just told her, I won't pay her the full value, and ten thousand plagues take me if I'll go a *liard** more.'

'You spoke differently not so very long ago! You told me you could muster the full amount, if you really had to.'

'You're drivelling, I never said that!'

'Sorry, pardon me! But think back! It was at Cluis* fair, and Monsieur Grouard the mayor was a witness!'

'He can't testify, he's dead!'

'But I might!'

'You'd never!'

'That depends.'

'Depends on what?'

'It depends on you.'

'How do you reckon?'

'The way I'm treated in your house will determine how I treat you, Monsieur Bricolin. I'm tired of your wife's insults and accusations; I know there are others you're not even open about, that your daughter is forbidden to speak to me, dance with me, come and see her old nurse at my mill, all sorts of annoyances I wouldn't mind if I'd deserved them, but that I find insulting because I don't.'

'Oh, is that all, Grand-Louis? Well, would a little present cheer you up, say 500 francs?'

'No, Monsieur!' exclaimed the miller briskly.

'Well, you're a fool, my lad. Five hundred francs in an honest man's pocket is worth more than a bourrée in the dust. So you insist on dancing with my daughter?'

'For the sake of my own honour, I do insist, Monsieur Bricolin. I've always danced the bourrée with her, in front of all the world. No one thought any the worse of it, but if now she insults me by refusing me, they'll think what your wife's already trumpeting about, that I'm dishonest and ill-bred. I've no wish to be treated that way. So it's up to you to decide whether you want to make me angry or not.'

'Dance with Rose as much as you like, my boy, dance away!' barked the farmer with mingled pleasure and malice. 'If that's all it takes to content you!'

'Well, we shall see!' thought the miller, satisfied with his revenge. 'The lady of Blanchemont is coming,' he said. 'Your wife, with her slanders, didn't give me enough time to tell her about her commissions. If she talks to me about her affairs, I'll tell you what she has in mind.'

'I'll leave you with her,' said M. Bricolin, getting up. 'Don't forget you can influence what she has in mind! Business bores her, she wants to have it over and done with. As for me, I'll go and find Thibaude and preach her a sermon about you.'

'Double rascal!' said Grand-Louis to himself, watching the farmer make his heavy way outside. 'Count on me for your stooge, will you! Oh yes, just for thinking me capable of that, I hope it costs you 50,000 francs, and another 20,000 besides!'

XXI. THE MILLER'S LAD

'My dear lady,' blurted the miller hastily, hearing Rose approaching behind Marcelle, 'I have two hundred things to tell you, but I can't spill it all out in two minutes! Besides, in this place the walls have pretty keen ears (I don't mean Mademoiselle Rose) and if you and I go for a stroll that'll look suspicious, so far as your business is concerned . . . But I've got to talk to you; how can we do it?'

'There is a perfectly simple means,' answered Mme de Blanchemont. 'I shall go for a little walk today, and I shall happen upon the way to Angibault.'

'Good, and if Mademoiselle Rose would like to show it to you . . .' said Grand-Louis just as Rose came in '. . . That is,' he added, 'if she's not too cross with me.'

'Oh, you great lummox! You'll get me a proper scolding from my mother!' exclaimed Rose. 'She's not said anything to me yet, but she never puts off till tomorrow what she can do today.'

'No, Mademoiselle Rose, no, have no fear. Your mama won't say a word this time, God be praised! I made my excuses, your papa pardoned me, he went off to calm Madame Bricolin down, and as long as you're not still angry with me for my foolishness . . .'

'Let's say no more about it,' said Rose, blushing. 'I don't hold it against you, Grand-Louis. Only, you might have made your excuses a little more loudly as you left; after all, you frightened me when you woke me up.'

'Oh, were you asleep? It didn't look like it.'

'Come now, you cannot have been sleeping, little slyboots,' said Marcelle, 'because you closed your curtains in a fury.'

'I was half asleep,' said Rose, trying to conceal her embarrassment under an air of vexation.

'What's clear, anyway,' said the miller with artless melancholy, 'is that she *does* hold it against me.'

'No, dear Louis, I pardon you, because you didn't know I was there,' said Rose, who had called Louis *dear* for so long when they were children together that she sometimes fell into the habit again when distracted, or by design. She was well aware that a single *dear* from her would transform her lover's sadness into an expansive joy.

'And yet,' said the miller, his eyes sparkling with pleasure, 'you don't fancy a walk to the mill today, with Madame Marcelle?'

'How can I, Grand-Louis, when Mama has forbidden me, for reasons of her own?'

'But your papa will permit it. I complained to him of Madame Bricolin's harshness; he doesn't like it either, and he promised he'd make *his lady* change her prejudices against me . . . I don't know her reasons either . . .'

'Oh, wonderful! if that's the way things went!' cried Rose spontaneously. 'We'll go on horseback, shall we, Madame Marcelle? You can take my little mare, and I'll take Papa's cob, he's very gentle and trots along quite fast.'

'And I want to ride, too,' said Édouard.

'That is a little more difficult,' answered Marcelle. 'I should not dare let you ride up behind me.'

'Nor I,' said Rose, 'our horses are a bit too lively.'

'Oh, I want to go to Angibault!' cried the child. 'Mama, take me to the mill!'

'It's too far for your little legs,' said the miller, 'but I'll take care of you, if your mother gives me her permission. We'll go ahead in my cart, and watch them bring in the cows, so these ladies can find cream waiting for them.'

'You can trust Louis with him,' said Rose to Marcelle. 'He's so good with children! I know a thing or two about it!'

'Oh, you were such a sweet thing!' said the miller softly. 'You should have stayed that way forever!'

'Thank you for the compliment, Grand-Louis!'

'I don't mean you're not sweet, just that you should have stayed little. You were so fond of me then! You couldn't stand to see me leave: you clung to my neck!'

'A fine thing,' sighed Rose, half distraught and half teasing, 'if I'd kept to that particular habit!'

'Well then,' said the miller, turning to Marcelle, 'I'll take the little fellow, is that agreed?'

'I entrust him to you completely,' said Mme de Blanchemont, placing her son in his arms.

'Oh, what fun!' shrilled the child. 'Alochon, you can lift me up even higher, so I can pick the black plums from the trees as we go along!'

'Yes, my lord,' said the miller with a laugh, 'on condition that you don't make me tumble out headfirst.'

Driving his cart and playing with Édouard, who made his heart throb with memories of Rose's little ways, her kisses, her mischief, when she was a child, Grand-Louis had just arrived at his mill when he saw Henri Lémor in the meadow. Lémor was coming to meet him, but turned round sharply and hurried to the house to hide, recognizing Édouard by the miller's side.

'Take Sophie to the field,' said Grand-Louis to the mill-lad, stopping some way from the door. 'And you, mother, amuse this child for me. Look after him like the apple of your eye; I've got a thing or two to do at the mill.'

He ran to find Lémor, who had hidden in his chamber, and who whispered, carefully opening the door, 'That child knows me; I had to avoid his seeing me.'

'And who the devil would reckon you'd still be here!' exclaimed the miller, barely recovered from his astonishment. 'When I said farewell to you this morning, I imagined you'd already be setting sail for Africa! What kind of knight errant or tortured soul are you, then?'

'Indeed I am a tortured soul, my friend. Have pity on me. I walked one league; I sat down by a well, I began dreaming, crying, and I came back: I cannot leave!'

'Well and good, that's the way I like you!' blurted the miller, pumping his hand. 'I've done that a hundred times! Oh yes, I've left Blanchemont a hundred times, sworn never to set foot there again, and then I'd always sit down along the way and bawl by some well that had the magic power of making me go back where I'd just come from. But look here, my lad, be careful: I reckon you'd best stay with us, so long as you can't make up your mind to go. That'll take some time, I can see. All the better, I've grown fond of you; this morning I'd have liked you to stay, you've come back, I'm glad and I thank you for it. But you've got to go off for a couple of hours. *The ladies* are coming.'

'Both of them?' exclaimed Lémor, understanding Grand-Louis's hint.

'Yes, both of them. I didn't get to say anything about you to Madame de Blanchemont. She's coming here to discuss the business of her money, not knowing that I want to talk to her about the business of her heart. I don't want her to find out you're here before I can be sure she won't take me to task for bringing you . . . And besides, I don't want to take her by surprise, specially not in front of Rose, she won't know a thing about it. So hide somewhere. They were just calling for their horses when I left. They'll have breakfasted as young ladies do, that is, like birds; their mounts won't have much weight to carry, they could be here any moment.'

'I shall leave . . . I am going!' blurted Lémor, pale and trembling. 'Oh, my friend! *She* is coming here!'

'I understand you perfectly! It makes your heart bleed not to see her! Oh yes, it's a hard thing, I agree! . . . If I could count on your . . . if you'd vow not to show yourself, not to move a muscle or a whisker the whole while they're here . . . I'd stash you away nicely, in a spot where you could see her but not be seen yourself.'

'Oh, my dear Grand-Louis, my excellent friend, I promise, I swear! Hide me away, I care not if it be under your millstone!'

'Devil take it! you'd not fancy that much, Grand'Louise is a bit harder in the bone than you are! No, I'll shut you up in a softer spot. You can climb up into my grainloft, and by the hole in the dormer window you'll see the ladies walking back and forth. I don't mind you having a look at Rose Bricolin, you can tell me whether you've seen any duchesses in Paris who're prettier than her. But just wait here till I see what's happening!'

And Grand-Louis climbed partway up Condé hill, from which one can see the towers of Blanchemont and almost the whole of the track that leads to them. When he was satisfied that the two Amazons had not yet appeared, he returned to his prisoner.

'See here, comrade,' he ordered, 'here's a two-sou mirror and a real miller's razor, you're going to shed your goatee. It's out of place in a mill, a nice nest for flour. And then if by ill chance somebody notices the tip of your snout, the change'll make you harder to recognize.'

'You are right,' exclaimed Lémor, 'and I shall obey you forthwith.'

'You do know,' the miller continued, 'that I've my own reasons for making you shear this black fleece of yours?'

'And what might they be?'

'I've just been thinking, and I've hit on a plan: you'll stay here with me till you decide to stop hurting my sweet lady and drop your cracked fancies about wealth. Even if you only stay a couple of days, it's important nobody knows who you are, and your beard makes you look like a city fellow, people will notice. I told my good old mother yesterday that you were a land-surveyor. That was the first lie as came into my head, and a foolish one it was. I'd have done better to have told her the true tale straight off. Well, nothing surprises my mother, and she wouldn't find it hard to believe that you'd changed from a surveyor into a mechanic. But you're going to be a miller, old fellow, it'll suit you better. You can keep busy, or look like you are, taking care of the mill; you must have acquaintances in that line of work. We'll say you're here to advise me on setting up a new mill wheel. You can be a useful acquaintance I've made in town. That way, your being here won't surprise anybody. I'm the deputy mayor, I'll be responsible for you, nobody will ask to see your papers. The constable is a bit of a Paul Pry, he likes a good gossip. But a couple of jugs of wine will quiet him down. That's my plan. Go along with it, or you're on your own.'

'I submit, I shall be your mill lad, I shall hide, anything rather than leave without seeing her again, if only for an instant . . .'

'Hush! I can hear hooves on the cobbles . . . clip clop . . . that's Mademoiselle Rose's black mare . . . clop clip . . . that's Monsieur Bricolin's grey cob. You're sufficiently shaven and washed, I assure you, you look a hundred times better that way. Run to the granary and close the dormer window shutter. You can look out through the chink. If my lad comes up, pretend you're asleep. A siesta in the hay is a little indulgence country folk are fond of, they reckon it's a more Christian occupation than daydreaming on your own with your arms crossed and your eyes open . . . Farewell! here comes Mademoiselle Rose. See her out in front! look how lightly and surely she's trotting along!'

'Beautiful as an angel!' said Lémor, looking only at Marcelle.

XXII. BY THE RIVERBANK

With all the delicacy of a frank and love-struck heart, Grand-Louis had given orders for the milk and fruit of the little collation to be served under a vine-arbour which adorned the front gate, just opposite from, and quite close to, the mill, so that Lémor, huddled in the grainloft, could see and even hear Marcelle.

The rustic meal was very lively, thanks to the mischievous intimacy between Édouard and the miller, and Rose's charming flirtatiousness with Louis.

'Take care, Rose!' whispered Mme de Blanchemont in the girl's ear. 'You are making yourself adorable today, and you can see perfectly well that he is becoming even more infatuated with you. It seems to me that you are making mock of my sermons, or else that you are becoming too involved yourself.'

Rose grew flustered and thoughtful for a moment but soon began her witty sallies again, as if she had decided inwardly to accept the love she inspired. In the depths of her heart there had always existed a brisk feeling of friendship for Grand-Louis; it was unlikely that she would have made sport of teasing him, had she not been aware of the possibility of deepening this fraternal amity in her being. The miller, though not wishing to flatter himself, was none the less instinctively certain, in his loyal soul, that Rose was too good and pure to torture him coldly.

He was pleased to see her so lively and animated, and he was miserable to leave her with his mother, as the last two to leave the table. But he had noticed Marcelle going a little way off and signalling to him secretly to follow her towards the other side of the river.

'Well, my dear Grand-Louis,' said Mme de Blanchemont, 'it appears to me that you are no longer quite so sad as you were the other day, and I have guessed the reason!'

'Oh, Madame Marcelle, you know everything, I can see, and I've nothing more to teach you. Indeed, you're the one who ought to tell me a thing or two, for it looks to me as if I can have confidence in you, and so I do.'

'I have no wish to compromise Rose,' smiled Marcelle. 'Women must keep each other's secrets. None the less I feel it possible to hope, with you, that it may not be impossible for you to gain her love.'

'Oh, if she did love me! . . . I'd be happy with that, I'd not ask anything more; for the day she told me that much, I'd die of joy!'

'My friend, you love her in noble and sincere wise, and this is why you should not hope to be repaid too generously before you have overcome the obstacles arising in the family. I presume that is what you have to discuss with me, and that is why I made haste to reply to your invitation. Come, time is precious, for no doubt they will rejoin us any moment . . . In what way can I influence the father's views, as Rose has given me to understand I may?'

'Rose gave you to understand that!' exclaimed the miller, transported by joy. 'So she's thought about that? She does love me? Oh! Madame Marcelle! and you didn't tell me right away? . . . Well, what do I care about anything else if she does love me and wants to marry me?'

'Gently, my friend. Rose has not progressed quite so far as yet. She has a sisterly affection for you, she wishes to overturn the edict against your speaking with her, and her coming here, and in short against your treating her as a friend, as she had done up until now. This is why she asked me to protect you from her parents and to take your part, at the same time demonstrating firmness in my dealings with them. So much do I understand, Grand-Louis: Monsieur Bricolin wants my land cheaply, and perhaps, if Rose did love you, I might be able to assure her happiness and your own by establishing your marriage as a condition of my agreement. If you think so, doubt not that I should be entirely happy to make this easy sacrifice.'

'This easy sacrifice! don't even think of it, Madame Marcelle! You may reckon you're still well off, so you can talk of 50,000 francs as a trifle. You've forgot that it's now a hefty portion of your means. And do you reckon I'd accept that sacrifice? Oh no, I'd rather give Rose up right now!'

'That is because you do not understand the true value of wealth, my friend; it is only a means to happiness, and the happiness which one can give to others is the surest and purest one can give oneself.'

'You are as good as our Lord, poor lady! but there is a surer and purer happiness still for you, the sort which you must ensure for your son. And what would you say, good God! if some day your dear Édouard had to renounce his hopes of some women he loved for lack of the 50,000 francs you'd sacrificed for your friends?'

'Although I take your sound reasoning very much to heart, there can be no absolute calculations for the future in respect of my material interests. My position is not fixed so rigidly as you imagine; in abstaining from a bad bargain I should lose time, and as you know, each day of hesitation carries me nearer to my ruin. By closing quickly I shall free myself from the debts that are destroying me, and no doubt one day there will be some profit in knowing that I made my decision without puerile regret or ill-advised parsimony. So you may see that I am not so very generous, and that I am acting in my own interests by advancing yours.'

'What a poor head for business you've got!' exclaimed the miller with a sad little smile. 'A heavenly saint couldn't do worse. You've got no common sense, begging your pardon, my dear lady. In a fortnight's time you'll find plenty of buyers for your land who'll pay the full price.'

'But will they be as solvent as Monsieur Bricolin?'

'Oh yes, that's his pride and joy, being solvent! *Solvent*! the great word! He reckons he's the only man in the world who can say, "Look at me, I'm *solvent*!" Actually he knows perfectly well there's plenty of others, but he just uses that to blind you. Don't pay him any mind. He's a crafty devil. Pretend you've struck a bargain with somebody else, even if it means false representations and contracts. I shouldn't stop at that, if I were in your place. All's fair in love and war, you've got to out-jew a Jew!* Will you allow me to act for you? In a fortnight, I swear to you, sure as this river's full of water, Monsieur Bricolin will give you 300,000 francs neatly counted out and a nice little bribe as well.'

'I should never be skilful enough to follow your advice, and I think it much quicker to make each of us happy in his own way, you, Rose, myself, Monsieur Bricolin, and my son, who will tell me some day that I did the right thing.'

'Fairy stories! All fairy stories!'* said the miller. 'You've no idea what your son will think in fifteen years about money and love. Don't commit this folly, Madame Marcelle; I shan't be a party to it . . . no, no, don't reckon on me, I'm as proud as the next man and stubborn as a sheep . . . and a Berri sheep at that! Besides, believe me, it would be a dead loss. Monsieur Bricolin would promise the moon and deliver nothing. Given your position, your contract of sale has to be signed before the end of the month, and it will certainly be more than a month before I could hope to marry Rose. For that she'd have to be mad about me, which she isn't. I'd have to expose her to gossip and scandal! I'll never be able to make up my mind to do that. How furious her mother would be! What a load of backbiting and amazement there'd be among her neighbours and friends! What wouldn't they say? Who on earth would understand that you'd imposed the condition on Monsieur Bricolin out of pure nobility of soul and holy friendship for us? You don't know how wicked men can be; and as for women, well! . . . your kindness to me . . . oh no, you can't imagine, and I'll not make bold to tell you what Monsieur Bricolin would make of it, him most of all . . . Or worse still, they'll say that Rose, the poor innocent! is in trouble, that she told you her secret, and that you gave her a dowry to save her honour . . . All in all, it's not possible, and I hope that's more than enough reasons to persuade you. Oh, no, that's not how I want to win Rose! It's got to happen naturally, and without giving anybody cause to gossip about her. I know perfectly well that there's got to be a miracle, making me rich, or a disaster, making her poor. God will come to my aid if she loves me . . . and you do think she might just love me?'

'But my friend, I cannot devote myself to feeding the flames of her love for you if you deprive me of the means to conquer her father's cupidity. I should never have begun if I had not thought of this plan; for encouraging this charming young girl in a hopeless affection would be a crime on my part.'

'Oh, yes, that's the truth!' exclaimed Grand-Louis, suddenly overwhelmed, 'and I can see I've lost my wits . . . Well, it wasn't about me or Rose that I wanted to speak to you, when I invited you here, Madame Marcelle; you were wrong to think so, in the goodness of your heart. I just wanted to talk to you about your own affairs, but you forestalled me by talking about mine. I let myself be carried along like an overgrown child, listening to you, and then I had to reply; but now I come back to my aim, which is to force you to take proper notice of your own affairs. I know about those of Monsieur Bricolin; I know his intentions and his burning urge to buy your lands, he won't give up, and if you want to get 300,000 francs off him you'll have to ask 350,000. You'll get it, too, if you hold on; but above all, don't let him have the property for less than its value. He wants it too badly, never fear.'

'I tell you again, my friend, that I cannot sustain this battle, and that although it has only lasted two days thus far, I am already at the end of my strength.'

'Fine, then you keep out of it. You shall put your affairs in the hands of an honest, skilful lawyer. I know such a one; I'll go and talk to him this evening, and you can see him tomorrow, without going out of your way. Tomorrow is the saint's name-day fête at Blanchemont. There'll be a load of people on the church green. The lawyer'll be there, chatting with his clients from the villages; you can go as if by chance into a house where he'll be waiting for you. You'll sign a power of attorney, you'll have a word or two with him, I'll have three or four, and you'll have nothing more to do but send Monsieur Bricolin out to do battle with him. If he won't give in, during that time your lawyer will have found another purchaser. You just need a bit of prudence to prevent Bricolin from suspecting that I've suggested this lawyer to you rather than his own, whom he's doubtless told you to hire and who maybe you've even been daft enough to accept!'

'No, I promised you I should do nothing without your advice.'

'And a good thing too! Well then, tomorrow at two o'clock by the church bell you'll be walking along the banks of the Vauvre, as if to have a better view of the fête from the bottom of the green. I'll be there, and I'll take you into the house of a discreet trustworthy person.'

'But my friend, if Monsieur Bricolin discovers that you are behind me in this business, working against his interests, he will dismiss you from his house and you will never see Rose again.'

'He'll have to get up early in the morning to find that out! But if he does . . . I've told you, Madame Marcelle, God will come to my aid with a miracle, all the more so because I'll have done my duty.'

'My brave and loyal friend, I cannot bring myself to expose you to such danger.'

'Don't I owe you something, when you were willing to ruin yourself for me? That's enough tomfoolery, dear lady, we're even now.'

'Here comes Rose,' said Marcelle. 'I barely have sufficient time remaining to thank you.'

'Oh no, Rose has just turned down the avenue with my mother, who'll keep her talking a while, for I've not done yet, Madame Marcelle, I've something quite different to tell you!

But you must be tired from walking so long. Now that the courtyard's empty and the mill has stopped, come and sit down here on this bench by the gate. Mademoiselle Rose thinks we're on the other side of the river, and she won't come back here till she's walked round the meadow. What I've got to tell you is even more interesting than business, and wants even more secrecy.'

Astounded by this overture, Marcelle followed the miller and sat down on the bench with him, just below the grainloft trap-door, so that Lémor could hear and see her.

'Tell me, Madame Marcelle,' stuttered the miller, now a bit nervous of starting on this topic, 'you know the letter you gave me?'

'Of course, my dear Grand-Louis!' answered Mme de Blanchemont, whose placid and slightly dull features suddenly went bright red, 'did you not tell me this morning that you had sent it?'

'Pardon me, excuse me . . . but I didn't exactly put it in the post.'

'You forgot it?'

'Oh, no, not a bit!'

'You lost it, perhaps?'

'Even colder. No, I did something better than drop it in a post-box, I delivered it to the address.'

'What can you possibly mean? The address was in Paris.'

'Oh yes, but I happened to run into the person it was destined for, and I thought the best thing was to give it to him directly.'

'Good Lord! how you make me tremble, Louis!' exclaimed Marcelle, going white again. 'Surely you made some mistake.'

'Nothing as foolish as that! It may be that I am well acquainted with Monsieur Henri Lémor! . . .'

'You know him! and he is in this region?' blurted Marcelle, not attempting to hide her feelings.

In a dozen words Grand-Louis explained that he had recognized Lémor as the traveller who had come to the mill, and as the man for whom the letter was intended.

'But where was he going? and what is he doing at ——?' Marcelle asked with difficulty.

'He was travelling to Africa. Just passing through!' answered the miller, wanting to test her out. 'That's the road for Toulouse. He was just going to the post office while the diligence had stopped for lunch.'

'And where is he now?'

'I can't tell you exactly where he is, but he's no longer in ——.'

'He is going to Africa, you say? But why so far away?'

'Precisely because it *is* far away. That's what he answered when I asked him.'

'The answer is clearer than you may think!' said Marcelle, with no thought of camouflaging her increasing agitation. 'My friend, you are not so unfortunate as you think! There are hearts worse broken than yours.'

'Yours, for example, my poor dear lady?'

'Yes, my friend, mine.'

'But isn't that somewhat your own fault? Why did you order the poor young man to wait a year without hearing a word from you?'

'What? Did he let you read my letter?'

'Oh never, he plays his cards close to his chest! But I went on at him, questioned him, guessed at it, and finally he had to tell me I wasn't far off. Blessed virgin! you see, Madame Marcelle, I'm very curious about the secrets of people I love, because unless you know what they're thinking, you don't know what you could do to help them. Am I wrong about that?'

'No, my friend, I am content that you should know my secrets, as I know your own. But alas! no matter how good your heart and will, you cannot help me. Answer me none the less. Did this young man give you any answer, either orally or in writing?'

'Oh, just a load of twaddle he wrote, I didn't think it worth bringing!'

'You have done me no service there! So I am not to know his intentions?'

'He just said to me, "I love her, *but* I am a brave man!"'

'He said "*but*"?'

'Well, maybe he said "*and*"!'

'That would be quite another matter! Try to remember, Grand-Louis!'

'Well, sometimes he said one, sometimes the other, because he repeated it a great deal.'

'This morning, you say? You mean you only left the town this morning?'

'I meant yesterday evening. It was late, and hereabouts we call it morning starting at midnight.'

'Good Lord! what does this mean? Why no letter? So you did see one that he wrote to me?'

'Not half! He ripped off four of them.'

'But what did these letters say? Could he not make up his mind?'

'Sometimes he said he'd never see you again, sometimes he said he was coming to see you right away.'

'But he resisted this temptation? Then he is indeed a brave man!'

'Come now, listen to me! He went through more temptations than Saint Anthony, but on the one hand I tried to change his mind, and on the other he was afraid of disobeying you.'

'And what do you think of a lover who does not know when to disobey?'

'I think he's too much in love, but he won't get any thanks for it.'

'I am quite unjust, am I not, dear Grand-Louis? My emotions have run away with me, I do not know what I am saying. But why, my dear friend, did you forbid him to follow you? For surely he thought of it.'

'Oh, indeed! He even went part of the way on my cart. But you must pardon me, I was afraid of putting you out.'

'You are in love, and you believe other lovers to be so strict?'

'Blessed virgin! what would you've said if I'd brought him back to the Vallée-Noire? For example, if right now . . . if I said to you that I'd told him to hide in my mill! Well, this time you'd deal with me as I deserved!'

'Louis!' cried Marcelle, rising with an air of exalted resolution. 'He is here, admit it!'

'Not at all, Madame, you're putting words in my mouth.'

'My friend,' she persevered, taking his hand gratefully, 'tell me where he is, and I pardon you.'

'And if that's so,' said the miller, a bit frightened at Marcelle's spontaneity but gladdened by her openness, 'you'd have no fear of what people might say about you?'

'When he had left me of his own accord and I was utterly downcast, I was capable of considering people's opinion, of foreseeing dangers, of creating strict duties for myself, perhaps even exaggerated ones; but now that he has returned to me, when he is near here, what do you wish me to think of and what do you wish me to fear?'

'Still, you must consider whether some act of folly will make your plans harder to carry out,' said Grand-Louis, making a sign to show Marcelle the dormer window above her head.

Marcelle lifted up her eyes and met those of Lémor, who was trembling, leaning towards her, about to jump down from the roof to shorten the distance.

But the miller coughed mightily, and with another gesture, indicating to the lovers that Rose was coming, with the mill-wife and little Édouard, 'Yes, Madame,' he said, raising his voice, 'a mill like this one doesn't bring in much money; but if I could just set up the big mill-wheel I've got in mind, it might bring in . . . 800 francs a year!'

XXIII. CADOCHE

The glance exchanged by the two lovers had been brief and blazing. A sovereign serenity followed. They were in love, they were confident in each other. All had been told, explained, and made good in the electric shock of this single glimpse. Lémor retreated to the back of the grainloft and Marcelle, mistress of herself now that she was happy again, greeted Rose calmly and without regret. She allowed herself to be led into the delicious spinney nearby, and after an hour's promenade she and her companion mounted up again and made their way

back to Blanchemont. But first she had whispered to the
miller, 'Hide him well, I shall return.'

'No, no, not too soon,' Grand-Louis had replied. 'I'll arrange a safe meeting; but let me take my own measures. I'll
bring your son back to you tonight and talk to you if I can.'

When Marcelle had left, Lémor emerged from his hiding-
place, dizzy with joy and emotion even more than with the
intoxicating smell of the hay.

'My friend,' he said buoyantly to the miller, 'I am to be your
mill lad, and I cannot pretend to be under your orders unless
I am seen to be working. So give me something to do, and you
shall soon see that a Parisian can be strong despite his puny
appearance.'

'Oh yes,' bantered Grand-Louis, 'when your heart's content, it strengthens up your arms a treat. Your affairs are
proceeding better than mine, my lad, and when we talk tonight in our room it'll be your turn to give me hope. But for
now, as you've said, down to work. I can't spend all my time
blathering about love, and you'll go mad from sheer joy if you
stay idle. Work is good for everybody;* it brings happiness
and makes you forget your troubles; all of which may well
mean it's part of the good Lord's plan for us all. Come on, you
can help me turn the mill-wheel paddles and set Grand'Louise
dancing. Her song has the power to put me back in good
spirits when I'm out of sorts.'

'Oh, my Lord! The child will recognize me!' exclaimed
Lémor, catching sight of Édouard, who had escaped from the
mill-wife's arms and begun scrambling up the steep staircase
of the mill on his hands and knees.

'He's already seen you,' replied the miller. 'Don't bother
hiding or pretending. He's not very sure he does recognize
you, rigged up like that.'

It was true: Édouard stopped, nonplussed and uncertain. In
the month since Marcelle had abruptly left Montmorency to
be with her dying husband, her son had not seen Lémor, and
a month is a century in the memory of such a young child.
True, the boy was unusually precocious in his development;
but without his beard, and with his face powdery with flour,
Lémor, disguised in his peasant smock, was barely recogniz-

able. Édouard stopped before him for a moment, as if turned to stone; but having met the harsh and indifferent gaze of the friend who would ordinarily run to him with open arms, he dropped his eyes with a sort of embarrassment and even fear, a sentiment which is almost always yoked with surprise in young children; then he came up to the miller, saying to him with his typical serious and meditative air, 'Who is that man?'

'Him? That's my mill lad, Antoine.'

'Have you got two, then?'

'Of course! I've got dozens of lads! That one is Alochon number two.'

'And Jeannie is Alochon number three?'

'Yes sir, general!'

'Is he a bad man, Antoine?'

'No, no! But he's a bit thick, a bit deaf, he doesn't play much with children.'

'In that case I shall go play with Jeannie,' said Édouard, going off happily. At four one has no conception of what it is to be deceived, and the word of those we love is stronger than the evidence of the senses.

Grain was delivered for the miller to grind into flour by that same evening. It belonged to M. Bricolin, and was contained in two sacks each marked with two enormous initials.

'There,' laughed Grand-Louis, this time with a certain bitterness, '*Bricolin of Blanchemont*, that is, Bricolin who lives at Blanchemont. But when he's bought the land I expect he'll put a little 'b' between the two big ones, meaning *Bricolin, baron of Blanchemont.*'

'Oh, so this is the grain from Blanchemont?' enquired Lémor, absently.

'Yes,' interjected the miller, guessing his meaning before he could go any further, 'this is the grain that will make the flour that will make the bread that will be eaten by Madame Marcelle and Mademoiselle Rose. They say Rose is too well off to marry a man like me, but I provide the bread she eats!'

'So we are working for *them*!' continued Lémor.

'Yes, yes, my lad. Mind what you're doing! No call to get slack! Devil take it! I shouldn't work so hard for the king himself.'

This perfectly ordinary coincidence in the mill's workings took on a romantic and poetic colouring in the young Parisian's mind, and he threw himself into helping the miller with such care and zeal that within a few hours he had entirely conquered the craft. He had no difficulty in adjusting to the simple, almost primitive mechanism of the place. He saw the improvements that could have been made to the rustic machinery, with a bit of ready money (forbidden fruit to the peasant). Soon he had mastered the dialect names of each piece and function of the machinery. Seeing him so busy and in such good standing with the master, Jeannie was a bit jealous and discomfited. But when Grand-Louis carefully explained to him that the Parisian was only there for a short time, and would not be taking over from him, Jeannie was reassured and even decided, good *Berrichon* that he was, to hand over a little of his work for a few days to this officious *compagnon.** He took advantage of it to bring Édouard back to Blanchemont, since the child was beginning to tire of the mill and to be frightened by so long a separation from his mother. The mill-wife had lost her power to amuse him, and when little Fanchon came to find him, Jeannie was not discontented to accompany the young serving-girl and the boy to the castle.

When the task was completed, Lémor, with his forehead bathed in sweat and his face aglow, felt himself to be in better trim and finer fettle than he had been for a very long while. The lengthy meditations that were consuming his youth had given way to the spiritual and physical well-being with which Providence rewards man's labours, when the goal is heartfelt and the fatigue proportionate to his strength. 'My friend,' he exclaimed, 'work is good and holy in itself; you were right to tell me so when we began! God requires and blesses it. It seemed sweet to work for my mistress's nourishment; oh, how much sweeter it would be to work at the same time to feed the human family as equals and brothers! If everyone worked for all and all for every one, how light our fatigue should be, and how beautiful our life!'

'Oh yes, in that case my profession would be one of the most genteel!' smiled the miller with a wry intelligence.

'Wheat is the noblest thing to grow, bread is the purest thing to eat. You might think that my work deserves some respect, and that on holy days they should put a crown of wheat-ears and cornflowers* on poor Grand'Louise, who gets no thanks at all at the moment; but what do you expect? *In the light of day today*, as Monsieur Bricolin puts it, I'm nothing but a mercenary for hire to him, and when he thinks of me he says to himself, "A man like that, with pretensions to my daughter! A wretch who grinds corn, when it's me as sows the wheat and owns the land!" And that's the real difference! My hands are cleaner than his, which shift manure, and that's the truth of it! Well then, my lad, our work's done, let's polish off some soup. I wager you'll find it tastier than you did this morning, as it'll be ten times saltier, and then I'll be off to Blanchemont with these two sacks, shall I?'

'What, without me?'

'Well, of course. Do you want to get yourself seen at the farm?'

'No one knows me there.'

'True. But what will you do there?'

'Not much; I shall help you unload the sacks.'

'And how will that help you?'

'Perhaps I shall see a certain person pass through the farmyard.'

'And if you don't see a certain person?'

'I shall see the house she lives in. I shall hear her name spoken, perhaps.'

'I reckon that's a pleasure you could have without going so far.'

'It's only two paces from here!'

'You've got an answer for everything. So you won't take any risks?'

'Do you imagine I do not love her? Would you take risks, if you were in my position?'

'Oh I might well do, if I was loved! Hang on a bit, you won't look at her like you did from the dormer window? You know, I thought you were about to set light to my grain, the way your eyes were burning.'

'I shall not look at her, not in the least.'

'And you won't breathe a word to her?'

'Under what pretext should I speak to her?'

'Won't you cobble one together?'

'I shall not so much as enter the farmyard if you forbid it. I shall observe the castle walls from afar.'

'That'd be best. I'll allow you to stand at the gate and smell the wind that blows about the castle, no more.'

The two friends set out at dusk; Sophie, loaded with the two sacks, walked before them in magisterial fashion. Grand-Louis, whose heart was heavy, said little, expressing his black thoughts only with great swishes of his whip through the shrubbery to right and left, full of wild blackberries and pale honeysuckle of a stronger scent than that found in our gardens.

They had just passed a group of cottages called the Cortioux when Lémor, who was driving along by the ditch at the road's edge, stopped suddenly, surprised to see a man stretched out under the hedge with his head pillowed on a well-filled beggar's scrip.

'Look out,' said the miller with no great surprise, 'you nearly drove over *my uncle*!'

Grand-Louis's deep voice woke the sleeper with a start. He sat up briskly, grabbed his long staff with both hands, and swore a vigorous oath.

'Don't get het up, Uncle!' laughed the miller. 'We're friends who want to pass, with your permission; for though all the roads belong to you, as you say, you wouldn't stop anybody using them, would you?'

'Oh indeed!' answered the man as he stood up, showing his gigantic height and repulsive aspect. 'I'm the best of the land-owners, wouldn't you say, *little one*? But it's abusing my kindness a bit to step on my face. Who is this unchristian soul, who doesn't notice an honest man stretched out in his bed? I don't know him, though I know everybody hereabouts, and elsewhere!'

And with these words the beggar eyed Lémor scornfully from head to foot. Lémor surveyed him in turn, with repugnance. He was a bony old man covered in filthy rags, with a pepper-and-salt beard scratchy as a hedgehog's armour. His tall tattered hat was topped by a knot of white ribbons and a bouquet of faded silk flowers, like a mock trophy.

'Have no fear, my uncle,' said the miller, 'the man is a good Christian!'

'And how do I know that?' answered Uncle Cadoche, taking off his hat to Henri.

'Come on!' said the miller to Lémor. 'Can't you see my uncle is asking you for a sou?'

Lémor threw an *obole** into the uncle's hat. The old man picked it out quickly and turned it round and round with his long thin fingers, in a sort of sensual ecstasy.

'That's a nice fat sou!' he barked with a nasty grin. 'Ten revolutionary decimes, maybe! Oh no! God be praised! It's one of my king's, Louis XV!* a king whose reign I've lived through! That'll bring me good luck, and you too, Nephew,' he added, resting his great twisted hand on Lémor's shoulder. 'Now you can say that you're one of my family, and I'd know you even if you were disguised from top to toe.'

'Well, goodnight, Uncle,' said Grand-Louis, throwing his alms in with Lémor's. 'Are we friends?'

'For ever!' answered the beggar in a solemn voice. 'You've always been a good relation, the best of all my family. So it's to you, Grand-Louis, that I intend to leave all my worldly goods. I've told you so many a time, you'll see if I don't keep my word!'

'I should think so, too!' quipped the miller. 'And the bouquet thrown in?'

'The hat, certainly! But the bouquet and the ribbon are for my last mistress.'

'Blast! I was particularly looking forward to the bouquet.'

'And I should hope so!' exclaimed the beggar, who had begun walking behind the two young men, at quite a good clip for his great age. 'The bouquet is the most precious item in the inheritance. It is blessed, you realize! from the chapel of Sainte-Solange.'*

'How can such a man as devout as you stand hearing him talk about his mistresses?' asked Henri, filled with profound disgust for this ridiculous character.

'Be quiet, Nephew,' answered Uncle Cadoche, glaring at him crosswise. 'You're talking tripe.'

'Excuse him, he's only a child,' hastened the miller, who liked to banter with his *great-uncle*. 'He's not got any beard on his chin, but he thinks he knows best! But where are you going so late, my uncle? Are you hoping to sleep at your own place tonight? It's a long way from here!'

'Oh no! I'm going this way to Blanchemont, for the fête tomorrow.'

'Oh, yes, true, that's a good day for you! You should *harvest* at least forty nice fat sous.'

'No, but enough, at least, to have a mass said for the good saint of the parish.'

'Still keen on masses, are you?'

'Mass and rum, Nephew, with a little tobacco, these are the salvation of body and soul.'

'I'm not saying you nay, but rum doesn't keep you warm enough to sleep in ditches like that at your age, Uncle.'

'Sleep where you find it, Nephew. If you get tired, you stop; you have a little nap on a rock or on your bag, if it's not too flat.'

'Looks to me like yours is round enough tonight.'

'Yes; you know, Nephew, you ought to let me ride on your horse, my bag is getting too heavy for me.'

'Oh no! Sophie has enough to carry. But give it me, I'll carry it to Blanchemont for you!'

'Right and proper! You're a young man, you ought to be serviceable to your uncle. Just a minute, is your smock clean?' he added with a disgusted air.

'Oh, that's just flour!' said the miller, taking the beggar's bag. 'It's on friendly terms with your bread. A thousand thunders! there's certainly plenty of old crusts in here!'

'Crusts? I don't get any. I'd like to see somebody try to give me one, I'd throw it back in their face, like I did once to that Bricolin female.'

'So it's since then that she's been afraid of you?'

'Yes indeed! she says I might set fire to her barns!' replied the beggar with a sinister air. Then he added in a wheedling voice, 'Poor good woman, God have mercy! as if I was an evil man! What wickedness have I ever done?'

'None that I know of,' answered the miller. 'If you had, you wouldn't be where you are today.'

'I have never harmed a soul, not a living soul,' continued uncle Cadoche, lifting his finger to heaven, 'and the proof is, I've never been apprehended for anything. Have I ever spent a single day in prison, all my life? I've always done the good Lord's will, and the good Lord has looked after me these forty years, while I've made my poor living.'

'Just how old are you, Uncle?'

'I don't know, my child, my certificate of baptism was lost, like so many others, but I must be past eighty. I'm about ten years older than Père Bricolin, though he looks older than me.'

'That's true, you're well preserved, and as for him... but then he's had such accidents as don't happen to everybody.'

'Oh yes,' sighed the beggar with deep compassion. 'He has had his misfortunes!'

'That's a story of your time, eh? You come from that part of the world, don't you?'

'Yes, I was born in Ruffec,* near Beaufort, where the accident happened.'

'And were you there at that time?'

'Oh, I should think so, holy mother of God! I can't think of it without trembling. We were so afraid then!'

'You were afraid? You always go about alone at all hours, on the roads.'

'Oh, at present, my dear son, what should a poor man like me be afraid of, when he's only got the few old clothes that cover his nakedness? But in those days I had a little something, and the brigands robbed me of it.'

'What? Did the rick-burners come to you too?'

'Nay, nay! I hadn't enough to tempt them; but I did have a little house that I let out to some farm labourers. When fear of the brigands began to spread round the country, nobody wanted to live there any more. I couldn't sell it; I hadn't enough money to keep it in good repair. It was falling into rack and ruin, and there were debts to be paid, that I couldn't meet. So my house, my land, and a pretty little hemp-field I had, they were all sold by the bailiffs; I left the country, and since that time I've wandered as one of God's children.'

'But you didn't leave the area altogether?'

'Of course not, people know me; I've got my clientele and all my family.'

'I thought you were alone in the world?'

'What about all my nephews?'

'Oh, that's true, I forgot; me, for example, and my comrade here, and all of us who won't refuse you your sou for tobacco. But tell me, Uncle, these rick-burners we were talking about, what sort of folk were they?'

'Best ask the Good Lord, my poor child; only He knows.'

'They say there were rich folk among them, well-dressed?'

'They say those folk are still alive, grown great and stout, with good land, good houses, men of worth in the country, but they won't give two *liards* to a poor man. Now if they'd been folk like me, they'd have been hanged!'

'That's true, Père Cadoche!'

'I was lucky not to be accused myself; for everybody was suspected in those days, and justice only hunts down the poor. Some were put in prison that were white as the driven snow, and when the real culprits were found, there came orders from on high, to let them go.'

'And why was that?'

'Because they were rich, I've no doubt. When have you ever seen anything but giving way to the rich, Nephew?'

'Truer still. Well, Uncle, we're nearly at Blanchemont. Where shall I take your sack of bread?'

'Give it back to me, Nephew. I'll go and sleep in the priest's stable; he's a holy man and never sends me away. He's like you, Grand-Louis, who've never given me a harsh word. And you'll be rewarded for it; you'll be my heir, I've always promised you. Except for the bouquet, I want to give that to little Borgnotte, you'll have everything, my house, my clothes, my begging-bag, and my pig.'

'Good, good!' exclaimed the miller. 'So I see I'll be *too* rich in the end, and all the girls will want to marry me.'

'I admire your good heart, Grand-Louis,' said Lémor when the beggar had disappeared behind the hedges of the pad-docks, cutting straight through them without looking for the path or worrying too much about the state of the fences. 'You treat this beggar as if he really were your uncle.'

'Well, why not? It gives him pleasure to pretend he's a grandfather and promise to make all the world heir to his wealth! And what an inheritance! His earthen hut where he sleeps with his pig, no more and no less than Saint Anthony* did, and his cast-off clothes that tug at your heart-strings! That should be enough to persuade Monsieur Bricolin and settle my fate nicely!'

'Despite the disgust which his personage inspires,* you none the less took his bag on your own shoulders to aid him. Louis, you are a true missionary.'

'No great matter! Is it right to refuse such a little service to a poor old devil who's still begging for his bread at the age of eighty? After all, he's a good man. Everybody looks out for him because he's honest, even if he is a bit hoity-toity, and has a roving eye.'

'So I thought.'

'Bah! What virtues do you expect such folk to have? All you can ask is that they don't have real vices and don't commit any crimes. Isn't his reasoning sound, despite it all?'

'Yes, in the end I was struck by that. But why does he think himself everyone's uncle? Is that an element of folly?'

'Oh no, it's a part he plays. Many a one in his trade puts on some little madness to make himself funny, or get attention, or amuse people, as they won't give alms out of charity or prudence. That's the sad way it is with us, the poor have to be the jesters at the gates of the well-to-do... But here we are at Blanchemont farm, comrade. Hang about, don't go in, take my word for it. You may well be master of yourself, I don't doubt it. But *she*'s not been warned, and she might let out a little scream or say something . . . Just let me warn her, at least.'

'But everyone's still up in the hamlet; won't they notice a stranger, just as much, if I sit here waiting for you?'

'Well then, you shall do me the service of going into the hunting-park; at this hour nobody else walks there. Sit down like a reasonable soul in some corner. When I go past, I'll whistle like I was calling a dog, begging your pardon, and you'll come out and join me.'

Lémor gave in, hoping that the ingenious miller would find some means of bringing Marcelle that way. So he walked slowly, under the overhanging trees, across the hunting-park, stopping frequently to listen carefully, holding his breath and turning around, in case a happy encounter might be imminent.

It was not long before he heard light footsteps seeming to skim over the grass, and a brushing of the branches convinced him that someone was coming this way. Hiding in the thicket to make sure he was not mistaken, he caught sight of a dimly defined shape approaching, that of a rather small woman. It is easy to believe what one wants to believe, and Henri, never doubting that this was Marcelle, sent to him by the miller, emerged and began walking to meet the phantom. But he stopped when he heard an unknown voice calling cautiously, '*Paul! Paul! Are you there, Paul?*'

Realizing his error, and fearing that he had happened upon another's assignation, Henri attempted to flee. But he trod noisily on some dry branches, and the madwoman caught sight of him. Still deep in her dream of love, she threw herself after him with the swiftness of an arrow, wailing in her pathetic voice, 'Paul! Paul! Here I am! Paul! It's me! . . . don't go! Paul! Paul! Why must you always leave me?'

XXIV. THE MADWOMAN

At first Lémor was not too much worried by his adventure. He imagined that under cover of night it would be no great matter to evade this woman, whom he had not observed sufficiently clearly to see as a lunatic. Naturally he flattered himself that he could run much more swiftly than she. But he quickly realized that he was mistaken, and that it required all the agility he could muster to keep her at a distance. Forced to cross the entire hunting-park, he soon found himself in the lower avenue, where Bricoline habitually spent long hours in her wanderings, creating bare patches in the grass with her steps. The fugitive, who had been hampered by roots barely covered with earth and rough dips in the path, now used all his strength to gain some ground. But when the madwoman was in the grip of her ardent thoughts she became as light as a dry leaf borne away in a storm. She followed him with such speed that Lémor, fearful of recognition, stunned and confused, decided to plunge once more into the shrubbery and attempt to lose himself in the shadows. But the madwoman knew every tree, bush, and branch in the hunting-park. During the twelve years of her life which she had spent there, there was no corner which her body had not penetrated in its mechanical fashion, even though her wits were in no state for reasoned observation. Furthermore the exaltation of her delirium made her perfectly insensible to physical pain. She would have left tatters of her flesh on the brambles without noticing it, and this near-cataleptic disposition gave her an unequivocal advantage over the man she wished to capture. Besides, she was so scrawny that she could glide like a lizard between the tightly packed trunks, where Lémor had to force his passage laboriously or, more often, turn aside altogether.

Seeing that he was in a worse plight than before, he emerged again into the avenue, closely pursued, and made up his mind to jump the ditch without realizing its breadth, covered as it was by thick undergrowth. He leapt, and fell on his knees in the brambles. But barely had he regained his feet when the phantom, who had crossed this obstacle with no effort and no concern for the rocks and nettles, was there at his side, clutching his clothes. When he found himself in the grip of this horrifying creature, Lémor, whose imagination was as vivid as that of an artist or poet, thought himself hag-struck as in a nightmare, and battling ferociously, he managed to rip away from the howling madwoman, and began bounding through the fields.

But she set out after him, running as nimbly over the rigid, prickly stubble of new-mown straw as she had over the forest floor. At the far end of the field Lémor vaulted over a new fence and found himself in an overgrown path that ran rapidly downhill. He had not taken ten steps when he heard the spectre behind him, wheezing, '*Paul! Paul! Why are you running away?*'

This flight had its fantastic element, which gained a stronger and stronger hold over Lémor's imagination. As he wrenched himself away from the madwoman's grasp, he had been able to glimpse her more clearly in the clear starlit gloaming: this bizarre apparition, this corpse-like face, these stringy arms covered in wounds, these long black locks drifting over the blood-stained rags. It never occurred to him that this unfortunate creature had lost her reason. He thought himself pursued by a jealous woman temporarily deluded into believing that he was someone else. He wondered briefly whether he should stop, to speak with her and disabuse her of her notions; but how then could he explain his presence in the hunting-park? Skulking through the shadows like a thief, would not a stranger such as he arouse suspicion at the farm from the start, and was he not obliged to avoid, above all else, such a scandalous and ridiculous arrival on the scene?

So he decided to run on, and this peculiar exercise continued half an hour without interruption. Lémor's thoughts boiled in his brain, and at times he thought he would go mad himself, when he observed the inconceivable obstinacy and the supernatural rapidity of this phantom hell-bent on his pursuit. It was like the tales of will o'the wisps and malicious fairies of the night.*

Finally Lémor came upon the Vauvre at the bottom of the combe. He was about to plunge in and swim for it, despite being bathed in sweat, reckoning on this obstacle to deliver him from the spectre at last. But just then he heard a ghastly howl behind him, chilling his entire being. He turned but saw nothing there. The madwoman had vanished.

Henri's first impulse was to profit from what was at best an instant's respite, by gaining enough ground to put the madwoman off his track entirely. But this appalling scream had left too painful an impression on him. Was it really that woman who had uttered it? The sound had nothing human about it, and yet what affliction, what despair it seemed to express! 'Had she wounded herself gravely in a fall?' wondered Lémor, 'or else did she think I'd drowned when she lost sight of me behind the willow? Was it a wail of anguish or of dread? Or was it fury that she could not follow me into the water, where she presumes I have thrown myself?

'But what if she herself has fallen into some ditch or over a precipice that I did not see, in my haste? If this unfortunate meeting cost the miserable woman her life? No, whatever follows, I cannot possibly abandon her to the horrors of her agony.'

Lémor turned and sought for the unfortunate woman, but in vain. The path he had clattered down ran along the outside edge of the hunting-park; the boundary was a tall hedgerow, not a ditch; there was no swamp or mire where she might have drowned. The sandy path bore no signs of a body's fall, so far as Lémor could see. He was still searching, lost in conjecture, when he heard a whistle repeated several times, as if someone were calling a dog. At first he barely noticed, so greatly absorbed and shocked was he by his adventure. But at length he remembered that this was the signal which he had agreed with the miller, and, despairing of finding his avenging fury, he replied to Grand-Louis's call with a second whistle.

'What on earth possessed you to go so far on your little stroll?' sputtered the miller in a whisper, when they had met up in the hunting-park. 'I told you not to budge! I've been looking for you a good quarter of an hour in this wood, I didn't dare call too loud, and I was losing patience . . . Look at you! all out of breath, and your clothes torn to shreds! Blast it, looks to me like my smock's had a hard time of it on your shoulders. Well, what is it? You look like a scared rabbit, or a man chased by goblins.'

'You've hit the nail on the head, my friend. Either what Jeannie has told me about these night-time phantoms in the Vallée-Noire is all rooted in some inexplicable truth, or I have had a hallucination. But for an hour now (it may be a century for all I know!) I have been doing battle with the devil.'

'If you weren't so stubborn about drinking nothing but water with your meals,' answered the miller, 'I'd think you'd got yourself into the right state for catching sight of the *Great Beast, the white lurcher bitch*, or *Georgeon the wolf-drover*. But you're too educated and reasonable a man to believe those stories. So something must really have happened. A rabid dog, maybe?'

'Worse than that,' said Lémor, recovering his wits bit by bit; 'a madwoman, my friend! a sorceress who could run more quickly than I and who disappeared, I have no idea how, at the very moment when I was about to throw myself into the water to shake her off.'

'A woman? oh! and what did she say?'

'She took me for a certain Paul who is dear to her, it would appear.'

'I thought as much! it's the madwoman of the castle. What kind of ass am I, not to have seen that you might meet her there? 'S truth, I forgot all about it! We're so used to seeing her trot around at night like an old weasel that we don't pay her any heed. Though it's a thing to break your heart, if you think about it! But why the devil did she light out after you? Most often she runs off when she hears someone coming. It must be her madness has got worse; she'd a bad enough dose of it before, poor girl!'

'Who is this unfortunate creature?'

'I'll tell you her tale later. Quick march, now! you do look worn out.'

'I think I broke my knees when I fell.'

'All the same, there is a ce*rtain person* waiting impatiently at the end of the path,' said the miller, lowering his voice still further.

'Oh!' exclaimed Lémor. 'I feel lighter than the night breeze!' And he tried to break into a trot.

'Slow down!' barked the miller, holding him back. 'Don't run on the grass. No noise! She's over there under that tall tree. Don't leave that spot. I'll patrol round there so you won't be taken unawares.'

'Is there some danger for her in coming here?' blurted Lémor in fright.

'If I thought so, I'd never have let her come! All the folk at the new castle are busy getting ready for the fair tomorrow. But at least I can keep the madwoman off you, in case she takes it into her head to come back and torment you some more!'

Henri forgot all that had occurred and ran to throw himself at Marcelle's feet, there where she was waiting for him under a stand of oaks, in the least frequented part of the wood.

There was no room for explanations in their first rush of effusion. Chaste and restrained, as they had always been, they none the less experienced a sort of intoxication which no human words could express. They were dumbfounded to see each other again so soon, having believed their separation almost eternal, but they did not attempt to make each other understand all their reasons for retracting with such haste their courageous and altruistic schemes. With mutual conjecture they understood what unbearable sufferings and irresistible forces had brought them running to each other, just at the moment when they had sworn to flee one another.

'Madman! who wanted to leave me for ever!' exclaimed Marcelle as she gave Lémor her beautiful hand.

'Cruel woman! who wanted to banish me for an entire year!' replied Lémor, brushing his closed lips to her hand.

And Marcelle realized that her resolution of one year's self-sacrifice had been more genuine, in her own mind, than the eternal exile to which Lémor had attempted to condemn himself.

As soon as they were able to speak, an effort of which they were only capable after a long period of gazing at each other in the silence of delight, Marcelle was the first to return to this truly praiseworthy plan.

'Lémor,' said she, 'this is only a sunbeam between two clouds. We must obey the law of duty. Even if we encountered no obstacle here to the security of our relations, there would be something profoundly irreligious in reuniting so soon, and we should see each other now for the last time before the expiration of my mourning. Tell me that you love me and that I shall be your wife, and I shall have all the necessary strength to wait for you.'

'Tell me not of separation now!' blurted Lémor impetuously. 'Let me savour this moment, the most beautiful of my life. Let me forget what came yesterday or what will come tomorrow. See how soft the night is, and how beautiful the heavens! How calm and balmy this place is! You are here! It is really you, Marcelle, not your shadow! We are both here! We found each other by chance and against our wills! It was God's will, and we were happy to obey, were we not? *both of us*? you as well, Marcelle, as much as I? Is it possible? No, I am not dreaming, for you are here next to me, with me, alone! blissful! We love each other so! We could not separate, we shall never be able to!'

'And yet, my friend . . .'

'I know! I know what you were about to say. Tomorrow, some other day, you will write to me and tell me what you wish me to do. I shall obey, as you know! But why talk to me about it tonight? Why spoil this moment which has no parallel in any of my earlier life? Let me persuade you that it will never end. Marcelle, I see you! Oh! I see you so well, despite the darkness! how much more beautiful you have become in three days . . . in the space of a single day, when you were already so beautiful this morning! Oh! tell me that your hand will never leave mine! I shall hold on to it so firmly!'

'Oh, you are right, Lémor! Let us be happy that we have found each other again, and let us not think yet that we shall have to separate . . . tomorrow . . . another day . . .'

'Yes, another day, another day!' exclaimed Henri.

'Do me the goodness of speaking softer,' said the miller as he came up to them. 'I can hear every word you say in spite of myself, Monsieur Henri!'

The two lovers remained there for over an hour, plunged into a pure ecstasy, concocting the sweetest dreams of the future and speaking of their happiness together, as if it were not to be interrupted but to begin the following day. The breeze shook down the perfumes of the night on them, and the serene stars passed above their heads without impressing on them the inevitable march of time, which never stands still in the hearts of happy lovers.

But the miller, after several signs of impatience, came up and interrupted them when the inclination of the polar star indicated ten o'clock on the celestial clock.

'My friends,' he said, 'I can't leave you here, or wait for you a moment more. I don't hear the cowherds singing in the farmyard anymore, and they're putting out the lights in the windows of the new castle. Only Mademoiselle Rose's is still alight, she's waiting up for Madame Marcelle before she goes to bed. Monsieur Bricolin'll be out here on his rounds with the dogs, as he does every evening before a fête. Let's go quickly.'

Lémor protested: he had only just arrived, he claimed.

'That's as may be,' said the miller, 'but do you realize I've got to go to La Châtre tonight?'

'How do you mean? On my business?' asked Marcelle.

'If you please! I want to see our lawyer before he goes to bed, and I don't want to see him tomorrow in the daylight for fear Monsieur Bricolin thinks I'm plotting against him.'

'But Grand-Louis, I don't want you to risk . . . for my sake . . .'

'Enough gab,' boomed the miller. 'I'll do what I please . . . Listen! I hear the lurchers yowling! Go back into the meadow, Madame Marcelle, and you and me, my Parisian, let's take the high road, if you please. Take to your heels!'

The lovers took a silent leave, too chary of reminding each other that this must be seen as their final meeting. Marcelle had not the stength to fix a time for Henri's departure, and as for him, he dreaded hearing her pronounce that date. Kissing her hand ten times in silence, he hastened to depart.

'Well? What'd you decide?' demanded the miller when they had reached the outskirts of the park.

'Nothing, my friend,' said Lémor. 'We talked of nothing but our happiness . . .'

'In the future; but what about the present?'

'There is no present, no future. All is one to lovers.'

'You're rambling again, I see. Well, I just hope you return to your right mind before long, and don't send me toiling and moiling about the woods again with your deadly sorceresses and suchlike. Here you go, my lad, this is your road. You can make your way back to Angibault on your own?'

'Perfectly well. But do you wish me to accompany you to town?'

'No, it's too far. One of us would have to go on foot, and that'd hold the other back, unless we did things the country way and both rode Sophie; but the poor beast's too long in the tooth, and besides, she's not had her feed yet. I'm going to look for her under the tree where I tethered her after pretend-ing to take the road back to the mill. Have you any idea of the worry it gave me, leaving poor Sophie in God's keeping like that? I hid her under the branches, but if some tramp decided to pinch her!—and all sorts come to the *assemblée*! While you were billing and cooing down there, Sophie was trotting through my brain! . . .'

'Well, let us go and find her together!'

'Oh no you don't! You're looking for any excuse to go back to the castle, you are! Go on, tell my mother she can go to bed with a quiet mind, I'll probably be home late. Monsieur Tailland the lawyer will ask me to supper. He keeps a good table, he's a fine man. That way I'll have time to tell him about affairs at Blanchemont, and Sophie can enjoy her nose-bag at his place, even if she's not got an appointment with him.'

Lémor did not press the matter. He was moved by affection and respect for the miller, and he preferred to be alone with his emotions. He felt a need to think of Marcelle calmly, and to retrace and begin anew the gentle dream he had just had at her feet. Thus he started off down the track for Angibault like a sleepwalker finding his way back to his bed. I cannot say whether he wandered off the track, whether he crossed the river on the bridge, whether he covered twice the necessary distance, whether he drifted off several times by wells. The night was sultry, and from the cock lancing his fanfare to echo around the cottage rooftops, to the cricket whispering mysteriously in the long grass, everything seemed to repeat, triumphantly though secretly, the cherished name of Marcelle.

But when he reached the mill, he was so shattered by fatigue that as soon as he had warned the good mill-wife not to wait up for her son, he threw himself down on the little bed which Louis had set up for him in his own room. Grand'Marie told Jeannie not to expect his master to rise before him, and to take Sophie to the stable; then she went to bed as well. But a mother's tenderness sleeps with one eye open, and when a thunderstorm rolled through the valley, the good woman awoke with a start, thinking she heard her son knocking at Jeannie's door, in the mill where he slept at night. When day broke she got up noiselessly and went to tell Jeannie not to make too much racket, since Grand-Louis, who had doubtless returned late, needed to sleep a bit longer than usual. Thus she was quite surprised and rather frightened when Jeannie answered that his master was not yet back.

'That's not possible!' she exclaimed. 'He never stays overnight when he goes to Blanchemont.'

'Oh, bah, our mistress! It was the evening before the fête. Nobody's asleep over there. The inns are open all night long. The *cornemuseux** come, playing their best marches. It sets your heart to dancing. You want it to be tomorrow already; you don't think of going to bed, you're afraid of waking up too late and missing a mite of the amusement. Our master's been having a fine time, he'll have been up all night long.'

'The master does not spend his nights in inns,' answered the mill-wife, shaking her head, after having opened the stable door to make sure that Sophie was not at her manger. 'I reckoned he'd come in without waking you up, Jeannie. He'd rather look after things himself than bother a child like you, as sleeps the sleep of the just. But he's not been to bed! He was tired enough the day before yesterday, he'd been a long way. He went to bed late the other night, and last night not at all! . . .'

The mill-wife went off to don her Sunday best with a profound sigh. 'Love, you little rascal!' she thought to herself. 'That's what's tormenting him and keeping him on his feet day and night. How will it all end for him?'

The Fourth Day

XXV. SOPHIE

The good mill-wife was absorbed in sad thoughts, and, as is often the way with elderly people, she expressed them aloud, as she trudged mechanically from her wardrobe to her chest of drawers, getting out her long bodice in the ancient style, and the checked calico apron that she had preserved carefully since her youth, valuing it all the more because in those days it had cost four times more than finer stuffs cost today.

'Don't worry, Mother,' said Grand-Louis, who had overheard her from the threshold, although she had not heard him arrive. 'All this would end as it will; but your son will always try to please you.'

'Oh, my poor child, I didn't see you!' exclaimed the millwife, slightly flustered, even at her age, to be taken unawares by her son with her long grey hair loose; for the peasant-women of the Vallée-Noire are extremely modest about showing their hair. But Grand'Marie quickly forgot her super-annuated prudishness when she saw her son's pale face and dishevelled condition.

'Lord Jesus!' she cried, clasping her hands together, 'how tired you look! Every drop of rain that fell last night must have landed on you! Eh? you're still soaked through. Go quickly, change your clothes. Why couldn't you find a house to shelter in? And what a hangdog face you've got this morning! Oh, my poor child, I'd think you wanted to make yourself ill!'

'Oh, no, Mother, don't torment yourself like this!' said the miller, forcing himself to speak with his usual gaiety. 'I did shelter the night with friends... people I had business with, who gave me supper. I only got this little bit wet afterwards, seeing as I came back on foot.'

'On foot! What have you done with Sophie?'

'I lent her to . . . *thingummy* . . . from . . . *thereabouts* . . .'

'Who do you mean, thingummy from thereabouts?'

'Don't you know? Oh, well I'll tell you later. If you want to go to the *assemblée*, I'll take the little black mare, and put you up behind me.'

'You were wrong to lend Sophie out, child. There's no match for her, you should spare her such things. I'd rather see you lend out both the others.'

'So would I. But there you go: that's how it worked out. Come on, Mother, I'll go and get dressed, and when you want to go, just call me.'

'No, no, I can see you'd no taste of sleep last night, and I want you to go and lie down a bit. We've plenty of time before mass. Oh, Grand-Louis, such a face! you really oughtn't to go about that way!'

'Have no fear, Mother, I don't feel ill, and I shan't do it often. But once in a while, you've got to try to forget.'

And the miller, even more distressed at having burdened his mother, whose concern and disquiet were never expressed in anything but a gentle, restrained manner, went to throw himself down on his bed with an angry movement that awoke Lémor.

'Are you getting up already?' asked Henri, rubbing his eyes.

'No, no, I'm going to bed, if you don't mind,' barked the miller, thumping the mattress with his fist.

'My friend! You have some trouble,' said Lémor, now fully awakened by the unequivocal signs of Grand-Louis's inner rage.

'Trouble! Oh, yes, Monsieur, I should think so, perhaps more than the thing warrants, but there we are, it hurts me more than I'd wish, I can't help myself.' And thick tears misted the miller's tired eyes.

'My friend!' exclaimed Lémor, jumping up from his bed and dressing in haste, 'some misfortune happened to you last night, I see it plainly! And here I was sleeping like a baby! My Lord, what can I do? Where shall I run?'

'Oh, don't run anywhere, there's no point,' shrugged Grand-Louis, as if embarrassed by his own weakness. 'I've run around enough last night for two of us, in vain, and here I am on my last legs, and all for this stupid business! But that's the way it is, you get just as attached to animals as people, and you miss an old horse like an old friend. You won't understand that, you're a town-dweller; but we peasants live with animals, and we're no diferent from them!'

'And you have lost Sophie, I understand now.'

'Lost, yes, you could say that; somebody stole her.'

'Yesterday in the hunting-park?'

'Precisely. You remember, I had an evil inkling of it! When you left me I went to the spot where I'd hidden her, which the poor beast, who's patient as a sheep, would never have left of her own accord... In all her days she's never broken a bridle or a halter. Hey presto, sir! Horse and bridle, both gone. I looked for her, I ran all about, nothing! And I didn't dare ask at the farm, that'd have given them food for thought! They'd have asked how I managed to lose the beast on the way, since they thought I'd already left. They'd have said I was drunk, and Madame Bricolin would have seized her chance to tell Mademoiselle Rose that I'd had a low adventure, unworthy of a man whose only thoughts are of her. At first I thought somebody was playing a prank on me. I went into all the houses. Practically the whole village was still out dancing. I wandered from one to another, I didn't try to hide. I went into all the stables, even the castle's, without anybody seeing me: no Sophie! At the moment Blanchemont is full of people of every stripe, and there's bound to be some clever scoundrel who came on foot but returned on horseback, thinking he's had a good enough time already, before the fête even started, so he won't care about seeing any more of it. Well, no point thinking about it any more. Lucky for me, I didn't do anything too stupid, despite all that. I hot-footed it to La Châtre. I saw the lawyer; it was a bit late, he'd finished his supper, and his digestion made him a bit stupid; but he'll be at the fête this afternoon, he promised me. When I left him, I did some more ferreting around, beating the bushes like a huntsman at night. I wandered around in the rain and thunder till daybreak, still hoping to find my thief hidden somewhere. Useless! I don't want to trumpet my misfortune about, it'll only create a scandal, and if it came to an inquiry, we'd look nice and clean, wouldn't we? with this tale of a horse hidden in the hunting park and left there over an hour for no reason I could explain. I left her a good way from your meeting-place, so that if she made a little movement, the noise wouldn't attract any attention to your part of the woods. Poor Sophie! I should have trusted her good sense. She'd never have budged!'

'So I am the cause of your misadventure! Grand-Louis, this troubles me even more than it does you, and you must allow me to make your loss good as soon as I can.'

'Hush up, Monsieur; I scorn the little bit of money the old beast'd be worth at a fair! Do you reckon I'd be so out of sorts about a hundred francs! Not a bit, *she*'s what I miss, I don't care about her price, she was beyond it as far as I'm concerned. She was so brave, so intelligent, she knew me so well! I'm certain she's thinking about me right now, and looking crosswise at whoever's grooming her! Well, I just hope he looks after her properly. If I was sure about that, I'd be pretty much comforted. But he'll groom her with the whip and feed her on chestnut shells! Because it's got to be some rogue from La Marche who'li take her off to his mountains* and pasture her in a field of rocks, instead of her pretty little meadow down by the stream, where she lived so contentedly and played the fool with the young fillies, she felt that sprightly when she saw the green grass. And my mother! she's the one who'll really be upset! and I shan't ever be able to give her a proper explanation of how this disaster happened. I haven't had the heart to tell her yet. Don't tell her till I've ransacked my brain for some story that'll soften the news for her.'

In the miller's innocent regrets there was something both comic and touching. Lémor, despondent at being the cause of the trouble, was so affected that the good Louis was obliged to console *him*.

'Come now,' he said, 'that's enough foolishness about a four-legged beast. I know it's none of your doing, and I've not thought for one moment of blaming you. Don't let it spoil your happy memories, my friend! It's no price to pay for such a beautiful evening as you had! And if I ever have such a rendezvous with Rose, I'll gladly ride a broomstick for a horse, the rest of my life! Don't tell Madame Marcelle any of this; it'd be just like her to give me a thousand-franc horse, and I'd hate that. I don't want to get attached to my beasts any more. There's enough trouble in life with people! So I'm telling you: think about your love-life, make yourself handsome for the fair, but in the peasant style, for they've got to get used to seeing your face around these parts. That'll be better than hiding, which would make folk suspicious right off. You'll see Madame Marcelle, but you certainly won't speak to her! Anyway, you won't get the chance, she won't dance, she's in full mourning! . . . but Rose isn't, heavens be praised! and I intend to dance with her till nightfall, since darling Papa consents. That makes me think I'd best grab a few hours' sleep so I don't look like a risen corpse. Don't worry about being quiet, you'll hear me snoring in five minutes.'

The miller was as good as his word, and at ten o'clock, when he was brought his black mare, who was far handsomer but less close to his heart than Sophie, he was already dressed in his fine linen coat for Sundays, with his chin neatly shaved, his complexion rosy and his eye sparkling. He clenched his robust mount between his strong thighs, with the mill-wife behind him, who had mounted with the help of a chair and Lémor's arm, feeling a thrill of pride at being the mother of such a handsome miller.

They had not slept must better at the farm than at the mill, and we are obliged to turn back a bit in order to inform the reader of the events which took place during the night before the fête.

Agitated equally by his distressing adventure with the madwoman and the intoxicating pleasure of seeing Marcelle again, Lémor had not observed that when they separated in the hunting-park, the miller was no calmer than he. Grand-Louis had found the farmyard full of movement and tumult. Two *pataches* and three *cabriolets*, which had transported all the Bricolin relatives between their sturdy sides, were lying tipped on their weary arms by the stables and middens. All the poor relations, eager to earn a pittance, had been summoned to help prepare the meal for the numerous hungry guests who were expected at the new castle. M. Bricolin was in the highest humour, his unwillingness to bear any expense having been bested by his desire to flaunt his opulence. His daughters, sons, cousins, nephews, and sons-in-law all took him aside, one by one, to enquire when they might expect the house-warming at the old castle, restored and freshly whitewashed, with the monogram of the Bricolins as a heraldic shield over the doorway. 'For after all, you will be the lord and master of Blanchemont,' they chanted in a banal refrain, 'and you'll administer your wealth a good deal better than all the counts and barons you'll succeed, to the greater glory of the new aristocracy, the nobility of sound money.' Bricolin was drunk with pride, and although, with a malicious smile, he answered his dear relations: 'Not yet, not yet! Perhaps never!' none the less he was already enjoying all the self-importance of a feudal lord. Having lost all qualms about the expense, he boomed out orders to his servants, his mother, his daughter, and his wife, puffing his stout belly out up to his jowls. The entire household was in a commotion: old mother Bricolin was plucking chickens, fresh-killed, by the dozens, and Mme Bricolin, who had at first been in murderous mood while she was trying to govern the tumult in the kitchen, was also beginning to brighten up at the sight of the copious meal, the well-appointed rooms, and the awestruck guests. Thanks to all this disorder, the miller was easily able to have a word with Marcelle, and she, pleading migraine, excused herself from the supper table and went out to meet Lémor in the hunting park while the festivities were going on.

As the table was being laid, Rose herself had found one or two excellent excuses for wandering out into the farmyard and saying a few friendly words in passing to Grand-Louis, according to her custom. But her mother, who never let her out of her sight, had found a means of sending the miller about his business with all due speed. Although she had been forced to obey her husband's commandment not to show the miller any ill grace, she assuaged her hatred, and tried to make Rose feel ashamed to be his friend, by ridiculing him in front of her other daughters and the rest of her relations, all malicious and rude, young and old. She was quick to confide to each one, as if for her ears alone, that this fine fellow from the

village flattered himself that he was to Rose's taste; that Rose
knew nothing about it and paid him no attention; that
M. Bricolin, unwilling to believe it, treated him far too well;
but that she had learned a curious fact from a reputable
source, that the *handsome miller*, the darling of all the country
hussies, had often boasted that he had the hearts of the richest
women he might court, this one and that, indiscriminately . . .
and on that score Mme Bricolin named names of women
present, laughing, with arms akimbo, in an acidic scornful
manner as she adjusted her apron.

On the distaff side of the family this secret had promptly
passed from mouth to mouth and ear to ear, to the Bricolins
of the other sex, so much so that Grand-Louis, who had no
other thought than to rejoin Lémor, soon found himself as-
saulted with witticisms of such spectacular dullness that he
could barely understand them, and accompanied in his retreat
by barely stifled sniggers and whispers of the highest impertinence. Having no idea why he had excited such gaiety, he left
the farm in an unquiet mood, and full of scorn for the thick
wit of the wealthy farmers gathered at Blanchemont that
evening.

In accordance with Mme Bricolin's advice, they took care
that M. Bricolin should not notice the conspiracy, and they
promised each other to persecute the miller the next day in
Rose's presence. It was necessary, her mother pontificated, to
humiliate this bumpkin in front of her, so that she learned not
to be too trusting and to keep the peasants at a distance.

After supper the strolling fiddlers were summoned, and
everyone danced in the courtyard in anticipation of tomorrow. It was during an interval's rest that the miller, feeling
nervous and anxious to be off to La Châtre, had reckoned that
the pleasure-party was over at the new castle, and forced the
two lovers to separate much sooner than they would have
wished.

When Marcelle returned to the farm, the amusements had
begun afresh, and with the same need for solitude and reverie
which Lémor had experienced in the *traînes* of the Vallée-
Noire, she went back to the hunting-park and strolled at her
leisure until midnight. The sound of the *cornemuse*, accompanied by the hurdy-gurdy,* is rather rasping to the

nearby ear; but from a distance, this rustic voice, singing what are often quite graceful motifs, made more original by a primitive sort of harmony, possesses a charm which works its way on simple souls and quickens the heartbeat of anyone who was rocked to its lullaby as a child. The strong vibration of the *musette*, though somewhat raucous and nasal, is made to complement and correct the sharp creak and the nervous staccato of the fiddle. Marcelle listened to them with pleasure for a long while, and observing that distance increased their charm, she soon found herself at the other extremity of the hunting-park, lost in a dream of a pastoral existence supported by love.

But she stopped abruptly: almost under her feet the madwoman was stretched out motionless on the groud, apparently dead. Despite the disgust aroused in her by the unimaginable filthiness of this miserable being, she decided, after having vainly tried to rouse her, that she would lift her in her arms and drag her as far as she could. She supported her against a tree, and feeling that she had not the strength to carry her any further, she was thinking whether she should go and call for help at the farm, when Bricoline began to rouse herself from her stupor and to lift her scarred hand to brush from her face her long black hair, bristling with grass and grit. Marcelle helped her to remove this thick curtain which hampered her breathing, and, daring for the first time to speak to her, asked her whether she was in pain.

'Of course I am in pain!' answered the madwoman with a dreadful indifference, as if to say, 'I am still alive'; then she barked imperiously, 'Have you seen him? He's come back. He won't speak to me. Has he told you why not?'

'He told me that he would return,' answered Marcelle, endeavouring to calm her mania.

'Oh, he'll never return!' shrilled the madwoman, getting up with a start. 'He'll never return! He's afraid of me. Everyone's afraid of me, because I'm very, very rich, so rich I've been forbidden to live. But I don't want to be rich; tomorrow I'll be poor. It's time this ended. Tomorrow everybody will be poor. You'll be poor, too, Rose, and you won't frighten anybody. I'll punish the evil people who want to kill me, shut me up, poison me . . .'

'But there are people who pity you and only wish you well,' said Marcelle.

'No, there are none,' replied the madwoman sharply, shaking in a ghastly manner. 'They're all my enemies. They tortured me, they plunged a red-hot poker into my head. They nailed me to trees, they threw me out of the tall towers on to the paving stones, more than two thousand times. They criss-crossed my heart with great steel needles. They flayed me alive; that's why I can't change my clothes without going through appalling agony. They wanted to pluck out my hair, because it protects me a little from their blows . . . But I'll have my revenge! I've drawn up a complaint! It took me fifty-four years to translate it into every language for all the sovereigns of the universe. I want them to bring back Paul to me, they've hidden him in their cellar and tortured him like they do me. I hear him screaming every night when they torment him . . . I know his voice . . . There it is, do you hear it?' she wailed, listening to the lively sound of the *cornemuse*. 'You can hear they're putting him through a thousand deaths! They want to eat him alive, but they'll be punished, punished! Tomorrow I'll make them suffer too, I will! They'll be in such pain that I might even have pity on them . . .'

And with these words, spoken with delirious volubility, the poor woman rushed off through the undergrowth towards the farm, leaving Marcelle vainly attempting to follow her quick course and her impetuous leaps.

XXVI. THE *VEILLÉE**

At the farm the dancing went on more stubbornly than ever. The servants had joined in, and a thick dust was rising under their feet, a circumstance that never prevents the Berry peasant from dancing with abandon, any more than do stones, sun, rain, or the fatigue of harvest and mowing-times. No other culture dances with such simultaneous gravity and passion. Watching them advance and retreat as they dance the bourrée* in their tight squares, with the gentle precision of a clock pendulum, one would never guess the pleasure they take in this monotonous exercise; still less would one suspect the difficulty of learning this elementary rhythm, which must be rigorously marked in every pace and with every movement of the body, whilst a great sobriety of gesture and an apparent languor must entirely mask the effort if perfection is to be attained. But after observing them for some while one is amazed by their indefatigable tenacity, one appreciates the sort of supple and naïve grace which preserves them from lassitude, and if one but observes the same personages dancing ten or twelve hours at a stretch without so much as an ache, one might think they have been bitten by tarantulas,* or realize that they love dancing with maniacal passion. From time to time the inner pleasure of the young men betrays itself in a strange cry, but their visages lose none of this imperturbable gravity, and occasionally, they slap their feet on the ground with such force that they bound up like bullocks, regaining their phlegmatic balance with a nonchalant grace. All of the Berry character is exemplified by this dance. As for the women, their task is to glide airily along, skimming the earth, all of which requires a greater degree of delicacy than one might imagine, and their graceful movements are imbued with a rigid chastity.

Rose danced the bourrée as well as an ordinary peasant woman, which is no mean compliment, and her father watched her with pride. Everyone was infected by gaiety; the musicians, plentifully plied with drink, spared neither their arms nor their lungs. The half-light of a fine night made the dancers appear more ethereal, particularly Rose, this charming girl who seemed to dance like a white gull skimming calm seas, borne away on the evening breeze. The melancholy of which all her movements partook this evening made her even more beautiful than was customary.

And indeed Rose, who was, deep down, a true peasant girl of the Vallée-Noire, in all her innocent simplicity, was enjoying the dancing, if only to practise for the numerous invitations which Grand-Louis would certainly put to her tomorrow. But suddenly the bagpipe-player tumbled off the cask which he had been using as a pedestal, and the residual

air in his instrument escaped with a bizarre whine that forced
the dumbfounded dancers to stop and turn towards him. At
the same moment, the hurdy-gurdy, which had been plucked
brusquely from the hands of the other minstrel, rolled under
Rose's feet, and the madwoman leapt away from the rural
orchestra, into which she had vaulted like a wild cat, bounding into the midst of the dancers and screaming: 'Death to the
assassins! death to the executioners!'—Then she threw herself
on her mother, who had stepped forward to restrain her, and
buried her talons in her neck. Mme Bricolin might well have
been strangled if old mother Bricolin had not seized the madwoman round the waist. Bricoline had never offered her
grandmother any violence, whether because she retained some
sort of unconscious instinctive love for her, because she recognized her alone among the crowd, or because she remembered
the efforts the good woman had made to further Paul's court-
ship. She made no resistance and allowed herself to be led
wailing into the house, her shrieks throwing all present into
consternation and terror.

When Marcelle arrived in the courtyard, having followed
the elder Mlle Bricolin as closely as she could, she found the
fête interrupted, the guests thunderstruck, and Rose very
nearly in a faint. No doubt Mme Bricolin also suffered, in the
depths of her being, if only to have this private wound exposed to all eyes; but in the ferocity with which she castigated
the lunatic and stifled the noise of her screams, there was a
violence more like that of a constable with a criminal than a
solicitous and despairing mother. Old mother Bricolin put the
same zeal into it, but more sensibility. It was a heart-rending
sight to watch the poor old woman, with her rough voice and
virile manners, caressing the madwoman and talking to her as
if to a little child: 'Come now, my darling,' she soothed her,
'you're good as gold, as a rule, you don't want to make
grandam unhappy, do you? Go to sleep like a good girl, else
I'll get cross and not love you any more.' The madwoman
neither understood nor so much as listened to these words.
Huddled at the foot of her bed, she sobbed dreadful howls,
and her disordered imagination persuaded her that she was
undergoing at that very moment all the punishments and

tortures which she had detailed to Marcelle in her fantastic tableau.

Marcelle, having seen that her child was still sleeping peacefully in Fanchon's care, was now most concerned about Rose, who had wandered off in fear and chagrin. This was the first time that Bricoline had let loose the hatreds stored up over twelve years in her disturbed spirit. At most once a week she had cried and wept when her grandmother decided to change her clothes. But those were the cries of a child, and these were the roars of an avenging Nemesis. She had never spoken to a soul, and now for the first time in twelve years she had made threats. She had never hit anyone, and now she had tried to kill her mother. For twelve years this mute victim of her parents' greed had kept her inexpressible griefs out of the way, and almost everyone had grown accustomed, with a sort of brutal indifference, to the deplorable spectacle. No one feared her any longer, everyone was weary of pitying her, all endured her presence as an inalterable nuisance, and if anyone had regrets, they kept them to themselves, or even from themselves. But the appalling illness consuming her inevitably had its worsening phases, and it had now reached a state in which her martyrdom was no longer private, but dangerous to others. It was time to do something about it. M. Bricolin, seated before his door, was listening with a distracted air to the gross condolences of his family.

'What a terrible misfortune for you,' they said, 'and one which you have endured so long, in your own house. That sort of patience is superhuman, but now you must decide to put her in a lunatic asylum.'

'They can't cure her!' he shook his head. 'I've asked them all. It can't be done: she's too ill, she'll die of it!'

'That would be the best for her. You can see yourself, she's too pitiful to live. But even if they can't cure her, it'll save you the trouble of having to care for her and see her declining. And she won't do you any evil. If you don't look out, she'll end by killing someone, or she'll kill herself under your very eyes. How appalling!'

'But what do you expect? I've said so a hundred times to her mother, but she won't let her be put away. Deep down she still loves her, believe me, you can understand it. Mothers always feel something for their children, it seems.'

'But she'd be better off there, really she would. They look after them ever so well these days. There are some lovely places, they lack for nothing. They're kept clean, they have work to do, they're busy, they're even given amusements, so it's said, mass and music.'

'In that case they're happier than we are,' sighed M. Bricolin. After a moment's reflection he added, 'And does all that cost a pretty penny?'

Rose had been affected deeply. With her grandmother, she was the only one who had not grown insensible to the misery of poor Bricoline. If she chose not to speak of it, it was to avoid accusing her parents of this moral parricide they had committed;* but twenty times a day she would be surprised by her own trembling rage at hearing her mother mouth those maxims of egotism and avarice to which her sister had been sacrificed. As soon as she had recovered from her fainting-fit, she tried to help her mother calm the lunatic; but Mme Bricolin, fearing that the sight would make too strong an impression on her, and having a vague instinct that excessive anguish might be contagious, sent her away with the strictness she maintained even in her moments of greatest solicitude. Provoked by the refusal, Rose returned to her bedchamber, where she walked up and down a large portion of the night, prey to a vivid sense of exaltation but unwilling to say anything of it to Marcelle, for fear of expressing herself too forcefully on the subject of her parents.

Thus the night that had begun with sweet joy was extremely painful for Mme de Blanchemont. The cries of the madwoman ceased at intervals but resumed again in even more terrible and frightening wise. When they did stop, it was not by degrees, gradually growing weaker, but abruptly, in the midst of their highest intensity, as if cut short by a violent death.

'Doesn't it sound as if they're killing her?' sobbed Rose, pale and barely able to stand as she walked up and down the room. 'Yes, it sounds like torture!'

Marcelle had no wish to tell her the atrocious tortures which the madwoman believed herself to be undergoing, and was actually suffering in mind if not in body. She kept the conversation in the park secret. From time to time she visited the sick woman; she always found her stretched out on the floor with her arms tightly laced around the foot of the bed, choked by the exhaustion of screaming, but with her eyes wide open and fixed, and her spirit evidently in great travail. Her grandmother, kneeling beside her, was trying vainly to put a pillow under her head or to slip a spoonful of sedative medicine into her twisted mouth. Mme Bricolin, sitting in an armchair opposite, was pale and motionless, bearing in her deeply worn but energetic features the marks of a profound grief which she was unwilling to confess, not even to God. Stout Chounette, standing in a corner, was sobbing mechanically without offering to help, nor did anyone think to ask her. There was a profound despair on all three faces. Only the madwoman, when she was not howling, seemed to be sapient, thinking her sombre thoughts of enmity. Snoring could be heard in the adjoining bedroom; but M. Bricolin's heavy slumber was not without agitation. From time to time it seemed to be interrupted by nightmares. Further off, along the dividing wall, old father Bricolin could be heard coughing and whimpering; a stranger to others' sufferings, he had barely enough strength left to endure his own.

At last, around three in the morning, the heavy air of the storm seemed to overwhelm the madwoman's exhausted constitution. She fell asleep on the floor, and was put to bed without waking up. It must have been a long while since she had tasted a moment's sleep, for she buried herself in it, and everyone was able to rest, even Rose, whom Mme de Blanchemont hastened to inform of the news.

If Marcelle had not had the opportunity to devote herself to poor Rose, she would have cursed the unhappy inspiration that had impelled her into this house, inhabited by greed and tragedy. She would have hastened to find some other lodging than this one, so antipathetic to idealism, so ugly in prosperity, so lugubrious in shame. But whatever fresh distress she might suffer there, she was resolved to remain as long as she could be serviceable to her young companion. Luckily the morning was peaceful. Everyone woke late, and Rose was still asleep when

Mme de Blanchemont, who had herself arisen only a moment before, received the following reply to the letter she had written three days earlier to her mother-in-law.

Letter from the Comtesse de Blanchemont to her daughter-in-law, Marcelle, Baronne de Blanchemont

My daughter,
May Providence, which has sent you such great resolve, continue to preserve you in it! I am not surprised at courage in you, although it is powerful. Do not think to praise mine. At my age one has not long to suffer! At yours... happily, one has no precise conception of the length and difficulty of existence. My daughter, your plans are praiseworthy, excellent, and as wise as they are needful; still more needful than you may think. We too are ruined, my dear Marcelle! and we shall not be able to leave any inheritance to our dearly loved grandson. The debts of my unhappy son surpassed anything you may know of them, anything we might have foreseen of them. We are temporizing with the creditors; but we must accept responsibility, although it entails depriving Édouard of the respectable fortune which he might have expected after our deaths. Educate him to lead a simple life. Teach him to create his own resources through his talents and to maintain his independence through the dignity which will allow him to endure misfortune. When he is grown to man's estate, we shall no longer be in this world. May he respect the memory of his aged relations, who preferred honour to pleasure and who will have left him no other inheritance than a pure name, beyond reproach. The son of a bankrupt would have had no other pleasures in life save contemptible ones; but the son of a guilty father owes at least some obligation to those who have shielded him from public shame.

'Tomorrow I shall write to you with the details, today I am still feeling the blow, from this realization of an unplumbed abyss. I tell it to you with few words. I know that you will understand all and endure all. Adieu, my daughter, I admire and love you.'

'Édouard!' exclaimed Marcelle, covering her sleeping son with kisses. 'So it was ordained that you should have the glory and perhaps the happiness of not succeeding to the wealth and rank of your forefathers! Thus do the great fortunes wrought over centuries perish in a single day! Thus do the former masters of the world, driven more by fate than by their own designs, themselves take on the task of accomplishing the decrees of divine wisdom, which works imperceptibly to render all men equal in power! May you understand one day, my child, that this law of Providence favours you, for it places you in the flock of sheep on Christ's right hand, and separates you from the goats on his left. God, grant me the necessary strength and wisdom to make a man of this child! To make him into a patrician, I had only to fold my arms and let wealth do the rest. As it is I have great need of light and inspiration: my God, my God, you have given me this task to carry out, you will not abandon me!'

'Lémor!' she wrote a moment later. 'My son is ruined, his relations are ruined. My son is a pauper. Perhaps he would have been a despicable and unworthy rich man. Now we must make him a courageous and noble poor man. Providence has reserved this mission for you. As things stand, do you still talk of abandoning me? Is not this child, once an obstacle between us, now a dear and sacred bond? Unless you found you no longer loved me in a year's time, Henri, who could oppose our happiness now? Have courage, my friend, and depart. In a year's time you shall find me in some cottage in the Vallée-Noire, not far from the mill of Angibault.'

Marcelle wrote these few lines in a state of exaltation. But when her pen traced the phrase 'unless you found you no longer loved me in a year's time', an imperceptible smile endowed her features with an ineffable expression. She attached the letter from her mother-in-law to this one for clarification, and, sealing both together, put them in her pocket, thinking that she would soon see the miller and perhaps Lémor himself in the peasant garb that suited him so well.

The madwoman slept the whole day through. She had fever, but that had not left her for a single day in the past twelve years, and this prostration, which had never been seen in her before, gave rise to hopes that the crisis had been favourable. The doctor who had been fetched from town, and who was accustomed to seeing her, did not find her ill in comparison to her ordinary state. Rose, greatly reassured, gave herself over to the sweet instincts of youth and dressed at leisure, with a great deal of coquetry. She wanted to be simple so as not to frighten off her admirer with a display of her wealth; she wanted to be pretty so as to please him. So she experimented with ingenious combinations, and succeeded in making herself modest as a daughter of the fields and beautiful as an angel in paradise. Without wishing to acknowledge it, in the midst of so much heartache, she had trembled slightly at the idea of losing this day, so full of laughter. At eighteen one does not lightly renounce the opportunity to intoxicate one's lover for an entire day, and without her own consciousness of it, this fear had melted into the sincere and deep grief to which her sister had subjected her. When she appeared at high mass, Louis had been watching for her arrival a good while. He had taken up his station where he should not lose sight of her for a moment. As if by chance she found herself standing next to Grand'Marie, and it was with tenderness that he saw her put her pretty shawl under the mill-wife's knees, despite the good woman's protestations.

After the service Rose adroitly took the arm of her grandmother, who rarely left her old friend, the mill-wife, when she had the pleasure of meeting her. Each year this pleasure became less frequent, as age made the distance from Blanchemont to Angibault more difficult for them to traverse. Old mother Bricolin liked a good chat. Always *given a dressing-down*, as she put it, by her daughter-in-law, she had a torrent of unused words to pour out on the mill-wife, who was less talkative but sincerely attached to her childhood companion, listening to her with patience and replying to her with discernment.

In this fashion Rose hoped to escape from the watchful gaze of Mme Bricolin for the entire day, and indeed from the society of her remaining relations, since her grandmother preferred to converse with other peasants, her own kind, rather than with the parvenus of her family.

Under the old trees of the castle mound, overlooking a charming site, the pretty girls crowded around the musicians placed in close pairs on their trestles. Giving way to the most jealous rivalries,* the bagpipers were waging battle with their arms and lungs, each playing in his own key and style with no thought for the dreadful cacophony produced by the assembled drones, each doing his utmost to drown out the melody and rhythm of his neighbour. In the midst of this musical chaos each quadrille of dancers remained staunchly at their posts, never confusing the music which they had paid for with that screeching two paces away, and never tapping their feet to the wrong rhythm, a true *tour de force* of ear and habitude. The greenwood echoed to no less haphazard sounds: some were singing at the top of their lungs, others were discussing business with great passion; some were drinking a friendly toast, others threatening to throw tankards at their neighbour's head, and the whole tableau was enhanced by two local constables making their rounds through the mobs with a fatherly air that sufficed to contain this peaceable population, who rarely come to blows whatever harsh words they may exchange.

The tight circle which had formed around the first dancers became even more crowded when the charming Rose opened the dance with the tall miller. They were the handsomest couple at the fête, and their exuberant but firm pace electrified all the others. The mill-wife could not help but remark on it to mother Bricolin, and she even dared to add that it was a tragedy if two such fine young people were not destined for each other.

'As for myself,' replied the old farm-wife, without a moment's hesitation, 'I'd not give two pins, if I was the mistress; for I'm sure your lad would make my granddaughter happier than she'll ever be with anybody else. I know Grand-Louis loves her; that's plain as day, though he's canny enough to say nought. But what can I do, my poor Marie! they think of nought but money in our house. I was daft enough to give all my wealth to my son, and since that day he pays me no more heed than if I was dead. If I'd done otherwise, I could marry Rose off in the way I think best, by giving her a dowry. But all I've got left is feelings, and that's valueless currency in our house.'

Despite the agility with which Rose passed from one group to another, attempting to avoid her mother and to find herself by sheer chance next to her admirer again, Mme Bricolin and her clique managed to join up with her and take up their posts around her. Her male cousins danced her off her feet, and Grand-Louis beat a prudent retreat, feeling that the slightest dispute would bring his temper to a boil. They had tried to bait him with wounding raillery, but the boldness of the Bricolins was no match for his calm blue gaze, his scornful calm, and his great height. When he had left, they mocked him to their heart's content, and Rose was amazed to hear her sisters, sisters-in-law, and numerous female cousins proclaim, in her presence, that this big lad looked a perfect fool, that he danced in ridiculous fashion, that he was puffed up with pretension, and that none of them would dance with him *for all the tea in China*. Rose had her pride. Her family had laboured so stubbornly to cultivate this fault in her that it was hardly surprising if she fell prey to it at intervals. They had done their utmost to corrupt and drag down her fresh and pleasant nature, and if they had not succeeded very well, that goes to show that there are some incorruptible spirits on whom the spirit of wickedness has little purchase. All the same, she was miserable at hearing her lover denigrated so thoroughly and bitterly. She lost her taste for dancing with him, and, pleading a headache, returned to the farm after having searched in vain for Marcelle, whose influence, she realized, would have restored her to calm and courage.

XXVII. THE FARM LABOURER'S COTTAGE

Marcelle waited for the miller at the bottom of the castle mound as he had advised. As the clock struck two, she saw him enter an overgrown garden, and signal to her to do likewise. After crossing this typical peasant garden, so badly maintained and thus so lush, green, and pleasant, she slipped though a gap in a hedge and entered the yard of one of the poorest cottages in the Vallée-Noire. This yard was about twenty feet by six, bounded at one end by the little house, at the other by the garden, and on both sides by outbuildings of rough timber and thatch, which served to house a few chickens, two sheep, and a goat, all the worldly wealth of the man who earns his bread from day to day and owns nothing, not even the wretched house he lives in and the narrow garden he hoes: he is the true country proletarian. The interior of the house was as impoverished as the exterior, and Marcelle was touched to see how the wife's house-proud courage had battled against the affliction of penury. There was not a single grain of dust on the uneven wood floor; the two or three sticks of furniture gleamed as if varnished; the little collection of earthenware dishes had been washed and placed carefully on the shelves. In the homes of most peasants in the Vallée-Noire the most genuine and utter misery is discreetly and bravely hidden under these conscientious habits of order and cleanliness. There, rural poverty is seen at its most affecting. One would find these paupers good companions. They inspire, not disgust, but interest and a sort of respect. It would require so little of the wealthy person's superfluity to end the bitterness of their lives, camouflaged by its appearance of poetic tranquillity!

This thought struck Marcelle to the quick when Piaulette came out to greet her, with a child in her arms and three others clinging to her apron; all of them in their Sunday best, fresh and clean. Piaulette (or Pauline) was still a young woman, and beautiful, although worn by the fatigue of motherhood and the absence of the necessaries of life. Never any meat, never any wine, not even vegetables for a woman who works and gives suck! None the less the children could have spared some of their robust health for Marcelle's son, and the mother had a smile of good nature and trust on her pale chapped lips.

'Enter our home and sit down, Madame,' she said, offering a rush-seated chair covered with a freshly laundered cloth of rough linen. 'The gentleman you're expecting to meet already came by, but when he didn't find you here he went off to have a look at the dancers, saying he'd be back right away. I'd like to offer you something while you wait! . . . Here are some plums I've just picked and some hazel-nuts. Go on, Grand-

Louis, will you take some fruit from my garden? I'd very much like to be able to offer you a glass of wine, but we don't grow grapes, as you know, and without you we wouldn't always have bread either.'

'So you are very poor?' asked Marcelle, slipping a piece of gold into the pocket of the little girl, who was touching her black silk dress with astonishment. 'And Grand-Louis, who is not enormously rich himself, comes to your assistance?'

'Him?' replied Piaulette. 'He's the best-hearted man the good Lord ever made! Without him we'd have died of hunger and cold these last three winters; but he gives us flour, wood, he lends us his horses to go on pilgrimage when one of us is sick . . .'

'That'll do, Piaulette, you'll make me look like a plaster saint,' the miller broke in. 'It'd be a fine thing for me to let a good worker like your husband starve!'

'A good worker!' exclaimed Piaulette, shaking her head. 'Poor fellow! Monsieur Bricolin tells everybody he's a shirker, as he's not strong.'

'Well, he does the best he can. I like men with a good will, so I'll always give him work.'

'That's why Monsieur Bricolin says you'll never be rich and that you must be cracked, taking on men in poor health.'

'Oh, so if nobody gives them any work, they ought to be left to starve? Fine reasoning!'

'But you know,' Marcelle added mournfully, 'what moral Monsieur Bricolin would deduce: *so much the worse for them*!'

'Mam'selle Rose is a kind girl,' replied Piaulette. 'She'd help the poor if she could, but she can't do any more than bring us a little white bread, on the sly, to make soup for my little boy. And I tell her not to, for if her mother caught her! oh! the awful woman! but that's the way of the world. There are evil folk, and good ones. Oh, here comes Monsieur Tailland! You won't have long to wait now.'

'Piaulette, remember what I told you,' said the miller with his finger on his lips.

'Oh!' she exclaimed. 'I'd have my tongue cut out before I'd say a word.'

'It's because, you see . . .'

'You don't have to give me the whys and wherefores, Grand-Louis. It's enough that you tell me to be silent. Come on, children,' she said to her three little ones who were playing on the threshold, 'let's go see the dancing for a bit.'

'This lady put a gold louis* in your little girl's pocket,' whispered Grand-Louis to her as she left. 'It's not a bribe to hush you up; she knows you can't be bribed. It's because she sees you're in need. Hold on to it, the child might lose it, and don't say thank you; the lady doesn't like compliments, that's why she kept her charity secret.'

M. Tailland was an honest man, very active for a *Berrichon*, a good businessman but a shade too much inclined towards the good life. He was fond of a comfortable armchair, a nice little snack, a good long meal, steaming hot coffee, and smooth roads without pot-holes for his cabriolet. None of these had he found at Blanchemont fair. But while cursing country pleasures, he had remained voluntarily for the entire day, to render services to some and do business with others. Within a quarter of an hour's conversation, he had speedily demonstrated to Marcelle the possibility, indeed the probability, of selling dear. But as for selling quickly and being paid in cash, he was not of the miller's opinion. 'Nothing happens quickly in our part of the world,' he said. 'All the same, it would be folly not to try to improve Bricolin's offer by 50,000 francs. I'll give it my all. If I haven't succeeded in a month's time, I might advise you, given your delicate position, to concede defeat. But I'll lay you a hundred to one that Bricolin, who's itching to be the lord of Blanchemont, will settle with you if you can pretend to be very ruthless, a savage but necessary trait, though one which I can see you're not well provided with, Madame. As for now, if you'll sign the power of instruction I've brought you, I'll be off, because I don't want to appear to be scheming against my colleague Monsieur Varin, whom the farmer would have advised you to instruct.'

Grand-Louis saw the lawyer out to the gate, and each went off his own way. It had been agreed that Marcelle would leave alone and last, a few minutes later, and that she would keep

the *huisseries** of the cottage closed, so that if any prying eye
saw their movements, the house would appear empty.

These *huis** of the cottage were stable doors, that is, a single
door cut in half, with the upper half acting as a window to
give air and light. In old-fashioned peasant dwellings glazed
casement windows, independent of the door, were unknown.
Piaulette's cottage had been built some fifty years before, for
people of some substance, whereas today even the poorest
folk, provided they live in a new house, will have French
windows and a door with a proper lock. In Piaulette's house
the stable door was fastened with a *coret*, a wooden bolt
inserted into a hole in the wall, from which come the terms
coriller and *décoriller*, that is, to close and to open.

When Marcelle had bolted herself in, she found herself in
the deepest darkness, and she wondered what sort of intellectual existence could be had by people who were too poor to
buy a candle, and who were obliged to go to bed at nightfall
in winter, or to huddle in the shadows during the day to stave
off the çold. 'I told myself that I was ruined, and so I believed,'
she said to herself, 'because I was obliged to leave my gilded
apartments, lined and hung with silks; but how many degrees
am I yet removed in the scale of social existences from this
pauper's life, which differs so little from that of the beasts! No
middle way between enduring the exigencies of the weather at
all hours, or burying oneself in the nothingness of mental
torpor, like a sheep in its pen! How does this unhappy family
occupy itself during the long winter evenings? Do they talk?
And what can they have to talk about but their misfortunes?
Ah! Lémor is right, I am still too rich to dare proclaim before
God that I have no reason to reproach myself.'

At length Marcelle's eyes grew accustomed to the darkness.
The badly fitting doors allowed a vague light to penetrate, and
it became brighter with each moment. Suddenly Marcelle
trembled: she was not alone in the cottage. But her second
shiver was not one of fear: Lémor was by her side. Unbe-
knownst to anyone, he had hidden behind the coffin-shaped
bed draped by serge curtains. He had found courage enough
to seek one last meeting with Marcelle, telling himself that he
must take his leave afterwards.

'Well, since you are here,' she said, masking, with a tender coquetry, the joy and emotion of her surprise, 'I shall say out loud what I was thinking just now. If we were reduced to inhabiting this cottage, would your love survive the enforced effort of the day and idleness of the night? Could you live deprived of your books, or unable to make use of them for lack of a drop of oil in the lamp, and of time during the hours when you would be busy in your work? After years of troubles and privations of all sorts, would you find this dwelling-place so picturesque in its delapidation, and the pauper's life so poetic in its simplicity?'

'I had precisely the same thoughts, Marcelle, and I was thinking of asking you the same thing. Would you love me if my utopias brought you to such a pass?'

'It seems to me that I would, Lémor.'

'Then why do you doubt me? Ah! you are not sincere in telling me that you would still love me.'

'I am not sincere?' sighed Marcelle, putting her hands in Lémor's. 'My friend, I wish to be worthy of you, that is why I forbear from romantic exhilaration, which can impel any-one, even a woman of the world, to affirm all, promise all, but to hold nothing sacred, and tell herself the next day, "Well, that was a pretty story." I do not pass a single day without interrogating my conscience in the strictest manner, and I believe that I am sincere when I tell you that I cannot envisage a situation, not even the horror of a dungeon, in which I should not love you to the point of suffering!'

'O Marcelle! My dear, great Marcelle! But why do you doubt me, then?'

'Because men's natures are different from ours. They are accustomed to other nourishment than tenderness and solici-tude. They require activity, work, the hope of being useful, not only to their family but to humanity.'

'But is it not therefore a duty to throw oneself voluntarily into the powerlessness of destitution?'

'Do we live, then, in a time when duties contradict each other? For no one can attain the power of the spirit without the light of instruction, or instruction without the power of money; and yet everything we enjoy, everything we acquire, everything we possess is at the expense of the man who can acquire nothing and possess nothing of celestial or material goods.'

'I am caught by my own utopias, Marcelle. Alas! What can I reply, except that we live in a time of huge and unavoidable inconsistency, when good hearts desire right but are obliged to accept wrong? There are myriad reasons for convincing ourselves, as do all the fortunate people in our time, that it is our duty to polish and prettify our own lives, so as to make ourselves active and powerful instruments to serve our fellows; that to sacrifice, debase, and annihilate one's self, as did the first Christians of the desert, is to neutralize a force, to extinguish a light sent by God for mankind's edification and salvation. But what arrogance there is in such reasoning, even if it seems correct in the mouths of certain enlightened and sincere men! It is an aristocratic way of thought. Let us conserve our wealth so that we can give alms, say the pious people of your caste. We are the ones, say the potentates of the Church, whom God has appointed for the enlightenment of men. We are the only ones, say the bourgeois supporters of democracy, who are sent to initiate the people into liberty! But only mark how little alms, enlightenment, and liberty these powerful people have given to the destitute! No! Private charity is impotent, modern liberalism is ignorant, the Church is inimical. I feel my spirit flag and my heart fail in my breast at the dilemma of how we can emerge from this labyrinth, those of us who desire truth and to whom society returns only lies and threats. Marcelle, Marcelle, let us love each other, so that God's spirit may not abandon us!'

'Let us love each other!' exclaimed Marcelle, throwing herself into her lover's arms; 'and do not leave me, do not abandon me to my own ignorance, Lémor, for you have forced me away from my narrow Catholic horizons, when I placidly put my trust in salvation, in the decision of my confessor above that of Christ, thinking I was excused from the full letter of Christianity because a priest had said to me, "That is a matter for the God of compromise." You have made me enter a vaster sphere, and now I shall no longer have a moment's peace if you abandon me without a guide in the pale dawn of truth.'

'But I know nothing myself,' replied Lémor disconsolately. 'I am the child of my time.* I do not possess the science of the future, I only know how to understand and comment on the past. Torrents of light have flowed by me, and like all things young and pure today, I ran towards these strong beams, which show up our errors but do not themselves give us truth. I hate evil, but I do not know what good consists in. I suffer, oh! I suffer, Marcelle, and only in you do I find the beautiful ideal that I should like to see reigning on earth. Oh! I love you with all the love that mankind repels, with all the devotion that society disdains, with all the tenderness that I cannot communicate to others, with all the charity that God has given me for you and them, but which you alone understand and sense as I intend it, when others are insensible or scornful. Let us love each other, then, without corrupting ourselves to side with the victors or lowering ourselves to be the vanquished. Let us love each other like two voyagers who cross the oceans to conquer a new world but do not know whether they will ever reach it. Let us love each other not so as to enjoy mutual egotism, as they call love, but to suffer together, to pray together, to seek together for what we two, poor birds lost in the storm, can do day by day to cast out this scourge that is dispersing our race, and bring together under our wings a few broken fugitives like us, full of grief and dread!'

Lémor was crying like a child as he pressed Marcelle to his heart. Marcelle, borne away by burning sympathy and enthusiastic respect, fell to her knees before him like a child in front of her father, crying:

'Save me, do not let me perish! You were here just now, you heard me consulting a man of wealth about affairs of wealth. I have allowed myself to be persuaded to struggle against poverty in order to rescue my son from ignorance and moral impotence; if you condemn me, if you can prove to me that my son will be better and nobler as a pauper, perhaps I shall have the dreadful courage to force him to suffer in body in order to strengthen his soul!'

'Oh, Marcelle!' exclaimed Lémor, forcing her to sit again and throwing himself in turn on his knees before her, 'you possess the force and resolution of the great saints or the proud martyrs of past times. But where are the waters of baptism to which we shall carry your child! The church of the poor has not yet been built, they live scattered lives, in the absence of all doctrine, following various whimsies: some are resigned by nature, others idolatrous through stupidity, still others fierce in vengefulness, some destroyed by every vice that licentiousness and brutalization can bring. We cannot ask the first beggar who passes by to place his hands on your son's head and bless him. The beggar may have suffered too much to be full of love, he may well be a robber! Let us keep your son out of the way of evil as much as we can, let us teach him the love of virtue and the need for enlightenment. Perhaps his generation will find it. Then it will be up to them to enlighten us, one day. Keep your wealth: how can I reproach you for it, when I see that your heart is entirely detached and that you regard it as deposited with you for later accounting to Heaven? Keep the little gold that remains to you. The good miller said the other day: "There are some hands that purify what they touch, just as there are some that dirty and corrupt everything." Let us love each other, let us love each other, and let us believe that God will enlighten us when the day comes. And now adieu, Marcelle, I see that you wish me to manifest that courage. I shall have it. Tomorrow I shall leave this gentle and lovely valley where I have lived so happily for two days, in spite of everything! In a year I shall return: whether I find you in a palace or a cottage, it will be for me to prostrate myself at your door and hang up my pilgrim's staff, never to take it down again.'

Lémor departed, and after a few moments Marcelle left the cottage in turn. But though she took precautions to hide her retreat, at the edge of the yard she found herself face to face with an ill-featured boy who was crouching behind a bush as if waiting for her to pass by. He looked at her fixedly with an air of effrontery, then, as if delighted to have surprised and recognized her, he set out at a trot in the direction of a mill situated on the Vauvre on the other side of the road. Marcelle, to whom this ugly face seemed familiar, remembered after some effort that this was the *patachon* who had recently led them astray in the Vallée-Noire and abandoned them in a swamp. This gingery head and ill-omened green eye caused her some disquiet, although she could think of no reason why the boy should want to keep track of her movements.

XXVIII. THE FAIR

The miller returned to the dance, hoping to find Rose relieved of her *mob of cousins*, as he put it. But Rose was sulking, put out with her relatives, the dancing, and perhaps herself as well. She felt guilty at not being strong enough to brazen out her family's jibes.

Her father had taken her aside that morning. 'Rose,' said he, 'your mother has forbidden you to dance with Grand-Louis from Angibault, but *I* forbid you to insult him this way. He's an honest lad, he wouldn't embarrass you; and besides, who could imagine anything between you and him? It's too *unproper*, and *in the light of day today* no one could possibly think that a peasant would dare press his suit with a girl of your station. So you may dance with him; we shouldn't humiliate our inferiors; we might need them one day, and it's best to keep them sweet, if it costs nothing.'

'But what if Mama scolds me?' blurted Rose, pleased with her father's permission but insulted by his motives.

'Your mother will hold her tongue. I've preached her a sermon,' boasted M. Bricolin, and in fact Mme Bricolin had not said a word. She did not dare to disobey her lord and master outright, which allowed her to be vicious in other people's company so long as she bowed before him. But since he had not seen fit to explain his position, she had no inkling of the importance he attached to keeping the miller as an ally in the diplomatic affair of acquiring the Blanchemont estate. She knew how to evade her husband's commands, and Grand-

Louis found her sarcastic condescension more aggravating than open warfare.

Annoyed not to find Rose, and counting on the protection of her father, whom he had seen returning to the farm, Grand-Louis went back there as well, hoping to find some pretext for conversing with him and divining the drift of his thought. But he was taken aback to find M. Bricolin talking heatedly in the farmyard with the miller of Blanchemont, whose mill was at the foot of the castle mound opposite Piaulette's cottage. Now only a few days earlier, M. Bricolin had broken off for good with this miller, who had enjoyed his custom for some time but who, he claimed, had shamefully robbed him of the full measure of grain. Whether guilty or innocent, this miller was sorry to lose the farm's business, and had sworn vengeance on Grand-Louis. He was on the look-out for some chance to do him harm, and now he had found one. The owner of his mill was that same M. Ravalard to whom the miller of Angibault had sold Marcelle's *calèche*. Puffed up with pride and eager to show off his carriage to his vassals, M. Ravalard had decided to inspect his properties at Blanchemont, but having no groom who could drive a pair of horses, he had engaged the red-headed *patachon*, who sometimes drove for hire and who claimed that he knew the highways and byways of the Vallée-Noire like the back of his hand. M. Ravalard had arrived the morning of the fair, after some difficulties but no accidents. He stabled his horses at the mill but did not put his carriage in the barn, for he wanted everyone to see it from the top of the castle mound and to know who owned it.

The sight of the gleaming *calèche* made M. Bricolin quite bilious: he detested M. Ravalard, his local rival in property. He walked down the path along the Vauvre to scrutinize and criticize the vehicle. Grauchon the miller, Grand-Louis's foe, came out to strike up a conversation with M. Bricolin, just as if they had never fallen out, and he deliberately niggled the farmer by pointing out how much higher a style his own master lived in. For the prosecution, M. Bricolin belittled the carriage, claimed that it was some cast-off old thing of the prefect's,* a ramshackle wheelbarrow, and that it might not leave the Vallée-Noire quite so spruce as when it arrived. For the defence, Grauchon lauded his landlord's taste and the merchandise's quality; then he revealed that it had belonged to Mme de Blanchemont and that Grand-Louis had negotiated the deal. The stupefied M. Bricolin heard all the details, including the fact that the miller of Angibault had persuaded M. Ravalard to acquire this luxury item by pointing out how furious M. Bricolin would be. Unfortunately this was all too true. On the way, M. Ravalard had chatted freely with the *patachon*. Hoping for a good tip and observing the townsman's intoxication with his new vehicle, the lad had talked about nothing else. Nothing could be handsomer, lighter, more pleasurable to drive than this carriage. It must have cost at least 4,000 francs, and it would be worth twice that. Pleasantly flattered by such naïve admiration, M. Ravalard had revealed to his guide all the details of the affair, and the driver had blabbed to Grauchon over lunch at the mill. Learning how much the miller of Blanchemont detested and envied Grand-Louis, he had spiked the account with venom, for the pleasure of gossiping and sounding like an authority, as well as on account of the bitterness he himself felt towards Grand-Louis, who had teased him cruelly for getting bogged down in the mire.*

Only a few moments after M. Bricolin had stalked off with a furrowed brow and a brooding air, Grauchon saw Grand-Louis and Marcelle go into Piaulette's cottage. This rendezvous smacked of guilty secrets, and Grauchon racked his brains to find another chance of doing down his rival. He set the *patachon* on sentry duty, and in an hour's time he had learned that Grand-Louis, a stranger who seemed to be the miller's new lad, the young lady of Blanchemont, and M. Tailland the lawyer had been closeted together in Piaulette's cottage; that they had all left separately after taking useless precautions against being noticed; all in all, that some plot was afoot, certainly something to do with money, because the notary was part of it. Grauchon was aware that this honest lawyer was the bugaboo of the Bricolins. Guessing at least half of the truth correctly, he hastened to make himself useful to Bricolin by telling him what he knew, and to offer his congratulations on the way in which the miller of Angibault was advancing the Bricolin fortunes. It was this report that Grand-Louis interrupted as he entered the farmyard.

In any other circumstances our honest miller would have faced down his accuser and forced him to justify himself. But when he saw Bricolin turn his back on him rudely and Grauchon look up at him with an impudent shifty air, he wondered with some concern what serious matter could have brought together these two men who, the evening before, wouldn't have *given each other the time of day*, as he put it, even if they'd met nose to nose in the narrowest alleyway in town. Grand-Louis had no inkling what was going on, or whether he was the object of this ostentatious snub; but something weighed on his conscience. He had tried to play games with M. Bricolin, pretending to negotiate with him for the sake of one or two dances with Rose, instead of rebuffing him proudly when he offered bribes to advance his interests at the expense of Marcelle's. Grand-Louis had left him with high expectations and deliberately tricked him to punish him for his outrageous offer.

'Well, I deserved to be found out,' he thought to himself. 'He that sups with the devil had best have a long spoon! My mother always told me that it was a bad habit countryfolk had, suchlike scheming, and I fell foul of it too. If I'd shown this blasted farmer I'm an honest man, as I am at heart, he'd have hated me for it, but I'd have had some respect off him, and maybe he'd have feared me more than he will now, when he's found out my weasel words! Grand-Louis, old mate, you've been a prize ass. Every wicked deed is a piece of foolishness; better hope you don't suffer too much for yours!'

In a state of torment, fear, and self-loathing, he went back to rejoin his mother on the castle mound, to offer to drive her back to Angibault. Vespers had finished, and the mill-wife had already left with some neighbours, having told Jeannie that his master should amuse himself a little longer but return at a reasonable hour.

Grand-Louis could take no pleasure in this authorization. Prey to a thousand anxieties, he wandered about till sunset, taking no pleasure in anything, waiting for Rose to reappear or for her father to announce what he intended to do.

Nightfall brings the best times for the village folk on the day of a fair. The constables, weary with doing nothing, begin saddling their horses; the townspeople and the folk from distant villages climb into their assorted vehicles and set off for home, so as to avoid bad roads at night. The pedlars pack up their wares, and the *curé* goes off contentedly to dine with some colleague who has come to see the dancing, sighing, perhaps, that he cannot partake of this guilty pleasure. Only the local people remain in possession of the spot, together with those few musicians who have not had a successful day, and who compensate by staying later. Now everyone knows each other, and once things have got started again, they make up for the lost time when they were separated, observed, and perhaps teased, by outsiders; for in the Vallée-Noire, anyone who lives beyond the radius of a league* is an outsider. Now all the little population set to dancing, even the elderly relatives and friends who would have been embarrassed to do so in broad daylight, even the portly barmaid from the inn who had exhausted herself serving her customers since dawn, but adjusted her smoke-stained apron and jigged with super-annuated grace; even the little hunchback tailor, who would have made the girls blush if he had hugged them earlier, but opined, grinning from ear to ear, that *all cats are black at night*.

Tired of sulking, Rose rediscovered her pleasure in these diversions, once all her relatives had left. But before returning to the fête, she wanted to see the madwoman, who had slept the whole day through, under the eye of plump Chounette. She tiptoed into her bedchamber and found her wide awake, sitting on her bed with a pensive, almost calm air. For the first time in a very long while, Rose made bold to touch her hand and ask her how she was keeping; for the first time in twelve years, the madwoman did not pull her hand away and turn her face moodily to the wall.

'My dear sister, my good Bricoline,' repeated Rose, emboldened and overjoyed, 'are you feeling better?'

'I feel quite well,' replied the madwoman abruptly. 'When I woke up, I'd found what I've been looking for *these fifty-four years*.'

'And what have you been looking for, dear?'

'*I have been looking for a bit of tenderness!*' answered Bricoline in a hollow voice, placing her finger on her lips with an air of mystery. 'I looked everywhere: in the old castle, in the garden, on the banks of the stream, down the sunken track, and most particularly, in the hunting-park. But it's not to be found there, Rose, and you're searching for it in vain yourself. They've hidden it in a great vault under this house, and we'll only find it under the ruins. I realized that when I was sleeping, because I think when I sleep, and I'm always racking my brains. So be of good cheer, Rose, and now leave me alone. Tonight, no later, I'll find my bit of tenderness, and I'll give you some. And then we'll be rich! *In the light of day today*, like the gaoler says that they've put here to keep us locked up, we're so poor that nobody will have us. But tomorrow, Rose, no later, we'll both be married, me to Paul, who's now the king of Algiers; and you to that man who carries sacks of wheat about and keeps looking at you. I'll make him my prime minister, and his job will be to burn. over a nice slow fire, that gaoler who always says the same thing and who's made us suffer so much. Hush, now, don't tell a soul about this. It's a great secret, and the fate of the African campaign* depends on it.'

This bizarre speech alarmed Rose considerably, and she dared say no more to her sister, for fear of inflaming her. She refused to leave her side until the arrival of the doctor, who was expected any moment, and she quite forgot her desire to dance, sitting pensively by the madwoman's bedside with her head lowered, her hands crossed in her lap, and her heart full of profound sadness. The two sisters formed a striking contrast, one so terribly ravaged by her suffering and so repulsive in her self-neglect, the other so carefully attired and glowing with freshness and beauty; yet there was some resemblance in their features, and both were now sad and serious, nursing, to different degrees, their resentment at having been crossed in love. Of the two, the madwoman was less cast down, with her wandering mind hatching fantastic hopes and projects.

The doctor arrived promptly. He examined the madwoman with the apathy of a man who has nothing more to suggest, nothing more to try, in a case which has long been hopeless.

'Her pulse is steady,' he pronounced. 'There is no change'.

'Pardon me, doctor,' whispered Rose, pulling him to one side. 'There is some change since yesterday evening, actually. She screams, she sobs, she talks differently than usual. I assure you, some great transformation is going on inside her. This evening she's been trying to get her thoughts together and express them, even if they are delirious ideas. Is this better or worse than her usual state of dejections? What is your opinion?'

'I have no opinion,' replied the doctor. 'One might expect anything in these cases, but one can predict nothing with certainty. Your family was wrong not to make the necessary sacrifices to put her in one of those establishments where men of science specialize in these exceptional cases.* I never claimed I could cure her, and now I think even the greatest practitioners would be hard pressed to do so. It is too late. I only wish to see her mania remain confined to silence and solitude, not degenerate into fury. So say nothing to her, do not encourage her to talk, for she may develop dangerous fixations.'

'This is dreadful!' exclaimed Rose. 'I dare not contradict you, but it's so terrible for her, always living alone, with everyone horrified by her! Now that she seems to be looking for some pity and sympathy, must we repay her need for affection with icy silence? Do you know what she just said to me? She told me that ever since her madness began (she says that was fifty-four years ago), she's been searching high and low for a bit of tenderness. Poor girl, one thing is certain, she's not found it!'

'And did she say that in a reasonable manner?'

'I'm afraid not, she jumbled together all sorts of frightening ideas and dreadful threats.'

'You can see, then, these outpourings of delirium are doing her more harm than good. Leave her alone, follow my advice, and if she wants to go out, make sure that no one impedes her usual wanderings. This is the only means of ensuring that yesterday's crisis does not recur.'

Rose obeyed regretfully; but Marcelle, who had retired to the bedchamber in order to write a letter and had found her companion sad and preoccupied, persuaded her to go out for a little distraction, promising that at the first cry or the first symptom of agitation from her sister she would send little Fanchon with the news. In any case Mme Bricolin was also busy in the house, and the grandmother urged Rose to come and dance one more bourrée for her before the *assemblée* ended.

'For you must know,' she said, 'I count every fair day now, because I know I may not see next year's. I want to see you dancing and enjoying yourself today, else I'll have sad memories, and that'll do me no good.'

Rose had not taken three paces on to the castle mound before Grand-Louis appeared at her side. 'Mademoiselle Rose,' he asked, 'has your papa told you something unpleasant about me?'

'No. In fact this morning he practically ordered me to dance with you.'

'But . . . since this morning?'

'I've hardly seen him; he's not said a word to me. He seems very preoccupied with his affairs.'

'Come then, Louis,' said the grandmother, 'aren't you going to ask Rose to dance? Can't you see she's hankering to?'

'Is that so, Mam'selle Rose?' enquired the miller as he took the girl's hand. 'Would it please you to dance one more time with me this evening?'

'Oh, I don't mind dancing,' she replied with teasing nonchalance.

'If you want to dance with some other fellow,' exclaimed Louis as he pressed Rose's hand to his thumping heart, 'you only have to say the word and I'll go find him for you!'

'Oh, does that mean you'd rather not be the victim?' replied the malicious girl.

'Is that what you think?' cried the miller in a transport of love. 'Well, you'll soon see whether my legs have gone to sleep!'

And he led, or almost carried, her out into the very middle of the dancers, where in a moment's time, forgetting their worries and constraints, they were gliding lightly along the grass, holding each other's hands a little more tightly than was strictly required for the bourrée.

But M. Bricolin had been waiting for this moment to maximize Louis's humiliation in front of all the village. The intoxicating bourrée had not yet finished when he shoved through the crowd of dancers and interrupted the bagpipe with a sign of his hand. 'Daughter!' he barked. 'You're an honest, respectable sort of a girl; so don't you ever dance again with folk you don't know the measure of!'

'Mademoiselle Rose is dancing with me, Monsieur Bricolin!' exclaimed Grand-Louis hotly.

'And that, my lad, is why I forbid it, just as I forbid you to ask her, or talk to her, or set foot over my threshold, or . . .' The farmer's thundering voice was suffocated by this sudden excess of eloquence, and while he was stammering in fury, Grand-Louis cut him short.

'Monsieur Bricolin,' he exclaimed, 'you're the master in your own house, so you've the right to order your daughter about, I suppose, or to keep me out of your house, but you haven't got any right to insult me in public without giving me a proper explanation.'

'I've got the right to do anything I like,' shouted Bricolin in exasperation, 'and that includes telling an upstart what I think of him!'

'Just who are you saying that to, Monsieur Bricolin?' roared Grand-Louis, his eyes flashing; for although he had told himself at the start of this scene, 'Well, here we go, I'm going to get what I deserve, at least a bit,' he could no longer bear these insults patiently.

'I'll say it to whoever I damn well please!' boomed Bricolin majestically, though suddenly nervous.

'Oh well then, tell it to the marines!' replied Grand-Louis, trying to laugh it off.

'Will you look at this lunatic!' called out M. Bricolin, drawing the group of curious spectators closer to him. 'Wouldn't you say he's trying to insult me because I won't let him talk to my daughter? Haven't I got the right?'

'Oh yes, you've every right,' replied the miller, forcing himself to draw away, 'but not without telling me why, and I'll wait till you and I have both calmed down before I call on you about that.'

'Oh, so you're threatening me, you wretch?' screamed Bricolin in alarm. Taking the onlookers as his witnesses, as if to invoke the aid of his clients and servants against a dangerous man, he sputtered, 'He's threatening me!'

'Heaven give me strength, Monsieur Bricolin,' shrugged Grand-Louis, 'you're not listening to a word I say.'

'And I don't want to! Why should I listen to an ungrateful wretch and a false friend? Oh yes,' he added, observing that this reproach had caused the miller more chagrin than anger, 'I tell you you're a false friend, a Judas!'

'A Judas? Well, hardly, since I'm not a Jew, Monsieur Bricolin.'

'How do I know that?' shrilled the farmer, growing bolder now that his adversary seemed to be weakening.

'All right, that's enough,' replied Grand-Louis in a tone of voice which stunned M. Bricolin into silence. 'No more insults; I respect your age, I respect your mother and daughter, more than I do you, perhaps; but I won't be responsible for myself if you get too carried away. If I wanted to, I could show that you're guilty of a great crime, even if I am guilty of a little one. But let's say no more, take my word for it, Monsieur Bricolin, we might be led further than we want. I'll talk to you later and you can listen to me then.'

'You're not coming to my house! If you do, I'll have you thrown out like a dog!' yelped M. Bricolin, once he saw that the miller, loping along at a fast clip, was well out of earshot. 'You're a cur, you've tricked me, you've plotted against me!'

Rose had stood pale and frozen with fear, hanging on to her father's arm; but now she was overwhelmed by a force of which she would not have thought herself capable a moment earlier.

'Papa,' she said, pulling him away from the crowd, 'you're angry, and you're saying things you don't mean. You shouldn't hang out your dirty linen in public. What you've done is very embarrassing for me, you don't seem to care about me.'

'About you? You?' blurted the stupefied farmer, overcome by his daughter's bravado. 'I've done nothing to shame you, it's no concern of yours. I'd allowed you to dance with this wretch, I thought that was all plain and above board, every-one did. I had no idea he was a scoundrel, a traitor, a . . . a . . .'

'As you like, Papa, but that will do for now,' exclaimed Rose, tugging his arm like a rebellious child. And she managed to drag him away towards the farm.

XXIX. THE TWO SISTERS

Mme Bricolin had not expected to see her family back so soon. Her husband had sent her home without telling her that he intended to make a scene; he did not want her screeching to detract from the majesty of his public role. So when she saw him crimson-faced with rage, panting, muttering under his breath; arm in arm with a very agitated and anxious Rose, whose eyes were swimming with irrepressible tears; both followed by the grandmother, trotting along with her hands gripped together in a nervous fashion: she drew back in sur-prise, lifted her candle up to the height of their faces, and barked, 'What is it then? What's happened?'

'What's happened is that my son's gone daft, and done a great wrong,' answered mother Bricolin, dropping on to a chair.

'Oh yes, oh yes, the same old song from the old woman,' sputtered the farmer, his anger somewhat strengthened by the sight of his better half. 'That'll do from you! Supper ready? Well Rose, are you hungry?'

'No, Father,' said Rose tonelessly.

'Oh, so I'm the one that's robbed you of your appetite?'

'Yes, Father.'

'That's a reproach, is it?'

'Yes, Father, so it is.'

'Come now, Rose!' exclaimed the farmer, who was as bene-volent towards his daughter as any man might be, but now found her somewhat rebellious, for the first time. 'I don't much like the way you're taking this. You know what I reckon, from your long face? or would you rather not know what I think?'

'Oh go on, go on, Father. Do tell me what you think; if you're wrong, it's my duty to defend myself.'

'What I say, Daughter, is that it'd be a poor thing for you to take that rascally miller's part, and that I'll break my stick over his back one fine day, if he comes sniffing round my house.'

'Father,' exclaimed Rose with a certain fire, 'I'll make bold to tell you, yes, even if you break your stick over *my* back, that all this is heartless and unfair; that you have humiliated me, as the instrument of your public vengeance, as if I were responsible for whatever wrongs you have or have not endured; and, finally, that all this hurts me and my grandmother a good deal, as you can plainly see.'

'Yes, yes, this hurts me to the quick, and it makes my blood boil, too,' said mother Bricolin with her frank manner, underneath which there was so much gentle kindness (and in this respect Rose was much like her, having a lively turn of phrase and an easy-going temperament). 'It *wounds my soul*,' the old woman went on, 'to see you abuse an honest lad that I love almost like one of my own, the more so as I've been friends with his mother and all his kin these sixty years... All good people, in truth! and Grand-Louis's never brought them any shame!'

'Oh, so it's that fine handsome gentleman who's making your mother grumble and your daughter cry?' Mme Bricolin asked her husband. 'Just look at her snivel! Oh yes, haven't you got us into a pretty pickle, Monsieur Bricolin, favouring that great donkey like you've done! Well, he's paid you back nicely! It's shameful, it is, your mother and daughter are taking his part against you, bawling for him as if . . . as if . . . Good Lord! I can't say no more, it'd make me blush.'

'Oh go on, Mother, say what you like,' exclaimed Rose, provoked beyond endurance. 'Since everyone else is busy humiliating me today, why shouldn't you too? I'm quite ready to say what *I* think, if you want to interrogate me seriously and sincerely about my feelings for Grand-Louis.'

'And just what are your feelings, Mademoiselle?' boomed the infuriated farmer in his most impressive tones. 'Tell us quickly, if you'd be so good, since your tongue's itching to speak.'

'My feelings are those of a sister and a friend,' replied Rose, 'and none of you can alter them.'

'A sister! The sister of a miller!' sneered M. Bricolin in a falsetto, imitating Rose, 'A friend! The friend of a peasant! Oh, that's a nice way to talk, quite proper for a girl like you! Devil take me, *in the light of day today*, if all the girls haven't gone stark staring mad! Rose, you're talking like they do in the asylum!'

At that moment plangent cries echoed in the madwoman's bedchamber; Mme Bricolin shivered, and Rose went as pale as death.

'Listen to me, father!' she exclaimed, gripping M. Bricolin's arm with some force. 'Listen carefully, and then you may laugh at young girls' madness! Then you may laugh about asylums, though you seem to forget that *a girl of our station* can love a poor man to such an extent that she slips into a state worse than death!'

'There, look, she admits it, she's telling all the world!' shrilled Mme Bricolin, torn between fury and despair. 'She's in love with that clodhopper, and she threatens us that she'll soon start raving like her sister!'

'Rose! Rose!' bellowed M. Bricolin, thunderstruck. 'Be quiet! And as for you, Thibaude, go and look after Bricoline,' he added in an imperious tone.

Mme Bricolin went out. Rose remained standing, her features in disorder, terrified by what she had just said to her father.

'Daughter, you're poorly,' stumbled M. Bricolin distractedly. 'You've got to get your good wits back.'

'Oh yes, you're right, Father, I'm not well,' sobbed Rose, bursting into tears and throwing herself into her father's arms.

Although M. Bricolin was taken aback, it was not in his nature to act tenderly. He patted Rose like a child to be calmed, not a daughter to be loved. He was smug about her beauty, her wit, and, most of all, the wealth he intended to settle on her. He would have preferred that she turn out ugly, stupid, wealthy, and enviable, than virtuous, poor, and pitiable.

'Little one,' he said to her, 'you've lost your usual common sense tonight. Go to bed, and when you wake up, the miller and your fine friendship will have left your head. True enough, his sister was your nurse, but good God! we paid her well enough. All right, the lad was your friend when you were children, but he was our servant, and keeping you amused was his job. Now that I'm minded to toss him out, *in the light of day today*, it's your duty to tell me I'm right.'

'Oh, Father!' wept Rose, still in the farmer's arms. 'You'll take that order back, I know. You'll let him give an account of himself, he's not guilty, that can't be, and you'll never make me humiliate my old childhood friend, the son of the good mill-wife who loves me so much!'

'Rose, this is starting to vex me considerably,' Bricolin barked as he wrenched himself away from his daughter's embrace. 'It's damn tomfoolery, making such a to-do over my throwing out some barefoot tramp. Go on, give me a bit of peace, leave off now. You can hear your poor sister howling, don't spend so much time worrying about a stranger when we've got trouble enough in our own house.'

'Oh, if you think I don't hear my sister's voice,' blurted Rose with a frightening look on her face, 'if you think her cries say nothing to my soul, you're wrong, Father! I hear them well enough, and think about them all too much!'

Rose walked out unsteadily, towards her sister's room. They heard her fall on to the hall floor. The two Bricolin ladies ran to her side in consternation. Rose had fainted and lay there, deadly still.

In haste they carried Rose into her bedroom, where Marcelle sat writing as she waited for her, having no idea of the tempest surrounding her poor friend. She lavished the most tender care on her, and was the only one who had enough presence of mind to send into the village to see if the doctor was still there. He came and found the young girl in a state of violent nervous contraction. Her limbs were rigid, her teeth clenched, her lips blue. She regained consciousness after his treatment, but her pulse oscillated between terrifying lethargy and ardent energy. Fever burned in her great black eyes, and she spoke agitatedly, to no one in particular. Marcelle was struck by hearing her repeat the name of Grand-Louis several times over, and she managed to evict the frightened parents so as to look after Rose on her own. Meanwhile the doctor took care of the elder Mlle Bricolin, who was beginning to present symptoms of mania like those of the previous evening.

'My dear Rose,' Marcelle soothed her, taking her in her arms, 'you are grief-stricken, that is the cause of your malady. Calm yourself; tomorrow you can tell me all that has happened, and I will do anything in the world to end your misery. Who can say whether I may not succeed?'

'Oh, you are an angel,' sighed Rose, sinking on to Marcelle's shoulder. 'But there's nothing you can do for me. Everything is lost, it's all broken off. Louis has been thrown out of the house; my father was his protector this morning, but tonight he hates him and curses him. I am so miserable!'

'So you do love him?' exclaimed Marcelle in astonishment.

'Of course I love him!' blurted Rose. 'How could I not love him? How could you doubt it?'

'Only yesterday, Rose, you said something different.'

'Oh quite possibly, I would have gone on saying something different if they hadn't persecuted me, if they hadn't pushed me beyond endurance as they did today. Just imagine,' she said in a rushed manner, her burning forehead in her hands, 'they tried to humiliate him in front of me, to drag him down in my eyes, because he's poor and has the gall to love me! This morning when they were teasing and mocking him, I was a coward; I was angry with them but I wasn't brave enough to show it. I let them vilify him and didn't come to his defence, I was almost embarrassed by him. And then I went home, suddenly I had a terrible headache, and I asked myself whether I'd ever have the strength to brave all these insults for his sake. I told myself I didn't want to love him any more, but then I felt as if I was going to die, as if this house, which I always thought was beautiful because I grew up here and I was happy here, as if it had gone all black, filthy, sad, and ugly, like it seems to you, I'm sure. I felt like I was in a prison, and last night, when my poor sister said to me, in her ravings, that our father was a turnkey who kept an eye on us so as to make us suffer, there was a moment when I felt as mad as she, and I could see everything my sister saw. Oh! that was so painful! And when I regained my senses, I realized that without my poor Louis there would be nothing pleasant or even bearable in my life. It's because I love him that I've been able to accept all my miseries so gaily, my mother's terrible moods, my father's hard-heartedness, the burden of our wealth, the way it only creates misery and jealousy all around us, and the terrible maladies that struck down my sister and my grandfather, all those years ago. All that seemed completely hideous to me when I imagined myself alone, not daring to love him any more, and forced to endure all that without the consolation of being loved by someone who's handsome, high-minded, wonderful, whose attachment would make up for everything else. Oh, it's impossible! I love him, I have no desire to cure myself of that any more. But I'll die of it, you know, Madame Marcelle; they've thrown him out, and no matter how I suffer, they won't take pity on me. I won't be able to see him any more; if I speak to him secretly, they'll scold me and jeer at me till I go out of my mind . . . My poor head, I thought it was so solid and sensible, and now it hurts so much I think it'll break . . . Oh, I won't let myself become like my sister, Madame Marcelle, never fear! I'd rather kill myself, if I thought I was developing her sickness. But I won't, will I? . . . And yet when I hear her scream, it rips my heart in two, it breathes fire and ice into my blood. A sister, a pitiful sister! she's got the same blood as me, and I feel her illness in my body, as well as in my soul! Oh, Lord, Madame, oh, God, can't you hear her! Listen! it's no good their shutting the doors, I can still hear her, I'll always hear her! . . . She's suffering so much, she still loves him, she's crying out for him! my sister, oh my poor friend, I knew her when she was so beautiful, so good, so kind, so gay, and now she's howling like a wolf!'

Poor Rose burst into sobs, and little by little the tears which had long been stifled, by a violent effort of will, became inarticulate cries and then piercing screams. Her features altered, her eyes seemed to wander and return, her tightly clenched hands gripped Marcelle's arm in a death-like vice, and at last she buried her face in her pillow, wailing in a heart-rending manner, imitating, as if by a fatal and irresistible instinct, the terrible cries of her unhappy sister.

Overwhelmed by this sinister echo, the family left the bedside of the elder sister for the younger's. The doctor came running, and since he was aware of what had transpired, he did not simply attribute this violent attack of nerves to the impression produced on Rose's imagination by her elder sister's lunacy. He succeeded in calming her; but when he found himself alone again with the Bricolins, he spoke to them severely: 'For a long while you have imprudently exposed this young girl to a very sad spectacle indeed. It would be opportune to relieve her of it, to send the elder girl to a lunatic asylum and to marry the younger one off, so as to lighten the melancholy which may otherwise seize hold of her.'

'What do you mean, Monsieur Lavergne!' exclaimed Mme Bricolin. 'All we want to do is marry her off! She's had ten chances, and even today her cousin Honoré was here, he's a very good match, one day he'll come into a fortune of 100,000 écus. If she was willing, he'd ask nothing better, and nor would we, but she won't hear of it; she turns down every man we present to her!'

'Perhaps that is because you have not presented the young man of her taste to her,' replied the doctor. 'I know nothing of it, and have no desire to intrude in your affairs; but you are well aware of the reason for the other one's illness, and I advise you most strongly to conduct yourselves in a different fashion with this one.'

'Oh, not this one!' spluttered M. Bricolin. 'That'd be too much, a beautiful girl like that, eh, Doctor?'

'The other was also a beautiful girl; or have you forgotten?'

'But really, Monsieur,' exclaimed Mme Bricolin, more irritated than shamefaced at the doctor's frank comments, 'do you actually think my daughter isn't right in the head? The other one's sickness was just an accident, she never got over the death of her lover . . .'

'Whom you would not allow her to marry!'

'Monsieur, you know nothing about it; maybe we'd have let her, if we'd known it'd turn out so ill. But Rose, Monsieur, she's a level-headed girl, a reasonable girl, and God be praised, this isn't an illness that runs in the family. There've never been any lunatics in the Bricolin family, as far as I know, nor in the Thibaut family! I've always had a strong, cool head myself; I've got other daughters like me; I've no idea why Rose shouldn't be like the rest.'

'You may take it as you will,' replied the doctor, 'but I tell you that you are playing with fire if you deny your youngest daughter's inclinations. She has a nervous temperament much like that of the eldest. And furthermore, although madness may not be hereditary, it is contagious . . .'

'Oh, very well! we'll send the other to a hospital, we'll make up our minds to do that, no matter what it costs,' blurted Mme Bricolin.

'And you mustn't do anything to provoke Rose, do you hear, wife?' said the farmer, pouring himself a good full glass of wine as a distraction from his domestic woes. 'There are some actors in La Châtre, we'll take her to see the comedy. We'll buy her a new dress, two if she likes. Hang it, we've got enough money, we don't need to refuse her anything! . . .'

M. Bricolin was interrupted by Mme de Blanchemont, who requested a private interview with him.

XXX. THE CONTRACT

'Monsieur Bricolin,' Marcelle began as she followed the farmer into a sort of untidy dark closet where his papers were piled up pell-mell with various agricultural implements and seed samples. 'Are you disposed to hear me out in a calm and peaceful fashion?'

The farmer had drunk a good deal to give himself courage before sallying forth to insult Grand-Louis on the green. When he came back he drank some more, to calm and refresh himself. In the third instance he had drunk to charm away the gloom spreading all about him and to drive off the dark notions gaining power over him. The sight of his blue-flowered earthenware jug, which sat permanently on the kitchen table, usually kept him in good countenance and helped him resist the first torpor of intoxication. When he found himself alone with the lady of Blanchemont, deprived of the assistance of his white wine, he was ill at ease. Automatically he felt round the writing-table for the glass that wasn't there. As he made to offer her a chair, he knocked two over. Marcelle noticed that his legs, his red face, his tongue and brain were the worse for drink, and despite the disgust which this accentuation of his characteristics inspired in her, she resolved to initiate a frank exchange with him, reminding herself of the proverb *In vino veritas.**

Realizing that he had barely heard her initial words, she returned to the attack. 'Monsieur Bricolin,' she said, 'I had the pleasure of enquiring whether you were disposed to listen calmly and benevolently to a rather delicate request I have to make of you.'

'What's the matter, Madame?' answered the farmer in a dull ungracious voice. He resented Marcelle greatly but was too weighed down with troubles to have it out with her at the moment.

'The matter, Monsieur Bricolin,' she continued, 'is that you have expelled the miller of Angibault from your house, and I should like to know the reason for your dissatisfaction with him.'

Bricolin was astounded at this open style of questioning. In Marcelle's manner there was a fearless sincerity which he always found difficult, and particularly now that he did not enjoy the free exercise of his faculties. Overpowered by a will superior to his own, he did the opposite of what he would have done if sober: he told the truth.

'I'm sure you know the reason for my dissatisfaction, Madame!' he replied. 'I've no need to tell you.'

'Am I the cause?'

'You? No. I'm not accusing you. You're thinking of your own interests, fair enough, like I do of mine . . . but I reckon it's a scummy trick to pretend to be my friend and all the while be giving you advice against me. Fine, listen to his advice, profit from it, pay for it, no doubt, and you won't go lacking. But as for me, I'll throw out the enemy who tries to do me down. That's all there is to it! . . . So much the worse for them as don't like it . . . I'm master in my own house; because, here we are, you see, Madame de Blanchemont, what I'm telling you is, every man for himself! Your interests are your interests, they're yours, my interests are my interests, they're mine . . . The scum of the earth is the scum of the earth . . . *In the light of day today* everybody looks out for himself. I'm master in my own house, and in this household, you've got your interests like I've got mine; if you're looking for allies against me, you won't go wanting, I can tell you . . .'

And M. Bricolin continued in this vein for ten minutes, fastidiously repeating himself without noticing it, forgetting the hundred previous times he had said exactly the same thing.

Marcelle, who had rarely seen a drunken man at close quarters and had never conversed with one, listened to him in astonishment. She asked herself whether he had suddenly degenerated into imbecility, and realized with dismay that the fate of Rose and her lover depended on a man who was hard-hearted and opinionated when sober, unhearing and stupid when wine had tempered his uncouthness. She allowed him to keep going over the same unattractive ground for some time, but when she saw that this could go on until sleep overcame him in his chair, she tried to sober him up by tugging on his most sensitive cord.

'Tell me, Monsieur Bricolin,' she broke in, 'you do very much want to purchase Blanchemont? And if I were to accept the price you offered, would you still be out of sorts?'

With an effort Bricolin lifted his dilated eyelids and stared at Marcelle, who, for her own part, was gazing at him with attention and confidence. Bit by bit the eye of the farmer cleared; his jowly distended face seemed to tauten; and one might have said that a veil descended over his features. He rose and made several turns round the room, as if to test his legs and collect his thoughts. He feared that he might be dreaming. When he sat down again opposite Marcelle, his attitude was firm and his complexion almost pale.

'Pardon me, *Madame la baronne*,' he said to her, 'what was it you just did me the honour of saying?'

'I was saying,' continued Marcelle, 'that I might conceivably let you have my land for 250,000 francs, if . . .'

'If what?' snapped Bricolin, with a lynx-like eye.

'If you promise me not to make your daughter miserable.'

'My daughter! What's my daughter got to do with it?'

'Your daughter is in love with the miller of Angibault; she is dangerously ill, she might lose her mind like her sister. Do you hear me, do you understand me, Monsieur Bricolin?'

'I hear you but I don't understand a thing. I can see perfectly well my daughter's got some sort of fancy in her head. That sort of thing changes from one day to the next, same way it began. But why do you take such an interest in my daughter?'

'What does it matter to you? Since you do not appreciate that one may experience friendship and compassion for a charming girl who is unhappy, perhaps at least you understand the advantages of being the owner of Blanchemont?'

'You're playing with me, *Madame la baronne*. You're mocking me. Today you spoke with my greatest enemy, Tailland the lawyer, he must have told you to make me dance to your tune!'

'Although he has no animosity towards you, he gave me information necessary to my position. Thus I know that I could find a buyer at very short notice, and that I *could* make you dance to my tune, as you put it.'

'And was it the miller of Angibault who got this fine adviser for you, without telling me?'

'What do you know about it? You might be mistaken. Furthermore, any explanation is unnecessary; if I am content with your offer, what does the rest matter to you?'

'But the rest . . . the rest, that's that my daughter will marry a miller!'

'As your father was, before he became tenant farmer to my family.'

'But he made money, and *in the light of day today*, I'm in a position to get a son-in-law who can help me buy your land.'

'To buy it for 300,000 francs, perhaps more?'

'So that's your condition, *skinny cat gnome*?* You want the miller to marry my daughter? What's your interest in all this?'

'I have already told you: friendship, the pleasure of making people happy, all sorts of things that will seem bizarre to you; but to each his own.'

'I know perfectly well, the late baron, your husband, he'd have paid 10,000 francs for a bad horse, 40,000 for a bad woman, if he'd a mind to. Those are the sorts of things a nob gets up to; but you can understand it, it was for himself alone, he got pleasure out of it; but making a sacrifice purely for somebody else's pleasure, for people that think nothing of you, that you hardly know . . .'

'So you advise me not to do it?'

'I advise you,' said Bricolin hastily, taken aback by his own clumsiness, 'to do whatever you like! There's no accounting for tastes! though all the same! . . .'

'But all the same, you distrust me, that much is clear. Do you think me insincere in my propositions?'

'Holy Mother, Madame! what kind of guarantee have I got? This is a queen's fancy, you might drop it tomorrow.'

'And that is why you should make haste to take me at my word.'

'She's right, God knows,' said M. Bricolin to himself. 'In her madness, she's cooler than me.' 'Well then, *Madame la baronne*,' he said, 'what guarantee will you give me?'

'A written agreement.'

'Signed?'

'Most certainly.'

'And as for me, I'm to promise that I'll marry my daughter to your protégé?'

'To begin with, you will give me your word of honour.'

'Honour? And then what?'

'And then you will immediately go and give your word to Rose, in the presence of your mother, your wife, and myself.'

'My word of honour, eh? So Rose really is head over heels?'

'Well, do you consent?'

'If that's all it'll take to give the little girl pleasure! . . .'

'There is one thing more . . .'

'What?'

'You must keep your word.'

The farmer's face altered. 'Keep my word ... keep my word!' he shouted. 'You doubt it?'

'No more than you doubt mine; and since you demand to have mine in writing, I shall ask the same of you.'

'In writing? How?'

'A promise of marriage which I shall dictate to you myself, which Rose will sign, and which you will sign as well.'

'And suppose Rose demands a dowry of me after all that?'

'She will renounce it, in writing.'

'That'll be a great saving,' thought the farmer. 'This damn dowry that I would have had to provide one day might have stopped me buying Blanchemont. Not giving her a dowry, and getting Blanchemont for 250,000 francs, that's 100,000 francs clear profit. Right, there's nothing more to bargain for. Besides, if Rose goes mad, I'll have to give up finding a son-in-law ... and I'll have to pay a doctor's fees ... And anyway, it's all too sad; it'd make me too miserable, seeing her get ugly and filthy like her sister. It'd be a matter of great shame for us, having two mad daughters. She'll be oddly lodged, that's true, but being lord of Blanchemont makes up for a good deal. They'll snipe at us, but won't they be jealous? Well then, let's be a good father. It's not such a bad business.'*

'*Madame la baronne*,' he said, 'suppose we tried to draft this document? It'll be an odd bargain, I've never seen the like.'

'Nor I,' replied Mme de Blanchemont, 'and I have no idea whether there are any models in modern legislation. But no matter, with good sense and trust, you know, we can draft a document that will be more solid than any a professional might draw up.'

'Oh yes, that happens all the time. A will, for example! it's not the stamped paper* that makes it official. Though I know I've got stamped paper here somewhere. I always do. You should always have some to hand.'

'Let me do a rough draft on ordinary paper, Monsieur Bricolin, and you should make one of your own; we shall compare them, negotiate if necessary, and then transcribe it on to stamped paper.'

'Yes, you do that, Madame,' replied Bricolin, who could barely write. 'You've got more learning than me, you'll make a better job of it, and then we'll have a look at it.'

While Marcelle was writing, M. Bricolin found a jug of water in a corner, and, without being noticed, he put it down on a corner cupboard, bent over and drank a certain quantity. 'You've got to have your head for such business,' he thought, 'I think mine's coming back; but cold water in the blood, that's a good thing to have for business, it makes you careful and suspicious.'

Marcelle, inspired by her heart and gifted with a great lucidity of intelligence in her generous resolutions, drafted a document which a lawyer might have seen as a masterpiece of clarity, even though it was written in clear French, though there was not a word of jargon, and though it was shot through and through with the most admirable good faith. When Bricolin heard it read out, he was struck by the precision of the document, which he had not dictated, but whose value and consequences he understood very well.

'Devil take all women!' he thought. 'It's true, when they do understand business—by chance, of course—they outdo the most cunning of us. I know that whenever I ask my wife what she thinks, she always picks up on whatever could leave a door open, in my favour or against me. I wish she was here now! But she'd slow us down with her objections. Well, we'll see, when it's time to sign. Now who'd have thought it?—this young woman, she reads novels, she's a republican, she's a madcap, but she carries off this lunacy so wisely. It's enough to drive you mad with astonishment. Let's have another glass of water. Pouh! Dreadful! I'll need some good wine after the bargain's struck, to restore my stomach!'

XXXI. AFTERTHOUGHTS

'I can't see any objection to that,' said M. Bricolin when he had listened attentively to a second and third reading of the document, with his eyes growing wider and clearer all the while, as he followed each line of the text which Marcelle had placed between them. 'There's just one little thing I'd like to change, and that's the price, Madame Marcelle; in truth, it's 20,000 francs too dear. I didn't think right away how much harm my daughter's marriage to the miller might do me. They'll say I'm ruined, because I've set her up so badly. It'll wreck my credit. And besides, this lad hasn't got the where-withal to buy wedding presents. That's another expense, 8,000 or 10,000 francs, as I'll have to bear. Rose won't want to do without a pretty trousseau, I warrant!'

'I warrant she will not care at all,' replied Marcelle. 'Listen, Monsieur Bricolin, she is weeping! Do you hear her?'

'I don't hear her, Madame, I reckon you're mistaken.'

'I am not mistaken,' said Marcelle as she opened the door. 'She is miserable, she is sobbing, and her sister is screaming! How can you hesitate, Monsieur? You have been presented with the means of enriching yourself whilst at the same time restoring her to health, sanity, perhaps life itself, and at a time like this you think to make further gains from the bargain! Truly!' she added indignantly, 'You are not a man, you have no compassion! Take care: I may choose to seek further advice and abandon you to the calamities which hang over your family as retribution for your avarice!'

In the whole of this vehement denunciation the farmer heard only the threat of breaking the agreement.

'Oh all right, Madame,' he sighed, 'take it down 10,000 francs, and we've got a bargain.'

'Adieu!' exclaimed Marcelle. 'I shall go and see Rose; consider your position, I have considered mine and shall not change it. I have a son, and am mindful that whilst thinking of others, I have no right to sacrifice him.'

'Sit down, Madame Marcelle, let poor Rose sleep. She's right poorly!'

'Go and see her yourself!' replied Marcelle fiercely. 'Perhaps it will convince you that she is not asleep. Perhaps her sufferings will remind you that you are her father.'

'I'm mindful of that,' answered Bricolin, terrified at the thought that Marcelle might change her mind if he gave her time to reflect. 'Come on, Madame, let's cobble this bit of paper together, so we can take the news to Rose and cure her.'

'I hope, sir, that you will give her your consent, pure and simple, and that she will never know that I have purchased it from you.'

'Oh, so you don't want her to know it's a condition we've agreed? That can be arranged! But then there's no point her signing the document.'

'Pardon me, she shall sign without fully understanding. It will be a sort of dowry which I shall settle on her betrothed.'

'It all comes down to the same thing. Makes no difference to me: Rose is sensible enough to understand that I wouldn't marry her off so daftly unless she got something out of it in the future. But what about the payment, Madame Marcelle, do you insist on it being cash?'

'You told me that you were in a position to afford that.'

'Course I am! I've just sold a big tenant-farm that was too far away for me to keep an eye on, got payment in full eight days ago, that's something you never hear of in our part of the world. It was a great lord bought it off me, those folk have got sackfuls of ready money. He was a peer of France, *Monsieur le duc de* ——, wants to make a park of my land and grow fat. That suited him, so I sold dear, only fair!'

'Never mind, you have the means?'

'I've got them in a scrip, fine handsome banknotes,' whispered Bricolin. 'I'll show them to you to calm your mind.'

And having bolted the doors, he took from his belt a huge scrip of glistening, greasy leather, wherein were piled up a quantity of notes drawn on the Bank of France. Astounded at the indifferent air with which Marcelle counted them out, he exclaimed, 'You know, it makes me edgy, having as much money as that in hand at a time! Good thing there aren't any rick-burners these days, and you can take the risk of keeping money at home several days before you invest it. I wear the scrip on me all day; at night I put it under my pillow, I sleep on top of it. I'm late getting shot of it, it's true. If I wasn't doing business with you this soon, I'd have bought an iron chest to lock it away before I invest it. As for trusting it to lawyers or bankers, I'm not such a fool! So I'd like to cobble together our bargain tonight, then I won't need to keep watch over this treasure any more.'

'I certainly hope that we can conclude matters immediately,' said Marcelle.

'What? Without consulting anybody else? What about my wife? And my lawyer?'

'Your wife is here; as for your lawyer, if you call him out, I shall be obliged to send for mine.'

'Oh, these damn lawyers'll ruin the whole thing, believe me, Madame! I know every bit as much as them, so do you, our document is sound, and if we get it registered, it'll cost us a damn fortune!'

'Let us dispense with that formality. I shall sell to you directly, without receipt.'

'Such an important bargain! It makes me tremble! But after all it's only a promise; what if we sign it?'

'It's a promise which is as good as a bill of sale. I am prepared to sign. Go and find your wife.'

'Yes, I better had,' said Bricolin to himself. 'I just hope it doesn't take too much time and the wind doesn't change during the hour's quarrel that Thibaude's sure to pick with me!'

'Are you going to see Rose, Madame Marcelle? Don't tell her nothing yet.'

'I certainly shall not! But will you permit me to drop her a hint, some hope of your consent?'

'At the stage we're at, that's reasonable,' answered Bricolin, whose cunning mind told him that the sight of Rose and her tears was the best means of keeping Marcelle firmly fixed in her generous intentions.

M. Bricolin found his wife considerably more accommodating than he had foreseen. Mme Bricolin was hard and shrewish; but though she was tighter-fisted than her husband in household expenses, she was perhaps less greedy than him overall. Sharper-tongued in her words, harder-faced in her appearance, she was more capable than he of right feelings when the occasion demanded. Furthermore, she was a woman, and maternal feeling, although disguised by her hard exterior, was still vividly alive in her breast.*

'Monsieur Bricolin,' she sighed, coming to meet him and taking him into the kitchen, where a meagre candle flickered mournfully, 'you find me in pain. Rose is worse than you think. She does nothing but wail and sob, like she's lost all reason. She's in love with this miller; it's God's punishment for our sins. But the harm's done, she's lost her heart to him, and she's just like her sister when the poor girl began to lose her wits. And the elder one's worsening too, I can't bear it any more. The doctor saw that she was making to break down the door, so he's made me let her go out and roam about in the hunting-park and the old castle, like always. He says as she's used to being on her own, always on the move, if we keep her shut in with all her folk about her, she'll go into a frenzy. But I'm deathly feared she might kill herself! She looked so wicked! She never says a word, but tonight she told us all the horrors of her life, right turned my stomach. It's dreadful to live like this! And when you think it was *being crossed in love* that caused it! But we raised all our girls the same! The others all got married like we wanted, they've done us proud; they're well off, they're sensible enough to be happy with their lot, even if their husbands have their little ways. But the first and the last are mule-headed, and since we had the ill luck not to realize we might lose the one, we'd best be careful and not go against the other one. I'd rather she'd never been born than marry that miller! But it's what she wants, and as going mad's worse than death, we must take her part. So I say to you, Monsieur Bricolin, I give my consent, and you must give yours. I just told Rose that if she absolutely insists on marrying that man I shan't stand in her way. It seemed to calm her down, though she didn't look like she rightly understood me, or believed what I said. So you'd best go to her and tell her the same yourself.'

'Well, there's a happenstance!' blurted the delighted Bricolin. 'Here, wife, read me this bit of writing, and tell me if anything's wanting.'

'Would you credit that!' exclaimed the farm-wife after reading the document. And after several similar exclamations she gathered all her icy will to read it again, with a lawyer's attention to detail. 'This document favours you,' she said. 'It'll stand up in court. You've no need to consult anyone else, Monsieur Bricolin, just sign. It's all profit and good fortune! It'll be the making of us, and Rose'll be happy too. They're

right to say that the Good Lord rewards fair intentions. I'd
decided to give her away for nothing to her lover, and now
we'll be paid for it! Sign, sign, old fellow, and pay up. That'll
put the bill into effect, and she won't have any comeback.'

'Pay already? Just like that? On the strength of a scrap of
paper that hasn't even got the notary's seal?'

'Pay up, I tell you! And publish the banns tomorrow
morning.'

'But suppose we could get the girl to see sense! Maybe she'll
be better tomorrow, and she might agree to marry somebody
else if we reason with her, if you know how to go about
it. Then they might say that this bill was a piece of madness
on my part, a bit of foolishness that couldn't bind my
daughter . . .'

'Then the sale would be null and void!'

'Remains to be seen! I could always make out a case.'

'You'd lose!'

'Also remains to be seen! Besides, what would it matter?
The sale would be suspended. You can always drag a suit out.
Madame de Blanchemont is impatient, you know. It'd force
her to deal with us.'

'Bah! They'll think badly of you if you come up with
something like that, Monsieur Bricolin. We'll lose our good
name and our credit. There's always profit to be had in being
straight.'

'Well, we'll see, Thibaude! Anyhow, go and tell your
daughter it's all settled. Maybe when no one's saying her nay,
she won't be so bothered about her Grand-Louis; because
frankly it feels to me like some little quarrel between her and
me that's put all this in her head. What do you reckon? He's
handled things in a cunning way, the miller! He knew how to
fiddle this lady's friendship and protection, I can't think
how . . . Not just a pretty face, is he?'

'I'll hate him as long as I live!' replied the farm-wife. 'But
there we are. So long as Rose doesn't go mad like her sister, I'll
cold-shoulder her husband and keep still.'

'Oh, her husband, her husband! . . . He's not there yet.'

'Might as well be, Bricolin, it's over and done with: go and
sign the paper.'

'And what about you? Have you got to sign as well?'

'I'm ready to.'

Mme Bricolin went cautiously into her daughter's bed-chamber, where Marcelle was waiting for her, and signed, together with her husband, on a corner of the chest of drawers.

When they had finished, Bricolin whispered with a look of ferocious triumph, 'Thibaude! The sale is valid, but the condition isn't! You didn't know that, though you reckon you know everything!'

Rose still had fever and intolerable migraine, but her nerves were calmer, now that the madwoman was outside and she could no longer hear her screams. When Marcelle had signed and handed the pen to her young friend, Rose had great difficulty in comprehending what was going on; but when she finally understood, she burst into tears and threw herself effusively first into her father's arms, then her mother's, and finally her friend's, whispering in Marcelle's ear, 'Dearest Marcelle, this is a loan which I accept; one day I shall be wealthy enough to acquit my debt, to your son.'

Grandmother Bricolin was the only one in the family who grasped the nobility of Marcelle's conduct. She threw herself at her feet and embraced them, without a word.

'Come,' whispered Marcelle to the old woman, 'it's not so very late, only ten o'clock! Perhaps Grand-Louis is still out on the green, and in any case it's not so far to Angibault. Could we send someone to find him? I do not dare to propose it myself, but perhaps he might arrive as if by chance, and once he was here he should be told about his happiness.'

'Leave it to me!' cried the old woman. 'Even if I have to go to the mill myself! I'll find the pair of legs I had when I was fifteen!'

Indeed, she went out and looked round the village herself, but she did not find the miller. She thought to send a farm lad, but they were all drunk, asleep in their beds, or in the tavern, incapable of movement. Little Fanchon was too timid to go out at night on the roads; and besides, it was not kind to expose the girl to the risk of encountering all sorts of folk on a fair night. Mother Bricolin was searching up and down the nearly deserted castle mound for someone old and wise enough to take on this commission when into her sight came Uncle Cadoche, who was just emerging from the porch of the church, where he had been murmuring a final prayer.

XXXII. THE *PATACHON*

'Out for a late stroll, Madame Bricolin?' said the beggar to the old farm-wife. 'You seem to be looking for someone? Your granddaughter went home a long time ago. Her papa certainly gave her something to be cross about today!'

'True, true, Cadoche,' replied the old woman. 'I've no money, but I believe they gave you something today at our house.'

'I'm not asking you for anything; my day's work is over; I drank three little glasses of wine tonight, and it's only made me walk the straighter. You know, Mère Bricolin, neither your husband nor that fat fellow your son can hold their drink like me, and at my age too. I wish you good evening. I'm going off to spend the night at Angibault.'

'Angibault? Cadoche, good fellow, are you going to Angibault?'

'Why's that so surprising? My house is a good two leagues from here, towards Jeu-les-Bois.* I've no need to wear myself out. I'm going to spend the night with my nephew the miller; they always give me a good welcome, never put me out in the haybarn like the other houses do, like your place, for example, though you're still rich enough, in spite of the rick-burners! Now at my nephew's place, there's a bed for me in the mill, and they don't fear that I might set fire to it... as they do at your place, because when you lack fire in your legs, you've got it on the brain.'

These allusions to the catastrophe of which her husband had been the victim made mother Bricolin's old blood run cold; but she made an effort to think only of her granddaughter and of better days to come.

'So you're bound for Grand-Louis's place?' she asked the old man.

'Yes indeed, to the best of all my nephews, my true nephew, my future heir!'

'Well then, Cadoche, as you're sober, and a friend of Grand-Louis's, you could do him a good turn. There's some pressing business, he's got to come and talk to me right soon; tell him that; I'll wait for him at the gate to the big farmyard. Have him saddle his mare, he'll go faster.'

'His mare? He's not got her any more, somebody stole her.'

'All right, tell him to come anyway! He'll be mightily interested in this business.'

'And just what is this business?'

'Oh, so now he wants *that* explained to him! Cadoche, there'll be a new twenty-sou piece for you, you can come for it tomorrow morning.'

'What time?'

'Whenever you like.'

'I'll come at seven. Be there, I don't like waiting.'

'Go on then!'

'I'm going. I shan't be more than three-quarters of an hour. You know, I've got better legs than your husband, Mère Bricolin, though I'm ten years older than him!'

In fact the beggar did set off at a good clip. He was just approaching Angibault when he found himself in a narrow bit of the road, just ahead of M. Ravalard's *calèche*, driven at great speed by the malicious red-haired *patachon*, who thought himself too grand to cry out a warning, and only drove his horses on all the faster.

It goes against the dignity of the Berry peasant to move aside for any vehicle, no matter what warning he is given or what difficulty there would be in moving aside for *him*. Uncle Cadoche was the proudest in the land. With his customary condescension from the heights of his grandeur, with his mocking gravity towards those to whom he held out his hand, he made a point of slowing his steps and keeping to the middle of the way, although he could feel the horses' hot breath on his shoulder. 'Move aside, you brute!' shouted the *patachon* at last, landing a great blow of the whip on the back of the old man's head.

The beggar spun around and grabbed the horses by the reins. They reared up so strongly that they nearly tipped the carriage into the ditch. And then there began a desperate battle between the beggar and the infuriated *patachon*, with the latter lashing out with the whip and swearing a thousand oaths, old Cadoche protecting himself from these assaults by ducking under the horses' heads and pushing at them by yanking hard on their bits, sometimes forcing them back, sometimes being forced back himself. M. Ravalard had begun by taking the role of the great gentleman, as is fitting for a man who was driving in a carriage for the first time in his life. At first he, too, swore at the insolent fellow who had dared to delay him; but the good heart of the *Berrichon* soon got the better of the arrogance of the parvenu, when he saw that the old man was insanely braving a real danger. 'Take care!' he shouted to the driver, leaning out of the carriage. 'Don't do any harm to that poor man!'

It was too late: maddened at being whipped from behind and pushed back from the front, the horses made a furious jump and knocked Cadoche down. Thanks to the admirable instinct of these generous beasts, they leapt over his body without touching it; but the two wheels of the carriage rolled over his chest.

The track was gloomy and deserted. It was too dark for M. Ravalard to make out the body, covered in earth-coloured rags, that lay stretched out behind his rapidly fleeing carriage, and the *patachon* himself had lost control of the horses. At first the bourgeois was full of fear that they might tip over; when the equipage was finally under control, they had left the beggar far behind.

'I hope you didn't knock him down?' Ravalard asked his coachman, who was still trembling with fear and anger.

'No, no,' said the driver, whether or not he believed what he was saying. 'He fell to one side. It's his own fault, the old wretch! but the horses didn't touch him, and he's come to no harm, or he would've shouted out. He'll have got off with a fright, and that'll teach him a lesson.'

'Should we go back and see?' asked M. Ravalard.

'Oh, no, no, sir; if they get so much as a scratch, these folk'll sue you. Even if nothing at all's wrong with him, he'll pretend his head's broke, so as to get a good deal of money out of you. I knocked into one like that a while back, he was patient enough to spend forty days in bed to get compensation from my gentleman for forty days' loss of work. He was no more sick than me!'

'Oh, they're clever, these folk!' agreed M. Ravalard. 'All the same, I'd rather not have a *calèche* than run anybody down. Next time, son, pull up rather than get into a fight like that; it's dangerous.'

The driver, who cared nothing for the consequences of the business, whipped his horses again to get away as fast as possible. He was not immune to terror and remorse, and he swore under his breath for the rest of the trip.

The miller, Lémor, Grand'Marie, and M. Tailland the lawyer had just come out of the mill at this moment. Lémor had decided to leave in the morning; he was spending the last night here, paying little attention to what was being said, and contemplating with a sweet melancholy the beauty of the sky and the reflections of the stars in the river. The miller, in sad and sombre mood, was forcing himself to be polite to the lawyer, who had just drafted a will for a tenant farmer a short distance away in the Vallée-Noire and had stopped at the mill on his way back, to light his cigar and the lamps on his cabriolet. Grand'Marie was in the midst of explaining to him that if he took another route he would avoid a long stony track, and Grand-Louis was assuring him that if he went over the difficult bit at a walk or on foot, leading his horse by the bridle, the rest of the way would be better. When it came to his creature comforts, the lawyer was what the local people call *fafiot*, an untranslatable word meaning a man who is both dawdling and pernickety. In order to learn how he could avoid a quarter hour of light fatigue, he had just wasted a quarter of an hour which he might have employed resting in his own bed.

He had come to the opinion that leading his horse on foot by the bridle was more tiring than remaining in the carriage and enduring the bumps, but that even the better of the two alternatives was worthless, and would do nothing for his digestion.

'Come on then,' said the miller, whose sad thoughts could not extinguish his native kindness and his obliging disposition, 'follow me, walking at your leisure, I'll take your horse and carriage up to the top of the road. When we've passed the vines, you'll have a fine sandy road all the way.'

As he was good-naturedly acting the groom, Grand-Louis was obliged to move the cabriolet aside, almost into the ditch, to let M. Ravalard's *calèche* speed furiously by. Preoccupied by his encounter with the beggar, M. Ravalard did not reply to the miller's friendly greeting.

'It's because he's got his carriage now that he doesn't know me!' Louis remarked to Lémor, who had followed him. 'Money, money! you make the world go round, like water does my mill-wheel. That damn *patachon* will smash the carriage to smithereens if he goes over our stones at that speed! No doubt he's got wine in his brain and money in his pocket. I don't know which one makes you tipsier. Oh, Rose, Rose! they'll get you to drink the poison of vanity, and in a little while maybe you'll forget me as well. Though she almost seemed to be in love with me tonight; her eyes were full of tears when they tore us apart. I shan't ever talk to her again . . . maybe she'll miss me . . . You know, I could be quite happy if I weren't so miserable!'

The horse Grand-Louis was leading swerved suddenly, and the miller was jerked from his reflections. Leaning forward, he saw something pale lying across the road. The horse stubbornly refused to go any further, and the shadowy *traîne* was so dark at this spot that Grand-Louis was obliged to tread gently on the shape, to see whether it was a heap of stones or a drunken man.

'Oh, Lord! My uncle!' he exclaimed, recognizing the beggar's tall figure and money-bag. 'Yesterday evening you were lying on the edge of the ditch, fair enough, but tonight you're right on top of the ruts! Seems you like this spot, but it's not the best bed for you. Come on, wake up now, come sleep at the mill, you'll be more comfortable there than under a horse's hooves.'

'This man is dead!' shouted Henri, lifting the beggar in his arms.

'Oh, never fear! He's often been through that particular death, it's an old acquaintance of his. He holds his liquor well, good old fellow that he is! but on feast days you drink more than's sensible, and as they say of wine, there's no friend so faithful that he doesn't betray you some day. Come on, let's leave him at the foot of this tree; we'll pick him up on the way back and take him to the house.'

Lémor touched the beggar's wrist. 'If I didn't feel a faint pulse,' he exclaimed, 'I'd swear he was dead! What! Is it not sufficient that he is sunk in misery, age and wanton ways? Must a shameful passion drag him under men's feet? And yet he is a human being!'

'Bah! You're hard on him like only a teetotaler can be! Who was it said that the poor man needs to drink so as to forget his troubles? I've heard that said somewhere; it's true enough.'

Just as Lémor and the miller were about to abandon Cadoche for the time being, he emitted a deep groan.

'Well, Uncle?' laughed the miller. 'Not feeling any better?'

'I am a dead man!' answered the beggar feebly. 'Have pity on me! Finish me off! . . . I am suffering too greatly.'

'It'll pass, Uncle. A little water and a good bed . . .'

'They crushed me, they rolled over my body!' the beggar replied.

'That's not impossible!' exclaimed Lémor.

'Oh, he's always saying things like that,' replied the miller, who had seen too much of the painful ramblings of drunkenness to be greatly concerned. 'Come on, Père Cadoche, did something terrible happen to you, seriously?'

'Yes, the carriage, the carriage . . . over my stomach, over my chest, over my arms!'

'Take one of the lamps down from the cabriolet and bring it over here,' the miller ordered Lémor. 'It may light up one corner, though it'll darken another; when we've got the lamp under his nose, we'll see if it's sickness or drunkenness.'

'No! not wine... not wine,' mumbled the beggar. 'They've murdered me, crushed me like a dog; I'm going to die of it.

May our Heavenly Father and the Holy Virgin and all good Christians take pity on me and avenge my death!'

Lémor brought the lantern over. The beggar's face was livid. His clothes were too ragged for another rip or smudge more or less to be any proof, but when they removed the rags that covered his chest, they saw traces of burning red on his wizened flanks; it was the iron bands of the carriage wheels, that had ploughed him like a field. But no blood was spurting out, his ribs did not appear to be broken, and his breathing was still unimpeded. He was even able to tell them about the accident, and he had sufficient strength to vomit up all the curses and oaths of vengeance that rage and despair could suggest to him, against the rich man in his carriage and the vile mercenary who outdid his master in cruelty and insolence.

'God be praised!' exclaimed the miller. 'You're not dead, my poor Cadoche, and we must hope that you won't die. Look, the right wheel went into the ditch, you can see its marks; that's what saved you; the carriage's weight went over on to the wheel, and not so much on you. It's a miracle the *calèche* didn't tip over on its side.'

'I did my best!' barked the beggar.

'Well, your malice has served you well, uncle. They didn't manage to crush you, and we'll get even with them, not with that poor M. Ravalard, who'll be as upset as you are, but with that wicked damn boy!'

'And think how many days' work I'll lose!' said the beggar mournfully.

'Good Lord! you might get more money walking about like that than the rest of us do working. But we'll help you, Père Cadoche; we'll take up a collection for you; as for me, I'll give you your weight in wheat; never fret. When you've had a misfortune, you shouldn't let fear finish you off.'

With these words the miller, aided by Lémor, placed the beggar in the cabriolet, and they brought him back slowly, avoiding the stones with extreme care. M. Tailland, who was taking his time climbing the hill for fear of getting out of breath, was astounded to see them coming back, but when he learned what the matter was, he lent them his cabriolet with a good grace, though not without some disquiet about the delay to which this accident would subject him and the fatigue which climbing the hill again would cause him, when he had already reached the top. But none the less he went down again to see if he could help his friends from the mill assist poor Cadoche.

When they laid the beggar down on the miller's own bed, he fainted. They gave him vinegar to sniff.

'I'd prefer the smell of *eau-de-vie*,' he said, as he came to, 'it's healthier.' So they brought him some.

'I'd rather drink it than breathe it,' he said, 'it's more fortifying.'

Lémor wanted to stop them. After such an accident, this fiery drink could and would provoke a terrible attack of fever. But the beggar insisted. The miller tried to dissuade him; but the lawyer, who had made so fine a study of his own health that he was entirely free from medical prejudices, declared that at this juncture water could be fatal to a man who might not have drunk a drop for fifty years; that as his ordinary beverage alcohol could only do him good; that he had no other serious condition than fear; and that the stimulant of a little drop would restore his senses. The mill-wife and Jeannie, who, like all peasants, also believed in the infallible virtue of wine and *brandevin** in such cases, agreed with the lawyer's assertion that the main thing was to keep the poor man content. Majority opinion ruled, and whilst they were looking for a glass, Cadoche, who was genuinely tortured by the thirst which great suffering brings, grabbed the bottle and drank more than half of it in one go.

'That's too much, that's too much!' shouted the miller, trying to stop him.

'What do you mean, nephew!' roared the beggar, with the dignity of a paterfamilias reclaiming the rightly exercise of his authority. 'So you measure out my share at your place? Are you tight-fisted about the assistance to which my condition entitles me?'

This unfair reproach defeated the prudence of the kind and honest miller. He left the bottle by the side of the beggar, saying, 'You can keep that for later, for now you've had enough.'

'Ah, you're a good relation and a worthy nephew!' said Cadoche, who appeared entirely restored by the *eau-de-vie*; 'and if I've got to die, I'd rather do it at your place, because you'll give me a decent burial. I've always been fond of a good funeral! . . . I take you all as witnesses, I order my nephew and heir, Grand-Louis of Angibault, to have me carried to the grave no more and no less honourably than I'm sure they'll do shortly for old Bricolin of Blanchemont . . . who won't outlive me long, even if he is younger . . . but who let his legs get burned back in the days when . . . Ah! ah! now tell me, the rest of you, haven't you got to be a fool, *getting your drumsticks grilled* for the sake of the money you've got put away! Though it's true enough he had some in the cast-iron pot! . . .'

'What is he saying?' enquired the lawyer, sitting in front of a table, and not ill-pleased to see the mill-wife preparing tea for the invalid, since he expected to have a nice hot cup himself to protect him against the night mists on the banks of the Vauvre. 'What's he on about with his grilled drumsticks and his cast-iron pot?'

'I think he's raving,' answered the miller. 'In any case, when he's not drunk or ill, he's old enough to drivel, and he thinks more about tales from yesterday than today's. That's how old men are. How do you feel, uncle?'

'I feel much better since that little drop, though your *brandevin* has no damn taste! Did you play a little trick on me and water it down for economy's sake? Listen, nephew, if you refuse me anything during my illness, I'll cut you off without a penny!'

'Oh, fine, let's talk about that *for a change*!' shrugged the miller. 'You'd do better to try to sleep, Père Cadoche!'

'Sleep? Me? I've no wish to,' replied the beggar, hunching himself up on his cushion and gazing round with bright eyes. 'I know my goose is cooked, but I don't want to die on my side like an ox. Oh yes! I can feel something heavy in my stomach, here, around my heart, like a stone. It bothers me, like an itch. *Meunière*! Bring me some compresses! Nobody's looking after me properly here, you'd never know I was your wealthy uncle!'

'Mightn't his ribs be crushed?' asked Lémor. 'Perhaps that is what weighs on his heart?'

'I don't know a thing about it, neither does anybody here,' answered the miller. 'But we could send for the doctor, who's doubtless still at Blanchemont.'

'And who'll pay for the doctor's visit?' snapped the beggar, who was as stingy as he was vain about his supposed wealth.

'I will,' answered Grand-Louis, 'unless he comes out of pure charity. No one will ever say that a poor devil snuffed it in my house for lack of the help a rich man would have had. Jeannie, saddle Sophie and go and get Monsieur Lavergne.'

'Saddle Sophie?' sneered Cadoche. 'You're just saying that out of habit, Nephew! Have you forgot? Sophie's been stolen!'

'Sophie's been stolen?' echoed the mill-wife, turning round sharply.

'He's rambling,' replied the miller. 'Don't pay any attention, mother. Tell me, Père Cadoche,' he added in a whisper to the beggar, 'how did you know that? Can you tell me anything about my animal and my thief?'

'Now who could know such a thing?' replied Cadoche with a pious air. 'Who is it that finds thieves out? Not the police, they're too stupid! Who could ever have said who it was that burned old Bricolin's legs and stole his cast-iron pot?'

'Yes, tell us that, Uncle,' answered the miller. 'You keep talking about those legs, you think about them a good deal. For some while now every time I meet you you come back to the same thing! and tonight you've thrown a cast-iron pot into the story as well. Now you never told me about *that*?'

'Don't make him talk!' said the mill-wife. 'You'll worsen his fever.'

In truth the beggar was feverish. Whenever his hosts turned away he swallowed a furtive gulp of *eau-de-vie* and put the bottle adroitly back under his bolster pillow against the wall. Yet he looked stronger by the moment, and it was a marvel to see how this iron constitution could endure, at such an advanced age, the consequences of an accident which would have shattered any other.

'The cast-iron pot!' he exclaimed, staring at Grand-Louis with a peculiar expression that caused him a sort of inexplicable fear. 'The cast-iron pot! That's the best part of the story, and I shall tell it to you.'

'Do tell, do tell, Père Cadoche, this interests me!' said the lawyer, examining him attentively.

XXXIII. THE WILL

'There was a cast-iron pot,' the beggar went on, 'an ugly old cast-iron pot that looked like nothing at all; but appearances are deceiving . . . In this pot, which was sealed up tight, and heavy! . . . oh, it was so heavy! there were 50,000 francs belonging to old lord de Blanchemont,* whose granddaughter's staying at the Bricolin farm now. And on top of that, in this pot, old Bricolin, who was a young man then, it was forty years ago . . . exactly! . . . had squirreled away 50,000 francs of his own, the proceeds of a good bit of business he'd done about some wool. Those were the days! they needed wool for the army uniforms. The lord's deposit and the farmer's profit were both in fine handsome louis d'or, twenty-four-franc pieces, with the head of good king Louis XVI, the ones we call *toad-eyes* because of the round shield on them. I've always liked those coins, I have! They say you lose out on the exchange, but I reckon you make a saving: 23 francs 11 sous is still worth more than a wretched twenty-franc *napoléon*. They were all muddled up together. But because the farmer loved his louis coins in their own right (and that's how you ought to love your money, my children) he'd marked all of his with a cross, to distinguish them from the lord's, when it came time to give them back. He was following the example of his master, who'd marked his with a simple bar, to amuse himself, so they said, and to make sure nobody swopped them. The mark was there . . . it's still there . . . Not a single one's missing; on the contrary, a few more have joined them! . . .'

'What the deuce is he on about?' exclaimed the miller, looking at the lawyer.

'Peace!' the lawyer replied. 'Let him go on, I think I'm beginning to understand. So then . . .' he encouraged the beggar.

'So then,' continued Cadoche, 'he put the cast-iron pot in a hole in a wall at the castle of Beaufort, and he bricked it up. When the rick-burners pursued him . . . Don't you go thinking that all those folk were scum! Some of them were poor, but there were rich men among them; I know them well enough, 'struth! Some of them are still alive today, and folk bow low to them. Among us were . . .'

'Among *you*?' blurted the miller.

'Be quiet!' ordered the lawyer, grabbing his arm forcefully.

'I mean, among them,' continued the beggar, 'were a judge, a mayor, a priest, a miller . . . I think there was a lawyer too . . . Eh, Monsieur Tailland, I don't mean anything against you, you were hardly born, nor against you, nephew, you'd have been too simple to do any such thing . . .'

'So the rick-burners got the money?' asked the lawyer.

'They never got it, that's the best bit. They grilled and browned poor Bricolin's drumsticks, the old turkey, it was frightful, it was a wonderful thing to see.'

'You mean you saw it?' exclaimed the miller, unable to contain himself.

'Oh no!' answered Cadoche. 'I didn't see it; but one of my friends, well, that is, someone who was there, he told me all this.'

'That's better,' said the miller, pacified.

'Have your cup of tea, Père Cadoche,' said the mill-wife, 'and don't gabble so much, it'll do you no good.'

'Go to hell with your warm water!' shouted the beggar, pushing the cup away. 'I can't abide these slops. Let me tell my story; I've had it on my mind a long time, I want to tell the whole thing once before I die, and you keep interrupting me!'

'It's true,' said the lawyer, 'this morning you started telling it under the arbour, and everyone turned their backs thinking, "Ah, here's Cadoche telling his story of the rick-burners again, let's be on our way!" But I find it fascinating and I should have liked to have heard the rest of it. So please go on.'

'You have to imagine,' said Cadoche, 'that this man I told you about, who was there . . . a bit against his will . . . he was a poor peasant, they'd dragged him along; and then when he took fright and tried to get away, they threatened they'd blow his brains out, if he didn't get back up on the horse they'd brought for him, with its shoes back to front so as to confuse pursuers . . . And when this man was at the spot, he threw himself into combing the place for the money. He preferred that to taking part in making a pig-roast of poor Bricolin, because he wasn't an evil fellow, this man I'm telling you about. 'Struth! that business wasn't to his taste, seeing it gave him the shakes . . . it was appalling . . . the condemned man screaming enough to deafen you, the woman in a dead faint, those cursed legs floundering around in the fire, I can still see them . . . There's not been a single night since when I haven't seen them in my dreams! In those days Bricolin was a strong man, he held himself so stiff that an iron bar in the middle of the fire was twisted by his feet . . . Oh, I swear before almighty God, I took no part in it . . . when they forced me to hold a cloth over his mouth the sweat poured off me, cold as ice . . .'

'Off you?' whispered the stupefied miller.

'Off the man who told me all this. So our man waited for the right moment to make himself scarce, and he set to searching everywhere, high and low, all over the house, tapping the walls with a pickaxe to see if there was a hollow space somewhere, and shattering and smashing like the other lot. But what do you reckon, he slips into a little pig-shed, with respect . . . and he's all by himself! Since that time I've always had a particular liking for pigs, I've raised one every year . . . He knocks, he listens . . . something still sounds hollow. He looks around . . . I was all by myself! He works over the wall, he digs away at it, and he finds . . . can you guess? The cast-iron pot! . . . We all knew it was Père Bricolin's money-box! The locksmith who'd sealed it up had blabbed, so I knew right away, it was the rose-pot! And it was so heavy! But no matter, my man found the strength of an ox in his arms and heart. He got clean away with his cast-iron pot, tiptoed off, not a word of goodbye to the others. And they've never seen him since in that part of the world. Oh, aye, he was playing a dangerous game! The rick-burners would have killed him with no more ado, if they'd found him out. He walked day and night, never stopped, never ate nor drank, till he came to a great wood, where he buried his pot, and he slept there, I've no idea how long. I was so worn out, carrying such a weight! When I got hungry I was in a right pickle. I hadn't a sou to bless myself with, and I knew that in the whole of my 100,000 francs there wasn't a single louis that wasn't marked! I'd looked them over, couldn't stop myself! and I knew right well, this damn mark would give it away, the police had been informed. Trying to scrape it off would've made matters worse. And then a poor devil, like him I'm telling you about, who tried to change a gold louis to buy a bit of bread at the baker's, that would've roused suspicion. So there was only one thing to do: he became a beggar. The police didn't do their duty so well then as today, the proof is that not a single one of the rick-burners was punished, though they never left that part of the world. A beggar's life is a good one, if you know how to go about it . . . I got a bit of wealth together, and I never wanted for nought. My man wasn't such a fool as to ask a locksmith to seal up his cast-iron pot; he buried it right in the middle of a wretched hut made of straw and earth, which serves him as a home, and which he built himself deep in the woods. For forty years nobody's bothered him, because nobody envies his way of life, and he's had the pleasure of being richer and prouder than all the folk as despise him.'

'And what good did his wealth do him?' asked Henri.

'He looks it over once a week, when he goes back to his hut where he's locked away the money he receives in alms. He keeps no more on him than he wants to spend on tobacco and *brandevin*. He has a mass said once a week, to pay the Good Lord back for the help he had, and with a good deal of wit and method he's got out of his difficulties. He's not so daft as to let a single piece of his treasure get out. It wouldn't give rise to any suspicions now that everyone's forgot the tale and they've given up trying to track down the money, but it would make folk think he's well off, and he'd get no more charity. There it is, my children, the tale of the cast-iron pot. What do you say to it?'

'Superb!' exclaimed the lawyer. 'And very useful to know.'

A deep silence followed this narrative. The bystanders gazed at each other, torn between surprise, fear, scorn, and a kind of mad desire to laugh, on top of all these other emotions. Cadoche, worn out by talk, had turned over on the pillow: his pale face was taking on a greenish hue, and his long stiff beard, still black enough to cast a shadow over his grubby features, gave him an eerie air. His hollow eyes, which, a moment before, had shot out flames while drink and delirium were loosening his tongue, now seemed to retreat into their sockets and to take on the glaze of death. His pronounced features, his long aquiline nose, his narrow lips, all of which might have been handsome in his youth, did not betoken natural cruelty, but a bizarre blend of avarice, cunning, distrust, sensuality, and perhaps even geniality.

'Well, is it a dream he's had?' said the miller at last. 'Or have we just heard his confession? Should we send for the doctor or the priest?'

'It is God's grace!' exclaimed Lémor, who was more attentive than the others to the beggar's transformed features and impeded breathing. 'Either I am much mistaken, or this man has only a few minutes to live.'

'I have only a few minutes to live?' barked the beggar, making an effort to lift himself. 'Who said that? Was it the doctor? I don't believe in doctors. They can all go to hell!'

He leaned over towards the wall and finished off his bottle of *eau-de-vie*; then as he turned back, he was seized with terrible pain, and emitted a cry.

'My heart's caved in,' he said, battling fiercely against his illness. 'It may well be I won't get over it. And if I never go back to my house again? What will become of it all? And my poor pig, who'll look after him? He's used to the bread they give me, I bring him some every week. There's a young girl living nearby who takes him out to the fields. The flirt! she's always making eyes at me, she hopes she'll inherit something from me. But it'll come to nought: here is my heir!'

And Cadoche stretched his hand out solemnly towards Grand-Louis.

'He's always been kinder to me than all the others put together. He's the only one that treated me like I deserve; who put me up in a bed, who gave me wine, tobacco, *brandevin*, and meat, and not their dry crusts of bread that I wouldn't touch! I've always practised one virtue: gratitude! I've always loved Grand-Louis and our Heavenly Father, because they did me some good. So I mean to make out my will in his favour, just like I always promised him. Mill-wife, do you reckon I'm sick enough to make out my will?'

'No, no, my poor fellow!' exclaimed the mill-wife, who in her angelic candour had taken the beggar's narrative to be a sort of dream. 'Don't make your will; they say it brings misfortune and hastens your death.'

'On the contrary,' spoke up M. Tailland. 'It does you good; it's comforting. It might even revive a dead man.'*

'In that case, lawyer,' said the beggar, 'I'll try your remedy. I'm fond of what I own, and I need to be sure it'll pass into the right hands, not go to the little hussies that play up to me, they'll get no more from me than the bouquet and the ribbon from my hat, so they can make themselves pretty on Sunday. Lawyer, take your pen and scribble it out for me in the right words, and don't leave anything out.

'I hereby give and bequeath to my friend Grand-Louis of Angibault all my worldly goods, my house situated at Jeu-les-Bois, my little patch of potatoes, my pig, my horse...'

'You have a horse?' asked the miller. 'Since when?'

'Since yesterday evening. It's a horse I found when I was out strolling.'

'It wouldn't be mine, by any chance?'

'As you say. It's old Sophie, who's not worth the ferrier's iron.'

'Excuse me, Uncle!' exclaimed the miller, half-pleased, half-annoyed. 'I'm fond of Sophie; she's worth more than... many folk! Blast it, so you had the gall to steal Sophie! And to think I trusted you with the key to my mill! Just look at the old hypocrite!'

'Be quiet, Nephew, you're talking codswallop,' replied Cadoche with dignity. 'A fine thing if an uncle hasn't the right to use his nephew's mare! What's yours is mine, since, according to my intent and testament, all that's mine is yours.'

'Oh all right then!' answered the miller. '*Bequeath me* Sophie, bequeath away, Uncle, I'll go along with it. All the same, it's a good thing you hadn't time to sell her . . . Pox on you, you old rascal!' he muttered beneath his breath.

'What are you saying?' replied the beggar.

'Nothing, Uncle,' said the miller, who had noticed that the old man had developed a sort of convulsive rattle in his throat. 'I was saying that you've done well: if it's your pleasure to go begging on horseback!'

'Have you finished, lawyer?' continued Cadoche in a muffled voice. 'You write slowly enough! I'm dropping off. Hurry up, you idler of a scrivener!'

'It is done,' said the lawyer. 'Can you write your name?'

'Better than you!' barked Cadoche. 'But I can't see. I need my glasses and chewing tobacco.'

'Here you are,' said the mill-wife.

'That's better,' he continued, rolling his tobacco around in his mouth with pleasure. 'That's given me strength. I'm not dead, you know, even if I am suffering like one of the damned.'

He cast his eye over the will and said, 'Ah! You've not forgot the cast-iron pot and *its contents*?'

'Certainly not!' replied M. Tailland.

'Then you've done well,' replied Cadoche with deep sarcasm, 'though all I said about it be no more than a tale to taunt you!'

'I knew it!' exclaimed the miller joyfully. 'If you'd had that money, you'd have returned it to its rightful owner. You've always been an honest soul, Uncle . . . even if you did steal my mare; but that was one of your little jokes; you'd have brought her back! There we are then, you needn't sign this bit of tomfoolery; I don't need your cast-off clothes, though they might make some poor man happy; or maybe you've got some relative I'd be robbing of your last few sous.'

'I have no relatives, I've buried them all, God be praised!' answered the beggar. 'And as for the poor, I detest them! Give me the pen, or face my curse!'

'All right, all right, please yourself!' sighed the miller, handing him the pen.

The beggar signed; then pushing the paper away with a gesture of horror, he shouted, 'Take it away, take it away! It feels like it's killing me!'

'Do you want me to rip it up?' asked Grand-Louis, about to do so.

'Not at all, not at all,' replied the beggar with a final effort of will. 'Put it in your pocket, my lad, perhaps it won't cause you any offence! Ah! where's the doctor? I need him to finish me off faster, if I've got to suffer like this!'

'He's on his way,' said the mill-wife, 'and the priest with him, as I sent for both of them.'

'The priest?' said Cadoche. 'To do what?'

'To give you some words of comfort, old fellow. You've always been a pious man, and your soul is as precious as anybody else's. I know right well the priest won't mind going out to bring you the sacraments.'

'So I'm in that state?' replied the dying man with a deep sigh. 'In that case, no foolishness! and let the priest go to hell, even if he is a good sort when he's drunk enough; but I don't believe in priests. I love our Lord and not the priest. The Lord gave me the money, the priest would have made me give it back. Let me die in peace! . . . Nephew, will you promise to beat that damn *patachon* to death?'

'No, but I'll give him a good hiding.'

'Enough talk,' said the beggar, extending his livid hand. 'I wanted to die talking, but I can't talk any more . . . Ah! I'm not so sick as you think, I'll have a nap, and then perhaps you won't come into your inheritance so soon, Nephew!'

The beggar dropped back on his pillow. After a moment there was a sonorous noise in his chest, a boiling sound. He went ruddy again, then pale. For a few minutes he moaned. His eyes opened, wide and frightened, as if death had appeared to him in visible form; then all at once, with a half-smile, as if he had rediscovered hope of life, he gave up the ghost.

The death of even the worst of men always has a solemn mystery about it which demands respect and silence in religious souls. There was a moment of dismay and even sadness at the mill, when the beggar Cadoche was dead. Despite his evil ways and peculiar habits, despite this peculiar confession they had just heard, which only the lawyer firmly believed, the mill-wife and her son felt a kind of warmth for the old man, because of the kindnesses they had grown accustomed to do for him; for if it is true to say that one detests others in proportion to the wrongs one has suffered from them, the reverse maxim ought to be accepted.

The mill-wife knelt down beside the bed and prayed. Lémor and the miller also prayed, in their hearts, that He who gives reparation and grace would not abandon the immortal, divine soul that had lived on earth in the abject shape of this miserable man.

Only the lawyer returned tranquilly to drinking his cup of tea, after having pronounced calmly, *Ite, missa est, Dominus vobiscum.** 'Grand-Louis,' he continued, 'you must go to Jeu-les-Bois right away, before news of this death arrives. Some of his own kind might destroy the hut and take the egg out of the nest.'

'What egg?' asked the miller. 'His pig, his change of linen?'

'No, the cast-iron pot.'

'You're dreaming, Monsieur Tailland!'

'Go and see anyway. And there's your mare!'

'Oh, my faithful old servant! I forgot, you're right. She's worth the trip for her good heart and our long-standing friendship. We're nearly the same age, she and I. I'll be off; I just hope he's not laughing at me from up above! He always was an old joker!'

'Go anyway, I tell you, don't be idle! I believe in the cast-iron pot; you might say I have a cast-iron belief in it!'

'But tell me, Monsieur Tailland, do you really think that scrap of paper you scribbled for your amusement is worth anything?'

'It's perfectly legal, I'll vouch for it, and it may make you the owner of 100,000 francs.'

'Me? But have you forgot that if the story is true, half of it belongs to Madame de Blanchemont and the other to Bricolin?'

'That's another reason for your errand. You've taken that on as a matter of restitution. So go and find it. When you've done this service for Monsieur Bricolin, he'd be a wicked devil if he didn't give you his daughter.'

'His daughter! Am I thinking of his daughter? Could his daughter be thinking of me?' exclaimed the miller, going red.

'Fine! Fine! Discretion is a virtue; but I saw you dancing together a little while ago, and I know perfectly well why her father separated you so abruptly.'

'Monsieur Tailland, get all that out of your head. I'm on my way; if there really is a nest-egg, what'll I do with it? Don't we have to make some sort of legal declaration?'

'Why? The formalities of the law were invented for those who have no law in their hearts. What would be the point of blackening the memory of this strange old boy who managed to pass himself off as an honest man for eighty years? Nor do you need to prove you're not a thief; nobody thinks you are. You will give the money back, and that will be the end of the affair.'

'But what if the old man has relatives?'

'He has none, and if he did, would you want them to inherit that which does not belong to them?'

'That's true; I'm just dazed by what's happened. I'll go and saddle a horse.'

'That won't be convenient for bringing back this famous cast-iron pot which is so heavy, so heavy! Are the roads passable in those parts?'

'Of course. From here you go to Transault,* then Lys-Saint-George, then Jeu. It's all commune roads, recently repaired.'

'In that case, take my carriage, Grand-Louis, and make haste.'

'What about you?'

'I shall sleep here while I wait.'

'You're a brave man and no mistake! What if the beds aren't good enough, you're a mite delicate!'

'So much the worse! A night soon passes. Besides, we cannot leave your mother to a tête-à-tête with this dead man, it is too gloomy; for you must take your mill lad with you. Two men aren't too many for the job, when there's money to carry.

You will find loaded pistols in the side-pockets of my cabriolet. I never travel without them, since I often have valuable things to carry. So be on your way! Tell your mother to make me some more tea. She and I will talk as late as we can, for this dead fellow is tiresome.'

Five minutes afterwards Lémor and the miller were en route for Jeu-les-Bois, through a dark night. We shall give them time to make their way there, and while they are travelling we shall go back and see what is happening at the farm.

XXXIV. DISASTER

Grandmother Bricolin was growing very impatient at the miller's delay. She had no idea that her messenger would never return to claim the wages she had promised him, and the reader will readily understand that at the moment of his death the beggar had forgotten to pass on the message she had given him. Finally, in a state of exhaustion and discouragement, she went back to find her elderly spouse, after having made sure that the madwoman was still wandering in the hunting-park, absorbed in her usual meditations and no longer adding her sinister plaints to the tranquil echoes of the valley. It was about midnight. A few unsteady voices sang out of tune as they left the inn, and the farm dogs did not bother to bark, apparently recognizing friends.

On the urging of his wife, who wanted to see the contract with Marcelle take immediate effect, M. Bricolin had given the *lady vendor* the scrip containing 250,000 francs—not without a good deal of suffering and terror. Marcelle received the venerable money-bag emotionlessly. It was so filthy that she only touched it with the tips of her fingers; weary of a business in which others' greed had inspired her with disgust, she threw it into a corner of Rose's desk. She had accepted this extremely prompt payment for the same reason which had motivated the purchaser: to set things in motion and to make sure of the girl's future, whilst preventing any second thoughts.

She told Fanchon to let Grand-Louis into the kitchen, whatever time he came, and to call her. Then she lay down fully
clothed on her bed, to rest but not to sleep, for Rose was still
very excited and seemed never to tire of blessing her and
telling her how happy she was. But the miller did not come,
and since the day's emotions had exhausted everyone, by two
in the morning the entire farm was sound asleep. Yet there
was one exception: the madwoman, whose mind had reached
a fever pitch she could no longer bear.

M. and Mme Bricolin had spent a long while talking in the
kitchen. The farmer had nothing more to fear, and feeling
chilled by all the water he had drunk, he picked up his jug
again, which he replenished from one hour to another, with
an unsteady hand, from a larger jug placed nearby, full of a
frothy blueish wine. This was the *mère-goutte*, the strongest
of the vintage, a detestable beverage, but one which the
Berrichon prefers to any other wine in the world.

Several times his wife had noticed that the pleasure of being
the proprietor of Blanchemont and the gay prospect of his
huge wealth were no longer bringing a sparkle to his dulling
eye, or tautening his jowls, and she had suggested he go to
bed. Each time he had answered, 'In a minute, I'll go, I'm
going,' but without getting up from his chair. At length,
having made sure that Rose was asleep, along with Marcelle,
Mme Bricolin could take no more, and she went to bed, still
vainly calling her husband, who no longer had the strength to
move and who could not hear her any more. Completely
drunk, in the stupor of a man who had mounted a sudden
effort to sober up but who had made up for it afterwards, the
farmer, with his hand on his jug and his head on the table,
snored energetically, lulling his wife, who was sleeping an
exhausted slumber in the next room.

Barely an hour had gone by when M. Bricolin felt he was
suffocating, that he was about to keel over. He had a great
deal of difficulty in getting up. He felt as if his lungs could get
no air, as if his burning eyes could see nothing, as if he were
undergoing an apoplectic attack. Fear of death gave him the
strength to drag himself to the door on to the farmyard; the
candle had snuffed itself out in its iron holder.

Having managed to open the door and stumble down the steps that formed a sort of primitive perron in front of the new castle, the farmer turned his stupefied gaze on his surroundings, without understanding any of what he saw. An extraordinary light filling the farmyard forced him to put his hand in front of his face; his dizziness increased at the contrast with the shadows from which he had emerged. At last, when the air had dissipated some of the fumes of the wine, his sense of strangulation gave way to a convulsive shudder, at first mechanical and merely physical, but soon the sort produced by inexpressible terror. Two tall columns of fire, visible through the clouds of smoke, were emerging from the barn roof.

Bricolin thought he was having a nightmare; he rubbed his eyes, he shook all his limbs; but yet these jets of flame rose skywards, and took on huge shape with a dreadful speed. He wanted to shout 'Fire!', but his tongue was paralysed and his throat lifeless. He tried to turn round towards the house, away from which he had taken several insensible steps. On his right hand he saw torrents of flame come out of the stables, on his left another column of fire crowned the towers of the old castle, and in front of him ... his own house was illuminated from within with a fantastic clarity, and the door that he had left wide open vomited out a black whirlwind, as from the mouth of a forge. Every building at Blanchemont was victim to arson, conceived on a magnificent scale. The fire had been lit in over a dozen different spots, and what was even more sinister in the first act of this strange drama, was that a deathly hush reigned everywhere. Bricolin, deprived of his strength and will, was left in dreadful solitude, contemplating a disaster of which no one else was aware. All the other inhabitants of the new castle and the farm had passed straight from the slumber produced by fatigue or drunkenness to the suffocation produced by smoke. The crackling of the fire was the only thing to be heard, apart from the tiles dropping with a shrivelled sound onto the hard earth. Not a single cry or moan made answer to these evil warnings. It seemed as if the fire would have nothing more to devour than empty buildings and corpses. M. Bricolin wrung his hands and remained mute and immobile, as if, overcome by this nightmare, he were making vain efforts within himself to wake up.

At last a single piercing cry rang out: a woman's cry.* As if set free from the enchantment weighing him down, Bricolin replied with a savage howl to this human voice. Marcelle was the first to realize the danger; she hurtled outside, carrying her son in her arms. Not seeing Bricolin or the rest of the fire, she deposited the child on a haystack in the middle of the farmyard, and, telling him firmly, 'Stay here! Don't be afraid!', she ran back into the house, despite the suffocating smoke that filled it, to fetch Rose from her bed, where she remained as if paralysed, unable to follow.

Then, with a man's strength, the small blond woman, exalted by courage, took her young friend in her arms and heroically carried this weight, far greater than her own.

At the sight of his daughter, Bricolin, who had only thought of his harvest and his livestock at first, running up and down the barns, remembered that he had a family, and, sobering up for the second time in an even more radical fashion than the first, he flew to the aid of his mother and wife.

Fortunately the fire had not broken out vigorously anywhere except the roof-timbers, and the ground floor, where the Bricolins had their living quarters, was still intact, except for Rose's separate apartment, which, being located lower down and near a woodpile, was burning rapidly.

Mme Bricolin, who had woken with a start, suddenly found all her physical strength and presence of mind. With the help of her husband and Marcelle, she brought out old Bricolin, who, believing himself surrounded by the rick-burners, howled with all his strength, 'I've got nothing more! Don't kill me! Don't burn me! I'll give you everything!'

Little Fanchon came resolutely to the aid of old mother Bricolin, who was soon able to help the others. They managed to rouse the tenant farmers and their servants, and no one perished . . . But all this took a long while, and by the time they were able to get help from the village and organize a bucket chain, it was too late: the water seemed to reanimate the fire's intensity and to send the sparks flying further. The huge stockpiles of cereals and fodder, with which the farm buildings were full to overflowing, flamed up with the rapidity of thought. The timbers of the old buildings seemed to ask nothing more than to burn. Almost all of the plentiful live-stock was too stubborn to be shifted, and was suffocated or burnt alive. All they could save was the body of the new castle: the tiles caved in and the battens were exposed, reduced to charcoal, raising the roof's scorched carcass over the still-white walls of the house.

The fire-engines arrived, that useless and belated resource in the country, rescue forces that are usually badly directed, badly organized, and whose hoses inevitably split at the first effort, for lack of maintenance or use. However, the firemen and the inhabitants of the hamlet did manage to clear the ground, to prevent the fire spreading, and to save the Bricolins' dwelling and furnishings. But what the fire had taken was a vast amount: the separate apartment in which Rose and Marcelle slept, all the farm buildings, all the live-stock, all the farm implements. No one was concerned about the old castle, whose roof burned but whose strong bare walls were their own best defence. One of the towers succumbed to the heat and cracked from head to foot. The thick ivy embracing the others protected them from final ruination.

Daylight was beginning to glimmer as the miller and Lémor came out of the beggar's miserable hut. Lémor was carrying the cast-iron pot, and Grand-Louis was leading his beloved Sophie, who had greeted his approach with a whinny of friendship. 'I've read *Don Quixote*,' remarked the miller, 'and now I feel just like Sancho when he got his donkey back. For two sous I'd follow his example, put my arms round my old Sophie's neck and flatter her shamelessly.'

'Grand-Louis,' said Lémor, 'you may be able to resist that particular temptation, but aren't you tempted to see whether this iron pot is full of gold, or stones?'

'I lifted the lid,' replied the miller. 'Something's shining in there, all right; but I badly want to get out of here before daybreak, or else the people who live in this wilderness, if any do, will see movements and take me for a thief. I'm trembling with emotion and pleasure, like a man who's brought somebody else's business to a good end; but I also feel pretty cool, like a man who isn't getting anything out of it himself. Let's go, Monsieur Henri. Did you put my pickaxe back in the carriage? Let me just take one last look inside. The hole's covered up nicely, you can't see anything, let's be on our way! We'll stop in some little glade if our beasts refuse to go any further.'

The lawyer's horse had done three blessed country leagues at a fast trot, and often at a gallop, over hilly and rutted roads, and he was so weary on the return journey that when our travellers got to the heights of Lys-Saint-George they were obliged to give him a breather. Sophie, whom they had hitched to the back of the cabriolet, was not accustomed to such a mad pace, and she was covered in sweat. The miller was touched. 'You have to show these beasts some humanity, and besides, I don't want our good lawyer to lose a fine horse in this business, when he's been so honest and clever. As for Sophie, never mind the iron pot; no iron pot can equal my old servant. Here's a nice shady bit of pasture, no sign of man or beast in it. Let's go in. I'm sure there's a bag of oats in the back of the cabriolet; for Monsieur Tailland thinks of everything, and he's not the man to set off without a bite of something. We'll have a quarter-hour's rest, and then we'll all be in a fresher state when we set off again. I'm afraid that when I let my uncle's pig loose (let anybody who wants it inherit it!) I forgot to pinch a few of its bread-crusts, and my stomach's so empty that I'd happily share Sophie's oats if I didn't think I'd be doing her wrong. I don't feel I've begun my new life as the miser's heir very well. I'm dying of hunger next to my treasure.'

While he was chattering away in his usual manner, the miller unbridled the horses and gave them their breakfast, in the oat-sack for the lawyer's horse and for Sophie, in her long bonnet of blue cotton, which he tied jokingly round her neck.

'It's strange how light my heart feels now,' he said, squatting down under the hedgerow and opening the cast-iron pot. 'Do you realize, Monsieur Lémor, my happiness is in here?— if the louis coins aren't just on top, and the bottom full of big sous. It frightens me; this is too heavy to be gold alone. Come on, help me count it all.'

The counting was quickly accomplished. The antique gold coins were rolled up in dirty scraps of paper, in thousand-franc quantities. When they unrolled them, Lémor and the miller saw the marks that the beggar had told them about. The money belonging to Père Bricolin had a cross on each coin, the deposit left by the lord of Blanchemont a simple bar. At the bottom were roughly 3,000 francs in silver coins of every description, and even a handful of big sous, the last the beggar had put by.

'These left-overs,' exclaimed the miller as he threw them back into the bottom of the iron pot, 'these are my uncle's fortune, your servant's inheritance, the widow's mite that the old scoundrel had no scruples about accepting, but that'll go straight back to the widow and orphan, I can promise you. And who knows if it isn't also the proceeds of theft? When you look at how my uncle, God grant him peace! pinched Sophie from me, I don't have a lot of faith in how clean this legacy is. Well, I'll take pleasure in giving alms! I don't often get the chance of that princely privilege! Do you realize, with 3,000 francs, in this part of the world, you can rescue three families from poverty and give them a secure living?'

'But you have not considered the rest of the deposit, Grand-Louis. Only think, with this huge sum, which Madame de Blanchemont does not really require for herself, you will put her into a position to make many people happy.'

'Oh, I'll leave it up to her, she'll set things rolling pretty quickly there! But there's another thing, something that tickles my vanity: the little nest-egg that Monsieur Bricolin will accept from me with such great pleasure. He won't put it to the most Christian use, but it'll do a lot to smooth over my dealings with him, they were in a right state last night.'

'You mean to say, my dear Louis, that now you may claim Rose's hand.'

'Oh, I wouldn't be too sure of that! If the 50,000 francs belonged to me, it'd be all right, at a pinch. But Bricolin is better at counting than you! He'll say, "Here's 5,000 pistoles* that belong to me and that Grand-Louis has brought back to me, he's only doing his duty. What's mine isn't his; so I've got another 50,000 francs in my pocket, and he's left with his mill Gros-Jean, same as before.'

'But will he not be astounded and touched by an honesty of which he himself would never be capable?'

'Astounded, yes; touched, no. But he'll say to himself, "This lad could be useful to me." Honest folk are indispensable to those that aren't honest, and he'll forgive me my sins; he'll give me back his custom, which is very important to me because it puts me in a position to see and talk to Rose every day. So you can see that though I've no illusions, I have reason to be pleased. Yesterday evening, when I was dancing with Rose, when she acted as if she was in love with me, I was so proud and happy! Well, now I've recovered yesterday's happiness, tomorrow's worries don't bother me. That's a good deal, Cadoche, old mate, believe me! You were always sure your iron pot would give me consolation, weren't you? Well, you thought you could make me rich, but instead you've made me happy!'

'But my dear Louis, since you are now bringing Marcelle a sum equal to that which she wished to sacrifice for you, surely you will now accept the concessions she was offering to make to Monsieur Bricolin?'

'Me? Never. Let's talk no more about it. It offends me. I won't be banished from the farm any more; that's all I ask. Look how pretty the treasure is! How it gleams! What a lot of relieved misery and appeased worry is in there! You know, there is something handsome about money after all, Monsieur Lémor! Admit it! Here, in the hollow of my hand, lies life for five or six pauper children!'

'My friend, I can only see what is really there: weeping, screaming, the tortures old Bricolin underwent, the greed of the beggar, his shameful pointless existence, entirely eaten up by the nervous contemplation of his theft.'

'Humph! you're right,' exclaimed the miller, thrusting the handful of gold back into the iron pot with repulsion. 'Think of the crimes, the acts of cowardice, the worries, the lies, the terrors, and the suffering rolled up in there! You're right, money is vile! Even the two of us are peering at it and counting it out secretly like a pair of highwaymen, armed with pistols, afraid of being attacked by other bandits or hauled off by the constables. Go on, hide yourself away, you wretched stuff!' he shouted as he replaced the lid. 'And let's be off, friend! Long live joy, this isn't for us!'

The Fifth Day

XXXV. THE RIFT

As they approached the valley of the Vauvre, our travellers observed over Blanchemont a huge sheet of heavy smoke, lit by the rising sun.

'Look how heavy the mist is over the Vauvre this morning,' exclaimed the miller, 'especially over the place we both want to see! That saddens me, I can't make out the pointed turrets of my good old castle, which makes an anchor-point for my thoughts as I do my rounds of the villages!'

After ten minutes the smoke, pressed down by the humid vapours of the morning, had crawled the entire length of the valley. Reining the lawyer's horse in briskly, Grand-Louis remarked to his companion, 'It's a funny thing, Monsieur Lémor, I don't know if I'm blind this morning, but stare as I may, I can't see the red roof of the new castle down below the towers of the old one! But I'm sure it can be seen from here; I've stopped here over a hundred times, and I can make out the trees around it. Hang on! have a look! the old castle's completely different! The towers look to me like they've been knocked down. Where in God's name is the roof? Devil take me! there's nothing left but the gable-ends! Wait! What's that red down by the farm? It's a fire! Yes, fire! and all those black things? . . . Monsieur Lémor, didn't I say to you, when we got to Jeu-les-Bois, the whole sky was red and it looked as if there was a fire somewhere. You told me someone was burning the peat-heaths, but I knew perfectly well there aren't any moors around here. Just look! I'm not having a dream! The castle, the farm, everything's been burned! . . . What about Rose? Rose! . . . Oh, Good Lord! And Madame Marcelle! and my little Édouard! and old mother Bricolin! My God! My God!'

And the miller, lashing the horse furiously, set off at a gallop for Blanchemont, unconcerned for once about whether old Sophie would be able to keep up.

The nearer they got, the more dreadfully certain the signs became. Soon they heard the sinister tale from the mouths of passers-by, and although everyone assured them that no one had died, both men, pale and fearful, pressed on in haste, the horse's progress too slow for their taste.

When they arrived at the bottom of the castle mound, the poor animal, panting and dripping sweat, could not manage the upward track at anything more than a walk. They stopped at Piaulette's cottage and jumped out of the cabriolet, intending to run up the hill on foot. At that moment, Marcelle emerged from the cottage and appeared before them. She was pale but calm, and her clothes bore no trace of burn-marks. Having spent the entire night helping human creatures, she had not made useless efforts towards extinguishing the fire. When he saw her, Lémor almost fainted for joy; speechlessly he took her hand.

'My son is here, and Rose is with the priest,' said Marcelle. 'She came to no harm, she is hardly ill any longer; she is happy despite her parents' consternation. The only thing that has been lost is money. That is very little, compared to the happiness that awaits her . . .'

'What do you mean?' asked the miller. 'I don't understand.'

'Go and see her, my friend, there is no reason why you should not, and hear the news from her own lips. I should not be the first to tell you.'

In a state of stupefaction, Grand-Louis ran off. Lémor entered the cottage with Marcelle and hurried to the bed in which Édouard was sleeping; Piaulette and her husband took care of the horses. The last of the Blanchemonts was resting peacefully on a pallet belonging to the poorest peasant of his domain. He no longer had a dwelling to call his own, and hospitality from the indigent was the only right he could claim at this moment.

'He wasn't in any danger?' exclaimed Lémor, kissing the tiny hands that were moist with a gentle warmth.

'This little fellow is made of solid stuff,' said Marcelle with a certain pride. 'He was not ill, he woke up in suffocating smoke, and he was never afraid. With me, he spent the night helping to rescue and cheer others, and despite his weakness and his innocence of misery, he devised kind acts, caresses, and naïvely angelic words of comfort for me and for all the frightened people who were shivering and howling all about us. And to think that I feared fresh air and excitement might be harmful to his health! This frail constitution houses a heroic soul, Lémor! He is a blessed child, marked by God at his birth to become a noble pauper!'

The child woke up at Lémor's touch, and this time he recognized his affection rather than his features: 'Oh, Henri!' he exclaimed. 'Why wouldn't you speak to me when you were playing that you were Antoine?'

Marcelle was starting to explain stoically to her lover the new disaster wreaked on the remainder of her fortune by this fire, when M. Bricolin entered the cottage with a tormented expression, his clothes all in tatters and his hands badly burned.

After his initial terror, the farmer had worked with desperate energy and boldness to try to save his cattle and harvest. A hundred times he nearly fell victim to his frantic dedication; he would not abandon his vain hopes until he found himself surrounded by a pile of ashes. At that point despair, discouragement, and a sort of fury seized his unfortunate brain. He had become like one possessed, and he rushed to Marcelle with a distracted air, confused of mind and halting of speech.

'Oh, there you are at last, Madame!' he stuttered. 'I've been looking all over the village for you, I'd no idea what had happened to you. Now listen here, Madame Marcelle... what I've got to tell you is very important . . . you can be as calm as you please, all this misfortune will land on your head, the whole tragedy is your concern!'

'I am well aware of that, Monsieur Bricolin!' replied Marcelle with some impatience. The sight of this rapacious individual was not particularly consoling to her at this moment.

'Oh, you're well aware of it?' spluttered Bricolin angrily. 'I'm well aware of it too! It's up to you to rebuild the Blanchemont estate and restock the cattle.'

'With what, if you please, Monsieur Bricolin?'

'With your money! Don't you have any money? Didn't I give you enough?'

'I have it no longer, Monsieur Bricolin! The money-bag went up in flames.'

'You left *my* money-bag to the flames? The money-bag I *entrusted* to you?' howled Bricolin in exasperation, striking his forehead with his fists. 'How could you have been so crazy, so *stupid*, not to rescue the money-bag, when you had time to rescue your son?'

'I rescued Rose as well, Monsieur Bricolin. I was the one who carried her out of the house in my arms. During that time the scrip burned; I do not regret it.'

'That's not true, you've still got it!'

'I swear to you, before God, that I do not. The chest it was in, all the furniture in the bedchamber, everything burned while I was rescuing the people in it. You know that perfectly well, I have told you, because you interrogated me about it; but you did not listen to me, or else you do not remember.'

'Oh, no, I remember,' said the farmer in confusion, 'but I thought you were playing a trick on me.'

'And why should I play a trick on you? Wasn't the money mine?'

'Yours? So you don't deny that I bought your estate from you yesterday evening, that I paid you for it, and that it belongs to me?'

'What gave you the idea that I am the sort of person to deny it?'

'Oh, begging your pardon, pardon, Madame! I'm not in my right mind,' muttered the farmer, pacified and discomfited.

'So I see,' said Marcelle in a scornful tone which escaped his notice.

'All the same, the repair of the buildings and the provision of fresh livestock are up to you,' he continued after a silence during which his ideas once more descended into confusion.

'One thing or another, Monsieur Bricolin,' shrugged Marcelle. 'Either you did not buy the estate, and it is up to me to make good the damage, or I sold it to you and have nothing more to do with it: choose!'

'That's so,' said Bricolin, slipping into a fresh stupor. Then he continued quickly, 'Oh, I bought it off you right and proper, paid for it, you can't deny that! I've got your deed as a receipt, I wasn't so daft as to let it burn, not me! My wife has it in her pocket.'

'In that case, you have nothing to worry about, and neither do I, for I have a copy of our deed in my pocket as well.'

'But you must bear the expense!' roared Bricolin with sombre fury. 'I didn't buy an estate with no buildings and no livestock. That's a loss of at least 50,000 francs!'

'I have no idea, but the disaster took place after the sale.'

'It was you set the fire!'

'Oh, very likely!' exclaimed Marcelle with icy scorn, 'and I threw the sale proceeds into the flames for my amusement!'

'Begging your pardon, pardon, I'm not well!' mumbled the farmer. 'Losing so much money in one night! But all the same, Madame Marcelle, you owe me reparations for my misfortune. I've always had misfortune with your family. For the sake of the money your grandfather left with him, my father was tortured by the rick-burners, and he lost 50,000 francs of his own money.'

'The consequences of that misfortune are irreparable, for your father lost his mental and physical health. But my family is entirely innocent of the crime committed by these brigands; and as for the loss of your money, it was generously recompensed by my grandfather.'

'That's true, he was a good master! And so you ought to do like him, you should make amends to me!'

'You care so much for money, and I care so little, Monsieur Bricolin, that I should satisfy you if I were in a position to do so. But you forget that I have lost all, down to the miserable sum of 2,000 francs which I had made from the sale of my carriage, down to my clothes and linen. My son cannot even say that he possesses nothing in the world at this moment beside the clothes that cover him, for I brought him naked out of your house; and if this woman you see before you had not taken him in, with sublime charity, and clothed him in the rough garments of one of her children, I should have been obliged to beg alms of you to buy a smock and a pair of wooden shoes for him. Leave me in peace, I beg of you; I have sufficient strength to bear my misfortune, but your greed makes me angry and weary.'

'That will do, Monsieur,' said Lémor, who could contain himself no longer. 'Go away, leave Madame in peace.'

Bricolin did not hear this command. He had dropped on to a chair, grasping at last that Marcelle was completely destitute and that his last hope of ransom was gone. 'So,' he howled in despair, striking his fists on the table, 'tonight I thought I'd made a good bargain, getting Blanchemont for 250,000 francs, and now this morning I'm 50,000 francs poorer in lost buildings and livestock! What that means,' he sobbed, 'is that the estate cost me 300,000 francs, just like you wanted!'

'I cannot think that this is my doing, or that I derive any profit from it,' said Marcelle coldly, her indignation abated by the sight of Lémor's, which she hoped to moderate by restraining her own.

'Is that all you've lost, Monsieur Bricolin?' asked Piaulette naïvely, astounded by what she had witnessed. 'If I was you, I'd make shift! This poor lady has lost everything, you're still well off, as well off as yesterday evening, and you're on at her for something more! It's a funny thing! If you get Blanchemont for 300,000 francs, even with your misfortune, you've still got it for a good price. I know plenty of folk who'd have given more for it.'

'What do you think you're saying?' spluttered Bricolin. 'Be quiet, you're nothing but a fool and a busybody.'

'Oh, thank you very much, sir,' answered Piaulette. Then turning proudly to Marcelle, she added, 'Never mind, Madame; since you've lost everything, you can stay with me as long as you like and share my black bread. I'll never begrudge it you nor send you away.'

'There, Monsieur!' exclaimed Lémor. 'Listen and be ashamed!'

'You know, I've no idea who you are!' shouted Bricolin. 'Nobody knows you in these parts; you look as much like a miller as I do a bishop. But you won't get far, my lad! I'll inform the constabulary, they'll demand your papers, and if you haven't any, so much the worse for you! The fire at my place was set maliciously, that's plain as day, everyone thinks so, and the public prosecutor is here to charge somebody. You're with a man who has a grudge against me, that's enough reason!'

'Ah, that really is too much!' blurted Lémor indignantly. 'You are the basest of men, and if you do not leave this house, I shall make you do so.'

'Stop!' called Marcelle, seizing Lémor by the arm. 'Have pity on this man, he has lost his reason! Be indulgent towards him in his misfortune, however badly he bears it: follow my example, Lémor, my patience is sufficient for the situation.'

Bricolin was not listening. He was cradling his head in his hands and moaning like a mother who has lost her child.

'And to think I never took out insurance because it was too dear,' he groaned pitifully, 'and what about my cattle, my poor cattle, that were so fine and fat! And a flock of sheep worth 2,000 francs, that I refused to sell at St Christopher's fair!'

Marcelle could not help but smile, and her equanimity aided Lémor in restraining his anger.

'Never mind!' blurted the farmer, rising abruptly. 'Your miller won't have my daughter!'

'In that case you will not have my land. The deed is clear and the conditions definite.'

'We'll go to court!'

'Well and good.'

'Oh, you can't go to court, you can't! You need money for that, and you haven't got any. And then you'd have to give the payment back to me, and how are you going to do that? Anyway your pretty little condition is null and void; and as for the miller, I intend to start by having him arrested and thrown into gaol; because I'm sure it was him as lit the fire, to get back at me for throwing him out yesterday. All the village wil be my witnesses, he threatened me . . . and this gentleman here . . .

that should do: police, police!' And he staggered out in a genuine delirium.

XXXVI. THE CHAPEL

Worried for the miller and Lémor, who might be drawn into a disagreeable and possibly serious business by Bricolin's blind vengeance, Marcelle persuaded her lover to hide, and Piaulette had just gone out to warn Grand-Louis to do like-wise, when they saw all the village folk, formerly dispersed around the green in conversation about the disaster, running together towards the farm.

'I know for a certainty, the deed's already done!' cried Piaulette, on the verge of tears. 'They've already arrested poor Grand-Louis!'

Lémor, acting immediately on his courage and loyalty, rushed from the cottage and hurtled up towards the castle mound. The frightened Marcelle followed him, leaving Édouard in the care of the eldest daughter of her hostess.

When they entered the farmyard, Marcelle and Lémor were thunderstruck by the scattered heaps of charred debris, the earth oozing water like black ink, and the crowd of exhausted, sodden, scorched workers, like spectres, preparing for further fatiguing effort: the fire had reignited in a little separate chapel between the farm and the old castle.

This new mishap seemed incomprehensible, for the building had remained intact until now, and if a spark had fallen on it during the blaze, the fire would not have smouldered quietly for so long in the stock of dry wood that was kept there. And yet flames were coming out of the interior, as if an audaciously implacable hand wished to destroy all, in front of all, down to the very last building on the estate.

'Let the chapel burn,' shouted M. Bricolin, frothing with rage, 'find the man who set the fire! He must be here, he can't be far away. It was Grand-Louis, I know it for a fact! I've got proof! Search the hunting-park! Seal off the hunting-park!'

M. Bricolin was unaware that even whilst he was consigning the miller to public prosecution, Grand-Louis, forgetting everything else and knowing nothing of the events outside, was in the presbytery, on his knees next to the armchair in which Rose had been laid, hearing from her own mouth the avowal of her love and the revelation of her father's bargain. In the general chaos the priest and even his maidservant had thrown their lot in with the fire-fighters, and only grandmother Bricolin had remained with Rose. Plunged into the purest intoxication, the young lovers were entirely oblivious to the tumultuous events unfolding around them.

A circle had formed around the chapel and the fire-engines had just begun work, when M. Bricolin, who had gone up as far as the arched doorway, jumped back in horror and keeled over on to one of his farm lads, who could barely support his weight. This chapel, formerly joined to the old castle, had retained some fine details of Gothic decoration which might have interested an antiquary. But this decrepit structure was no match for such intense heat. Flames were licking out the windows, and the delicate rose traceries began to split off with a great cracking. Just then the half-opened door was shoved open from the inside. The onlookers saw the madwoman, with a little lantern in one hand and a torch of burning straw in the other. She made her slow way out, having put the finishing touch to her work of destruction: walking in a grave fashion, her eyes fixed on the earth, seeing no one, entirely preoccupied by the joy of revenge, long calculated and coldly executed.

An over-conscientious constable marched up to arrest her, grabbing her by the arm. Now the madwoman saw that she was trapped in the crowd: she held her firebrand aloft to the constable's face, and he was forced by this unexpected defence to let go his hold. Then, her impetuous agility again to the fore, her face mirroring hatred and fury, the fugitive Bricoline leapt forward into the chapel with garbled oaths. They tried to follow her, but no one dared go in. She passed through the flames as nimbly as a salamander and clambered up the little spiral staircase that led to the tower. There she appeared, fanning the fire, which was too dilatory for her taste. Soon she was surrounded on all sides. In vain they played the hoses, trying to water the roof. It had recently been repaired, with zinc flashings. The water ran straight down it and barely penetrated the building. Thus the fire must have been smouldering away inside, and the hapless Bricoline suffering atrocious tortures as she burned slowly. But she appeared insensible, and they heard her singing a dance-melody she had been fond of in her youth, which doubtless she had danced with her lover, and which entered her mind again at the moment of her death. Not a single cry was heard from her; deaf to the screams and pleas of her mother, who was writhing from side to side, forcing the onlookers to restrain her from running to join her daughter, she sang for a long while. Then she appeared on the tower one final time. Recognizing her father, she called out to him:

'Ah! Monsieur Bricolin! It's a fine bright day for you, *the light of day today*!'

Those were her last words. When the fire was brought under control, they found her calcified bones on the stone floor of the chapel.

This appalling death finally unsettled M. Bricolin's mind and broke his wife's courage. They thought no more of arresting anyone, and for the entire day, forgot completely about Rose, mother Bricolin, and her elderly husband. Shut in with the priest, M. and Mme Bricolin refused to see anyone, and only emerged when they had drunk the full bitter measure of their grief.

XXXVII. CONCLUSION

Marcelle had sufficient presence of mind to foresee that it would be dangerous for Rose, ill and exhausted as she was by so much emotion, to learn about the appalling death of her sister. She suggested to the miller that he should pack her quickly in the lawyer's cabriolet and take her to his mill, with her grandmother and the elderly invalid, whom the good old woman would not leave. Arm-in-arm with Lémor, who was carrying Édouard, Marcelle followed shortly after.

For several days Rose had sharp attacks of fever every evening. Her friends never left her for so much as a moment, and, having successfully kept from her the sight of Cadoche's funeral, conducted with all the ceremony which the old beggar had demanded, they kept her in ignorance of the madwoman's death until she should be able to endure the news; but for a long while afterwards she did not learn the horrifying circumstances.

Marcelle consulted M. Tailland about the validity of the deed she had drawn up with Bricolin. The lawyer's opinion was not favourable. Since a marriage was a matter of public process, it could not be made a condition in a private contract of sale. If there are invalid clauses, the sale remains valid and such clauses are reckoned not to have been inserted in the contract. Such are the terms of the law. M. Bricolin had been well aware of them before he signed.

After three days the mill witnessed the arrival of the farmer, with a pale face and hangdog expression, weighing half as much as before, sine he had even lost the desire to drink so as to give himself courage. He seemed incapable of anger; yet no one knew his intentions in coming to Blanchemont, and seeing that Rose was still very weak, Marcelle was frightened that he might have come to force her back, with outrageous speech and manner. All the mill was taken aback, and everyone came out *en masse* to confront him and prevent him from entering, unless he announced his peaceful intentions.

He began by ordering mother Bricolin coldly to bring his daughter back immediately. He had rented a house in the village of Blanchemont and was beginning the work of reconstruction. 'The mere fact that I'm ill lodged,' he said, 'is no reason to deprive me of my daughter's company or for her to refuse to help her mother. That would be an unnatural feeling in the child.'

While he was speaking Bricolin was glaring fiercely at Grand-Louis. It was clear that he wanted to get his daughter away from the miller, without a scene, but that he intended afterwards to trumpet his bitterness abroad and accuse Grand-Louis of having kidnapped her.

'That's fair enough,' said Mère Bricolin, who had taken on the task of replying. 'Rose has been asking to return to her father and mother for some time now, but as she's still poorly, we wouldn't let her. I reckon she's in a fit state to follow you today, and I'm prepared to accompany her, with my husband, if you have a place to put us. Just give Madame Marcelle time to prepare the girl for both the pleasure and the shock of seeing you again. As for me, I've something private to tell you, Bricolin; come into my bedchamber.'

The old woman took him into the bedroom which she was sharing with the mill-wife. Marcelle and Rose had been made comfortable in the miller's room. Lémor and Grand-Louis slept luxuriously in the hay.

'Bricolin,' the good woman began, 'this rebuilding will cost you a pretty penny! Where'll you get the money?'

'What business is it of yours, Mother? You've none to give me,' answered Bricolin brusquely. 'Of course I'm short at the moment, but I'll borrow. I never have trouble getting credit.'

'Oh yes, but at heavy interest, that's the way, and then by the time you've got to pay it back you'll have more expenses, all necessary and inevitable. That'll weigh you down, and you won't know how to get out if it.'

'Well, what do you want me to do? Do you expect me to put my harvest in my shoe next year and shelter my animals under a broomstick?'

'How much will it cost, all that?'

'God knows!'

'About how much?'

'Between 45,000 and 50,000 francs, at least: 15,000 to 18,000 for the buildings, as much again for the livestock, and then there's what I lost on the harvest and my profits for this year!'

'Yes, that's about 50,000 francs, I reckon that too. Well, tell me, Bricolin, if I gave you the money, what would you do for me?'

'You?' barked Bricolin, whose eyes had taken on their usual alacrity. 'Have you made some household savings that you've kept from me, or are you drivelling?'

'I'm not drivelling. I have 50,000 francs in gold that I'll give you, if you let me marry Rose off according to my taste.'

'Oh, ho! It's always the miller! All the women are crazy about that bear of a man, even the eighty-year-olds!'

'Fine, fine, have your little joke, but do what I say.'

'And where is this money?'

'I gave it to Grand-Louis to keep,' said the old woman, who knew that her son was capable of snatching it out of her hands in a drunken moment, if he saw it in the flesh.

'Why Grand-Louis, why not to me or my wife? Do you intend to make him a donation, if I won't do your bidding?'

'Other people's money is safe in his hands,' said the old woman, 'for he had the money without my knowing it, and brought it back to me when I thought it was gone for ever. It belongs to my husband, but you had him declared legally incompetent, and since he and I bequeathed our property to whichever of us survived, under the old law, I have the disposal of it!'*

'You mean it's been recovered? That's impossible! You're mocking me, why should I listen to you?'

'Listen,' said mother Bricolin, 'it's a strange story.'

And she told her son the entire history of Cadoche and his legacy.

'And the miller brought the money back to you, when he could have kept mum?' cried the stunned farmer. 'Well, that's very honest of him, very handsome! We must give him a present.'

'There's only one present he wants: Rose's hand, since he's already made her a present of his heart.'

'But I won't give her any dowry!' yelped Bricolin.

'That goes without saying, did anybody ask you to?'

'Show me the money.'

Mother Bricolin took her son to see the miller, who showed him the cast-iron pot and its contents.

'And so,' exclaimed the farmer in amazement, revived by the sight of so many gold coins, 'Madame de Blanchemont isn't in utter destitution?'

'Thanks to the grace of God!'

'And to you, Grand-Louis!'

'Thanks to Père Cadoche's little fancies.'

'And you, what do you inherit?'

'Three thousand francs, of which a thousand is for Piaulette and the rest will go to set up two other families nearby. We'll all work together and share the profits.'*

'That's a stupid thing to do!'

'No, it is practical and just.'

'But why don't you hang on to the thousand *écus* for wedding presents to give to... your wife?'

'It would feel like stolen money to me; and even though it's only the product of alms-giving, you're very proud; would you want Rose to cover her body with dresses that have been paid for by the whole country's sous, given in charity to a beggar?'

'You wouldn't have to tell them where it came from! . . . Well, then, when's the wedding, Grand-Louis?'

'Tomorrow, if you consent.'

'Let's publish the banns tomorrow, give me the money today, I need it.'

'Not a bit of it! Not a bit!' exclaimed the old farm-wife. 'You'll have it the day of the wedding. Tit for tat, my lad!'

The sight of money had cheered M. Bricolin greatly. He sat down at table, drank a toast with the miller, embraced his daughter, and got back up on his nag, between two wine-sacks, to go and direct his masons at their work.

'After all,' he smiled to himself, 'I still got Blanchemont for 250,000 francs, you could even call it 200,000, because I haven't got to give my youngest daughter a dowry!'

'And as for us, Lémor, we shall build as well,' said Marcelle to her lover when Bricolin had departed. 'We are well off; we have enough to build a pretty little country house, where *our* child will get a good education; for you will be his tutor, and the miller will teach him his craft. Why should the boy not be both a working man and an educated person?'

'And I, too, have much to learn,' said Lémor. 'I am ignorant; I shall read and instruct myself in the evenings. I am a mill lad; I like the craft, and shall keep to it during the day. How wonderfully healthy our Édouard will grow, with such a life!'

'Well, Madame Marcelle,' said Grand-Louis, taking Lémor's hand, 'you were the one as said to me when you first got here (it was eight days ago, no more, no less!) that your idea of happiness was a nice modest little house, with thatch on the roof and green meadows all around it, like mine; a simple life, not too much encumbered, like mine; a son doing good work, not too dim-witted, like me . . . And all that here on our river Vauvre, which has the honour of pleasing you . . . and next to us, who're good neighbours!'

'And all on a communal basis,' said Marcelle, 'for I will not hear of any other arrangement!'

'Oh, that's impossible! Your share, at the moment, is bigger than mine.'

'You reckon incorrectly, miller,' said Lémor. 'Mine and thine, between two friends, are nonsense, like two and two making five.'

'Well, then I'm a rich man and a scholar!' replied the miller. 'For I have Rose's love, and you'll talk to me every day! Didn't I tell you, Monsieur Lémor, that it would take a miracle for everything to come right? But I wasn't reckoning on uncle Cadoche.'

'Why are you dancing like that, Alochon?' asked Édouard.

'Because, child,' laughed the miller, lifting him up, 'when I cast my nets, in the brightest part of the water I caught a little angel who'll bring me happiness; and in the muddiest bit, an old devil of an uncle, whom perhaps I can ransom from purgatory!'

EXPLANATORY NOTES

5 *far niente*: doing nothing. The walk in question could well have been through the flooded countryside of Berry, near Sand's home at Nohant. In June 1844, Sand had already signed a contract for the novel which was to become *The Miller of Angibault* but had not yet decided on her title and subject. The inspiration for the flood scenes which dominate the early chapters of the novel may have arisen from heavy rains which caused the River Indre to overspill its banks on 24 June.

in our valley . . . Angibault: the Vallée-Noire, 'Black Valley', a region on the River Indre and its tributaries in Berry. The mill of Angibault was 4 km. (2 1/2 mls.) west of Sand's home at Nohant, and 7 km. (4 1/2 mls.) north-west of the town of La Châtre.

M. de Robespierre: Maximilien François Marie Isidore de Robespierre (1758–94), Jacobin leader and orator, closely identified with the Reign of Terror even though he was not its architect. The allusion is unclear. Perhaps Sand means that the old mill-owner was unwilling to decapitate any of his vegetation, taking the lesson of the Terror thoroughly to heart.

the castle of Blanchemont: often identified with the ruined castle of Sarzay, 2 km. (1 1/4 mls.) south of Angibault.

6 *twenty leagues*: roughly 80 km. (50 mls.).

1852: written between the end of June and the middle of August 1844, at Sand's usual highly disciplined pace, *The Miller of Angibault* was serialized between 21 January amd 19 March 1845 in the journal *La Réforme*. In April of that year it was published by Desesart in two volumes. This Notice was written for the illustrated Hetzel edition of the novel, which appeared in 1853. See Note on the Text.

7 *Solange*: Solange Dudevant-Sand, later Clésinger (1828–98), Sand's daughter (probably by her childhood companion Stéphane Ajasson de Grandsagne, not her husband, Baron Casimir Dudevant). Named after the favourite saint of Berry, Solange was nevertheless not the family favourite: Casimir harangued her as a 'harlot's daughter', and her older brother Maurice (1823–89) was Sand's preferred child. Indeed, Sand wrote in later life that she regarded Maurice's wife, Lina, as her true daughter, not 'the other'. This dedication to the then six-

teen-year-old Solange makes some amends for Sand's consistent preference of Maurice, and its sentiment is touching. But it comes rather late: *The Miller of Angibault* was after all Sand's nineteenth published novel. Relations between Solange and her mother, often stormy, deteriorated further in 1847, when Solange married the sculptor Jean-Baptiste-Auguste Clésinger despite Sand's well-founded trepidation. Clésinger was often violent towards Sand, once punching her in the chest in pursuit of further dowry. Chopin's rupture with Sand widened the breach still further: he took the Clésingers' side in the dowry dispute and remained in hurtingly close contact with Solange, who was present at his deathbed, whilst Sand was not aware that he was dying. The Clésingers separated in 1852; their two daughters both died young (see Intro., p. 14). In 1871 Solange wrote to her mother that her childlessness was 'a despair which lodges like solitude in the heart, and which burrows and spreads like a cancer as one grows older. To grow old alone is awful for a woman.' Despite the unhappy circumstances of her life, Solange has universally been portrayed as a villain—blamed alternately by chauvinist biographers for luring Chopin away, or by more feminist-minded scholars for greed and failure to support her mother emotionally.

9 *The First Day*: just as Sand parcels out the last of her bucolic novels, *Les Maîtres Sonneurs*, into 'veillées' (evening entertainments), so she divides this, the first of her bucolic novels, into 'journées'.

The high Romantic style of this first chapter is quite at odds with the rest of the novel, and the modern reader may well be put off: isn't this just the sort of sentimentality for which Sand's name has become a byword? In fact, Sand may well be parodying the conventions of the Romantic novel here; or possibly she is sugaring the pill of socialist doctrine which the reader will later have to swallow. Most plausibly, the Parisian couple are set up in this first chapter as straw men: their overwrought dialogue and overnice ideas will fit them ill for founding a rural utopia. If reform is to come, it will not be from the urban intelligentsia. See also the note to p. 54.

13 *Do you mean to submit to the yoke again*: this passage recalls Sand's attack on the institution of marriage in her first published novel, *Indiana*.

16 *worthy to redeem . . . alone*: this theme of a female Messiah recurs throughout Sand's novels. The eponymous heroine of

Lélia (1833) is given the name Annunziata—the chosen one—
when she becomes a nun. Lélia's former lover Sténio says of
her campaign to redeem the convict Trenmor, 'You voluntarily
became his friend, his consolation, his good angel; you went to
him, you said, "Come unto me, you who are accused, I shall
return to you the heaven which you have lost! Come unto me,
who am without spot or blame. I shall make clean your sins with
my hands!"' (*Lélia*, Paris: Calmann-Levy, 1839 edn., 1. 39) The
plots of *Mauprat* (1837), *La Petite Fadette* (1847) and *Laura*
(1862) likewise hinge on male reformation through female
moral agency. *Mauprat* concerns a Heathcliff-like wolf-boy who
is taught to control his temper and libido by his cousin, herself
equally prone to the family fiery spirits but saved by feminine
sensibility—as he is in the end by hers. The heroine of *Laura*
symbolizes the middle way between the extremes of scientific
rationalism and romantic sensibility, both embodied by men.
Fadette is conventionally seen as the tale of a tomboy awakened
to proper feminine mental health by the love of a good man, but
actually Sand remarks of the relationship between Fadette and
her lover, Landry, 'she taught him reason'. (*La Petite Fadette*
(Paris: Livre de Poche, 166))

17 *all of them can now read*: literacy rose sharply, particularly
among French women, in the mid-nineteenth century. In 1830
roughly 85 per cent of men and 60 per cent of women were
literate; by 1848 the corresponding figures were 87 and 79 per
cent. (James Smith Allen, *Popular French Romanticism: Authors, Readers and Books in the 19th Century* (Syracuse, NY:
Syracuse University Press, 1981)) In the seven years between
1827 and 1835 alone, government spending on education performed an exponential leap from 50,000 to over 1.5 million
francs. A study of the book trade by Edmond Weroet remarked
that all of France had become 'an immense reading room'. (*De
la librairie française*, quoted in Smith Allen, 154)

20 *scorn for courtesans*: sympathy for courtesans and prostitutes
recurs throughout Sand's work, beginning with *Lélia* (1833), in
which Lélia and her courtesan sister Pulchérie frequently satirize
male hypocrisy about prostitution. The Sand scholar Béatrice
Didier has pointed out the link with Sand's vigorous critique of
marriage in *Indiana*.

21 *Italiens*: the Théâtre des Italiens, or Opéra-Comique, in the
Boulevard des Italiens.

22 *wastes of Sologne*: a district west of Berry, bounded by the River
    Loire to the north and the Cher to the south. In the 1840s it was
    still largely marshland, until the swamps were reclaimed and
    forestation undertaken during the reign of Louis Napoléon.

   eighty leagues from Paris: about 320 km. (200 mls.).

   five or six leagues hence: 20–5 kms. (15 mls.).

23 *Montluçon*: a town on the Cher, about 50 km. (30 mls.) south-
    east of La Châtre, the nearest town to Angibault.

   Château-Meillant: about 12 km. (8 mls.) east of La Châtre.

   Ardentes: north-west of Angibault, between Châteauroux and
    La Châtre.

   far away . . . four full leagues: this is both satirical and telling:
    16 km., or 10 mls., is not, of course, 'very far away'. Marcelle's
    grand designs, so clear in Paris, become progressively muddled
    the longer she stays in the country, and this is the first blow to
    her plans: she cannot even find her rural utopia.

   La Berthenoux: about 8 km. (5 mls.) north-east of Angibault.

   palace of the Corybantes: the Corybantes were priests of Cybele.
    In Plato's dialogue describing the period just before the end of
    Socrates' life, the *Crito*, they are said to hear imaginary flutes in
    the air, which obsess them. Thus, the palace of the Corybantes
    is mythical and delusive.

24 *Château of Corisante*: in the Romantic period, opera had a great
    popular vogue, so that even a groom might have heard it. This
    may be a reference to *Corisandre*, a three-act opera with libretto
    by Linières and Lebailly and music by Langle.

25 *his clear blue eyes*: in the previous paragraph the miller's eyes
    were black. Sand is not always scrupulous about her characters'
    physical appearance: in the earlier novel *Lélia*, the poet Sténio
    starts out with black hair but ends up a blond, like the poet
    Alfred de Musset, who became Sand's lover during the writing
    of the first draft.

   adherence of his head-covering to his head: Sand's wry wit now
    begins to appear, elbowing out the high style of the first chapter
    and a half. So does the political theme of incomplete rural
    transformation: the Revolution has lessened the peasant's defer-
    ence, but he is not its long-term beneficiary. That privilege
    belongs to the rich peasant Bricolin, who takes his first bow in
    Chapter 8.

26 *alochon*: mill-wheel paddle.

27 *calèche*: a light four-wheeled carriage with a folding hood.

patache: an unsprung cart for transporting goods, further described by Sand in the paragraph which follows.

29 *Labreuil*: or la Brewille, 5 km. (3 mls.) north-east of Angibault.

Corlay: 3 km. (2 mls.) north of Angibault.

traînes: the term used in nineteenth-century Berry for sunken lanes covered by foliage. In a letter to Mazzini, dated 28 July 1847, Sand distinguished between a *traîne*, wide enough for a wagon to pass, and a *traquette*, or footpath.

Automedon: in the *Iliad*, the charioteer of Achilles.

30 *Indre*: principal river of Berry, which rises south of La Châtre and flows into the Loire west of Tours, just north of the castle of Azay-le-Rideau.

Couarde: a black, narrow, deep stream, called 'Couarde' (Cowardly) because it runs under heavily wooded banks and appears to be crouching in fear.

dead man's stone: *pierre des morts*, a hollow stone at the foot of the wayside cross, in which each burial party that passes deposits a rough wooden crucifix.

32 *Bucephalus*: horse of Alexander the Great.

37 *La Fontaine*: Jean de La Fontaine (1621–95), fabulist, poet, and dramatist.

39 *English garden*: Sand is contrasting the English preference for the picturesque in garden style (as compared to the formal French garden) with the genuine prodigality of nature.

40 *galette*: girdle-cake.

44 *Nohant*: the hamlet surrounding George Sand's family home, 6 km. (4 mls.) north of La Châtre (Indre), with a fourteenth-century church, a farm, and an inn.

their son . . . army: Revolutionary and Napoleonic conscription had helped to raise literacy, since recruits had to declare publicly, and embarrassingly, if they could not read and write. The male literacy rate was 87 per cent in France by 1848, far higher than in most European countries. The female rate was a respectable 79 per cent, however, indicating that more widespread education in the wake of the Revolution was an even more potent factor than the ongoing conscription. (James Smith Allen, *Popular French Romanticism*, 153)

it wasn't the thing in my day: Grand'Marie would have been born well before the Revolution, probably around 1765 (she is seventy-five when the story opens in about 1840—making it improbable, incidentally, that she should have a twenty-five-year-old son). Female literacy increased by about 50 per cent between 1790 and 1870.

48 *a sounder basic education*: Grand-Louis would have been born about 1815, and thus would have benefited from the extension of primary schooling which began after the Revolution and continued throughout the Napoleonic period. In one of the poorest districts of Paris, whose rates were by no means the highest in France, 72 per cent of conscripts said they could read and write in 1829 (and when testing began in 1850, no more than 3 per cent were found to be lying). Wealthier areas had male literacy rates approaching 100 per cent. Berry would probably have been somewhere in between. A writer for the *Universel* noted in 1829, 'Reading has now reached the blacksmith's shop, the quarries, the sheds of wood-joiners' apprentices, and the stonemason's closet.'

49 *Sunday . . . fish all morning long*: note how little conventional religious observance figures in the good character of Grand-Louis, although in Chapter 11 he professes a deeper sort of religion.

50 *neither holly nor broom*: symbols of hospitality; the holly grows so abundantly in France that it is even used as winter fodder for cattle.

54 *the novel she wanted to live*: this phrase illustrates Sand's cleverly self-referential use of the novel's theme and diction to characterize the city-dwellers. Sand presents Marcelle's romantic egalitarianism as literally just that: taken straight out of a *roman*, a novel. This ties in with the overblown style of the first two chapters, written in the genre of the high Romantic novel.

55 *Marches*: *la Marche berrichonne*, in the direction of Boussac, south-east of La Châtre, on the Bourbonnais borders (marches).

the picturesque aspect of the old castle: the contrast between the ruined castle and the grubby workaday farm of the *nouveaux-riches* Bricolins symbolizes the conflict at the novel's centre between idealism and materialism: or more precisely, the disillusioning choice between the old castle (picturesque, but the vestige of feudal injustice) and the 'new castle' (soulless, and the possession of the now-ascendant rural bourgeoisie).

57 *Liège*: about 25 km. (15 mls.) south-east of Tours.

60 *Bourges*: about 55 km. (35 mls.) north-east of Angibault.

62 *The Parvenu Peasant*: from *Le Paysan parvenu*, title of an unfinished novel (1735) by Pierre Carlet de Chamblain Marivaux (1688–1763). Marivaux's peasant rises through making his fortune in the metropolis; Sand's exploits the decadent aristocracy of the metropolis and makes his fortune on his home turf.

65 *Mme de Blanchemont's fortune*: Sand may well be drawing on the similar near-ruination of her own family's estate by her husband, Casimir Dudevant. The provisions of the Napoleonic Code had radically reduced women's property rights, along with many of their other civic entitlements. On her marriage the Code dictated that Sand should surrender all control of Nohant to her husband, although she retained its legal title. At the time of their formal separation in 1836, Dudevant, the illegitimate son of a minor Gascon noble, who brought little wealth into the marriage, contested the title to the estate as well, although his faulty administration of it had reduced its value considerably. He was awarded Sand's Paris properties; she retained Nohant, but it took her many years to restore the lands and their tenants to any degree of prosperity.

66 *your chambermaid*: Sand italicizes this phrase (*fille de chambre*), perhaps to highlight Bricolin's ignorance: Suzette is a lady's-maid (*femme de chambre*), but Bricolin has never encountered a high-class servant of this ilk.

67 *in the light of day today*: au jour d'aujourd'hui, M. Bricolin's favourite, idiosyncratic phrase, almost impossible to translate. George Sand had thought of using it as the novel's title.

livres: old francs.

70 *Le Blanc*: about 70 km. (45 mls.) west.

79 *250,000 or 300,000 francs*: this would not have seemed a great deal to a member of the metropolitan aristocracy: Balzac reckoned that a fashionable woman of the period needed a minimum of 25,000 francs a year to live in Paris.

81 *Bois de Boulogne*: former royal park on the western outskirts of Paris.

82 *the infancy of Jupiter in the sacred grottoes*: according to Greek myth, Rhea, mother of Zeus (Roman Jupiter) gave birth to him in a cave on what is now Mt. Ida in Crete, to save the baby from his father, Cronos, who had swallowed all his previous children. She presented Cronos with a stone in swaddling clothes, which he swallowed instead. When Zeus reached manhood, he overthrew his father, forced him to vomit up the stone and the other

children, and banished him. Marcelle has similar hopes for
Édouard: that he will overturn the corrupt regime of his father.

84 *his milling-fee*: the miller charges in kind, not in money. Sand
appended a note to the text at this point: 'Millers are never paid
in the Vallée-Noire; they take part of the grain, more or less
faithfully according to the milling-fee, and they are generally
more honest than M. Bricolin allows. When they have a good
number of customers, they can set by much more than they need
for their own consumption and start a little grain-business.'

88 *as it's often been in the past*: with the coronation of Charles X
in 1824 and the resurgence of the Jesuits, sacrilege was made a
capital offence.

92 *Bricoline*: the eldest daughter, called, after the custom of the
country, by the feminine form of the family's surname (as her
mother is called Thibaude). George Sand may have been drawing on her own advocacy and protection of a girl with learning
difficulties called Fanchette, who had been abandoned by the
nuns.

96 *to line our pockets*: the rather didactic passage which this question introduces represents Sand's own socialist opinions (see
Introduction). What gives the dialogue spark is the personages
conducting it: both women.

97 *a king can do anything*: Rose reflects rural bourgeois satisfaction
with the Orleanist regime, instituted in 1830 after the more
extreme ultramontane regime of Charles X. Louis-Philippe, the
'Citizen King', encouraged trade, agriculture, and industry; opposition to him was largely confined to secret societies in Paris.
Alexis de Tocqueville wrote of the pragmatic Louis-Philippe,
'He was enlightened, subtle, flexible; because he was open only
to what was useful, he was full of proud disdain for the truth . . .
having no belief in himself, he had none in the beliefs of others.'

I am only an ignorant woman: this conventional disclaimer may
indicate the limitations of Sand's feminism.

99 *put out to nurse with his sister*: a subtle indication of the
Bricolins' social pretentions?

100 *assemblées*: rural balls. Dancing was a widespread pastime in
Berry: the importance of the bourrée (see note to p. 206) and the
social kudos accorded to the players of the accompanying
cornemuse (see note to p. 197) are described in the final novel of
Sand's rural series, *The Master Pipers*.

103 *all that for a man's love*: in this passage Sand develops, with
telling realism, the theme of all-pervading village gossip which
will play an even stronger part in the last novel of the series, *The
Master Pipers*.

104 *twenty leagues from here*: about 80 km. (50 mls.).

with his friends, horses, dogs and mistresses: it is hard to dispel
the sense that Sand is describing the great loves in the life of her
husband, Casimir Dudevant. Marcelle goes on to complain that
her husband fobbed her off with tales of woe whenever she
asked for details of Blanchemont, and there are parallels in the
speculative losses and maladministration of the Nohant estate
which occurred under Casimir's tenure.

107 *to become a mechanic*: Sand had great respect for those who
worked with their hands. She encouraged the proletarian poets—such as Poncy and Perdiguier—to whom she gave financial
support and introductions to literary networks to retain their
craft.

109 *he fled from me in panic*: the theme of class division in love
recurs frequently in Sand's novels, from *Valentine* (1832), in
which a young noblewoman leaves her husband for a com-
moner. In *The Miller of Angibault*, which Sand called her 'arch-
socialist and communist' novel, the device is more than merely
dramatic, however. Marriage between the classes symbolizes
their future fusion.

110 *to use up my own fortune*: although Sand devoted over
£1,000,000 to socialist causes, we should be careful not to
identify her too closely with Marcelle. Sand's 'fortune' was
largely earned from her writings; the estate at Nohant was often
more a source of expense than of income, particularly with her
many donations to peasant families. In 1847, for example, she
wrote to her half-sister, 'You may get some idea of how much to
give to the poor this year by the misery you see in your own part
of the world. It is the same here, if not worse. I think it will
absorb all the income from Nohant.' Further, Sand, unlike
Marcelle, was able to identify herself as working class on her
mother's side, of the stock of the bird-sellers on the Quai
d'Orsai. She belonged to the ordinary people 'by blood, as much
as in heart', she asserted, and was grateful to have 'a warmer
blood in my veins' than that of the aristocracy, despite her royal
cousins on the wrong side of the blanket. Nevertheless most of
Sand's contacts were with the artisan class, rather than the

proletariat. As in England, where the artisans were the backbone
of the Chartist movement, this was the class to which reformers
looked for social progress; but whether these were the 'ordinary
people' is perhaps another matter.

110 *the little comfort that remains for both of us*: the dilemma of
how extensively she should donate to socialist causes troubled
Sand as well. Pierre Leroux's *Revue sociale*, a socialist journal
for which she was the principal backer, also absorbed a potentially infinite amount of her income. In the same 1847 letter in
which she estimated that aiding the peasants at Nohant would
absorb all of the estate's income, she wrote to her sister that she
would not be giving her daughter, Solange, or her foster daughter, Augustine, lavish weddings: 'This is not the time to pay for
violins, but to give bread.'

111 *some speak of . . . fraternity and community*: Rousseau, Fourier,
and the French revolutionary Babeuf, perhaps, who championed
an agrarian communism. Sand was well versed in social and
political thought. At convent school her 'director of conscience',
the Abbé de Prémord, had advised her, 'Read the poets, they are
all religious. Have no fear of the *philosophes*, they are all powerless.' Of the 'powerless' philosophers, Sand had read Locke,
Condillac, Montesquieu, Bacon, Aristotle, Pascal, Montaigne,
Condorcet, and Rousseau by the time she was eighteen. The
social Christianity advocated by Chateaubriand in *Le Génie du
christianisme* was another early influence. Sand's Christian socialism is evident in a letter which she wrote to her cousin
Apolline Vallet de Villeneuve, explaining why her daughter,
Solange, was not marrying one of her own station: 'We understand nothing of rank and birth. We do not believe in them, we
see genius descend from heaven just as God pleases, and we do
not find the precepts of social distinctions in any page of the
Evangelist; quite the contrary.'

wisest sages of antiquity: perhaps a reference to the proto-
communism of Plato's *Republic*.

I know nothing of politics: an ironic claim after this lengthy
political diatribe! Marcelle mirrors Sand's own ambivalence towards women's involvement in politics. In the days of the 1830
revolution she protested that she, too, knew nothing of politics,
which was not a woman's proper domain; but at the same time
her correspondence is full of political news. In the 1848 revolution Sand served informally as minister of information, but
scorned the attempt made by feminists to put her name forward

for the National Assembly. Like many male socialists of her time, she feared that the vote for women would give strength to conservative factions. Class equality came first. 'Should women participate one day in politics?' she wrote in a letter to the provisional government central committee in April 1848. 'Yes, one day, I believe as do you, but is this day near? No, I do not believe so, and for the condition of women to be thus transformed, it is necessary that society be radically transformed.'

112 *decked with garlands like a pagan god*: 'The Fathers of the early Church bitterly condemned this pagan custom of ornamenting statues of gods. Minutius Felix explains the matter clearly and admirably. The medieval Church re-established these idolatrous practices, and today's Church continues the lucrative speculation' (Sand's note). Marcus Menucius Felix, late 2nd–early 3rd century AD, was probably the earliest Latin apologist for Christianity. His *Octavius* is a dialogue between the pagan Caecilius Natalis and the Christian Octavius Ianuarius.

we poor women, who can only weep for all this: in a letter of 1830 Sand, still avowedly apolitical, asked if women had at least the right to weep for Poland after the crushing of the revolution.

113 *under various titles*: in Europe and North America the 1840s were the heyday of utopian socialist communities, often of a Fourierite or Owenite stamp. Sand shares Marx's distaste for them.

Saint-Simonians and the Fourierites: Claude-Henri de Rouvroy, comte de Saint-Simon (1760–1825) was the author of *Du système industriel, Catéchisme des industriels*, and *Nouveau christianisme*. Saint-Simon's collectivism was tempered by a confidence in the new ascendant classes of scientists and engineers, whereas Sand's confidence lay with the artisans. In addition Saint-Simon thought the Englightenment attack on theology was the foundation of progress, whereas Sand's socialism was firmly Christian. Charles Fourier (1772–1837) was the author of *Théorie de l'unité universelle* (1822). His utopian community, the 'phalanstery', perhaps incurred Sand's displeasure because of its excessive regimentation: it would consist of 1,610 people, who did twelve different jobs each day and ate nine meals.

117 *the pursuit of the absolute*: *la recherche de l'absolu*, an overriding theme in French Romantic literature (cf. Balzac's 1834 work of that title). Despite the novel's high Romantic devices, such as the personage of the madwoman herself, Sand is sceptical of

where the pursuit of the Romantic absolute leads: to lunacy for those who persist in it. Marcelle herself is absorbed in the pursuit of absolute social equality and a rural utopia, and during the course of the novel she will have to modify her own *recherche de l'absolu*. The metaphor of the alchemist reinforces the image: the alchemist's preoccupation was also a chimera, of course.

120 *to look for work and exercise his craft*: Lémor's travels call to mind the tour of France by Sand's contemporary, the socialist feminist Flora Tristan (1803–44), in order to set up a national network for her Workers' Union, the precursor of the Socialist International. Tristan's tour began in May 1844, shortly before Sand started work on *The Miller of Angibault*. Although Sand disliked Tristan's feminism, they both espoused socialism, and Tristan made even greater sacrifices for it than Sand did: she died of typhus at Bordeaux. The workers of the city erected an obelisk to her memory, inscribed 'Liberté-Égalité-Fraternité-Solidarité'. After Tristan's death Sand helped to support her daughter Aline, who became the mother of the painter Gauguin.

125 *superb dahlias*: dahlias were a recent and fashionable import into France at this time, and hence a suitable choice for the slightly pretentious Robichon. Sand herself had first encountered them only a few years before, when she was presented with some by a neighbour.

132 *Marchois*: see note to p. 55. 'The inhabitants of *la Marche*, rightly or wrongly, are in such bad odour with their Berry neighbours that *Marchois* is a synonym for scoundrel' (Sand's footnote).

133 *and his lady*: the Virgin Mary. Compare the English carol, 'I saw three ships': 'And what was in those ships all three? Our Saviour Christ and his lady.'

Berrichons: natives of Berry.

écus: crowns (three francs).

Mers: Mers-sur-Indre, about 6 km. (4 mls.) north-west of Angibault, in the direction of Châteauroux and Ardentes (which may well be the town referred to as ——).

140 *Cross . . . Saint James's Path*: 'The Cross is the constellation of the Swan, and Saint James's Path the Milky Way' (Sand's footnote). The Swan is Cygnus, containing the bright star Deneb.

143 *Christian communists of the early era*: Sand had explored the Christian basis of socialism in earlier works, such as *Spiridion* (1838). She was influenced by, but ultimately dissatisfied with, the work of the Abbé Félicité Robert de Lamennais, whose *Paroles d'un croyant* has been called (by Harold Laski) 'a lyrical version of the *Communist Manifesto*'.

150 *one cannot oneself be chaste*: at the time the novel was written, Sand was herself living chastely with Chopin, after their initial passion (what Sand called in a letter of September 1838 'the delicious fatigue of a happy love'). The death of his father in 1844, the year of the novel's composition, left the composer deeply depressed, as did his recurring bouts of illness; at one point he locked himself in his room at Nohant, refusing to see anyone but Sand. She found the absence of relations frankly difficult, but insisted that she remained faithful to Chopin; his doubts and possessive jealousy, however, created distance between the lovers and played some part in their rupture in 1847.

152 *our master*: 'In our part of the world, old women still follow the ancient custom of saying "*our master*" when speaking of their husbands. Those of the present generation say "*our man*"' (Sand's footnote). Despite Sand's interest in Berrichon dialect, she denied that she was seeking to revive old language or to create a new one. 'I have never sought to create a new language or a new style. Although many critics have claimed it of me, I am always astonished at the way they complicate things, when the only inspiration for artistic production ought to be the simplest idea, the most ordinary circumstance' (Preface to *La Mare au Diable*, 1845). Here, as often occurs despite the stereotypes about her writing, Sand eschewed Romanticism and embraced classical principles.

Le Blanc: see note to p. 70.

153 *assignats*: during the Revolution large estates and church lands were nationalized. Those which were not sold for cash were exchanged for paper bonds (*assignats*) issued on their security. Financiers, lawyers, and country bourgeois—millers, brewers, and wealthy farmers—made considerable fortunes in speculating on the *assignats*.

161 *liard*: half-farthing.

162 *Cluis*: about 12 kms. (8 mls.) south-west of Sarzay (Blanchemont).

171 *out-jew a Jew*: although the French phrase 'avec les juifs comme avec les juifs' is a stock idiom, Louis's use of it, and his later outrage at M. Bricolin's insinuation that he might be Jewish, make him something of a flawed diamond. The Berry characters are given livelier lines and sounder sense than the Parisian visitors throughout *The Miller of Angibault*, but they are not depicted as noble savages. They are stolid, generally trustworthy, but conservative and small-minded. In *The Master Pipers* both their prejudices and their virtues are contrasted with those of the wild, inspired men of the Bourbonnais forests, only 20 km. (12 mls.) distant, but another country. (It may also be worth noting that Sand herself was not entirely free of anti-Semitism, as was shown in her barbed parting comments at the end of her relationship with the Jewish publisher Buloz.)

fairy stories: the French critic Béatrice Didier, editor of the annotated Livre de Poche version of *Le Meunier d'Angibault*, notes very perceptively at this point: 'The miller represents the realistic attitude of the man who knows how useful money is, and how hard to earn, in contrast to Marcelle and Henri, who symbolize idealism and Romanticism. But this makes it clear how misleading it would be to regard Marcelle alone as George Sand's mouthpiece. The miller is also George Sand.'

178 *Work is good for everybody*: here again, in addition to expressing the socialist view that working with one's hands was noble rather than dishonourable, the miller speaks for Sand, who wrote three novels a year until old age forced her to cut back to two. Throughout her life Sand kept to a regular discipline of composition and revision. At sixty she still described work as 'my mainstay, my nourishment, my all'. After fifty novels, a lengthy autobiography, a career in journalism, and fifty stage plays, she regretted that she had not written more. Only Balzac bested Sand's output, and he lacked the handicaps of an inferior education, a rash marriage, early motherhood, and the burden of caring for two consumptives (Chopin, and Sand's companion in later life, the engraver Alexandre Manceau).

180 *compagnon*: this term has a very specific meaning, not conveyed by 'companion'. The *compagnonnages* were traditional guilds of skilled workers, with local branches throughout France. By 1844 they were already declining in the rural areas because of lack of work and the migration of many workers to the towns.

Other associations were beginning to replace the *compagnon-nages*, such as mutual aid societies, Sociétaires de l'Union, and Flora Tristan's embryo Workers' Union (see note to p. 120). Sand had dealt with the theme of *compagnonnage* in her *Compagnon du tour de France* (1840), which Walt Whitman reviewed for his newspaper, *The Brooklyn Daily Eagle*. It became his bedside reading, and he was so enamoured of her picture of artisan life that he posed in his father's carpenter costume for his portrait in *Leaves of Grass* (1855).

181 *a crown of wheat-ears and cornflowers*: Sand may be alluding to rural customs of well-dressing, or, more heretically, dressing the cross, that is, decking the church crucifix with flowers. If that is the parallel, Grand'Louise becomes the equivalent of the cross and the miller's work his Passion.

183 *obole*: a farthing.

Louis XV: (1710–74).

Sainte-Solange: see note to p. 7.

185 *Ruffec*: about 10 km. (6 mls.) east of Le Blanc (see notes to pp. 70 and 152).

187 *Saint Anthony*: either the Christian monk and hermit, born in Egypt about AD 250, or the Franciscan monk, born in Portugal in 1195.

disgust . . . inspires: Lémor is remarkably fastidious about actual beggars, given his frequently professed love for humanity in the abstract.

190 *malicious fairies of the night*: Sand was enthralled by Berry's many legends of sorcery, a theme which recurs at greater length in *La Petite Fadette* (1848). The hero Landry is led off the safe track through a ford at night by a will o'the wisp, *ignis fatuus*, a phosphorescence caused by methane rising from marshy ground. He is rescued by Fadette, who has been taught wise-woman lore by her grandmother; she pulls him through the water and back on to safe ground with a force which, like Bricoline, she appears too slight to possess. Uncle Cadoche is the sorcerer figure in *The Miller of Angibault*.

197 *cornemuseux*: travelling players of the *cornemuse* (see note to p. 100), a mouth-blown bagpipe. The French *cornemuse* is simpler than the Scottish bagpipe, with a chanter for carrying the tune and one or two drones (the bass drone often being silenced when the bourrée is played). This is the true folk-instrument; the more elaborate *musette* was developed for court use. The

cornemuseux formed a secret and highly professional guild, whose way of life is at the centre of *The Master Pipers*.

201 *mountains*: to the inhabitants of the plain, like Grand-Louis, *la Marche berrichonne* was a region of mountains and wild men. Sand drew on the contrast between 'the plain, which sings in the major key, and the mountain, singing in the minor' once again in *The Master Pipers*.

204 *hurdy-gurdy*: not a barrel-organ, but the *vielle*, a lute-shaped instrument with the strings sounded by a resined wheel rather than a bow. The instrument has survived longer in France than in other European countries, and is still played today in Berry.

206 *Veillée*: evening entertainment of dancing, singing, or story-telling.

bourrée: dance, probably originating in the nearby Auvergne, in quick duple metre with a single upbeat. The form was used in opera and ballet by such composers as Lully and Rameau and, like the gavotte, often comprises one of the movements of a suite (e.g. Bach's French suites). Sand was a great partisan of the bourrée, as this passage reveals; frequently the dance was performed in the square before her house at Nohant.

207 *bitten by tarantulas*: in Italy and southern France the bite of the tarantula spider was thought to cause a potentially fatal disease which could only be cured by violent dancing. Samuel Pepys wrote of a meeting with a gentleman who 'is a great traveller, and, speaking of the tarantula, he says that all the harvest long . . . fiddlers go up and down the fields everywhere, in expectation of being hired by those that are stung'. In the nineteenth century this folk dance was codified by composers such as Chopin, Liszt, and Weber into the tarantella, a rapid dance in 6/8 time.

210 *this moral parricide they had committed*: note the parallel to the madwoman's attempt at matricide.

215 *jealous rivalries*: the jealousy of musicians is a major theme of *The Master Pipers*, whose central character, the musician Joset, is often thought to mirror Chopin's sexual and professional jealousies. Chopin was loath to recognize the worth of any living musician, with the possible exception of Berlioz. He refused to return the esteem of Schumann and Liszt, pronouncing the latter 'an excellent binder who puts other people's works between his own covers'. Despite the myth that depicts Chopin and Liszt as close friends, the admiration was largely one-sided.

219 *a gold louis*: in full, louis d'or, a gold coin issued in the reigns of Kings Louis XIII–XVI (that is, 1640–1793).

220 *huisseries*: stable-type doors. See also the following note.

   huis: archaic term for door, still used in legal phrases involving *huis clos*, closed doors, such as *entendre une cause à huis clos*, hear a case in camera, and as in Sartre's play.

223 *child of my time*: *l'enfant de mon siècle*, an apparent echo of *Confession d'un enfant du siècle*, by Sand's former lover, Alfred de Musset. But *enfant du siècle* is no more Musset's invention than *mon semblable, mon frère* is Charles Baudelaire's: Sand used the epithet *enfant du siècle* before Musset, in her *Lettres d'un voyageur*, and *son semblable, son frère* in her *Winter in Majorca*, well before *Les fleurs du mal*.

226 *prefect's*: local government official, chief executive of the *département*.

227 *in the mire*: note how in this chapter Sand juxtaposes the reality of village niggling to the high-flown ideals of the Parisian reformers in the previous chapter.

229 *a league*: about 4 km. (2½ mls.).

230 *the African campaign*: against the resistance of Abd el-Kader, who had declared a *jihad* or holy war against French colonization of Algeria.

231 *men of science . . . exceptional cases*: although the madwoman is a Gothic figure, and a necessary engine for the dénouement of the plot, she also symbolizes the destructive mercenary character of industrial society. Many commentators of the period linked the rise in insanity to financial competition, speculation, and unemployment. As the most advanced industrial nation, England was thought to have the highest degree of insanity, but these changes were occurring all over Europe. The head of one asylum wrote, 'I doubt if ever the history of the world, or the experience of past ages, could show a larger amount of insanity than that of the present day' (Dr John Hawkes of the Wiltshire County Asylum, quoted in Elaine Showalter, *The Female Malady*, Virago, 1985, p. 24).

243 *In vino veritas*: in wine lies truth.

246 *skinny cat gnome*: another of Bricolin's malapropisms: he means *sine qua non*, 'without which, nothing', the basic condition without which the deal will be void.

247 *not such a bad business*: note how Sand stops short of portray-
ing Bricolin as a total monster in this interior monologue. His
affection for Rose comes a poor third to his financial calculations and his social snobbery, but it is there.

stamped paper: official forms with the notary's stamp.

251 *alive in her breast*: this is the counterpart to the passage in the
previous chapter in which Sand tempers her portrayal of M.
Bricolin's villainy with his genuine if belated paternal warmth.
Sand sounds perfectly conventional in her stress on maternal
instinct, and indeed she believed firmly in separate male and
female natures, identifying women with the private realm and
the heart, men with public life and the head. Therefore she
publicly opposed female suffrage, and refused with considerable
rudeness a request from notable feminists of 1848 that she stand
for the Assembly.

255 *Jeu-les-Bois*: about 12 km. (8 mls.) north-west of Sarzay
(Blanchemont), near the forest of Châteauroux.

262 *brandevin*: an *eau-de-vie* made from wine.

265 *belonging to old lord de Blanchemont*: this inheritance, which
will play a crucial part in the dénouement, is thus rightly
Marcelle's, from her grandfather, as is the remaining land at
Blanchemont. Whatever she has, and whatever she gives away,
are hers by right; all she has from her husband are debts. Again,
the parallel with Sand's own situation is notable.

270 *revive a dead man*: note how skilfully Sand relieves the high
tragedy of the beggar's narrative and impending death with the
comic self-interest of the lawyer.

273 *Ite, missa est, Dominus vobiscum*: 'Go, the mass is ended, the
Lord be with you.'

274 *Transault*: about 6 km. (4 mls.) north-west of Sarzay
(Blanchemont).

278 *a woman's cry*: throughout the novel it is women who act, for
good (Marcelle, old mother Bricolin) or ill (the madwoman).
Although the novel has fairy-tale elements in it, the roles are
reversed from those in Sleeping Beauty or Cinderella: the once-
robust and grossly masculine Bricolin is as if under an enchantment in this scene, from which he is delivered by a woman,
Marcelle. With the exception of the miller, all the male characters do nothing at the crucial moment: Cadoche fails to deliver
the message, Bricolin cannot save his farm, Lémor is a superfluous dreamer.

281 *pistoles*: a pistole was a gold coin equivalent to a louis (see note to p. 219).

296 *I have the disposal of it*: the elderly Bricolins married under the law of the *ancien régime*, that is, before the Napoleonic Code effectively abolished married women's property rights. They each left their property to the surviving spouse. Old mother Bricolin inherits the property because her husband has been declared legally incompetent, just as she would have if her husband had died. Thus Rose is finally liberated from her father by her peasant grandmother, not her aristocratic friend Marcelle or her suitor Grand-Louis. In this final twist of the plot feminism coalesces with agrarian socialism.

297 *We'll all work together and share the profits*: notice that it is Grand-Louis who puts communism into practice at the end of the novel; Lémor's elaborate schemes remain so much hot air.

THE WORLD'S CLASSICS

A Select List